HOLLINGSWORTH ISLAND SERIES

HOLLINGSWORTH ISLAND

IN THE PRESENCE OF ANGELS

DEAN HAMILTON

Cover Art by Karen Phillips and Bublish
Distribution by Bublish

ISBN: 978-1-647045-89-0 (paperback)
ISBN: 978-1-647045-88-3 (eBook)

To my wife, Jayne. . . Always

CHAPTER ONE

Lindsay Featherstone continued to appear to Cole in his dreams. And just when he thought the moment was tangible, Cole abruptly awoke in a cold sweat, as she disappeared in a burst of shimmering dust and the wind carried her ashes across a darkened sea.

It had been just over six months since Cole Hollingsworth's triumphant return, following the manner in which he had put William Gaines—former CEO of Hollingsworth Enterprises—in his place. This had, for the most part, downplayed the $50,000,000 scam Lindsay's father, Jacob Featherstone, had swindled out of the company. Hollingsworth Enterprises, with its powerful grip on the news and publishing world, had adroitly downplayed the event as just a bad investment. The fact that the newly formed volcanic landmass in the Caribbean Sea had been named Hollingsworth Island, after Cole's heroic exploits to find the truth about his parents' deaths, tended to overshadow the young executive's inexperience. Yet, it was Cole himself who wanted to keep the Featherstone scam low-key, not to divert blame from himself, but rather to avoid tarnishing the Featherstone name. He couldn't bear the thought of people thinking badly about the woman he loved. The sacrifices she had made for him alone were worthy of sainthood.

In truth, the cryptic note Jacob had sent him, apologizing and promising the experience would make Cole a better businessman had, in fact, been prophetic. It had made him a savvier and more experienced leader. Yet, the more profound changes in Cole came from Lindsay's gifts. His womanizing, playboy days defined by excessive alcohol abuse and partying were now behind him.

Cole had recently discovered where Jacob and his wife, Margaret, were hiding out but had declined to pursue a legal recourse, even though his best friend and personal attorney, Art Barkley, had pressured him to do so. The country they now lived in had sketchy extradition laws with the United States, and the money was located in untraceable, offshore accounts. Partners in the con, the Cunningham brothers, however, had proven more elusive. They were nowhere to be found. It was an expensive lesson, but a lesson well learned. Cole would never again be taken advantage of like that.

A sudden knock on Cole's door startled him. Distracted from his daily reflections, he shouted something inaudible, irritated by the intrusion. Another interloper wanting something from him, no doubt. His increasing isolation brought with it a growing concern from his staff and his board of directors. Whispers of reclusiveness filled the hallways. What had happened to Cole while he was away to have changed him so dramatically? He wasn't talking about it, so the only thing left was speculation. Grace Foster, his executive assistant and close friend, was becoming concerned as well.

"Cole, may I come in?" Grace implored, wondering what his response would be today.

Cole hesitated before answering. *I can't keep ignoring her,* he thought. "Yes, Grace, please come in."

Grace entered tentatively, unsure of which Cole she would find—the charismatic leader or the despondent recluse. Unshaven and dressed in casual, beach-looking garb, he sat behind the mahogany desk that had once been his father's, twirling a miniature umbrella, the kind often found in tropical drinks. Ever since his return to Newport, Rhode Island, he had developed a fascination with the colorful little toys, almost to the point of an obsession. Other miniature umbrellas lay scattered about his office haphazardly.

What do they mean to him? Grace wondered. Clearing her throat, she approached. "Mr. Hollingsworth." Grace had started calling him *Mr.* since he became CEO of the family-controlled empire. "I. . . I noticed on your calendar that you have a board meeting scheduled today, in the main conference room, right after lunch." She hesitated, stumbling to find the right words. "Is there anything I can do to help you prepare, sir?"

Cole placed the umbrella down on his desk, staring intently at it for a long moment.

"For one thing, you can call me Cole. You remember my first name, don't you?" He gazed back at Grace, his face tilted so that one eye was on her and the other on the umbrella. "There's no need to be so formal." After a moment of hesitation, Cole added, "Did I ever tell you about the legend behind these miniature umbrellas and how they came into existence? It's really quite an interesting story." Cole said it as if this subject was more important than the impending board meeting.

"No, Mr. Hollingsworth, um, I mean, Cole. I don't believe you have," Grace replied, wondering why such a trivial thing would even occupy a minute of Cole's attention. They were just some silly marketing device to promote the illusion of being in the tropics when customers were really just in some local watering hole or a chain restaurant. Then it hit her. *Tropics!* There must be a connection somehow. After visiting the Caribbean and the Bahamas, Cole had returned a changed man. At first, his return was like that of a conquering hero, with his photo on the cover of a dozen magazines.

The headlines more or less read: "Billionaire Cole Hollingsworth risks his entire inheritance to find the truth. In the process, he becomes the first human to step foot onto the first landmass formed on Earth in a hundred million years. They're naming the volcano after his family."

The photo of Cole limping toward his rescuers in a threadbare wetsuit, with a makeshift cane under one arm and his other hand gripping a crushed diving helmet, instantly turned him into the poster child for survival magazines worldwide. His handsome, rugged good looks making him a heartthrob for millions of women. Brave, sensitive, and rich—who could resist a man like that?

"You were about to tell me about the legend behind the miniature umbrellas?" Grace said slyly, hoping this might get her boss to open up a little.

"Was I?" Cole replied, a dazed, far-off look in his eyes.

For an instant, Grace thought she saw moisture appear in those dark, rueful eyes. But focus returned immediately.

"It's not important." He brushed the toy into his wastebasket, as if it were no longer relevant to him.

Intuitively, Grace knew differently and made a mental note to confront him another time. There had to be a connection somehow.

"I think I should get cleaned up. Wouldn't want to appear unprofessional to our upstanding members of the board, would I?" Cole said, sarcastically. Members guided by the former CEO Bill Gaines, whose primary goal was to amass great personal wealth. Cole had replaced one director with his attorney, Art Barkley, and he planned to replace more when the time was right.

"Grace, I'm headed home to change. Will you please email me the agenda for today's meeting. I should be back before one o'clock." Cole rose quickly, disappearing out of the office without further comment.

Grace retreated to her own office to send the requested email, feeling even more conflicted.

CHAPTER TWO

C OLE HAD RECENTLY STOPPED driving his Maserati GranTourismo GTS, his $2.8 million street-legal racing machine that liked to talk back to him. Purchased at the Italian auto factory, the car was installed with an interactive voice control system that just happened to contain a sexy woman's voice with an attitude. Lindsay had ridden in it and somehow made a connection with Serena, the car's voice. The two became instant friends, united in their cause to belittle Cole and change his behavior.

Driving the supercar now was too painful, so he chose to drive his SUV, a benign reflection of Cole's former, flamboyant personality. Though expensive to most, the BMW somehow seemed beneath Cole. It wasn't loud, it wasn't flashy; it was simply the "Ultimate Driving Machine" according to BMW's marketing team. It would do. There were already so many lookalike vehicles in Newport that Cole felt he blended into the local landscape, something his Maserati would never allow.

Guiding his car up the snakelike drive along the cliffs near Rhode Island's famous Cliff Walk area, Cole arrived at his three-tiered home overlooking the Atlantic Ocean. The mansion appeared small when compared to the other estates dotting the landscape in this area of Newport. Former presidents of the United States had lived here, along with captains of industry from very old, very wealthy families. Cole's house was modern and stark and had been nicknamed the Lighthouse due the amount of light that escaped the large, glass facades that covered much of its structure. It had been featured in numerous architectural magazines. The warmth from the golden cascade of light that normally illuminated the property had gone cold and dark, as if abandoned. No staff remained, aside from the occasional house cleaner. There was only Cole, haunted by the ghosts of recent memories.

Cole spoke into a wireless voice system, and the fourth of five garage doors silently swung open. Pulling in, he parked the SUV between Serena and a Ducati racing motorcycle, which he also chose to no longer drive, after the mysterious disappearance and death of his parents at sea. If things kept going at the current rate, it might not be long before Cole was forced to rely on public transportation; his spotless, urethane-lined garage more a car museum than a collection of drivable, luxury automobiles.

After taking a quick shower and shaving, Cole slipped into charcoal gray slacks, a black-and-white pinstriped shirt, and a black sports coat. He glided past his tie rack without so much as a glance. Cole detested wearing ties. They were useless garments, only good for catching spilled bits of food or drinks. Walking down the three flights of stairs, he pulled up the board meeting agenda on his smart phone. The usual opening review of previous minutes by the company secretary, a brief review of their financial performance from the previous quarter, and. . . and someone was going to be outlining a plan of how to *use*—substitute the word *benefit*—from the newly named Hollingsworth Island? This was totally unexpected. Who had been working on this little project without his knowledge or his permission?

Cole quickly dialed his executive assistant. "What the hell is the last agenda item about? Were you aware of this, Grace?"

"I received an email from one of the directors that you had requested the assessment, otherwise I would have asked you about it myself. I thought you knew. . ."

"Which director?" Cole demanded.

"Walter Barrett," Grace said, hesitating as she perused the list. "It doesn't appear that he's scheduled to attend the meeting today. He's out of town."

"That's just great. Do you know who's making the presentation?"

"No idea," Grace replied.

"I should arrive in about twenty minutes. I'll call Walter on my way over."

"Yes, Mr. Hollingsworth," Grace said, concerned over the harshness in Cole's voice. Cole's suggestion of informality hadn't lasted long.

Barrett's phone rang six times before going to voicemail. After giving the number, the line went dead. Barrett was not a direct employee of Hollingsworth, rather he was one of four outside board members, as most large corporations typically had. Like so many other outside members, Walter was a lawyer who mostly gave legal advice when called upon to do so. He received a healthy per diem for attending the meetings and providing advice, along with a generous stock option program all board members loyal to William Gaines had been given.

If Walter wouldn't be part of the island proposal discussion, why had he lied to Grace about Cole's knowledge of it. And why wasn't he attending the meeting? Was this just a coincidence—or was it something more? Perhaps, Walter was the most expendable of all the board members. Something didn't feel right about this.

It had only been six months since Cole's return. The volcano was still too unstable to have any people other than scientists on the island, or the professional security personnel positioned on speedboats protecting the surrounding waters and shoreline. Out of the blue, someone at Hollingsworth Enterprises had concocted a plan for its use? It was not even clear what country held domain over the landmass, since it was located outside of any country's territorial waters.

Cole's car skidded to a stop in the parking garage below Hollingsworth's headquarters. Slamming the car door, Cole walked briskly to the elevator. Once inside, he pressed the button to the top floor, where upper management offices and the boardroom were located. As the elevator slowly ascended—it seemed to take longer than normal—Cole wondered why he was so upset by these circumstances. Was it that his authority had been circumvented, a typical male ego thing, or did it have to do with the island itself and that Lindsay had played such an important role in creating it? It was Lindsay's Island, Cole thought, not his, even though his family name was attached to it. Attempting to clear his head, he stepped out of the elevator, coming face-to-face with Grace, who was patiently awaiting his arrival with a mug of strong coffee in her hand.

CHAPTER THREE

A T COLE'S INSISTENCE, THE board meeting came to order immediately. The normal banter that preceded such meetings was quashed. Cole turned toward the company secretary.

"Mr. Jackson, will you please read the minutes from our last board meeting?" Cole paused. "We'll delay the financial review and any other pieces of business and then go straight to the last agenda item about Hollingsworth Island," Cole said, his expression insistent.

Eyebrows rose, and a hush fell about the room. Cole had sucked out whatever air remained in the musty old boardroom, as if a giant vacuum cleaner had just powered on. Grace stared at her boss, mesmerized by a faint, incandescent light that appeared to surround his body. She recalled seeing this once before, after his return, when he became emotionally supercharged.

Grace abandoned the tray she'd brought in containing hot coffee, fresh fruit and pastries, silently exiting the double doors. Once outside, she drew in a long breath, steadying herself. Things seemed out of sync after her boss had returned, like time had been altered. The initial excitement of Cole's heroic homecoming had faded within weeks. The world around her seemed heavier, darker, as if Cole had brought back an intolerable blanket of despair—or perhaps a curse.

Cole's first official actions of demoting Bill Gaines, appointing Art Barkley as a new director and president pro tem, and promising the employees a bright new future in electronic publishing, despite the Internet glasses debacle, had infused the company with hope. People were actually smiling and talking about the possibilities. It seemed infectious. Yet, day by day, the optimism was quietly evaporating, as if a mysterious force was draining the company of the energy to sustain itself.

Grace closed her eyes, remembering Cole before he had ventured out on the exploration to find the truth about his parents' disappearance. She had always liked him, even with his playboy reputation. She knew he was better than that. Her fondness for him had turned to great respect after his return. He was becoming his own man, finally. But what was happening to him now? If only he would talk to her about the experience. She knew she could help. She murmured a prayer and moved on toward her own office, awaiting the fateful results of the board meeting. She didn't have a good feeling about it.

After the minutes had been read, Cole stood at the end of the table, facing Bill Gaines, who was still chairman of the board but more of a lame duck than anything else, at least for now. Cole had allowed him to stay on but had stripped him of operating power over the company. That belonged to Cole now. The only board member Cole trusted was Art Barkley, one of the shrewdest attorneys in Rhode Island. Cole knew Art had his back; he had proven that during the expedition to the Caribbean. Art had spent a small fortune to reach Cole, surviving an encounter with pirates and the near sinking of the frigate Cole had been on, and had helped plan their escape from San Salvador. Art had also been instrumental in helping Cassie Thomas, Lindsay's closest friend and fellow diver, slip away undetected back to Australia. And now, Art would be called upon to help Cole assess any contentious actions of the board—or the ex-CEO Bill Gaines, who sat silently across from Cole like a viper about to strike. Cole could sense the loathing roiling under Bill's skin.

Cole began. "Does anyone here know where Walter Barrett is?" This question seemed to surprise everyone except Art, who Cole had called to brief on his way back to the office. The room remained silent, as the few members who were in the know realized Cole had already connected some of the dots. This was a concern. How had he found out so quickly?

"Well?" Cole demanded. Art quickly scanned the faces of the seven directors in attendance for a hint of recognition in their eyes. He noticed three who flinched ever so slightly. Bill Gaines remained implacable. Art knew he must be involved, but for a corporate warrior like Gaines, this was child's play. As a poker player, he was a master. There were many in the company still astonished at Cole's apparent coup when he'd demoted the longtime CEO and seized control for himself. It was a bold move, and many respected Cole for his boldness, but still, Gaines had his supporters throughout the organization, many of them silent. Bill was, however, the first person to speak.

"Cole, I believe Walter is out of town on a family emergency. It's not like him to just disappear. It must have been important. I'll look into it personally for you," Bill said magnanimously, attempting to separate himself from whatever Cole was irritated about. It was also an obvious move to change the subject from Walter's sudden disappearance. Six months ago, Cole would have believed Gaines, but no longer. He glanced over at Art, whose eyes were slightly squinted. That was all the confirmation Cole needed. Art didn't believe Gaines, either.

"Thank you, Bill. I appreciate that," Cole said. *Don't reveal your hand,* Cole's father had often told him. Cole was learning how to play the game.

"Well then, what can you tell me about *Hollingsworth's* plans for the new island? I must say, I was stunned when I saw it listed on today's agenda," Cole said, emphasizing his last name over the full name of the company. It was clear by the way he asked the question that Cole was insinuating it was his decision, not Bill's—nor anyone else's for that matter.

"A couple of us have been monitoring the progress of the scientific community on the island. There remains a lot of chatter about it and great public interest. We didn't want to bother you with it, since you're, um, still acclimating to your new responsibilities. Just wanted to keep an eye on it, especially since our name is associated with it." This was Bill's attempt to return serve—that they were simply doing their job for the benefit of the company. Two of the board members nodded their heads in agreement but appeared to prefer silence, allowing Gaines to carry the ball forward.

"I see. Now that that's clear, can you enlighten me as to what possible plans *we* could have for the newly formed volcano?" Cole changed the vernacular from island to volcano to emphasize it might not be usable—or inhabitable—for years to come.

Perfect, Gaines thought, and the slightest hint of a smile flashed across his lips. This was exactly what Gaines had hoped Cole would ask.

"As you've directed since your return, all of us at Hollingsworth Enterprises have been tasked with researching and recommending ways to reinvent the company for the benefit of its shareholders and the communities we serve. Michael"—he gestured toward his fellow director seated at the middle of the large boardroom table, "came up with a great idea, if I do say so myself." Bill intentionally complimented Michael, so as not to encourage Cole to believe this was really his own idea. *Spread the recognition around a little*, Bill thought.

"As I was saying," Bill continued. "With all the scientific news spreading around about the island, we thought it would be a great idea to start a publishing division focused on science. Since our name is prominently associated with the new landmass, what better way to introduce news articles or even a magazine?" Bill sounded almost giddy with enthusiasm. "This would benefit the world and could be a big success. Scientific journals haven't exactly been bestsellers, they're too technical. But with a different spin, this one could become popular."

Hushed laughter emanated from a few of the board members. Bill continued, "With the entire planet interested in this incredible event, we are the ideal enterprise to undertake it. We would develop a new website and start a daily blog. It would be great exposure and a new source of advertising revenue. But most importantly, the information must be accurate, supporting the scientific study and informing the public, otherwise we'll lose credibility."

Bill ended his report on an uplifting note. First two, then three, then all of the board members began to clap—all except Cole and Art.

It was beautifully orchestrated. The former CEO was in top form again. He had won this round. If Cole argued strongly against the proposal, he would come across as a sore loser. He hadn't been prepared for this, hadn't seen it coming. He was too preoccupied, lingering in his own delusions.

"Interesting concept, Bill. And just where will all of this credible information come from?" Cole asked, casting Michael a disdainful glance, letting him know that he knew this was much more Bill's idea than Michael's.

"We've been having a dialogue with one of the top scientific teams studying the island. They are interested in ensuring the public receives accurate information about the newly formed volcano and the vast secrets it holds. They also feel strongly that more publicity will result in more money for research and exploration. When we told the team we had been thinking along the same lines, they became interested in collaborating with us. Thus, the idea was developed for a new website and possibly a scientific journal where their findings could be published," Bill stated convincingly.

On the surface, it all sounded on the up and up. And it might have been—if it wasn't connected to Bill. But Cole knew better. The more the former CEO articulated his newly acquired, altruistic desire for informing the uniformed public, the more Cole sensed that something much deeper lay beneath the surface. Something that could only be motivated by profits.

"I'll take it under advisement, and we'll reconvene in a couple of weeks, after Art and I have had the opportunity to research this idea further. Thank you for your proposal," Cole said, effectively ending the discussion. The remainder of the meeting passed without further incident—no one wanted to rock the boat.

CHAPTER FOUR

ART FOLLOWED COLE OUT of the boardroom, leaving Gaines and the rest of the board members to themselves. Cole marched directly into Grace's office, ushering Art in before practically slamming the door. Grace jerked back in her chair, stunned by the abrupt intrusion. A moment of tense silence followed.

"How did it go?" Grace asked tentatively, bracing herself for Cole's rebuttal.

"How did it go! How do you think it went?" replied Cole, as if Grace could read his mind.

"Mr. Gaines, um. . ." Grace trailed off, the name sticking in her throat, as though frozen there by Cole's glare.

"Yes, Mr. Gaines is up to his old tricks. Smoke and mirrors, his personal game of camouflage. He has something secretive up his sleeve and, as usual, is making it seem like something else, something for the benefit of the company. And he's doing it all behind my back!" Cole's glare had turned to a scowl. Grace rolled her eyes. Art stood by, fidgeting but saying nothing.

"What do you think it is this time?" Grace asked.

"He wants to use Hollingsworth Island to help us launch a new scientific division to our publishing efforts. Wants to inform the public—or so he says.

He and some of the other board members have been communicating with a team of hotshot scientists stationed on the island doing research who apparently want their work to be published. Gaines sees this as an opportunity for more advertising revenue," Cole said.

Grace considered this, and it must have been the look of agreement on her face regarding Bill's plan that sent Cole over the top.

"What? You think Gaines's idea is a valid one?" Cole shouted.

Grace appeared to shrink back into her chair but had no place to hide. She wanted to lash back at her boss for being such a jerk but thought better of it.

"Hold on, everybody," Art said. "Let's all calm down. I think it's fair to assume Bill is hiding something. But before we speculate too much, my vote is to find out more on the QT, before we confront him."

Cole immediately turned on Art, as if he had become the enemy, too.

"Cole, I'm on your side, bro. Let's just give this some thought. What would *you* like to do?"

Cole appeared to calm down now that his opinion was being sought. He turned and walked toward the window, staring out at the city skyline, suddenly lost in thought. Silence fell over the room as Cole stood stiff-backed, gazing out into space.

"I think a little trip back to the island is in order." Cole faced his companions. "Think you can handle that, bro?"

Art nodded. Grace's eyes widened. Cole appeared resolute. He was going back to the Caribbean—but for what reason?

CHAPTER FIVE

AFTER ART HAD LEARNED the names of the scientists who were communicating with Gaines, he and Cole made plans to leave, while Grace kept the event low-key. Something about a publishing company for sale in Mexico—which was legit and priced right—but not where the twosome was ultimately heading. They would land in Mexico City on Cole's personal plane, a Dassault Falcon 7X SuperJet, then switch to a charter and fly to Puerto Rico, the largest island near the newly formed volcano. Most of the communication hubs for the research being conducted were located on the eastern side of Puerto Rico.

From there, a chartered boat would take them to Hollingsworth Island. The trick was not to be recognized but still be given clearance to the island, which was carefully guarded from outsiders. That would take a combination of influence and money—none of which were in short supply in Cole's world. The plan was to approach it from a scientific perspective, and the carrot dangled would be a large endowment fund to further the ongoing research. Once it was announced, scientific teams would descend like seagulls on beached crabs. Art would meet with a few of the leading teams, and, somehow, the scientists working for Gaines would get the nod as the finalists, without knowing who was responsible for it. They wouldn't really care anyway—only that they got the money and, eventually, the recognition. The scientific community wasn't really that different from any other industry or sport. It was all very competitive. Success was what mattered, and there was nothing better than money to ensure that would happen.

Plans were made quickly, false identities and passports secured, and the twosome was ready to depart in two days. When Gaines found out, he was naturally suspicious, but upon contacting the publishing company in Mexico that was for sale, they confirmed everything Cole had said and said they were eager to start negotiations with Hollingsworth Enterprises. It sounded like a reasonable opportunity, and the fact that Cole would be gone for a week or more allowed Gaines additional time to operate without Cole looking over his shoulder.

CHAPTER SIX

A s THE FALCON SOARED higher into the sky, heading southwest, Art turned to Cole. "So, you think Gaines bought into it? He's a tough guy to fool."

"I was worried about that, but after talking to the owners of Mexicali Publishing, I warned them they should expect a call from Gaines and to be convincing. Even if we don't acquire them, I promised them financial aid in the short term until they either get back on their feet or sell to a legitimate buyer. In any case, we'll have some amount of equity in whatever results. They're too important to the area to shut down," Cole said.

"Nice job, Cole. You're more like your father than I thought. That's exactly what he would have done," Art said, but with the slightest hint of sarcasm. Cole bristled but said nothing.

After a few moments of silence, Cole asked Art, "How did you manage to get the falsified documents so quickly?"

"It's all in who you know. Though I mostly represent corporations in business related law, some of the folks I've worked with are. . .how should I phrase it? Less than scrupulous," Art replied, smiling.

"Okay, that's all I need to know. Whatever you did worked, and we got what we needed."

A moment later, their flight attendant appeared, who had until now remained inconspicuous. Cole's mouth dropped open at the sight of Sydney Swanson, one of the socialite twins turned Ralph Lauren models and a former conquest of Art's. As Cole was about to lay into Art for bringing her along, Shelby, the other half of the gorgeous twin sisters, appeared, smiling and holding cocktails for the men.

"Well, you didn't think we were going to let you gents have all the fun, did you?" Sydney said, gushing with enthusiasm. Shelby did one of her infamous curtsy's, allowing her cleavage to be at eye level with Cole. Both women were decked out in Lauren aviation attire—which left little to the imagination—donning captain's hats at angles atop their windswept, strawberry blonde curls.

Cole groaned as Shelby handed him a scotch on the rocks, his choice of liquor. Seeing the two sisters again brought back bittersweet memories of Lindsay. Cole had played an integral part in Art's attempt to get both sisters in bed at the same time, on the night that Lindsay had reentered Cole's life. And, in some odd, twisted sort of way, the twins had played a minor role in the entire adventure. They were with Cole and Art to the end, deplaning the jet on Cole's arrival back in the States, after the volcano had formed. The fact that they had parlayed that not-so-coincidental episode into lucrative Lauren modeling careers hadn't escaped Cole's attention. What did it matter, anyway? He was happy for them—and Art was eternally grateful to Cole for allowing that to happen. He was on their good side again, and what Art had been doing with that little maneuver was anyone's guess.

Cole glanced over at Art with disapproval pasted on his face. Art sat and shrugged his shoulders as if to say, *I had no idea, boss.* Cole shook his head as Art accepted a mai tai from Sydney, apparently already in a festive, tropical mood.

As the girls disappeared into the plane's galley, Art smiled sheepishly. "I'm willing to share, ol' buddy."

"How dare you bring them with us," Cole accused. "This is a critical business trip, and—I don't think I need to tell you—top secret. With our luck, we'll be on the front page of a fashion magazine, or worse, a scientific journal, before you can say, *Bill Gaines scores again!*" Cole said, furious.

"Cole, I made them swear not to say or do anything to get us in the news. They know what we're doing is important but don't know what it is." Art hesitated. "Actually, they've been bored ever since. . . well, since we were all together the last time in San Salvador. But back to the subject—don't ever underestimate what beautiful and smart women can do in the way of persuasiveness. They are both committed to helping us. They're on board as part of the team."

Cole stared at Art for a long moment. "You should have been a salesman, you son of a bitch."

"What do you think a lawyer is?" Art laughed and took a long drink, just as Cole spotted the miniature umbrella hanging on his glass.

Cole's head began to spin, lost in a delusion of Lindsay and the mysterious Cantina de la Noche in San Salvador. There, where the proprietor of the cantina gave him the umbrella with the mermaid attached to the tiny silver pole, telling Cole to *look for her elsewhere, you will not find her here.* Her words had been prophetic. That mythical cantina was rumored to suddenly materialize in the back alleys of San Salvador, but only at a moment of greatest need.

"Cole. . . Cole? Are you okay?" Art asked, mildly shaking his friend by the shoulder. Cole blinked twice, then fully opened his eyes, unsure for a moment of their location.

"Where were you, buddy?" Art asked, concerned. "One moment we were talking, and the next you looked like you were in another world."

Cole cleared his head. "Just a memory, Art. . ." Cole's voice trailed off, a flood of pain sweeping across his face. So many sleepless nights had passed since his return to the States. So many restless nights, lying awake, wanting nothing more than Lindsay by his side.

"You miss her, don't you?" Art asked, with more compassion than Cole had heard in a long time.

Although Art was his best friend, he was often cold and seemingly indifferent to what others were feeling. All of his adult life, Art had trailed in Cole's shadow—watching the notorious playboy in action, jealous of all his accomplishments and fame. When Cole did something wrong, nobody seemed to care. When Art did likewise, he was chastised for being an overbearing attorney who cared little about anything or anyone except himself. Art watched silently as Cole's gaze returned to the porthole and out into the limitless sky of blue. Cole was one of the winners of the world—handsome, charismatic, wealthy beyond what most people could even imagine. Art flashed back to one of his favorite bands, Steely Dan, and the lyrics to *Deacon Blues.*

Something about names for the winners of the world, which Cole certainly was. And something about the losers. Which group did Art belong to?

And yet, Cole had somehow chosen Art to be his closest friend. Art smiled regretfully and turned away. The sound of the twin turbo fans of the powerful jet engines droned on as the Falcon rocketed toward its destination. *But where are we really going?* Art considered. And what would they find when they arrived? A mysterious volcanic island, one that somehow held the secret Cole was holding onto so fiercely? They weren't really going to invest in a floundering printing company or to thwart Bill Gaines's self-serving interests. No, Cole was going back to find Lindsay again. Art was sure of it.

CHAPTER SEVEN

T HE FALCON LANDED SAFELY at General Mariano Matamoros Airport, a local airstrip that catered to pilot enthusiasts and private airplanes. There would be little commotion caused by the arrival of an expensive private jet. Employees of the airport knew to keep their mouths shut and their eyes focused elsewhere. Their salaries were paid as much by the bribes of the travelers as they were by company paychecks.

The Falcon taxied toward a private hanger and stopped fifty yards away. Art had arranged for the jet to be stored inside and kept out of view while they completed their business in the area. It hadn't been cheap, but it was Cole's money after all. There would be no questions, no complaints, no mention of it. A blank check in the hands of a top attorney, known to have some very unscrupulous clients. Nothing to worry about.

Art handed an envelope to the attendant who suddenly appeared out of the hanger. A brief conversation and a handshake followed, as Cole deplaned and headed for a beige, nondescript Jeep Cherokee. A few minutes later, luggage was loaded into the back compartment, while the Swanson sisters and Art climbed inconspicuously into the SUV. Sydney and Shelby had changed into dark gray sweat suits with no visible labels, their hair tied up under baseball caps. The driver spoke both Spanish, his native language, and fluent English. He also knew the area well and asked no questions.

Art sat in the front passenger's seat, with Cole sandwiched between the twins in the back seat. It was going to be a long ride of just over twenty hours to Puerto Morelos on the easternmost tip of the Yucatan Peninsula. They would make the drive in two days, stopping at a small town midway to catch a few hours of sleep. After arriving in Puerto Morelos, they would spend the night, before catching a charter plane to Puerto Rico the following day. It was there where they would assume new identities and become invisible, no longer members of Rhode Island's social elite. Art had even managed to obtain forged documents for the Swanson sisters, no doubt as much for his own entertainment as for their aid in accomplishing Cole's objectives. So much for Art pretending not to know the twins were on the plane.

Art checked them into a motel around midnight in the Tabasco region of Mexico, where the terrain became more remote. Four rooms, next to each other. Their driver had gone for takeout food, and they ate in their rooms. The Swanson sisters were becoming restless, still confused about what this trip was all about and wondering what the hell they were doing in the middle of nowhere. This wasn't the way Cole normally traveled. Art talked the women down, but tension was mounting by the hour. The twins would not stay placated much longer without some reasonable explanation.

The sun rose far too early the following morning. The women were barely awake before being offered hot cups of coffee and an assortment of day-old Mexican pastries and then being ushered into the SUV, hitting the road with the glow of the eastern sunrise not yet faded. Cole sat in the front seat today, while Art did his best to keep the sisters entertained and under control in the back. Their driver sipped coffee, said nothing, and drove headlong into the bright sun, imposing its brilliant light directly into their faces. It was only eight in the morning, but the temperature had reached the mid-eighties, and the humidity was sweltering.

Art, who had suddenly become an expert on Mexico, recounted the history of the area's violent and colorful past, while the others pretended to listen. Occasionally, the driver would peer back at Art through the rearview mirror and chuckle, a subtle reminder that Art really didn't know the area all that well, but said nothing to correct him.

Ten hours into the drive, Shelby couldn't take any more and blurted out in near desperation, "How much longer? I can't stand any more driving! We didn't sign up for this."

Sydney was about to chime in with her two cents when the sound of sirens and red flashing lights caught them from behind. The driver slowed and pulled over to the dirt shoulder of the two-lane road, allowing the police to pass unobstructed. However, the state police car slowed as well. Cursing in Spanish, the driver came to a full stop. He turned to his passengers and whispered to them to remain calm and let him do the talking, just as two uniformed men approached the driver's window with pistols raised.

"Shit!" Art cursed under his breath. The women went stone silent, fuming. Could it get any worse?

Cole remained calm, retrieving a small satchel from his backpack and placing it between his legs for easy access if needed. He had intentionally filled it with hundred-dollar bills, which had come in handy during previous trips to the tropics. Somehow, despite all his previous antics, he had never been officially arrested. He intended to keep it that way.

The driver rolled down his window while looking up at the officers, who looked about as friendly as the sea pirates who had shuttled Art to the frigate in search of Cole after he had gone missing with Lindsay. It had taken all the money Art could conjure, along with his $20,000 Rolex watch and a threat to throw Art out of the helicopter before the mercenaries had let him board the ship.

"Hello officers," the driver said politely in English, but with his best Spanish accent. "Was I speeding?" he asked nonchalantly.

"Please get of the car, the rest of you stay seated," the taller of the two men commanded.

The driver cracked open the door as the police moved back. He stepped onto the packed dirt surface, handing the officer his license. The tall man took a cursory look.

"What are you doing with four Americanos in this part of the country? Are you hiding from someone? This looks very suspicious, you know."

The driver tipped his hat in a sign of submission. "I'm a professional driver and chauffeur." He handed the cop his business card verifying his statement. "These people are headed to the port town of Puerto Morelos for some R&R and a little fishing."

"No one drives to Puerto Morelos through this godforsaken desert. Everyone flies there. Now do you want to tell me what you're really doing out here?" the policeman said as he inched closer, gun still in hand. His partner moved nearer to the car and peered in at the passengers menacingly. He was brandishing his firearm as well.

"Sir, the two women suffer from air sickness and don't do well on airplanes, so they hired me. It's really not that unusual. I've made this same trip many times before," the driver lied.

"Where are you coming from?" the cop said.

"Mexico City. We left two days ago," the driver said.

"And how did these women get to Mexico City if they hate flying? They obviously aren't Mexican citizens. I suppose they walked?" the taller man said. The cop's partner snorted.

"Actually, they took the train from Los Angeles, in a luxury cabin. They, um, are well off and have a lot of free time," the diver said, deciding it was time to subtly bring money into the conversation. "Their gentlemen friends flew into Mexico City to meet them before heading out to Puerto Morelos."

At this cue, both Shelby and Sydney removed their baseball caps, as if the heat was getting the better of them, and their long, strawberry blonde curls fell about their shoulders as they shook their heads in unison. The officers' eyes widened, as though startled by this turn of events. Wealthy *and* beautiful—and stranded out in the middle of the Mexican desert. The cop who was guarding the car returned to his partner's side, whispering something into his ear.

The driver turned his head slightly, back toward Cole, smiling and rubbing his thumb and forefinger together, out of view from the police.

Cole acknowledged with a faint nod of his head. *Now we're getting somewhere*, he thought. The shakedown was only minutes away now, and Cole was prepared.

"Now that you two fine policemen know there is nothing out of the ordinary or illegal going on, I'd like to introduce you to two of the top Ralph Lauren female models. Would you like to meet them personally?" the driver asked slyly. "Part of their trip will include photo sessions in the resort areas of Mexico. You've heard of Polo Fashion, haven't you?" the driver said. The cops nodded, almost too eagerly. "They are introducing their new summer swimwear collection, and what better place than the coast of Mexico, no?"

"Ladies, please come out and meet two of Mexico's finest," the driver said, ushering the women out of the car with a hand gesture. Slowly, Shelby, then Sydney, exited the Jeep, moving seductively toward the officers. Both women smiled and took positions next to each man, snuggling up a little closer than was necessary.

Art could barely hold back a grin as the tough-talking *policia* melted into submission, as though entering their first strip club. The women glowed as they removed their bulky sweat suits, revealing tight tank tops and hot-pink shorts emblazoned with the Polo logo.

"What do you think? Do you like these?" Shelby asked, turning in a circle. The police stared open-mouthed at the models.

Art stepped out of the car, toting a 35mm digital camera. "Gentleman, how about a photo with the girls? I'm sure they'd love to send you personally autographed pictures once we reach our destination," Art said.

The officers didn't seem to care that Art and Cole were stepping out of the car without being instructed to do so. They continued to gawk at the models as the women circled around them, occasionally touching their arms.

"Time to pose, girls," Art said enthusiastically. The girls snuggled up closely to the two men, while Art snapped off a dozen photos. "I think that should do it," Art said, lowering the camera. By this time, the officer's heads were spinning.

Cole stepped forward, introducing himself as Bradley Harris, a talent scout accompanying the models. His forged ID would confirm the name if needed. Cole looked the two men squarely in the eyes and let them have it with both barrels.

"Gentlemen, thank you for stopping us and making sure we were safe. It's great to know the local police are so concerned. We've really enjoyed meeting you, and thanks for being such good sports with the photos and everything. Don't be surprised if your pictures end up being published. I think that would be a great promo, don't you?" Cole paused. "In addition, we'd like to make a little donation to the local police charity." Cole handed each man twenty $100 bills, folded in half. "I'm sure you'll make good use of it. If there's nothing else, we must be on our way. We're hoping to make Puerto Morelos before dark."

Shelby and Sydney kissed both officers on the cheek and moved away, entering the car. The three men followed close behind. After tipping his hat toward the police, the driver started the Jeep and slowly drove away, while the girls waved back smiling, leaving the stunned officers standing alone and wondering what the hell had just happened.

CHAPTER EIGHT

T HE REST OF THE trip remained uneventful, other than the twins' moods improving remarkably. They were again laughing and talking about their new modeling careers and the crazy things that were happening to them. While sipping drinks and sitting on the veranda of their modest hotel, Art complimented the driver on the way he'd handled the situation with the police.

"By the way, how did you know these two gorgeous women were Lauren models?" Art couldn't help but ask.

"It's all in a day's work, *señor*. I make it my business to know who I'm driving around, you know. Especially, when it is people as famous as you are. But not to worry, I never reveal anything that will jeopardize my clients' business. That would mean professional death for me. But, at times, I may reveal just a little to help out in a particular situation," the driver said, and he smiled at the thought of the model incident earlier that afternoon.

Later at dinner, both Art and Cole raised their glasses in salute to their driver's resourcefulness. The girls leaned forward and gave the driver a hug. Art thought he saw the driver blush, but he refrained from commenting.

Dinner passed rather quickly, as the food was substandard and no one wanted to drink excessively. Art and Cole needed some time alone to finalize their plans and needed clear heads over the next couple of days. All said their good nights, and plans were made to depart at seven in the morning. The driver would take them to a small strip airport to catch their charter plane to Puerto Rico and then depart the premises quickly so no one would have a chance to question him, especially if the police officers had called in their planned arrival.

After a brief rehash of tomorrow's events, Cole retired to his room. Art, on the other hand, appeared to be headed for the twins' room, which they predictably shared. Art had personally seen to that little detail.

Cole lay in his bed, eyes wide open. He was closer now. Closer to the place where he and Lindsay had faced an event nearly unexplainable. Cole had survived. Lindsay, apparently, had not. Yet, he could feel her presence next to him, feel her protective wings wrapping around his body and carrying him to safety. With each breath he took, he could sense her—smell the faint saltwater scent of her skin, feel the luxuriousness of her thick, auburn hair. Her slate gray eyes boring into his, imploring him to face the truth, to be a better man. All of which he had done, but too late. They were still an ocean apart. Was that ocean closer now, as he navigated his way back? Back to the island—back to her. He slowly drifted off to sleep, spending a restless night searching for the woman he loved in the frigid, murky depths of the ocean.

Morning arrived with the scent of hot coffee wafting in from the open windows of Cole's room. Art was pounding on his door, driving Cole to action. Cole was already showered and packed. He slipped on a pair of blue jeans and a tropical shirt, laced up his boots, grabbed his duffle bag, and flung the door open. Art was smiling, standing flanked by the twins, leaving little doubt as to what had transpired during the night. Art handed Cole a cup of steaming coffee without saying anything, turned, and headed toward the Jeep, which was already running with the air-conditioning on high. The morning was strikingly bright and already muggy. It was going to be a long, hot day, in more ways than one.

Shelby blushed, as if she knew what Cole was thinking, while Sydney looped her arm through Cole's.

Sydney looked up at him. "Are you ready, Cole?" she said, in a manner that unnerved him. Lindsay had said the same thing to him before their first descent in their world-class submersible into the depths of the ocean. Did she know? Had Art confided in the twins last night that this trip was not just to see the volcano and to identify the best scientific team, but an attempt to discover a deeper secret. Cole suddenly felt a sense of relief wash over him, that his burden might be shared by others who cared about him. He patted Sydney's arm and smiled, but he said nothing. They headed to the Jeep, arm in arm.

There was little conversation between the group as the Jeep bounced along the pothole-filled road south of Puerto Morales, dust flying up from the all-terrain tires, forming a billowing dirt cloud behind them. The trip to the remote location would take a little over two hours, and then they would pay cash and board a cramped seaplane. Art only hoped this charter was more reputable than the unscrupulous group he had dealt with on San Salvador. He'd brought extra cash this time just in case.

When they arrived, Art's apprehension was well justified. From the grungy-looking shack that evidently served as the office to the three, weather-beaten seaplanes on the dirt runway nearby, the place screamed of decline. The two Mexican men sporting sawed-off shotguns sitting to the right and left of the front entrance did little to encourage the group. The driver stepped out of the Jeep and approached them cautiously.

Cole could barely hear the exchange in Spanish, which quickly grew heated. The driver turned back to Cole with a disgruntled expression. Cole knew immediately what that meant and nodded. They really didn't have much choice in the matter. Cole turned to Art, who had apparently figured it out on his own and was reaching for his locked briefcase.

Cole gestured for the driver to return. As he approached, Cole asked Art how much cash he had. Art said twenty-five thousand. Cole turned to the driver. "How much?"

"After they saw you *gringos* and that there are two women included, they have demanded an extra five thousand each. Twenty thousand total."

"That's fucking highway robbery!" Art exclaimed. "Especially after how much this cost to begin with. Tell them twenty-five hundred each and not a penny more. We'll find another charter."

The driver looked over at Cole, who nodded. Art handed the driver ten thousand. Before the driver walked back to the men, he instructed the group to pick up their bags and return to the Jeep. They needed to appear resolved.

From the interior of the car, they watched as the driver negotiated the deal. There was a lot of yelling and pointing back at the Jeep, and possibly even a few threats made, but in the end, the extra money won out. There was a handshake, the transfer of the cash, and then the driver waved the group out of the car. The deal was done.

As the twins passed by the Mexicans, one of the gunmen made a comment in Spanish, accompanied by a hand gesture that looked disgusting. His partner laughed raucously.

The driver lingered until it appeared it was safe and his clients were headed to the largest of the seaplanes. He strolled back toward his car but waited until the plane was airborne before leaving. Whispering good luck in Spanish and making a sign of the cross, he pondered what was really going on here. It appeared this leg of their journey had been successfully navigated, but what lay ahead might be even more fraught with danger. To successfully pass through the security of the volcano in disguise might prove more challenging, especially for someone as famous as Cole Hollingsworth.

CHAPTER NINE

T HE CHARTERED FLIGHT WAS, for the most part, low-key. The pilot spoke broken English, when he spoke at all. The amphibious floatplane appeared to be more mechanically sound than it looked, which was a good thing. The time-honored saying that appearances can be deceiving popped into Cole's head, and it was certainly true in this case.

After an hour in the air, the men relaxed, although the girls' expressions didn't follow suit. White-knuckled and tight-lipped, the Swanson sisters clung to their seats, incensed, their moods diminishing as quickly as the shoreline behind them.

Why all the secrecy? Shelby wondered. This entire trip was becoming more and more convoluted. Cole was hiding something, and Art wouldn't fess up. Shelby resolved to get to the truth and exchanged a look with Sydney. Something unspoken passed between the women, something only identical twins were capable of communicating. They would discuss it when—and if—they landed safely. There would be no more cavorting with Art until they knew more.

Two hours later, Hollingsworth Island became visible in the distance, dwarfing the seascape and the shoreline of nearby Puerto Rico from this height, even though that shoreline was more than two hundred miles away.

Cole's companions gasped in unison. The scene looked more akin to a Hollywood blockbuster movie, like *Jurassic Park* or *King Kong*—something created with special effects that could not possibly exist in the real world. As they flew in much closer, they could see that its uppermost peak was shrouded in clouds. Its barren cliffs looked like alligator skin, cracked and leathery and barren. Black, hardened lava flows streaked its shoreline, like fissures intertwined with flat spaces—all visible through binoculars from this distance. In a word, the volcano was *massive*.

Art and the women had seen pictures of it on TV or in magazines, but they were still totally unprepared for what they now saw firsthand, as the pilot flew them closer.

Cole looked on breathlessly, and even though he had walked on its surface as recently as six months ago, he was taken aback by its enormity. The volcano was mesmerizing, almost hypnotic. It had changed dramatically in a way he was unable to articulate or even begin to understand. No wonder the world's top scientists were enthralled to the point of abandoning all other projects they had been working on. Nothing compared in scope. Even the pilot, who had seen it many times, appeared dumbfounded, whispering something to himself in Spanish that sounded like a prayer—or a warning of something otherworldly.

"How soon until we land?" Art questioned the pilot.

"Veinte minutos," came the reply, in a voice that sounded unsteady. The pilot abruptly veered right and began heading to a small, private airstrip, near Isabela, as though he wanted nothing more to do with the island. After he began his descent, with the volcano behind them, the group could still feel a strange power emanating from its massive form, like a giant, electromagnetic field—powerful forces in constant opposition to each other.

Cole felt it the most. It was unnerving. Could it be Lindsay calling to him, beckoning him back? Was she really inside?

After a bumpy landing, the seaplane taxied to a stop near a small grouping of ramshackle buildings posing as hangers and an office. If anything, this airstrip appeared substandard compared to the one they had just left.

But they had made the journey safely, and they were now closer to their final destination. However, the real challenge lay ahead—could Cole and Art make it onto the new island unrecognized? If the media learned of Cole's return, the world would soon know about it, too, along with Bill Gaines and his collaborators.

Thirty minutes later, an aging van, looking more rusted than painted, pulled up. This was to be their mode of transportation to the city of Isabela, on the northeastern tip of Puerto Rico, and the Parador Villas, if they could be considered villas at all. A limo could have been summoned—they were available for the right amount of cash—and an upgraded hotel, but Cole had instructed Art to keep it as low-key and remote as possible. Close to the ocean and tucked away on a small inlet, the Parador offered separated bungalows with few amenities, resulting in more privacy.

Art had booked the rooms but began to grow anxious as the driver neared their destination. He had already anticipated the twins' reaction to the motel—as if top Lauren models would be forced to stay at such a dive. Fortunately, he had reserved separate rooms for all four of them. He doubted there would be further romantic liaisons with the women after they saw the place but hoped that one of them might weaken, so the more he could keep them separated, the better.

The driver unloaded their luggage near the cramped front office, accepted a tip from Art, and quickly drove away. Instinctively, the driver knew something was amiss. Why would four Americans rent an out-of-date, amphibious plane and fly in basically undetected to a remote airstrip from an even more remote airstrip? It had to be something about the mysterious new island. He wanted nothing to do with it. *Crazy Americans!* he thought as he drove off. Ever since the volcano had erupted violently out of the ocean, strange things were occurring—things he couldn't understand or remotely explain. Rumors were spreading about what was taking place inside the volcano. Unnatural things. The driver shuddered for a moment then tried to force the sensation away. A stop at a nearby cantina would help ease his anxiety. He knew just the place.

After checking in and a twenty-minute tirade from the twins directed at Art about their new accommodations, the women stomped off to cool down. Art shrugged and looked over at Cole.

Cole shrugged back at Art as if to say, *what did you expect?* Cole picked up his duffel bag and headed toward his bungalow. Art stood solitary for a few minutes, trying to collect himself and figure out a way to placate the twins. Frustrated, he turned toward his bungalow, which was adjacent to Cole's.

Each building housed two rooms. About fifteen yards separated the brightly colored buildings, which were garish looking against the earthy shades of ocean, sand, and the willowing grass surrounding the villas. In between, tattered, wooden picnic tables stood at tilted angles on the uneven ground. In the distance, Art glimpsed families near the water, frolicking on the beach, carefree—or so it seemed. Art envied their naivete; life seemed so much simpler for them. What had he gotten himself into?

CHAPTER TEN

E VERYONE KEPT TO THEMSELVES until the dinner hour rolled around. Art was fidgeting and pacing the wooden floor of his room. The old planks creaked under his weight. Cole sat at a small desk, studying a map of the area and taking notes, wondering what the next few days would bring. God only knew what the twins were up to.

Cole's cell phone rang, disturbing his contemplative state.

Art practically shouted at his friend. "Cole, I can't take much more of this. Let's grab a beer. I'll meet you at the cantina near the office. I'll be there in five."

Cole's phone went silent. This was the last thing he needed—Art coming unglued. Normally calm and collected, something was clearly bothering him. At first, Cole assumed it was the Swanson sisters' outburst that had rattled his friend. But the more he thought about it, the more it seemed like something else. Cole closed his laptop and headed out the door, locking it behind him.

The Parador's cantina was basically a deck with wooden pillars supporting a thatched roof. A collection of mismatched ceiling fans rotated lazily, circulating the damp air. The view down to the beach on the left revealed the sparkling waters beyond, which was probably the only redeeming quality about the place. With temperatures in the eighties and the humidity even higher, the air was hot and sticky. Thankfully, the rooms were air-conditioned, although the small in-wall units were pretty outdated. Droplets of water fell silently from the corners of the metal boxes to the ground below, forming small puddles—the perfect breeding ground for mosquitos.

When Cole arrived, Art was already seated at a table next to the railing, with a sweating bottle of beer clutched in his hand. It had been a short five minutes. Art turned his head toward Cole but said nothing. He motioned toward the waiter to come take another drink order. The young man moved tentatively forward, with a small notebook and a pencil tucked behind his ear. The kid couldn't have been more than sixteen, with dark skin, dark hair and eyes, and dressed in khaki shorts and a short-sleeved, tropical shirt. His English was broken, but he seemed to understand better than he spoke. Cole ordered a bottle of Old Harbor, the same beer Art was drinking, a local beer brewed in Puerto Rico that had a quite a kick to it.

Cole sat pensively, waiting for his drink to arrive, while Art gazed out toward the inlet and the ocean beyond. "So ol' buddy, what's on your mind? You seem troubled," Cole said.

Art's eyes twitched, but he remained mute, refusing to face Cole, as though contemplating what to say or searching for the right words. After a long moment, Art turned to his friend, his face contorted in a look of concern.

"What are we really doing down here, Cole? And don't tell me it's because you are all that interested in setting the scientific world straight on the volcano, or that Gaines is doing something that will significantly hurt Hollingsworth Enterprises." Art said, his expression unyielding.

Cole gazed back at his friend with resolve, as if his authority had just been questioned. His expression softened. If he couldn't confide in Art, then who could he? Cassie Thomas was halfway around the world, hiding out in Australia somewhere. Grace, who was not only his personal assistant but his close friend, didn't know the truth, and. . . and Lindsay was gone. His parents were dead. Cole had nobody. He hadn't felt this alone since that fateful day—the day Lindsay had saved his life and forfeited her own. The pain came cascading back, as if a giant wave had just crashed over his world, splintering it into pieces, the hollow feeling inside becoming more insufferable with each passing day.

Cole looked away, emotion choking off his ability to even speak the words he knew Art was waiting to hear.

Art pressed on, not letting his friend off the hook this time, even if it meant alienating him. He needed Cole to face the truth, to say it out loud. It was the only way they could get to the truth—the awful truth that Lindsay was gone forever. "So, what is it, Cole?" Art's tone more insistent now.

Cole slowly turned back toward Art and opened his mouth to explain what he was feeling when suddenly the Swanson twins approached. They were still looking betrayed, but dressed casually, silently indicating they were ready to unwind a bit. It was either that or stay camped out in their rooms, being miserable. If anything, the women had proven themselves adaptable.

Cole turned back toward Art, cutting him off with a single word. "Later."

Art frowned but had little choice. His mood changed immediately as he faced the twins—all smiles and looking repentant. "You two feeling better?" Art questioned. "Hey, I'm really sorry, but this was the only way. We can't be recognized. I promise I'll make it up to you later."

The twins appeared unconvinced, looking irritated and pouting like little girls. They had that act down to perfection and Art fell for it every time.

Cole looked on in amusement. *The games people play*, he mused. "Anyone up for a drink?" Cole asked, gesturing the server over.

The twins yielded, ordering a couple of designer martini's, which completely befuddled the young server. Not wanting to appear lame in the presence of such beautiful women, he nodded and returned to the bar. A few minutes passed before he returned with two screwdrivers, topped with cherries and orange slices. He smiled sheepishly, offering the sisters their drinks.

Shelby was about to object, but she noticed the expression on Cole's face, silently instructing her to accept it. She grabbed the drink, along with her sister's arm, and headed for the pool.

Art ordered two more beers, and the men headed out to join the women, who were sitting on lounge chairs facing the water, complaining about something.

For a long, unbearable moment, the foursome stared silently out at the shimmering ocean, which changed hues as the sun dipped low to the west. Tiny, twinkling lights encircling the cantina sprung to life, although nearly a third of them were burned out. The young server began lighting the tiki torches lining the nearby pathway leading to the restaurant, the pungent odor of kerosene suddenly filling the clammy air.

"In spite of our accommodations, it's still beautiful, isn't it?" Art remarked, while waving his arm across the inlet as though drawing a curtain back to reveal something altogether new—a panoramic canvas painted with glorious colors.

Both women sighed, but they nodded their agreement. What could they do about it, anyway? They were here for something more, something they didn't fully understand, but they intuitively knew it was important. They knew it was for Cole, otherwise they would be leaving on the first plane out tomorrow morning—with or without Art.

"Anyone hungry?" Art asked. It was getting late, and they had a lot to accomplish tomorrow. "Why don't we head back up to the cantina, and I'll buy you the best food this fine establishment has to offer."

Both women looked up at Art as though he was joking. "If their cuisine is like their martinis, I can hardly wait," Sydney quipped.

"Did you make reservations, Art?" Shelby added. "Otherwise, the wait may be hours!"

"Now, now, ladies, let's be civil. Before you know it, we'll be sitting at Breeder's back home, sipping French champagne and devouring Maine lobster. A few nights of roughing it won't do you any harm," Art replied, grinning.

But what Art and the twins did not yet understand was that day might never come.

CHAPTER ELEVEN

MORNING CAME SLOWLY, TOO slowly for Cole. His night had been restless, his dreams fraught with visions of Lindsay morphing into a myriad of supernatural beings—sometimes an angel of shimmering light, other times a gargoyle-like creature of evil. Irritated and sleep-deprived, Cole stood groggily in the shower, endeavoring to come to his senses as the ice-cold water slowly turned tepid. Normally, this would have infuriated him, but the shock to his body seemed to revive him. He dried himself, got dressed, and headed to Art's room.

Art appeared ready to get started, handing Cole a plastic cup of steaming coffee. A platter of mangos, papayas, and *quesitos* that looked at least a day or two old sat atop the small wooden table next to the bed.

Cole accepted the coffee gratefully and was about to reach for the Puerto Rican pastry, when he spotted something dark scuttling across the platter and then down a table leg before disappearing into a crack in the wall. Cockroaches! What next? He quickly retracted his hand.

"What's the matter, Cole? My breakfast not up to your liking?" Art questioned.

"No, it's fine. Thanks, Art. Just not hungry this morning. I'll grab something later."

Art shrugged but took no further offense. He grabbed a manila folder out of his briefcase.

"These are the names and contact information of the people I will be meeting with today to arrange the next leg of our journey. I hope to secure a driver and a sturdy watercraft to get us to the island. I've made a duplicate copy for you, in case anything happens or I run into trouble." Art paused. "We also need to secure a location for meeting with the scientific teams. This endeavor has to look legit. . . and we do have to choose the team we'll be working with to convince Gaines we are moving forward, right?" Art glanced at Cole to see if he was engaged in their plan, or even listening.

Cole nodded, but he seemed disinterested. Clearly, something else was occupying his thoughts.

"Cole, are you with me on this? It's the only way we will be able to get you on that island, and—correct me if I'm wrong—that is what you want, right?"

Cole hesitated, then focused his rather intimidating gaze squarely on Art. "Yes, it is essential I reach the volcano undetected. Nothing short of that will be acceptable. Do we understand each other?" Cole replied sternly, as if the selection of the scientific team was the furthest thing from his mind.

Art regarded his friend—his boss—for a long moment, while doubt began to creep back into his head. He was sure now, more than ever, that Cole's agenda was different than his. He believed Cole had been legitimately interested in controlling the outcome of this mission so that Bill Gaines would not gain more control of Hollingsworth Enterprises under the guise of creating a new scientific division of the company that he would lead. They had been clear about that before departing Newport. To thwart the chairman's attempts to win the loyalty of more board directors by establishing himself as the visionary that could lead the company to new heights and increased profitability. Now Art wasn't so sure.

After the two men finished discussing the last few details, Art left the room and headed to the front office to await transportation to a cantina in town, where he would meet with his initial contacts. They had texted him the location, time, and place the previous evening. Art didn't know what the men looked like, but they had indicated they would recognize him, so he put his faith in these strangers to fulfill their end of the deal. He was paying them a shitload of money, so he felt fairly certain they would produce—they had been recommended as *reliable*.

As he waited outside the tiny lobby of the Parador Villas, Art wondered if the word *reliable* meant the same thing in this part of the world as it did in the US. Intuitively, he didn't think so. All of the contacts he used for under-cover work or clandestine meetings in the States he trusted implicitly. But he knew them personally, and they had never let him down. His experiences thus far in the Caribbean had been disastrous—starting with the Charter fiasco in Cockburn Town that had disappeared with his money when he was initially trying to find Cole in San Salvador, to the sea pirates that had fleeced him out of his remaining cash, including his $20,000 Rolex, to fly him to the *USS Truett*, the frigate Cole was staying on with Lindsay while searching for the truth regarding Cole's missing parents. Art shuddered at those memories.

A moment later, a weather-beaten taxi pulled up. The driver opened the door, indicating that Art should enter, but said nothing. Art clung to his locked briefcase more tightly than necessary, determined to hold onto Cole's money until he was sure they would receive what they paid for.

CHAPTER TWELVE

Bored and anxious, Cole made his way down to the pool area, where Sydney and Shelby were sunning themselves. Their choice of swim-wear was not family friendly—at least not to the scattering of parents and kids nearby—but what the hell. They looked gorgeous and sexy, and, in Cole's mind, it was okay to look. One of the boys, who looked to be eleven or twelve, was pointing out the twins to his younger brother and smiling, while their mother looked on derisively.

Cole joined the women, sitting on an available lounge chair next to Shelby. "Good morning, ladies," Cole greeted them cheerfully. "Did you two sleep well?"

Shelby looked over, her eyes covered by designer sunglasses. She forced a smile. Her flawless, white teeth gleamed in the sunlight.

"Nice swimsuits," Cole offered. "Those boys over there are admiring them as well. I wonder what they're thinking?" Cole smirked.

Sydney glared at Cole. "What is it about boys and men always thinking the worst of women—always thinking about sex."

"Can you blame them, when they are fortunate enough to see two world-class models with next to nothing on sitting right in front of them? We males just don't possess the fortitude to look away," Cole replied good-naturedly.

This comment elicited a hint of a smile from Shelby, who was never one to turn down a compliment, no matter how salacious, from someone like Cole.

"Get out of here, Cole," Sydney said, not really being serious.

"Okay, okay, I know when I've worn out my welcome. I think I'll head down to the beach and wait for Art's call. By the way, you look like you're getting a little sunburned. You might want to turn over. I think the boys would like that view as well!"

Shelby threw the hardcover book she'd been reading at Cole's head. He ducked just in the nick of time, and then he headed down to the beach, as all eyes were now squarely on the sisters.

The main beach was to the left, curving around the shallow inlet, acres of sand sparkling under the hot sun, as if containing crushed diamonds. The waves of azure seawater rolled in one after another, forcing kids to run up the slope to avoid the advancing ocean. Seagulls squawked overhead. It was the picture of serenity; families spending a carefree day on the shoreline, while the stresses and anxieties of their everyday lives melted away, at least temporarily.

Cole was about to head out when he spotted a rickety-looking, wooden staircase to his right, leading down the side of the cliff. He hesitated for a moment, realizing he had not seen it there previously, and he had been at this exact spot yesterday. Intrigued, he approached, noticing a wooden sign attached to one of the railings, its letters faded to the point of being almost illegible.

UNSAFE * DANGEROUS RIP TIDES * NO LIFEGUARD ON DUTY

Surprisingly, the sign was in English, but with no Spanish translation.

Cole stared down at the shaft-like, spiraling stairway leading to a secluded section of beach not previously visible. The only thing separating him from the climb down was a fraying rope loosely attached to both railings. The patch of discolored sand below was surrounded by jagged rock walls, reminding Cole instantly of the treacherous cavern at the bottom of the ocean Lindsay had taken him to. The Puerto Rico Trench, nearly five and a half miles underwater at its deepest point, known as Milwaukee Deep. This was the location where Cole had passed through the portal, experiencing multiple encounters with his dead parents, and where he had ultimately lost Lindsay to the shifting tectonic plates giving birth to the massive volcano nearby.

How Cole had survived that event, rising at breakneck speed to the ocean's surface, protected only by Lindsay's wings, still eluded him. Magical wings, jewel-encrusted wings, protecting him from the unrelenting pressures of the deep ocean, where no human could survive for more than a few seconds without the assistance of a world-class submersible. But here he stood, as evidence of Lindsay's mysterious powers. Powers no one knew about but Cole—with the possible exception of Cassie Thomas, Lindsay's fellow diver and best friend. And even Cassie did not understand the full extent of what Lindsay had done to save Cole, the love of her life.

Cole unhooked the limp rope, taking a tentative step on the first rung of the stairway, testing his weight against the aging plank, unsure if it would hold him. It creaked and sagged a bit but withstood the intrusion. Slowly, Cole descended the stairway, gripping the railing tightly in case one of the planks snapped.

Reaching the bottom safely, Cole felt a strong wind gust in his face, forcing more seawater to the beach, raising the level of water in the protected cove. The waves hit with much more force than just around the corner, on the other side of the rock wall. The perfect combination to create rip currents, as they were officially called. Cole was familiar with this phenomenon, having spent a lot of time at tropical beaches and on the water. He knew they could be dangerous to the uniformed, who would normally panic if caught up in one. He strolled closer to the waterline cautiously, wondering what had drawn him here. It seemed he was destined to discover this place, but for the life of him, he could not understand why.

The hair on Cole's neck stood on end as he heard his name whispered from behind. He froze. And then he heard it a second time.

"Is that you, Cole?" The voice was more insistent now. His mother had spoken those very same words to him when he and Lindsay had passed through the portal to another dimension. Cole whirled around, half expecting to see his mother, or perhaps Lindsay, but to his utter shock, he was staring at the Cantina de la Noche, the mythical bar from the back alleys of Cockburn Town on San Salvador Island. The bar that had previously appeared to him at a time of great need.

The Cantina was pressed up against a recess in the jagged rock wall, out of sight of prying eyes. Suddenly, he was staring at the infamous bartender, a legend that remained steadfast with the locals of San Salvador and beyond. The elegant, silver-haired women was dressed in brilliant gaucho clothing, ageless in her eternal beauty. A *señora* who had fled Spain after an incestuous liaison with Spanish royalty that had resulted in two male children. She had opened the most famous brothel in Argentina, then run out of town to avoid persecution, ending up in San Salvador.

She was known for a specialty unlike any other—the ability to see into men's deepest desires. They would pay her the asking price, and she would pass a drink to them, adorned with miniature umbrellas painted with their country's flag—something she never got wrong—with the name of the partner they were seeking, whomever or whatever that partner needed to be. The men would disappear inside her building and reappear sometime later, but not near the cantina. The price was steep, but these solitary, forlorn men didn't hesitate to pay what she asked. There was no negotiation. The experience was exquisitely sublime, eventually driving many of her clients to madness when they could not find the cantina again.

The authorities had finally caught up with her and her two sons, who worked the bar, and publicly hanged them. At the time, it was major news in the Caribbean and South America, but the event eventually faded with the passing years.

Stories of the legend ultimately returned after random sightings of her doing business in various locations, in the very same cantina Cole was now facing. The myth held that she and her sons would reappear at a time of great need for someone facing a momentous impasse. She had appeared to Cole when he was seeking the truth about Lindsay—a truth that had eluded him until the very end.

Cole stood, weak-kneed and open-mouthed, as he continued to gaze at the *señora*, not believing his own eyes. How could this be possible?

She smiled back seductively, beckoning for him to approach. This could be the reason he was guided to the staircase—her powers were drawing him to the cantina. . . to her.

Cole moved forward, more out of instinct than conscious thought, until he reached the front of the wooden bar, which was shaded by a thatched roof with its ceiling fans slowly turning. He took a seat on one of the stools, placing his hands palm up on the bar top, as though submitting to her will.

Her hands reached over, covering his protectively, as she gazed deeply into his eyes, searching. "What brings you back to me, Cole?" she asked, as if she didn't know.

Cole sat breathlessly, unable to speak, while pondering how to express his wishes. There was really only one—to reunite with Lindsay—but Cole supposed not even this otherworldly gypsy-witch, or whatever she was, could fulfill his deepest desire this time.

She smiled knowingly, at the same time that Cole noticed her sons were conspicuously absent. She released his hands and began to mix a drink for him—a gin and tonic with lime—the same drink he had ordered previously. He recalled her sons doing the same, artfully creating the perfect drink. After he had dropped two $100 bills on the bar as payment for the drink and a bit of information, he had questioned her as to why her sons were not in school and suggested she use his money to further their education. That was before he learned of the witch hunt and hanging, before Lindsay had told him about the legend.

Curious, Cole couldn't help but ask, "Where are your sons?"

"I took your advice and sent them off to boarding school. I figured this wasn't the life for them after all. Thank you for your recommendation. They write to me, occasionally, so I know how they are doing. Good boys, they are," she replied ruefully, as though her soul had been permanently damaged by their absence.

"I see. Perhaps that is best," Cole said respectfully.

"Perhaps. Now, to the reason you have sought me out?"

Cole was momentarily stunned by the question, as if *he* had sought her out. It was more like she had found him. After further thought though, it occurred to Cole that she was right. However unconscious, he'd wanted frantically to find her again. For she had read his mind somehow, reached deep into his very soul, seeking his deepest desire. Perhaps once introduced to a man, she had the uncanny ability to reconnect with her patrons—that's what she called her customers—and so felt Cole's desperate need.

After completing Cole's drink, she topped it with a miniature umbrella—the American flag painted artfully on its top. There was something unrecognizable hanging from the tiny, silver pole. The bar mistress refrained from sliding the drink forward, smiling seductively at the handsome man, as if she might want him for herself. Her allure was impossible to ignore. Cole caught on quickly, recalling their previous encounter.

"So, what do I owe you, *señora*?" Cole asked, reaching for his wallet.

She didn't hesitate to answer. "It just so happens that school tuition is due for my sons, and the best schools don't come cheap, as I'm sure you understand," she said, her gaze unfaltering. She was obviously alluding to Cole's own expensive, Ivy League education.

Cole couldn't help but smile. She was a master of negotiation—and intrigue. She could undoubtably school Art on the topic.

"How does five hundred sound?" Cole replied.

"That will be sufficient. Five hundred for each boy, no?" She hesitated for a moment. "For I hold the *key* to what you seek."

Cole had felt ripped off last time, handing over two hundred for a drink and little more. However, he understood this woman more clearly now and knew instinctively she held information he would not find elsewhere.

"It would be my pleasure. Please pass on my regards to your beautiful sons." Cole extracted ten $100 bills from his wallet and slid them across the bar, without regret.

She accepted them nonchalantly, bowing her head slightly in acknowledgement of his payment. In return, she slid his gin and tonic over, watching, expressionless, as he plucked the miniature umbrella out of the glass.

Cole fondled the item attached, twirling it in his fingers. His eyes widened. It was literally a *key* after all. It looked to be fashioned from bronze or fine copper and studded with tiny, deep-red gemstones that appeared as if they were on fire, reminding him of the lava flow from the volcano. He gazed back at the bartender, puzzled. "What is this for?"

"As I said, it is the key to finding your true desire—nothing less, nothing more. If you choose to use this key, it will come at a great personal cost to you. So be forewarned."

Cole frowned. "Haven't I already paid the ultimate price? And I'm not referring to the money I have given you. Why would you say that to me? What am I supposed to do with this key?"

Upset, Cole stood, stepping down from the barstool and staring back at the woman with ire building in his eyes. More questions, vague answers; this was her stock in trade—or so it seemed.

"You will use it to open the door you are searching for. You will first need to discover and solve certain clues before you learn the door's true location. It may take on many guises. There is an extraordinary price to be paid for immortality. More than that I cannot say."

Cole stared, open-mouthed, then turned in disgust, attempting to hold his anger in check at this woman who was offering only questions and contradictions if she could even be believed. *What clues, and where do I find them? Immortality? What did she mean by that?* he pondered, becoming even more conflicted.

Cole walked closer to the water, contemplating his next move. In the far distance, he noticed sudden bolts of lightning streak through the darkening sky, illuminating the upper rim of the volcano that was visible from two hundred miles away. *Hollingsworth Island?* Cole shuddered at the sight as all went quiet around him. Even the crashing waves on the nearby rocks were muted. For an instant—a fleeting second—he thought he saw diamond-studded wings spreading atop the volcano, paralyzing him in place. The scene vanished as quickly as it had appeared. *Was that a sign? His first clue?*

Cole turned back to further question the woman. He needed more information, and he wasn't about to take no for an answer. Horrorstruck, he stared at the bartender as she gradually disappeared into mist, along with her cantina, leaving only an empty space of undisturbed sand where the structure had just been. Cole dropped to his knees, gazing blankly at the side of the rock wall, petrified. There was no portal to enter. No visible way to get back to Lindsay. Only unanswered questions—and riddles.

Through clouded eyes, he spotted something square materializing out of thin air, forming atop the sand where the cantina had stood. It was small, boxlike, and ebony in color. Cole approached it cautiously. He dared not touch it, although it beckoned to him, as though it wanted to be picked up. Surely it had been left by the woman. The more he stared at it, the more frightened he became. For a long moment, he just gaped at the mysterious object, frozen. The *box*, for lack of a better description, glimmered in the sunlight, like it was made of dark glass or something similar.

Gathering courage, Cole picked the object up warily, waiting for something extraordinary to happen. It felt smooth to the touch, yet emanated a strange warmth, like it had been exposed to a high temperature but was in the cooling process. Then it dawned on him that it was made of obsidian— cooled lava rock turned to glass. As he peered more closely at its edges, he noticed carvings inlaid into its surface that appeared darker and looked like letters or symbols of some type. Strange symbols. *What did they mean? Was this one of the riddles the woman had alluded to?*

Cole scrutinized the box, searching his mind to connect something that might make sense. Recalling one of his favorite books, *Lord of the Rings,* by J.R.R. Tolkien, an image of runes popped into his head. *Could these be the same?* It didn't seem possible—runes were thought by many to be fictional, simply the imagination of a fantasy writer. The imagination of many fantasy writers, actually. Such images were often born of myths, which may have had some basis in truth. Perhaps they were real. And yet, this only added to Cole's consternation.

More importantly, why had this object been left for him?

CHAPTER THIRTEEN

T HE TAXI DROPPED ART off near the entrance to an alleyway in a seedy
part of town. Isabella, known for its beautiful beaches and a few posh
resorts, contained an uglier side, tucked away from the eyes of tourists, as
if it didn't exist. Most streets here were narrow. Most buildings small and
old. Perhaps it was better this way, out of sight. Art tipped the driver, who
nodded his thank you but still refused to speak. He pointed a crooked finger
down the alley then drove off hurriedly.

Art clung to his briefcase, strolling tentatively down the darkened,
narrow alleyway. Few doors offered signs of welcome. Most were closed
for business or shuttered behind thick, metal bars, back entrances to places
people like Art would never go. Places where it was possible to purchase all
manner of objects—inanimate or living.

To his left, near the end of the alley, Art noticed a flickering neon sign
above an open door, sporting an image of an ancient dragon in green light.
Below the image, the words *Dragon Cantina* glowed fluorescently in orange. He had arrived.

When Art entered, he felt momentarily blinded, like he had just entered
a movie theater after the overhead lights had been turned off. This place
made the alley look positively glowing with light. He focused in on more

neon lighting behind the bar until his vision adjusted. Not only was the place dark, it was dingy with a scattering of wooden tables and chairs facing the bar. A stage stood to the left, with a stripper's pole visible through the smoked-filled room. The stage was deserted; apparently, it was still too early in the morning for there to be much action going on.

Art scanned the room for a sign of the men he was to meet—though he had no idea what they looked like. Many of the tables were occupied by one or two men, drinking beer and smoking—men who had just left work at a packing plant or shipping warehouse, working the graveyard shift. Too early to find sleep, too late for more normal means of entertainment, they sat and drank, trying to forget the lives fate had handed them. Lost lives, lives of addiction, only finding solace at the bottom of a glass, the end of a cigarette, or a needle discretely tucked away.

A man, one of two, seated at the corner table to the right of the bar, gestured toward Art. Neither man was smoking, and they appeared to be drinking coffee, or at least some form of hot beverage, as steam spiraled up from their cups. Evidently, they had just arrived as well.

Art strolled over to them, unable to avoid the stench of beer, stale tobacco, and sweaty bodies from nearby customers. He sat himself with his back facing the front of the building, sliding his briefcase between his legs and under the table. Art extended his hand for introductions, but the gesture was not returned. *Rude*, he thought, then he remembered where he was. This was purely business being transacted in a clandestine spot—there would be no friendships or lasting relationships formed today. Money would be exchanged. They would go their separate ways and most likely never see one another again. If Cole needed something more, Art would make another connection. Each negotiation would be separate so there was no connecting the dots.

"Gentlemen," Art began in his serious, courtroom tone. "I assume you understand my needs?"

The man on the right, the man who had not gestured to Art, nodded his head. He was obviously the negotiator. The other man, the muscle.

Art focused his gaze on him. There would be no mention of Cole, no mention of anyone else. As far as they were concerned, Art was making the deal for himself, although they probably knew better. Why complicate matters?

Art continued, "To confirm, I need a go-fast boat with a well-connected, skilled boatman who will keep his mouth shut and avoid the authorities. I need official papers allowing two men access to the volcano with the accompanying forged passports and paperwork that have already been emailed to you." Art purposely omitted the name Hollingsworth Island, even though that was what everyone was calling it.

The man on the right nodded as if he totally understood and as if he had already obtained these requisites. Just as Art was about to continue, a Spanish woman approached to take his order.

"I'll have an espresso, with artificial sweetener, please." Turning his head back to face the men as if she no longer existed, Art spoke in a hushed voice. "In addition, I need a meeting place in Isabella to conduct interviews. A place that's decent but won't be noticed, and I'll need it registered to a fake name. Reserve it for one week and pay for it with cash. Lastly, I need a driver and a car at my disposal twenty-four seven for the next ten days." Art paused, scrutinizing the men's facial expressions. "Are we on the same page?"

The man on the right nodded.

Art leaned in. "I believe the agreed upon payment was $150,000 cash, so don't try and fuck with me. I've had enough of that bullshit down here. If you do, or if you're services don't live up to expectations, I know how to find you, and I promise you that you will not like what happens next. *Comprendes?*"

Both men nodded this time.

Art slid the briefcase forward under the table until it was within reaching distance of the man on the left, while handing the man on the right a burner cell phone. The man on the left slid a similar looking briefcase back toward Art, containing the necessary documents and contacts, already prearranged.

"Here's a temporary, prepaid cell phone you can use to reach me, should you have an emergency. Otherwise, I don't expect to hear from either of you again." Art repeated the number to his temporary cell phone rather than writing it down. "You can excuse yourselves and count the money if you'd like while I enjoy my espresso. That said, I believe our business is concluded."

"No need, *señor*, we trust you," the man on the right replied in broken English. The two men stood, bowing slightly, then headed for the front door, leaving Art to his coffee.

Art dropped a twenty-dollar bill on the table and did likewise.

CHAPTER FOURTEEN

C OLE CONTINUED STANDING ON the deserted beach, staring at the box and contemplating what to do next. He couldn't go back to the Swanson sisters as if nothing had happened. They would pick up on his mood change. Cole's cell phone vibrated. It could only be Art. Retrieving the phone from his pocket, he hit accept, his eyes still transfixed on the box. Art's voice sounded on the line.

"Cole, I have the documentation we need and a location where we can meet with the scientific teams. We'll shortly have a boat and a driver. Everything looks legit."

"Good news. Everything go okay?" Cole asked.

"More or less. You should have seen the bar where we—"

"I'll call you later," Cole muttered, cutting his friend off, as though his story of seedy bars and clandestine meetings meant nothing to him. He couldn't concentrate on anything but the mysterious object he held or the conversation he'd just had with the infamous bartender. Or had he? Had she actually been there, or was it merely one of those implausible dreams he had experienced so often in Lindsay's presence—dreams that felt more real than reality. Had this box—or whatever it was—been lying here for years, awaiting discovery by some unlikely passerby? It might have been a remnant of a long-ago shipwreck, swept onshore by the rising tide. It was, after all, a very remote, desolate cove that would be difficult to detect.

Still confused, Cole supposed it was time to head back to his room to await Art's return. It would give him additional time to study the box. Yes, that was all this was—just a box from some bygone era. He would bring it back to Newport and have one of the curators at RIMOSA, the Rhode Island Museum of Science and Art, give it a once-over. It might be a valuable artifact, in which case he would donate it for study and exhibition and be done with it.

Cole headed back to the stairway, coming to an abrupt halt, stunned to see that it, too, had vanished into thin air. He looked up at the jagged cliff as the realization washed over him that he was trapped. The only way out looked to be by water. But weren't there dangerous rip currents out there? At least, that's what the sign above had noted. He looked back. The tide was rapidly encroaching inland.

"Damn it!" Cole cursed, then he recalled Art saying something about a boat during their brief conversation earlier. Quickly dialing Art's cell, he prayed Art would answer. He didn't think he had much time left, and no one, including the Swanson sisters, knew his location.

The phone rang once and then went silent. Cole looked at his phone just as the power went dead. "Shit!" Cole cursed again. *How long had he been out here?* Gazing at the sky, the sun had shifted dramatically westward. The morning, along with the afternoon, had drifted away, while Cole lingered in the cove, seemingly oblivious to the passing of time. There was no way he could attempt to climb out—that could only result in a crippling fall. Swimming seemed to be the only recourse, which meant he would have to leave the box. He would need all his limbs and strength to have the slightest hope of surviving the menacing ocean current. He supposed it was now or never. There was no need to delay or let the tide intrude farther.

Cole placed the box in a small opening about six feet up in the rock cliff, then turned to face his newest nemesis, the roiling ocean. The ocean that had cost him so dearly over the past year.

Taking a few deep breaths, he headed toward the surf with sheer determination. Inwardly, he called on Lindsay to guide him. He didn't expect her to, but it couldn't hurt to hope. He was certain her spirit was somehow nearby. She had saved him from the ocean before, perhaps she would be there for him again.

He stepped into the surf just as the waves were receding and was about to plunge in headlong when he spotted a gray object bobbing up and down about seventy-five yards away. Cole stopped, focusing his gaze out at the darkening ocean. His breath caught in his throat. As the next set of waves began to roll in, a rubber inflatable appeared to be riding atop the largest of the whitecaps, moving toward him.

Cole dropped to his knees, thunderstruck. Wasting no more time, he stood and sprinted back as fast as he could, given that he was running on sand. He grabbed the box, then hurried forward, awaiting the lifesaving arrival. The arrival that only Lindsay could have summoned. *Were they really only an ocean apart?*

He panicked as he waded into the water, realizing that he may only have one shot at this. Cole grabbed at the raft, flinging the box in first, then thrust his body, with every ounce of strength he could muster, into the inflatable, struggling to pull himself in. He began to slip backward as the waves receded with the pull of a strong current—even stronger than he'd expected. With one hand, he managed to grab a strap tied down to the side pontoon, clinging desperately to the side as the raft plunged back into the churning sea. He reached his free hand over the pontoon but could not find anything more to hold onto. Seawater pummeled his face, stinging his eyes and filling his open mouth with salt water.

As Cole was dragged half-submerged back to sea, another set of waves crashed headlong into the raft, turning it sideways. Blinded by the rushing water, Cole grabbed the same strap with his other hand and somehow managed to get a grip. Then he held on for the fight of his life. A life that seemed to be slipping away with every passing second, as he took in more seawater. He had no idea where he was now, only that if felt like he was slipping farther and farther away from the shoreline as the sky continued to darken.

As Cole's strength weakened, he continued to drift out to sea. Finally, after what seemed like hours, the ocean turned calm. Eventually, he gathered the strength to drag himself inside of the inflatable. To his shock, he spotted the box intact and resting on the bottom of the raft, tucked in behind the motor mount. Something about this particular raft seemed familiar, like he had been in it before. It had two sets of seats, equipped with an outboard motor. Peering over the side, he spotted the Gerace Institute logo emblazoned on the outside of the pontoon in vivid green lettering, contrasting against the gunmetal gray of the neoprene rubber.

But how could this be possible? This was the raft that he first traveled on from Redemption Bay to the *USS Truett*—Gerace's naval-grade frigate that he, Lindsay, Ryan Walker, and Cassie Thomas had used to search for Cole's dead parents. This inflatable belonged in San Salvador, not Puerto Rico. The two locations were over two hundred miles apart. Even more confusing was how it had appeared out of nowhere. This was the craft that was used by Dr. Andres Almquist, the arrogant oceanographer who had first greeted Cole upon his arrival to San Salvador—and then left immediately when it appeared something was going on between Lindsay and Cole.

Too drained to take action, Cole rested, attempting to regain his strength. He had barely survived the experience. It occurred to him that Almquist must be among the scientists stationed near Hollingsworth Island, studying it. Would Art be interviewing him later as part of their selection for the grant? That fact alone brought a smile to Cole's face, as he took stock of his whereabouts. Turnabout is fair play, after all.

The first stars began to form in the blue-velvet sky. Cole could barely see lights coming to life on the distant shoreline. He was still a long way out, but he had survived, and he was sitting in a motorized craft in which to make his way back. It could have been far worse. He fired up the engine and set course for the Parador Villas, certain that many questions awaited.

Forty minutes later, still in his wet clothes and clutching the box under his arm, Cole opened the door to his bungalow, hoping to go unnoticed so he could freshen up. No such luck. Art was sitting out on the tiny front porch of his adjoining bungalow, sipping a beer, awaiting Cole's return. He almost looked nonchalant—if such a thing was possible with Art—as though Cole's return in wet clothes well after dark, with no communication in nine hours, was nothing to be concerned about.

Art raised his bottle and motioned toward Cole. "A little late for a swim, don't you think?" Art said, sarcastically. "Were you swimming in the ocean? I didn't see you down at the pool. The girls have already eaten and retired for the evening, so it's just you and me, bro." Art pulled out another bottle of beer and tossed it in Cole's direction. Cole adeptly caught it with his free hand.

"Give me a minute to clean up, and then we'll talk." Cole entered his room, more to hide the box than a burning desire to shower and change clothes. He knew Art would grill him for information. He chugged down the beer as he towel-dried and changed into shorts and a polo shirt—courtesy of the Swanson sisters. He could have done without the hot-pink color, but it was the thought that counted. He grabbed a small bottle of scotch from the minibar, dropped a couple of ice cubes in a glass, and headed outside to face his friend. A friend who would undoubtably not believe what he was about to tell him.

"So ol' buddy, what have you been up to?" Art questioned, as if preparing himself for another one of Cole's outrageous explanations.

"This and that. I climbed down a staircase that didn't exist. Found the Cantina de la Noche and the gypsy-witch who inhabits it. Had a lengthy conversation with her. Dropped a grand for one drink and an umbrella. Then..." Cole's voice trailed off. *The umbrella*! He'd totally forgotten about it in all the confusion that had followed. There was a key attached. "Excuse me, Art. I'll be right back."

Art stared blankly as he watched his boss rush back to his room. He then popped open another beer, deciding it was going to be a long night.

Cole rummaged through his shirt and jeans, retrieving his cell phone. Thankfully, it was enclosed in a watertight case. Then he found it—the tiny umbrella crumpled up in the front pocket of his jeans. The key was still attached. And then it hit him like a lightning bolt. This key must open the mysterious box he had found after the cantina vanished. It all made sense. Picking up the box, he examined it closely under the light of the bedside lamp. He turned it around slowly, then upside down, but he couldn't see a keyhole, at least not the traditional type, but knew the two items must be connected. He decided to sleep on it and not tell Art for now. Five minutes later, he returned to sit with Art, as though nothing had just happened.

"Sorry Art, I had to charge up my cell phone. It went dead, and I'm expecting an important email. Now, where were we?" Cole said matter-of-factly.

Art continued to gaze quizzically at his friend, realizing again that Cole had his own agenda he was not yet sharing with him. He needed to play it cool, if he was ever to truly understand what Cole wanted—or how he could help him get it.

Art would go through the motions of selecting a scientific team, communicating with the executive team back in Newport, and doing anything else he needed to do in order to bring Cole the peace he was seeking. Without that, he knew Cole would never be capable of running Hollingsworth Enterprises—or anything else for that matter.

"Okay, Cole. Can we start over?" Art said.

"What, you didn't believe my story? Art, I'm amazed." Cole attempted to look wounded. "Okay, if you insist. It really isn't all that interesting. I sat with the twins for a bit by the pool, grabbed some food, then went to the beach to relax and wait for your call. At low tide, I noticed more beach was exposed to the right, near a wall of rock, and decided to explore. I found a secluded cove, which I would not otherwise have seen. I spent time thinking about … about a lot of things, actually. I took a nap, and when I awoke, the sun was setting, and the water had risen dramatically. The beach had disappeared, and I was basically trapped. I'd left my cell phone on and it had run out of power, so I couldn't contact anyone. I tried to climb up the cliff, but it was too steep, so I gave up. No boats seemed to be sailing by, so I eventually decided to swim out. It took me a couple of attempts, but I finally made it. And now I'm here." Cole hesitated. "Grab me a beer, would you, Art?"

Art handed Cole a beer, leaned back in his chair, and laughed. "If that is the truth—and I highly doubt it—what have you been doing for the past two hours? I don't think you swam out in total darkness," Art replied, unconvinced.

"No, really, Art, that's what happened. Next, I headed down the beach to that outside bar and had a few drinks while trying to dry out a bit. The experience of being trapped in that cove kind of unsettled me. For a while, I felt helpless."

"Since when have *you* felt helpless?" Art smirked. "What was it you were carrying when you tried to sneak by me? At least you can tell me that."

Cole gazed back at Art, sternly. "Actually, I can't. But I will at some point, I promise." With that, Cole put an end to Art's questions. "Now, tell me about your day," Cole said, as if he were speaking to a spouse after returning home from a long day at work.

Art shook his head in disbelief. "It's getting late, Cole, and I've had a few too many of these," Art said, raising his bottle. "I'll see you in the morning. Pleasant dreams." Art disappeared into his room without another word, leaving Cole alone to confront his own disturbing thoughts.

CHAPTER FIFTEEN

B ILL GAINES CALLED AN early morning meeting with the board members who were still in Newport. He'd heard nothing from Cole or Art, and things didn't feel right. There should have been some communication by now on their findings regarding the printer in Mexico they were visiting. But there was no news, and Gaines was intent on finding out why, even if it meant a trip to see for himself.

After the board members had assembled, which just happened to be the men supporting the chairman, he brought the meeting to order, dispensing with the usual protocols and the reading of the last meeting's minutes.

"Gentlemen, thank you for coming on such short notice. I'm concerned with Cole's progress in Mexico. I have not had any communication, and it's been nearly a week. Has he contacted any of you?"

Each of the four men shook their heads, but remained silent, awaiting what Gaines might say next. They were loyal to him but needed to tread carefully, as this was still Cole's company and they could ill afford to offend the majority owner.

"I see. . ." Gaines said, unconsciously stroking his chin. Gaines turned toward his closest ally. "Michael, will you please contact Cole today and see if you can find out anything on their progress and what they're doing. I now believe their agenda has changed and the possible acquisition of the Mexican printer is no longer their top priority," Gaines said accusingly.

Michael cleared his throat, not particularly pleased he had been given this assignment, but he knew all too well that when the chairman asked for something, he expected results, or there would be hell to pay.

"If I may ask, Bill, why do you suspect this? What else would they be doing in Mexico?" Michael questioned, hoping to gain more insight as to what Gaines was concerned about.

"Michael, I don't think it has anything to do with Mexico. Although, I did call the owner and he did confirm that Cole and Art were scheduled to meet with him and that he was serious about entering into an agreement with us. But this initial fact-finding trip shouldn't have taken more than a couple of days." Gaines frowned, pausing for effect, to add drama to the situation. "No, I think this concerns Hollingsworth Island. I believe Cole is taking the lead on this project and leaving the rest of us out, even though it was *our* idea." Gaines left out that it was actually his idea, wanting to sound inclusive of the others.

"Excuse me, sir, but why would Cole do that? It doesn't seem he has anything to hide, and he did compliment us on the idea originally," Michael said, respectfully.

"Yes, I suppose he did, but I think he has a completely different idea of what he wants to do with the island. After all, it does bear his family name. I've come to believe that he wants it for a very different use, one that will benefit him and not us. I don't believe he actually liked our idea. He may only have agreed to it so he could get a leg up on us and divert the potential windfall profits away from the company and its shareholders. In my mind, this is a breach of ethics."

This was a grave accusation against the primary shareholder of the company, and it sent a shockwave through the boardroom.

Donald Frasier, an attorney and one of the senior board members, spoke up. "Bill, Cole doesn't own the new island, nor does Hollingsworth Enterprises. While he may exert some amount of influence on what ultimately happens with the landmass, that really is a global decision yet to be made. We may be overreacting here."

Gaines went quiet, his expression implacable. This subject really hadn't been discussed yet, at least not in a formal board setting. To date, they'd primarily discussed how Hollingsworth Enterprises could profit from the island, since the company name was so closely associated with it. At some point, this connection would begin to fade, when the larger questions were answered, so it was imperative they acted swiftly.

Long moments passed while each board member contemplated Gaines's assessment, along with the question Donald has just raised. That question couldn't be ignored. This was serious shit, and they were walking on a tightrope here. One slip, and they could be sent packing. Fail to support Gaines, and the consequences could be equally disastrous.

Rather than challenge the chairman, Michael stood up, to the relief of the other three men. "I'll try contacting him this morning and report back to you as soon as I hear anything."

Gaines nodded, turned, and departed the boardroom without further comment. Michael and Donald exchanged glances, while the other two board members looked on with concern, now convinced that Gaines was again preparing himself to challenge Cole for power. It hadn't taken long.

CHAPTER SIXTEEN

T HREE TAPS ON COLE's door rousted him out of bed. He'd spent a restless night again, thinking about all that had happened. What kept him from sleep most was the sudden appearance of the cantina, the discovery of the box-like object, and, perhaps the most confounding of all, the implausible rescue at sea when the unmanned Gerace inflatable miraculously appeared. Again, it all seemed dreamlike. For all he knew, it had been a dream—if not for the box resting on the nightstand beside him. That was real and impossible to deny.

"Cole, are you awake?" Art asked from the other side of the door. "Are you going to hide out in your bungalow all day?" He sounded irritated.

Cole appeared at the door in a cheaply made bathrobe, sporting the Parador Villas logo. It wasn't exactly the Beverly Hills Hotel type of robe Cole was accustomed to.

"Couldn't sleep. What time is it, anyway?" Cole asked, groggy.

"It's ten o'clock, and the twins are getting restless. They want breakfast and are waiting for you. Then they want the hell out of this dump."

"Art, please take them to breakfast and bring me back some fruit, pastries, and a large, hot coffee when you're finished. I'll be ready by then. We'll figure out what to do next." Cole closed the door in Art's face, further aggravating him.

"Cole, it's about time we contacted Gaines!" Art shouted through the closed door, attracting the interest of a few passersby. "He has got to be suspicious by now, unless you've had any contact with him. I certainly haven't."

Art's directive was met with utter silence. Then, he heard the shower being turned on. He stomped off, totally frustrated, to notify the girls that Cole would not be joining them for breakfast—just another sign of Cole's increasing reclusiveness.

The twins were less than pleased when they were informed Cole would not be joining them for breakfast and that it appeared he would be headed out on another excursion—maybe with Art, maybe not.

"So, what are we supposed to do all day, Art?" Shelby said, fuming. Art went silent, considering the women's request.

"They have some great shopping in the downtown area near the Plaza Resort. Designer shops," Art replied timidly. He had quickly formulated a plan on his way up to the cantina. "I suggest you make a day trip there. . . and please, use my credit card for payment. Buy whatever you want. Now, let's order some food and you can be on your way. I'll call a car for you."

The girls forced their smiles but were not totally disappointed. Free shopping at designer shops couldn't be all bad.

Art ordered takeout food for Cole, paid the check, and politely excused himself. As he walked away, he called the front desk and ordered a limo to come pick up the women. He didn't think they'd appreciate riding into the finer part of town in one of the beat-up cabs that frequented this part of the island.

When Art reached Cole's room, he was sitting on his deck, dressed and ready to go, but where to still eluded Art. Art handed Cole the takeout and the hot coffee and sat down beside his boss, with his own large cup of coffee cradled in both hands. The coffee here was brewed on the strong side, which was a good thing. He needed to see a little fire back in his friend, who had become more listless within the past couple of days.

"So, where to, Cole?" Art asked.

Cole looked over at his attorney sharply, his mouth full of pastry, then returned silently to his eating. When finished, he returned his gaze to Art.

"Girls okay?" Cole said.

"I sent them shopping with my credit card. I think they'll be fine for another day. We should treat them to a nice dinner tonight in one of the swanky restaurants in town. I don't think they'll settle for another meal at this place."

Cole nodded. "Art, can you call our driver. I'd like to get started. We need to see the place where we'll be conducting the scientific interviews and start setting up the meetings. I also want to inspect the boat you hired and meet with its skipper today. Once we've completed those tasks, I'll contact Gaines with an update. I've already received an email and voice message from Michael, his most loyal board member. It appears they're getting more than a little anxious. We'll need to come up with something believable so Gaines doesn't decide to fly down here himself. That's the last thing I need."

Finally, some action, Art thought. "I'll call the driver right away." He rose to make the necessary contact. As he was dialing the number with his prepaid cell phone, he spotted the twins in front of the lobby, decked out in sexy outfits, heading toward a black limo already waiting for them. At least that hadn't been screwed up.

Art returned moments later, only to find that Cole had disappeared. He opened Cole's bungalow door, but there was no sign of him inside either. "Great!" Art exclaimed, wondering what Cole was up to now. Instinctively, Art looked toward the ocean, spotting a solitary figure standing near a cliff and staring out to sea, as though expecting something to happen. His first inclination was to give his friend some time, but the more he thought about it, the more he needed to reengage Cole and become a team again. It was the only way Art could help him.

Art strolled down to the cliff, remaining silent for a moment before addressing Cole, but soon found that wasn't necessary.

"I know you're there, Art." Cole said, without turning around. "Just give me a minute, then we can go."

Art crossed his hands behind his back, watching wordlessly, until Cole turned in his direction.

"What were you looking for, Cole?" Art asked compassionately. Again, Cole's behavior hinted of pain, of confusion, of something he was unwilling to share but that was clearly eating him up inside.

"Just thinking," Cole replied.

"I get that. . . but what were you thinking about?" Art asked, pushing his friend to open up a bit. "And please don't tell me, *this and that.*"

Cole smiled apologetically. He understood what his silence was doing to Art, but he just couldn't confide yet. Hell, he didn't even know what he was going to do next, or if his loosely formulated plans would have any chance of success.

"I was thinking about Lindsay, actually," Cole said.

At last, some honesty, Art thought. "What about Lind—"

Before Art could complete his question, Cole was striding swiftly past him, back up to the bungalows, tight-lipped. Art sighed heavily.

"I'll be right back, Art," Cole said, as he walked inside his room. Art thought he heard the door handle lock.

Cole placed the artifact in the safe inside the closet, grabbed a few incidentals, and returned outside. Art was standing rigidly, hands on his hips.

"You didn't have to lock your door, Cole. I wasn't going to sneak in. I'm sure you have a valid reason to hide whatever it is you're hiding."

"I do. Thanks for understanding, Art. Has our driver arrived yet?" Cole said nonchalantly, as if his behavior was perfectly normal.

The pair headed up the dirt path toward the lobby. A white, nondescript Ford van was parked near the entrance, its engine running. *Rumbling obnoxiously* might have been a more apt description. There were no markings on it, no signs of recognition, just a layer of dust covering the outside, as if the vehicle hadn't been washed in months. The passenger's door flew open. This was obviously going to be their driver.

Art opened the door to the second set of seats for Cole to enter. There were no windows beyond the two front doors, so Cole would basically be hidden from view. Art stepped into the passenger's seat and introduced himself. The two men shook hands. Art refrained from introducing Cole. There were no questions, as though the driver already understood his instructions. Cole nodded at the driver as a sign of hello. The van sped away.

Mario Hernandez, the driver, was burly, with dark skin, closely cropped black hair, and a scruffy beard. Dressed in denim jeans and a black sweatshirt, he fit in. No one would suspect him of anything or know that he was a world-class bodyguard who wouldn't take shit from anybody yet would remain low-key unless pressed into action. Art had made sure of that and had been explicit in his demands from the beginning. Not that they would necessarily run into trouble, but in this part of the world, anything could happen, especially with someone as rich as Cole Hollingsworth. Art's primary job was to keep Cole's identity as secret as possible for as long as possible, and he took nothing for chance.

Mario appeared to know where he was going, and in short order, they had reached their destination, which was in a section near the shoreline that housed industrial buildings and some office space, much of it vacant. It was on the remote side, attracting little attention. Still, a few of the newer office buildings were nice enough and well maintained, as though their landlord was hoping to attract new occupants.

Cole tapped Art on the shoulder. "Any chance we can begin the interviews later today?"

Art was dumbfounded by the abruptness of the question. Did Cole actually think he could put this together in a matter of hours? Confidential letters had been sent out to each potential member, with NDA agreements that needed to be signed. Art turned around, staring at his boss with one of his patented looks of disbelief.

"You're joking, aren't you? I don't even know where these people are at the moment, probably on the island or maybe somewhere in town," Art said.

Cole stared back and the look on his face made it clear he was dead serious.

"Art, I know you can do this. Each team has a leader, right? Contact that person and tell them the schedule has moved up to today and that the first teams that show up will be looked upon favorably."

Art cursed under his breath, realizing he needed to follow his boss's orders. Opening the passenger door, Art jumped out with briefcase in hand and headed toward a cement bench in front of one of the buildings for some privacy. Cole remained quiet, while Mario stared straight ahead, appearing unconcerned.

Twenty-five minutes later, Art returned, with a satisfied expression. "We have two teams that are available today. The first one can be here in about an hour."

"Good job, Art," Cole said. "Why don't you get set up inside whatever office space we've rented so that you can be ready to go when they arrive."

"What will you be doing, Cole?" Art queried.

"I have a little phone call to make—need to check back with the office," Cole said. It was time to call Bill Gaines.

Art nodded, relieved that Cole was finally making contact with the chairman.

Cole left the van and headed down to the water's edge to make his call. Mario accompanied Art inside, and they began to set up for the meeting. Fortunately, the office space already had most of the requested prerequisites: a long conference room table with hookups for laptops, a video monitor hanging on the wall, a full water cooler stood in one corner. Art flipped on the air conditioner to cool down the stuffy room.

"Mario, can you please head to the nearest market and pick up some refreshments and sodas. I doubt there's a Starbucks anywhere close, so I guess we'll need to pass on containers of coffee, unless you can find some," Art said, then realized Mario may never have heard of Starbucks, much less seen one.

The driver nodded and headed out the door, leaving Art alone. When Cole returned, there were two minivans parked outside the small office near the rear of the building. He suspected they contained the first scientific team they would be interviewing. He directed Mario to park nearby.

Cole donned a set of wireless headphones that would allow him to overhear the conversations inside, through a device Art was wearing. The scientific teams wouldn't suspect anything, since they had been invited to present their plans and relevant findings, with the winner receiving a sizeable grant to continue their research into the mysterious volcano. There would be other teams still working independently, but the chosen team would be represented by Gerace Institute, anonymously paid for by their benefactors, namely Cole Hollingsworth. But no one would know about that side of it, as Cole had already consummated the agreement with Dr. Voteli, the institute's director. Cole had helped the director out many times and had been especially helpful after the whole messy incident with Lindsay and the loss of the *Harbinger II*, their very expensive submersible. Many had called for Voteli's ouster after that, but Cole's support was pivotal in avoiding that outcome, and the director owed Cole big-time.

The first team entered the building shortly thereafter and introduced themselves. Art opened his briefcase, extracting a thick folder with each person's professional and personal background meticulously researched. In addition, Art possessed a list of detailed questions he would present to each team, which had been crafted by a few top oceanographers, biologists, and geographers. Art and Cole both knew these teams would not be fooled by amateurs and the interviews needed to look legit, even though they had basically selected the winner. But no one would ever know that.

In the meantime, the results and vital information from all the teams interviewed would be invaluable going forward. Something that could take months to discover on their own. The plan was to organize a team with the right mix of scientists with a well-articulated agenda that would be presented by Gerace to the public, as well as to governments, through the vast Hollingsworth publishing empire. At least, that was the plan—but plans had a way of changing.

This is where Bill Gaines came in. He would head the new scientific magazine, both traditionally published and online. That would keep him busy and become the basis for a nice bonus for him and a few of his loyal supporters, each of whom were motivated by a singular principal: greed.

Cole was counting on this, as he cultivated his own agenda of discovering what was actually happening inside the volcano, which was currently being tightly controlled—and if there was the slightest possibility of reconnecting with Lindsay.

CHAPTER SEVENTEEN

C OLE LISTENED ATTENTIVELY AS Art questioned the two teams throughout the afternoon while recording their conversations. The interviews
would last a couple of hours each. The room had been set up with wireless
connections to laptops and video screens all of which would be needed to
adequately present their evidence and plans for future research into the
new landmass. Six teams had been selected to participate, and two interviews would take place each day until completed. In the event that further
meetings were necessary, they were prepared for that. There was more at
stake here than just getting the money to advance their research, and each
team understood that. The winning team would become famous and, to a
point, household names in the eyes of the public, which couldn't seem to get
enough news on the towering volcano. Scientists turned celebrities, what
could be wrong with that?

The winning team that had already been selected included Andres
Almquist, the oceanographer Cole had met on the beach at Redemption
Bay, before departing on the deep-sea diving adventure that had quite literally changed his life. Once Cole had confirmation that Almquist was on
a specific team, the decision was basically made. Almquist was intelligent,
accomplished, and arrogant. He also coveted the spotlight. He had shared

a romantic relationship with Lindsay prior to Cole reuniting with her—a relationship that Lindsay had broken off prior to the death of Cole's parents. Cole suspected that Almquist held this against him.

One might question, then, the reason Cole and Art would select a would-be adversary. It had been Almquist's initial observation that had impressed the pair and had garnered some support from others in the scientific community, although eventually discarded. Andres believed the peculiar theory that as the volcano continued to discharge large amounts of molten lava into the ocean, the water cooled far too quickly, and that this phenomenon was actually a form of recycling, that it was the act fueling the volcano's massive growth, as if it was feeding itself.

This theory went against the grain of all conventional wisdom and so couldn't sustain itself due to diminishing interest, which in effect, meant diminishing funds. With Cole's financial assistance, Andres could continue his research, with Cole in the shadows with access to every detail. For some unexplainable reason, Cole believed this theory might actually be true. It would, after all, be Lindsay's influence. Basically, it was Lindsay's actions that created the volcano in the first place, and Cole believed she was still somehow connected to the island in inexplicable ways.

For the next two days, the teams presented their findings and how they planned to continue their research and what they hoped to discover. All six teams did a credible job, with two teams standing above the rest. The group that included Almquist was intentionally selected last to present. Though the most controversial, the other members of the team were brilliant in their own right. The team's open-mindedness and its experienced scientists made the decision appear to be legitimate, although there would certainly be ruffled feathers once the announcement was made. Gerace would take a couple of extra days to make the announcement, wanting to appear genuine in their desire to be fair, including callbacks to three of the teams with additional questions.

After the first day of interviews concluded, Mario chauffeured Cole and Art to a remote dock at the northern tip of the city to meet their new skipper and to inspect his craft. Although his go-fast boat looked worn, it possessed all the requisite ingredients: stealthy, well-built, fast. Painted a drab black with splashes of bright colors and a catamaran hull, the Eliminator 36 Daytona belied it's 169-mph top speed and outstanding handling qualities. It had ample room in the bow to carry extra cargo. Its captain looked much the same—experienced, strong, and determined, with a scruffy beard and piercing dark-blue eyes that penetrated even the most challenging of gazes. He was ruggedly handsome. A large bowie knife hung low on his right hip. It was obvious he had seen his share of action, and it appeared he would be unaffected by dangerous missions. On the way over, Mario had vouched for the man, who went by the nickname of Gamer, as the best boatman on the eastern shoreline of Puerto Rico and beyond. He hadn't come cheap, but by the look of him, Cole immediately felt a sense of relief wash over him. Money had its benefits.

Cole reached out his hand in a sign of solidarity and the boatman took it, surprising Cole with the strength of his handshake. Gamer smiled politely and nodded but said nothing. He had been instructed not to ask too many questions or to pry into his new boss's business. He had not been told who Cole really was, but Cole suspected he knew. There were not too many secrets that men of his occupation did not know, especially when it came to their neck of the woods. He reminded Cole of the driver who took them from Mexico to the remote airstrip from which Cole, Art, and the twins had flown safely into Isabella unannounced. Quiet but highly confident in his own abilities.

After a brief pause, Gamer shook Art's hand, nodding at Mario as though he was approving of his customers as well. Mario nodded back, then turned toward the Ford van.

"Gentlemen, it is a pleasure to meet you. I am at your beck and call." Gamer hesitated. "And your secrets are safe with me," he added in slightly broken English, hinting of an Eastern European accent.

Art suddenly wished he had hooked up with Gamer before he had been hijacked by sea pirates on his attempt to find Cole on the USS *Truett* to warn

him about Gaines discovering the scam that Lindsay's father had successfully pulled. Although men like Gamer lived in a shadow world and were
mostly invisible, they were as valuable as anyone and worth the expense.
Art immediately liked the man and made a mental note to add him to his
list of trusted contractors.

Mario and Gamer. We've struck gold, Art mused. Even though Art
didn't fully understand the plan—he was piecing it together little by little—
he had an odd sense of confidence in this pair of unlikely companions. And
that somehow their skills may just be tested in the days to come. He couldn't
say exactly why, just intuition gnawing at him.

CHAPTER EIGHTEEN

"COLE, IT'S GOOD TO hear from you. We were getting worried," Gaines said in a tone disguising his true feelings. "What's been the holdup?"

"I'm afraid there are complications with the Mexican printer none of us anticipated. When we got wind of it, we needed extra time to sort it all out. I didn't want to call you until I had foolproof evidence."

"What complications are you referring to?" Gaines asked, as if this was nothing more than a smokescreen or delaying tactic on Cole's part.

"I'm afraid they have ties, however well disguised, to a major drug cartel, including their partial ownership in the printer through a shell company. I'm glad Art was with me. His contacts back in the States were able to get proof of the connection. Basically, the cartel has invested funds to keep the printer afloat in return for favorable press coverage down here. The more forward-thinking and successful cartels, I'm told, are investing vast amounts of cash in legal businesses—much like the Mafia in the US did years ago—to appear more legitimate, rather than just relying on brute force."

"Well, that's just fucking great. So, what are your recommendations now? I assume you're coming back shortly," Gaines said, applying pressure to Cole to return immediately.

"Actually, no. We are still awaiting a couple of documents to be emailed to us before we confront the owners of the printer. We've spent a few days touring their facility and looking at the books. It's actually a decent setup, with relatively new equipment. Obviously, they've invested the cartel money in new printing and prepress equipment, so they are up to date technologically. There also appears to be an untapped market down here for more than just commercial printing of magazines. Packaging primarily, along with a push into Arizona and Southern California."

"Hold on, Cole. You're actually considering getting into bed with a drug cartel? You're joking, of course." Gaines sounded shocked, but it had taken his attention away from what Cole and Art were really doing in Mexico, at least for the moment—and it sounded too bizarre to be fabricated.

"No, not if the cartel is going to stay involved. If we could buy out their shares, which aren't worth a lot, and give them a reason to look elsewhere, it might work. We believe the printer could become highly profitable and give us a presence in a market we don't currently service well. Also, it might be a great investment if we get your idea of a scientific division on-boarded to cover the discovery of Hollingsworth Island. To have a printer in the same vicinity that we would control could be a huge asset," Cole said convincingly.

Silence on the other line indicated that Gaines was giving this some thought. If nothing else, Cole had bought he and Art more, precious time.

"What's your next move, Cole?" Gaines said.

"As soon as we have the necessary documents, we plan to call a meeting with their board to discuss options. We'll confront them in a nonthreatening manner and decide where to go from there. I got the impression they would like to replace their current silent partner with us, although they haven't confided in us who exactly that partner is just yet," Cole said. Then he added, "We'll probably be here for another couple of weeks if things move along. We'll need to bring down an accounting team at some point."

"Are you sure about this?" Gaines asked, still not fully convinced.

"Bill, I think it's worth pursuing. Nothing ventured, nothing gained," he said. Then, changing the subject, he asked, "How are things going up there?"

"Things are fine, just a few board members getting anxious to move forward with the scientific publication and make a commitment to a scientific team in Puerto Rico to start working with."

"Speaking of that, as long as Art and I are down here, we would be happy to make an introduction. Not to take any thunder away from your idea, Bill. You'll get full credit. In fact, I'd like you to oversee the new division, should we work out the details," Cole said slyly. This was the opportunity he had hoped would present itself in his discussion with Gaines. The timing was perfect, and Gaines really couldn't refuse the majority stockholder and CEO without coming off as noncooperative and self-promoting—both of which he was blatantly guilty of in the past.

"Cole, I'm not sure about that. You're needed back here as soon as possible. I really feel like—"

Cole interjected, "Nonsense, Bill. You and the team are more than capable of running the ship while we're away. Besides, there's always email and cell phones. There's no shortage of connectivity down here. I'll be sure to keep you informed along the way. There's no need to worry. Selecting a top scientific team will be our next priority. In fact, I know one of the top oceanographers who's currently studying the island. I met him on my trip with Lindsay Featherstone to search for my parents' sunken yacht. You might know his name. Andres Almquist?" Cole said, having discovered that Andres was the man Gaines and his cohorts had been communicating with in secret, before they presented this idea to the board and Cole.

Gaines smiled at hearing Andres's name. This might work out after all. "Yes, I've heard of him but never met the man. He's been in the news lately with some theory about the island's changing nature. He seems well respected."

"Then it's decided. We'll organize some meetings down here to get started. If we run into any roadblocks, we'll contact you for advice," Cole said, as if the matter was now closed.

"Okay, but please give me a report on your progress every couple of day so I. . . I can keep key people informed at headquarters."

"Will do, Bill. I've got to go. I'll be back in touch in a couple of days."

Both men hung up, with Cole feeling that he'd won this round, while Gaines was left with the uneasy feeling that he'd just been manipulated.

CHAPTER NINETEEN

G OOD TO THEIR WORD, Art and Cole accompanied the twins to the best restaurant they could find in the Plaza Resort, which turned out to be a clever move. The sisters, decked out in new designer outfits—as if they needed any more—were stunning, parading around the lobby and restaurant to the admiration of nearly every guest. Even staff members stopped momentarily to gawk.

Cole subtly chastised Art for the additional attention—attention they did not need—but Art defended his behavior and suggested Cole leave immediately for the discreetly placed table he had reserved at the posh restaurant. Art would accompany the sisters around for a while and then meet Cole later. Cole agreed.

Twenty minutes later, the sisters were seated facing the rest of the tables, while Cole was seated behind a wall adorned with plants, making him almost invisible to anyone but the waitstaff.

For the next two hours, while the foursome consumed a five-course, gourmet meal, with stellar wines paired perfectly, the men heard little else but details of the shopping extravaganza. Art hadn't seen the receipts yet, and quite frankly, he didn't want to. All that counted was the women were happy and reengaged. Maybe a stay down here wasn't quite so bad, after all—as long as Art's credit card remained available.

After a decadent dessert was served, accompanied by glasses of Drouet et Fils French Cognac, at a cost of $500 per bottle, Art was beginning to feel lucky. It had been long enough since anyone here had enjoyed intimacy—at least that was Art's perception—and things could get spicy if he played his cards right. He might even consider letting Cole in on the action. God knows he needed it.

After the dessert plates were cleared and a second snifter of Drouet et Fils had been poured, the twins excused themselves for a powder room break. Art turned toward Cole with his newly concocted plan.

"Hey, bro, how about we book ourselves a suite and spend the night? I think the twins would like that. What do you say?" Art asked, expectantly.

Cole gazed at Art with a sympathetic smile, knowing his friends were here to help him and that they deserved downtime so as not to be monopolized by Cole's personal agenda.

"Okay, Art. I have no problem with that, but I won't be attending. When the women return, I'll head to the men's room and you can set it up. If they accept, please call Mario to meet me out front. I'm headed back to my bungalow."

"But, Cole, don't you want to—"

"No," Cole said sternly. "I need time alone to think."

"Will you at least stay and finish your drink?" Art asked.

"Sure, I can do that." Cole paused. "But let's not have a repeat of the plan you concocted after our tennis match in Newport, because I'm not coming over later. Do this on your own, and I'll appear as supportive as I can. I'll go book you a room."

Art frowned, but there was little he could do once Cole made up his mind. Art fidgeted, awaiting the women's return, as Cole disappeared to the front desk. The women finally showed up, refreshed and renewed, highlighting their expertly applied makeup from earlier beauty treatments, compliments of Art's credit card.

"Where's Cole?" Shelby questioned, noticing the empty chair.

"He's booking a suite for the night. Thought you two gorgeous women would enjoy a night in a great room, rather than the Parador, as good as it is!" Art smirked. This instantly brightened the twins' mood.

Cole returned to the table but didn't take his seat. "You are all set up in the presidential suite. I hope you have a good night's rest," Cole said invitingly. "I'm sorry I can't join you, but I have a major report to complete for the board of directors, which I promised Gaines I'd have on his desk first thing in the morning. It was the only way I could keep him from coming down here himself. I hope you will forgive me." With that final comment, Cole wished them a pleasant evening and strode away, failing to finish his drink.

Once again, the twins seemed more than a little upset that Cole would not be part of the revelry, but anything was better than another night in one of those fleabag bungalows. Both women sighed at the same time and then finished their drinks. Art wasn't a bad lover, and he had grown on them over time. In fact, Sydney had begun to develop feelings for him, although she was not about to admit it.

Art paid the check, adding a bottle of Dom Perignon to be brought to their suite—a little added insurance, in his mind.

Mario was waiting for Cole outside the main lobby. In fact, he had been there since shortly after the limo had dropped the foursome off. He wasn't about to leave Cole and his group unattended and vulnerable. Cole was pleasantly surprised to see him there at the ready. He slid into the back seat of the van, exchanging a cordial greeting, and the twosome sped away in the darkness.

While Cole didn't need to submit the report, it was a legitimate excuse for leaving early. He was determined to find the secret to the boxlike object and the key the cantina mistress had left for him. He'd come to the conclusion it was not some artifact that washed up on shore years ago and was convinced it was intended for him and him alone.

The bartender had said something about riddles. Cole didn't particularly care for riddles and had never been adroit at solving them, so he had paid little attention when they presented themselves. But this riddle might be the most important one of his life. He was also convinced solving it would somehow lead him back to Lindsay. The more time he spent near the new volcano, the more he felt a strange pull toward it, as if Lindsay was calling from beyond the grave. Calling for him.

They were still connected somehow, but for the life of him, he couldn't quantify just how. How does one even begin to measure the supernatural? It was more than just the feelings of love that existed between them. Cole was grounded in facts. It was a lifelong learning path he had been forced into and dutifully followed. But now, this was more a matter of faith. There was that word again—*faith*. A word Lindsay had used on more than one occasion. Faith in her. Faith in the greatest mystery of all—life after death—and finally, faith in himself to be a better man, that his life's purpose had not yet been fully revealed to him. And just as he was beginning to understand, he'd lost Lindsay, leaving Cole alone to discover this paradox himself. *One riddle in exchange for another*? Cole wondered.

After entering his bungalow, Cole picked up the mysterious box, fondling it as he restudied its engravings. Once again, he searched for a keyhole, but none was apparent. The letter-like carvings—runes, he was sure—held the secret to unlocking it. He fired up his laptop and began to research the subject. Somewhere, there must be a clue hidden in the mountain of articles and theories available online. Again, he flashed back to the *Lord of the Rings* trilogy, filled with mysticism and obscure rune-speak. More convinced than ever, he believed the answer lay within that text, somewhere among the pages. All great adventures from Tolkien's remarkable mind hinted at larger truths, of things shrouded in mystery, of deeper meanings. That was one of the things that attracted Cole to his work. But Cole had never delved further to discover those meanings, not being a spiritual man. Somehow Lindsay had changed him, forced Cole to face the spiritual world and consider the concept of faith in his own life. And now. . . now it seemed inescapable.

While reading an interesting article online about the concept of moon runes, a language that was used in The Hobbit, it suddenly occurred to Cole that perhaps exposing the box to some different sort of light or location might present a clue to opening the strange container. Like Lord Elrond, the elf king, had done with Frodo's map, under the light of a moon phase that was the same as the day the runes had been written, revealing the moon runes and the key to entering Mount Doom. *But expose the box to what?* Cole pondered.

He rotated the object slowly under the table lamp's light, but nothing happened. Of course, it couldn't be that simple. Next, he took it outside, lifting it up to a bright, nearly full moon. Again, nothing. Would pointing the box directly toward the sun work? He'd need to wait until morning. Or maybe the trick was with sound instead of light. Possibly a high-pitched sound? Music? All would have to wait until tomorrow. Cole was grasping at straws now and he knew it. He again consulted his laptop to see what museums housing relics and antiquities might exist in or near Isabella that he could visit tomorrow. Growing more frustrated and tired, he decided to sleep on it. He could start fresh tomorrow.

At four in the morning, Cole bolted upright in bed, awakened by a vivid dream. He had been scuba diving in the pristine waters of the tropics, chasing after what looked to be a mermaid—a mermaid with luxurious, auburn hair. The creature occasionally stopped to allow Cole to catch up, only to dart forward with a powerful thrust of its tail fins, leaving Cole behind again. On and on the chase went, until the sea creature abruptly stopped in an area of intense, underwater light, as though some external force was illuminating it. The space was gleaming with a brilliant, aquamarine light source. Something was suspended inside the space, its blurred image made difficult to discern by the oscillating current surrounding it. Just as Cole was getting close enough to identify the object, he awoke, breathless.

Had the mermaid been Lindsay, leading him again to a point of discovery? Why this dream and why now? Cole contemplated. Still a bit dazed by the sudden awakening and the lack of sleep, Cole sat upright in his bed as though spellbound. And then it hit him like a shockwave. It was the box suspended in the light! It had to be. The mermaid, or whatever the hell it was, had shown him the means to read the runes. Underwater! Of course, it made sense. Why hadn't he thought of it earlier? It was the only logical answer. This box of runes was not covered in moon letters, it was covered in water letters.

His excitement built quickly. Hurriedly, Cole jumped in and out of the shower and then dressed. It was still dark outside; Cole would need to wait a few more hours before he could test his theory, but at least he had something to go on.

Cole dialed Gamer's cell. "Good morning, Gamer. I apologize for calling so early, but I need your assistance, and it really can't wait."

Gamer sounded groggy but recovered quickly, responding to his new employer's call as if it had been expected. "Yes, sir, what is it you need?"

Cole smiled. This was a no-nonsense guy who was ready to assist in the spur of the moment. He needed more people like Gamer in his life. "I need a full-blown scuba diving outfit, including tanks with at least two hours of breathable oxygen. My size is—"

Before Cole could finish his sentence, Gamer interjected. "I know your size, sir. I'll have the required gear in less than thirty minutes. Where would you like it delivered?"

"Actually, I'd like to meet you to get it. I'm calling Mario to come pick me up, and then we need a place to meet. I need you to take me to a spot in the ocean, but I'll need your help to identify it. Is the Eliminator ready for departure?"

"Of course. Meet me at the location where we were first introduced, and we can leave immediately," Gamer said, without any hesitation.

"See you in a few," Cole replied. Then he dialed Mario, who was apparently already awake, by the sound of his voice. *Had he been alerted somehow?* Cole wondered.

Ten minutes later, the van drove up, headlights darkened, stopping about fifty yards away from the Parador's front office. A quick flashing on and off of the van's lights signaled Mario's arrival to Cole, who walked silently toward the driver, carrying the watertight metal briefcase he had used to carry cash. Cole climbed in, and the van eased away from the darkened lot.

"Thanks for showing up so quickly, do you know where we're going?" Cole said.

"Of course, boss. I've already spoken to your skipper, and he is expecting us shortly." This brief exchange ended the conversation. The pair remained silent until they arrived at the dock where Gamer's boat was moored. The pier was small, shabby, dimly lit, and isolated. It was the perfect location.

Gamer approached with the scuba diving equipment, thinking Cole would need to change in the van. Mario opened the back doors for Cole. Gamer handed the expensive, neoprene diver's suite to Cole, along with a pair of Oceanic diving boots.

Cole exited the van a few minutes later, decked out in the all-black gear, looking stealth-like. As he neared the men at the dock, Gamer did a double take.

"Looks like you've worn this type of gear before," the boatman said, eyeing Cole in the tight-fitting suit accentuating his muscular body.

"You might say that," Cole replied, with a hint of sarcasm. The first streaks of sunlight appeared on the horizon, turning the black ocean water dark azure and tinging the low-hanging clouds with fire. *Lava fire,* Cole thought.

"The rest of your gear is already on board," Gamer said.

Cole turned to Mario. "Thanks for the ride. I'll call you when I return."

"But, *señor*, I can wait here for you—"

"That won't be necessary. The less attention we attract to this location the better. I trust you understand," Cole said.

Mario bowed his head in concession, with an expression that suggested he was letting his employer down.

"Really, Mario, it's okay. Who better than Gamer to bring me back safely?"

Mario nodded, turned, and headed back to his van. A moment later, the van disappeared from view in the lingering darkness.

Rather than ask his boss where he wanted to go, Gamer waited for Cole to speak. Cole turned to his skipper; his expression unsure. "I'm not quite sure how to describe where I want to go, so please bear with me." Cole hesitated. "I'm looking for a very specific spot in the ocean. A spot underwater that might be illuminated somehow. I. . . I don't know how better to define it."

Gamer looked down, remaining silent, as though he was searching his memory for such a place, if it even existed. A few minutes passed before he looked up, smiling.

"Bioluminescence," Gamer said. "That is what we are looking for."

"Bioluminescence?" Cole asked, confused. "What exactly is that?"

"The short definition would be visible light made by living animals. It exists in the open oceans, mostly," Gamer said.

Cole's lips parted in surprise. Gamer was the last person he thought would come up with an answer like this, and again Cole couldn't help but smile. "You really are something, my friend. Of course, it makes sense. Are you sure you wouldn't like to join one of the scientific teams?" Cole joked.

"What, and miss all of this cloak-and-dagger stuff! I say, leave the scientific junk to the geeks."

"I couldn't have said it better!" Cole paused. "I know. . .um, I *knew* somebody who would have really liked you." Cole went silent as thoughts of Lindsay shot through his mind. A wave of mind-numbing sadness crossed Cole's face. This expression did not go unnoticed by the skipper, but he didn't press further. Cole momentarily lost his connection to the present.

"So. . . so do you know of any place nearby that might contain living animals that light up?"

"Actually, I do, but we must move quickly. These types of organisms mostly hide out in the darkness in deep water during the day, then head toward the surface at night to feed. But some should remain since it is still very early," Gamer said.

Cole again stared at the boatman, dumbfounded, wondering if this shady character might have been someone else in a different life. "So, what are we waiting for?" Cole said with a renewed sense of urgency.

"Hop in, sir." Gamer pointed toward the two rear seats of his boat, then climbed in behind the steering wheel, firing up the twin turbo engines.

A throaty roar from the exhausts resounded in the stillness. A group of seagulls took fight in alarm. Gamer eased out from the pier with the running lights switched off. It was still fairly dark where the water met the land, and the twosome headed out to sea, unnoticed.

Unnoticed to all but Andres Almquist, who had been secretly watching from a distance.

CHAPTER TWENTY

AFTER ANDRES'S GROUP HAD been awarded the grant from Gerace Institute to study the volcanic island, Bill Gaines had contacted him with his suspicions about what Cole was really doing down here. In addition to the generous grant money, Gaines had promised the scientist a big payday and individual recognition for the scientific discoveries that would be made. The recognition was more important to Almquist, but the money wasn't a bad bonus. In return, Andres would keep the chairman updated on Cole's every move—not that Andres needed much motivation. He didn't like Cole, for a variety of reasons. Nor did he particularly care for Gaines, but at least Gaines had earned his wealth.

Gamer adroitly led Cole to a spot within a hundred miles of the mysterious volcano's western shore. The ocean water was still changing hues but was dark enough to reveal a strange luminosity emanating from deep underwater.

Cole had donned the twin oxygen tanks, Atomic Aquatics professional deep-sea swim fins, and a Kirby Morgan diving helmet, the same brand he had worn with Lindsay on their last dive. Cole vacillated when Gamer had handed him the helmet, wondering if the boatman knew more than he was letting on. Finally, he got a Yamaha Seascooter, commonly known as a diver propulsion vehicle, with a mountable underwater camera attached. Also included with the scooter was a detachable Hammerhead Carbon Speargun, for a just-in-case emergency, Cole supposed. There was no shortage of high-tech gear here. Gamer had thought of everything.

"I'm guessing you'll need to descend about two hundred feet to reach maximum illumination," Gamer said. Then he added, "You don't have a lot time, so be on your way."

Cole entered the water and started the scooter, descending straight down through layers of dark, shimmering water, heading to one of the strangest sights he had ever seen. Glowing incandescently, strange, glutenous life-forms floated in circles, lighting up the water at the level where it was beginning to turn murky. Cole had experienced this shifting layer of the ocean's clarity multiple times in the *Harbinger II*, the world-class bathyscaphe he and Lindsay had used to venture to the deepest caverns in the Atlantic Ocean, and beyond. Life below this invisible line changed dramatically, as the ocean's creatures adapted to their environment and the rapidly increasing pressures of the deeper layers. Cole instinctively knew that he could not dive much deeper and so began to level off. Detaching his briefcase and the speargun, he jettisoned the scooter topside. He could swim back.

Unlocking the briefcase, Cole removed the strange box he'd discovered near the cantina. The gypsy-witch had foretold his future in a most mesmeric manner, telling him he needed to discover clues and solve riddles to understand just what that future held for him. And he supposed now was the time to begin the journey she had set him on.

Cole thrust out the box at arm's length, exposing it inside the eerily glowing light source. At first, nothing happened, nothing changed.

Gradually, the box began to emanate heat from its core. A small area changed color, revealing a keyhole. Cole's eyes widened. He'd brought the key the Cantina mistress had given him, just in case. He slipped it into the hole. It fit like a glove. Too quickly, the intensity of the searing heat burning his hands forced Cole to release the box. Just as he feared he was about to lose it to the denizens of the deep, the box did something quite unexpected.

It floated, unsupported, and began to change color again—the mysterious glyphs changing shape and transforming into something altogether different. The object was forming a new shape, morphing into a triangular silhouette. Cole gazed in amazement at the transformation taking place.

The box turned a brilliant shade of crimson, spewing fire-like sparks from its jagged top. Before Cole realized what was happening, the box had taken on the shape of the newly formed volcano, expanding in size right before his eyes. The new structure continued to grow, adding exquisite detail to its landscape as it enlarged exponentially. It now looked like a three-dimensional, topographical map, detailing fissures, mountainous slopes, torched soil—and something else.

Materializing in the center of this mystical object, a human form took shape—or at least, that's what it looked like to Cole at first. But this was no ordinary human. The apparition appeared more like an abomination—with massive wings of fire attached to broad shoulders and its long, twisted mane of hair seemingly on fire as well. An elongated, sinewy body hovered midair, while its right arm pointed wickedly curved fingers downward, to what looked like an opening or cave approximately a third of the way up the volcano's slope. The key was still protruding from that space.

The creature's eyes were as black and cold as glistening obsidian from an ancient lava flow long since solidified. Hollow, dreadful eyes that filled Cole with horror as they locked in on his, paralyzing him instantly. The fire angel, or whatever it was, spoke no words, made no facial expression, only continued to point at the opening as if to say, *Come find me, if you dare.*

The mysterious, conjured shape slowly began to draw in on itself, collapsing until it disappeared from sight. So too the box vanished. Cole was left alone, suspended in the water as the light from the luminescent creatures surrounding him also began to fade. Gradually, feeling returned to Cole's body, and he began to ascend upward, but not of his own volition. Something—some external force—was guiding him to safety. Cole relented, allowing whatever was controlling him to have its way.

CHAPTER TWENTY-ONE

G AMER EXTENDED A HAND to help Cole slide up to the step at the aft of his boat. Cole clambered in, a distressed expression on his face, as if he had just seen a ghost from his past. He wiggled out of the straps holding the oxygen tanks to his back, pulled off the swim fins, and placed the diving helmet on a side seat. He noticed the scooter was tied off to the side and was glad he hadn't cost the skipper that expensive piece of equipment.

The men stared at each other for a moment, Cole wondering when Gamer would ask him about the dive, and Gamer waiting for his boss to speak first. Cole broke the silence. "You were right. I found a sphere of light cast from the living organisms. It was something to behold, actually. Thank you for leading me to it. It was. . . it was illuminating, if I do say so." Cole cast the skipper a peculiar smile, suggesting that was all the information he would get.

Gamer nodded, understanding. "Where to now, sir?"

"Please call Mario. I need to return to the Parador Villas."

"Consider it done," Gamer replied, then headed back to shore, the Eliminator slicing through the gentle waves like a hot knife through butter. Minutes after reaching shore, the nondescript van reappeared. It occurred to Cole that Mario hadn't left after all but had instead hidden his van behind one of the vacated warehouse buildings nearby. These guys were at the ready twenty-four seven. *Don't they have lives elsewhere?* Cole wondered. Maybe a payday like this didn't come along very often, and they were just trying to make the best of it, insuring there would be more substantial paydays to come. Cole shook the uncomfortable thought away. He decided he would trust them until he couldn't.

As Cole left with Mario in the van, and Gamer set off from the pier in the *Ocean Shark*, Andres finished scribbling a few notes in his journal, then left to compose an email to Chairman Gaines. Andres didn't fully understand what Cole was doing or what he may have accomplished, but what he'd just witnessed was more than a little interesting. Evidently, Cole had developed diving skills during his time with Lindsay. These skills were apparently coming in handy in his search to discover the mysterious secrets of the volcano—mysteries that Andres, too, was convinced existed.

After first checking Art's room, Cole opened the door to his bungalow. He figured it was still too early for Art's return with the twins, and he was glad for the privacy. What he had just discovered in the shadowy light of the ocean's early morning luminescence continued to baffle him. The image of the map, the fire angel, the secret opening he believed was revealed to him, burned an imprint into his mind, like looking at the sun without eye protection. Every time he closed his eyes, the image reappeared, stinging his brain, as if someone had poured scalding water on it. Perhaps the image existed extemporaneously so that he would not forget.

Cole knew intuitively that he had to find that entrance if he had any hope of entering the volcano and reconnecting with Lindsay. From all the scientific information they had gathered so far, supported by satellite photos of the volcano's crater, there appeared no other way to enter safely. Streams of new molten lava poured out from the upper rim randomly, spewing down what looked like tunnel chutes, emptying into the ocean below, steaming, then cooling quickly. Then, according to Almquist, the lava was being recycled and fueling the mountain's relentless growth.

The top of the volcano reminded Cole of the Darvaza gas crater, a remote firepit near the Caspian Sea, that burned continuously, fueled by leaking gases that could not be extinguished. He recalled seeing videos of this phenomenon on the Natural History channel. Why it had stuck in his memory, he wasn't sure, other than that it seemed so *unnatural.* Like a portal to the earth's core—a rare glimpse into the planet's deepest secrets. Cole had promised himself he would visit the spot someday, but the pain of losing Lindsay in the subterranean fire storm that had consumed everything around them as they were thrust up to the ocean's surface was a wound still far too raw. Cole blinked, and the image of the Darvaza crater vanished.

To date, there had been no way discovered to safely gain entrance to the inner chambers of the volcano. Had Cole just discovered the only viable entry point? Had the gypsy-witch from the cantina ensured Cole could find it? And finally, was Lindsay behind it all, orchestrating everything from inside? Cole shuddered at the idea.

Sitting at the wooden desk inside his room, Cole sketched out a rough drawing of Hollingsworth Island, to the best of his memory. Closing his eyes, he allowed the turbulent imagery of the fire angel to reappear in his mind's eye. Locking in on where he thought the secret opening would be in relationship to the overall height of the volcano, he drew an X approximately a third of the way up the mountain slope. Now all he needed was to get a current assessment of the volcano's height, and then he might be able to speculate on its location. The underwater map that had been revealed to him had spun around, apparently indicating the back side of the mountain, facing due east.

He could get the elevation from his scientific team, but Almquist was on that team and might question why Cole needed this information. Cole trusted the Swedish scientist about as much as he trusted Bill Gaines. Cole would assign this task to someone else. Art seemed to be the logical choice—he was a master of getting information out of people. Gamer might be capable—he seemed to know much more about science than he let on— but Cole feared that if the skipper could be bought for a higher price, his knowing exactly what Cole was searching for could be a risk. But he would need Gamer to take him to the far side of the island undetected. That was enough for him to concentrate on. Cole wouldn't let him know where and when until he had obtained the information he needed to move forward.

A quick succession of knocks on Cole's door stirred him out of his meditative state. It could only be Art. Cole rose to let his friend inside. He didn't bother hiding his drawing. It was time to let Art all the way in. He could not continue on this journey unaided. Cole needed someone he had absolute trust in when it came to crunch time. Art was that person. He had earned it.

"Hey, Art," Cole said, ushering him inside. Cole took a quick glance outside to confirm Art hadn't been followed before closing his door and locking it. "Before we get started, why don't you tell me about last night. I'm sure it's a great story," Cole said, allowing Art time to brag, or gloat, or whatever he wanted to do.

Art appeared momentarily stunned, thinking this was a bit odd for his boss. Normally, Cole would ignore Art's exploits, or worse, chastise him for his transgressions with the Swanson sisters. But he seemed legitimately interested this time. Art stuttered, which was not something he was accustomed to doing.

"Um. . . it turned out to be quite the night, though not at all what I expected. We enjoyed a glass or two of fine champagne—courtesy of Hollingsworth, thank you—then ended up talking most of the night—"

"What exactly did the three of you talk about?" Cole interrupted, thinking that Art would never have tolerated that. But then, he had done the same thing with Lindsay—twice.

"This and that. Mostly about you." Art paused to catch Cole's reaction, who remained stoic. Art continued, "The sisters wanted to know more about you and Lindsay. Your relationship. What actually happened in San Salvador. They're convinced this trip is really about that, no matter what we tell them. You know, for all their glitz and cavalier attitudes, they're very smart women. It's just that their looks have always overshadowed that side of them, so they've relied on that to get where they are."

Cole considered Art's words. His thoughts turned to Lindsay. Beauty, brains, courage—all things shaped by her unfailing desire to change, to make something of herself on her own. In the case of the twins, their lives had paralleled Cole's. Born into influential families, given great educations, they had obviously not felt the burning desire to escape that life—just as Cole had refused to. In a man's world, what Sydney and Shelby possessed could open doors closed to so many others with just a smile. He couldn't blame them. Hadn't he done the very same things? Cole smiled ruefully.

"So, what did you tell the women, Art?" Cole asked.

"What do you think I told them, when even I don't know what really happened?" Art said accusingly. "I did tell them this trip was primarily for you to find answers to Lindsay's disappearance but that I didn't possess the details to fill them in."

"Did that placate the sisters?" Cole asked.

"No, not really, but I think they believed me. What else could they do, except leave?" Art glared at his friend without realizing it, but his gaze didn't escape Cole.

"Well, bro," Cole mimicked Art's oft-used vernacular, "that's all about to change. Have a seat, you're going to need one. Would you like a beer?"

"Cole, it's ten in the morning. I—" Art saw the gravity in his friend's eyes. "Yeah, okay, I'll have a beer," he said, just as Cole removed two bottles from his ice chest. He tossed one in Art's direction, who caught it and immediately opened the twist off cap, chugging about half of it, before he eased himself into the wicker chair opposite the desk.

"Let me take you all the way back to my week with Lindsay and everything we experienced in the Caribbean. It's probably best to listen to the entire story without interruption. They'll be time for questions after," Cole said.

Cole interlocked his fingers, placing his arms on the wooden desk, and stared intently into Art's troubled eyes, wondering if Art would truly believe him, or if he, like the twins, would want to catch the next plane out of here and be done with Cole's desperate search for a dead woman.

CHAPTER TWENTY-TWO

C OLE PATIENTLY LED ART through the improbable tale, beginning with Lindsay convincing him to fly to the tropics in search of his parents and how they might somehow save them. He described the *Harbinger II* in detail, and the frigate that transported them into the Bermuda Triangle area. Art nodded when the *Truett* was mentioned, having spent some time on it. Cole told him about the first dive, to set the stage for what was to follow. Art's interest grew with each new detail, as though he was following an interesting lecture on the rigors of deep-sea diving. When it came time to divulge what had occurred on the subsequent dives to the bottom of the Atlantic, Cole paused. He tossed Art another bottle of beer and took a deep breath.

"Art, what I'm about to tell you will seem like fantasy fiction, like a book or a movie. But I swear, on my parents' grave, it's what I experienced. To be honest, I don't believe it myself sometimes. It seems more dreamlike than real, but I am convinced it happened as I'm about to describe to you."

Art shot Cole a sideways glance, as if nothing could be that implausible. So far, what Cole had told him seemed reasonable, even logical. Art gestured with his free hand for Cole to continue, assuming his boss would reveal how they found his parents' shipwrecked yacht, along with some rational explanation about how the new volcano was formed. All in all, Art appeared nonplussed.

"On our second dive to the bottom of the ocean, we entered the Milwaukee Deep, in the Puerto Rican Trench, the deepest trench in the Atlantic Ocean. It is second only to the Mariana Trenches in the Pacific and the Challenger Deep. The trench was cavernous, but Lindsay managed to maneuver us through the treacherous cliffs and rock outcroppings by sheer skill. And then. . . then she revealed to me a subterranean portal that defies description. A huge, diaphragm-shaped anomaly that was actually the entrance to another dimension. I can't begin to describe it accurately. It pulsated like it was alive and was deep ebony in color. After studying it for a time, Lindsay took me back up to the surface to give me additional time to process what we'd just seen. I actually didn't believe her. I thought the tremendous pressure and sheer darkness of the ocean floor distorted things."

At this last bit, Art stood, raising one hand, as if to stop Cole from continuing on, and appeared to be harboring either a cynical question or serious doubt. Cole cautioned him to keep quiet and then continued.

"On our third dive, we actually entered the portal, by shocking the submersible with 275,000 volts of electricity and reversing the craft's polarity. We drifted for a while—I have no idea how long—in a tunnel of sorts, where I swear time stopped and no instruments worked. It was like riding on a cushion of air in total darkness. Then, all of the sudden, we shot through to the other side and into another dimension—at least, that's what Lindsay called it. She had been there before, several times. Art, that's when I first heard my parents' voices calling to me. I swear to God. . ."

Art's eyes widened and he struggled to keep quiet. Given the incredulous look on his face, Cole sensed he wasn't buying any of it.

"Maybe we should take a break, Art. Go outside and get some fresh air, and we'll continue on in a few."

Art didn't need much convincing. He rose, turned, and headed outside to clear his head. This wasn't making any sense. He doubted he could possibly believe Cole's story without corroboration—and where was he going to get that?

Lindsay was gone, most likely dead. Cassie Thomas was hiding out somewhere in the Australian outback, and Ryan Walker—well, Ryan could be almost anywhere. All conveniently missing in action. As Art stood gazing out at the ocean, it occurred to him that Cole was most likely making this up to keep him engaged in his search for Lindsay and his mind off of company matters. Fabricating a story so that Cole could pursue some personal quest that he wasn't going to tell anyone about anyway—at least not the truth about it. Art and the twins were simply pawns in Cole's secretive game. And all for what, really?

Art returned to see Cole still seated, staring pensively at what looked like a hand-drawn map. Cole pushed it aside.

"Are you ready to continue, Art?"

Art nodded reluctantly and took a seat.

"As I was saying, we entered this other dimension and, just as I was beginning to gain my bearings, the tectonic plates nearby shifted, causing the entire area to collapse, like it was being torn apart. We barely escaped with our lives. Shortly after that, Gaines and Jack Saunders arrived on the *Truett*, and I learned the details of Jacob Featherstone's scam. It nearly killed me. I decided to leave the following morning, but somehow Lindsay and her friends convinced me to stay another day. To take one more dive." Cole paused as a wave of grief swept over his face. It was that last dive that sealed Lindsay's fate—and his.

"So, Lindsay and I headed back down to the trench the next day. And what we discovered was literally beyond description. I found my parents. . . well, not in the flesh, but their spirits or something. We spoke, and then they faded away. Lindsay told me they'd needed to reconnect with me one more time before they passed on to their final resting place. Just as before, the space around us began to self-destruct. But this time, it was far more violent, and we lost the *Harbinger*. We cast out an underwater flare, which ignited a massive explosion beneath us, and a layer of the earth's crust came crashing up, and we rose up on it from the ocean floor to the surface. Lindsay protected me somehow from the extreme pressure of the deep ocean. I think I passed out. When I awoke, I was lying on this. . . this incredible new island, alone. I wandered around, dazed, until eventually Cassie and Ryan found me and rescued me, taking me back to the *Truett*. And the rest, I think you already know." Cole went silent, refusing to tell Art the part about Lindsay morphing into an angel and her reanimation to come back for him. He instinctively knew Art would not believe him and would probably walk out and not return.

Art's mouth had dropped open, without him knowing, while he listened to the tale unfold. *Was Cole serious?* he wondered. He appeared to be. Art really didn't know how to respond. He just sat and stared at his friend, dumbfounded.

"So, what do you think happened to Lindsay?" Art finally asked. This was the real issue in Art's mind.

"I don't really know, and that's the main reason I'm here. It's the reason I must gain access to the volcano. Art, I'm going inside. I'm working on a plan with Gamer. We leave in the morning."

"But, Cole—"

"No buts, Art. I believe I know where there's an entrance. You remember the mysterious-looking box I brought back from the cove the other day? Well, with Gamer's help, I discovered its secret. While underwater yesterday, all was revealed to me." Cole grabbed his drawing so Art could see where he thought the entrance was.

"I just need one piece of information from you. I need to know the current elevation of the volcano. I would have asked our scientific team, but I don't want Almquist to know what I'm doing. Can you snoop around today and get me that number? Then we can calculate the approximate location of the opening."

Art appeared paralyzed, as he contemplated Cole's further descent into madness. Minutes passed while Cole awaited his friend's response. But nothing came, only silence—and disbelief.

"Art? Did you hear me?" Cole asked, his voice more insistent.

Art rose, casting Cole an incredulous glance. "I'll do what I can." Art turned and headed out without another word, as if he too was fading, like Cole's parents before him.

CHAPTER TWENTY-THREE

ART RETURNED AT HALF past one with the requested information. It hadn't been much of a challenge. The height of the volcano was being measured throughout the day, every day. At first, Art thought this was odd, but when it was explained to him that the mountain was continuing to grow in stature, he supposed it made sense. Art scribbled the elevation—35,814 feet—on Cole's drawing, then added, as of today.

Cole was shocked by the number. He had recently done research on the tallest mountains in the world, and at 35,814 feet above sea level, Hollingsworth Island was almost 7,000 feet taller than Mount Everest, the tallest mountain in the world. When Cole had learned that Everest was very close in height to the depth of Milwaukee Deep, the deepest point in the Puerto Rican Trench, the similarity had unnerved him, although he couldn't say exactly why. A premonition? There must have been some connection, as if it was a balance, a mirror reflection of what lay below the ocean and above it, as though the ocean was a centering point. And now. . . now to learn that Hollingsworth Island was almost identical in height to the depth of Challenger Deep, the ocean's deepest location in the Mariana Trench system, was more than a little coincidental. Challenger Deep measured 35,814 below sea level at its deepest point. The commonality of these measurements was disconcerting.

Balance. The concept resonated in Cole's head. From the tallest to the deepest. And what lay in between? He thought he was about to find out—if he could somehow reconnect with Lindsay.

"Thanks, Art. This is a big help." Cole sat back down at his desk, laid a ruler on the map, and started drawing lines from top to bottom and left to right in an attempt to triangulate a specific spot on the drawing. Cole scribbled numbers on the map, then took out his phone and performed a couple of calculations. Appearing satisfied, he looked up at Art.

"I've got it. Now we just need to find its general vicinity on the eastern slope of the island, and then we'll need to climb about 11,750 feet up the side of the volcano. It should appear like a cave opening, but I expect it will be fairly well hidden." Cole was talking excitedly now, assuming Art would be accompanying him.

"Hold on, bro. If you think I'm climbing a third of the way up the side of an active volcano and then going inside, you're fucking crazy. No way!"

"But, Art, I need you on this. You can't abandon me now," Cole said.

"The hell I can't. I've gone along on everything up until now. But there is a line that I just won't cross. I'm sorry, Cole, but this is my final decision. You've got Gamer and Mario to help you. They're both a lot tougher than I am. I'm the brains, not the brawn, on this expedition," Art said defiantly.

Cole slumped, defeated, having little comeback. Art was probably right. This might very well be a suicide mission, but he had been so excited about the possibility of finding Lindsay again—something deep inside was telling him he was getting close—he had overlooked the dangers.

The time had come to finish his story about Lindsay, in a final attempt to entice Art or to further alienate him, Cole could not predict. But if the outcome of tomorrow's events ended badly, at least Art would understand why Cole had to try.

"Art, there's more to the story about my experiences with Lindsay, and I think it's the appropriate time to tell you. Whether you choose to believe me or not, there's nothing more I can do, other than to tell you the truth."

Reluctantly, Art sat back down in his chair, reconciled to the fact that he was about to learn more implausible accounts that were rapidly turning Cole's story into high fantasy—not unlike the Tolkien novels Art knew Cole held a fondness for.

"Where to begin. . ." Cole said in a whisper, as though talking to himself. Taking a deep breath, he continued. "After Lindsay learned of my parents' disappearance in the Caribbean, she convinced Dr. Votelli of the Gerace Institute to let her take their advanced submersible, the *Harbinger*, to search for them, since she was in the area doing research. That's when she originally discovered the portal in Milwaukee Deep. She made several successful dives and finally gained entrance through it, and it was there she found evidence of not only my parents, but of the afterlife. Before you say anything, Art, just humor me, okay?"

The next part would be the toughest, Cole knew.

"On her last dive, the portal collapsed, and she didn't make it out. She perished inside, searching for my parents. Sometime later, she appeared to Cassie in a dream, then made contact with her while Cassie was scuba diving. According to Cassie, she came back for me. To help me find closure with their deaths so that I could move on with my life. She took me inside the portal to connect with my parents one last time. As I told you previously, she protected me as we rose up from the deepest trench in the Atlantic—not as the Lindsay you met at the Newport Yacht Club, but rather as what I can best describe as a water angel. I witnessed the transformation take place right before my eyes. I'll never forget it. She encased me in her shimmering, diamond-studded wings and kept me safe until we reached the surface. In the process, Hollingsworth Island was born from the fiery core at the center of the earth." Cole went silent to allow Art time to process this information.

"And now you know the full story. I believe her spirit exists inside that volcano. And I must know the truth. I must see if I can reconnect with her or if she is truly gone. If I don't, I'll never be able to function as anything but a lost soul, searching endlessly. I don't expect you to understand, Art, but the sacrifices she made for me. . ." Cole trailed off, unable to continue.

Art gazed into Cole's eyes, his steely, disbelieving glance slowly turning to one of compassion for his troubled friend. Whether what Cole had just explained was true or not, at least he now understood what had been torturing him since their return to Newport after the island had been created. That fact alone seemed to validate Cole's story in some inexplicable way.

Instead of responding, Art rose and approached Cole, wrapping his arms around him, just as Lindsay must have done, attempting to protect him from his overwhelming despair. It was done. No more secrets existed between them.

"I'm sorry, Cole. So very sorry. I will not question you again about your reasons for being here. And I will do everything in my power to help you—short of climbing inside of that volcano."

"Fair enough," Cole countered. "I do need you to carry on, should something, um, unexpected happen to me. Besides, who's going to take care of the twins?" Cole joked, attempting to lighten the somber mood.

Art released Cole from his embrace, instantly struck with the feeling that things between them were about to change dramatically. "Speaking of the twins, I'd better go check on them. Don't want them to feel neglected."

It didn't take long to reconnect. Art found them sunning themselves near the pool and looking bored. They could only get so tan, after all. "Hey, you two are looking lovely today. Sleeping in the presidential suite last night must have done you some good." Art had hardly finished speaking when Shelby spoke up.

"What's up with Cole? Did he get his report done for Mr. Gaines? We were thinking that a drive to San Juan down south would be fun. We need a change of scenery. This place is depressing us." The look on Sydney's face confirmed that she was feeling the same as her sister.

Twins, Art mused. *When one is unhappy so is the other.* "Cole is preparing for a side trip early tomorrow morning, but I'd be happy to accompany you two to San Juan. I'll call a car. How long until you're ready?" Art said.

"Art, you've just spent half a day with Cole. What is going on with him?" Shelby said, growing disgusted with Cole's reclusiveness. "Doesn't he like us any more?"

"No, it's not that at all. He thinks you're both great. This is really an important trip for him. The future of Hollingsworth Island is at stake here. He can't screw this up. Please be understanding," Art pleaded.

"Okay, but if things don't change soon, we're out of here," Sydney said, as though the smallest incident might set them off and flying back to Newport.

Art didn't want that to happen. Besides the hope of renewed intimacy with the women, Art still possessed a feeling they had a role yet to play that would help in some unknown manner. But just what that role would be eluded him for the time being.

The threesome agreed to meet up at the cantina bar in an hour for a drink before departing to their destination. Art arranged for a modest town car to pick them up. He knew they wouldn't even consider Mario's van, but a flashy limo would attract unwanted attention.

The afternoon was growing muggy, as thunderclouds formed on the distant horizon, casting long shadows over the shimmering water. The women were decked out in slinky sundresses of bright yellow and green, resembling some of the tropical birds found in this part of the world. The bright colors contrasted nicely with their deeply tanned skin, driving Art crazy. When would they finally give in to him? He had thought last night in the presidential suite would be the perfect time, but that hadn't happened. While the girls were getting ready, Art had researched the poshest hotels and restaurants in the San Juan area. He planned to make his next attempt there. Cole would be out of sight and out of mind. There would be no shortage of adult drinks, and no shortage of adult activities, Art hoped.

The town car arrived not a minute too soon. The twins were already growing restless. The driver opened the rear doors for them. The inside was pleasantly well appointed, something that didn't go unnoticed by the twins. There was a nicely stocked bar on one side, and the seats were plush leather. Fresh flowers adorned the opposite side. *Not a bad ride*, Art thought. Lively flamenco music played in the background as if to suggest, *Let's get this party started.*

The car drove away, while Andres Almquist watched from inside his nondescript SUV, wondering what Cole was up to. No doubt he was up to no good. And why had he stayed behind rather than departing with his close friends? Perhaps a surprise visit to Cole's bungalow might be in order. As part of the Hollingsworth funded scientific team, there was no reason for Almquist to avoid Cole. Andres was one of the few people who knew about Hollingsworth's involvement, thanks to Gaines. Maybe he could learn something newsworthy to report back to the chairman. He needed to feed Gaines information if he wanted to keep things going his way.

Cole was in the process of dialing Gamer's cell phone when a knock on his door delayed him. Art had informed him of the trip he and the twins were taking, and they must be gone by now. Who in the world could it be? Cole glanced through the peephole, shocked to see Andres Almquist standing on his front porch. *What the hell does he want?* Cole wondered. Reluctantly, Cole opened his door.

"I hope I'm not disturbing you, Mr. Hollingsworth. Do you have a few minutes?"

What could Cole say, other than yes? "Come in, Andres. What brings you to my humble abode?" Cole said, making light of his low-end digs. "By the way, how did you find me, if you don't mind my asking?" Cole was actually surprised to be discovered.

"I called your office. I hope you don't mind. No one seemed to know if you were here, but I had heard rumors, um. . .through some scientists that you and your close friend, Art Barkley, were remaining in this area to ensure the scientific team selection was being conducted properly. And by the way, thank you very much for selecting us. It is a great honor." Andres went silent, awaiting Cole's reaction.

Cole didn't buy this explanation for a second. It could only have been through Gaines that Almquist found out—and that meant this arrogant son-of-bitch was working directly with the chairman. Spying for him.

"I see, well that makes sense, I guess. What is it you want, Andres?" Cole said in a tone indicating he was not pleased with the intrusion. Cole gestured toward a chair and then returned to the desk, where he quickly grabbed the hand-drawn map and folded it up.

Andres watched intently but could not discern what the large sheet of paper contained. "Well, sir, I just wanted to check in to see if there is anything of special interest you would like us to concentrate on. I must admit I'm a bit surprised that the type of monotonous research we are conducting would be of interest to an influential businessman such as yourself. But then, the island bears your family name, after all," Almquist said, smiling indifferently.

Cole wanted to strangle the bastard, and he probably would have if he could have gotten away with it. His thoughts turned to Mario. He'd probably enjoy ripping this scientist's head off. Gamer, too. Cole had requested an identity check on his skipper after he appeared to be so well educated, especially when it came to oceanography. His office had emailed Cole back with Gamer's real name, Nikolai Kavrikov, which meant nothing to Cole, other than it being of Russian or Ukrainian descent. But it might mean something to Almquist.

"As was explained to you during the preliminary science team qualification meetings, we are most interested in reporting the facts to the public. To keep them informed of the island's formation and its changing nature. After all, nothing like this has taken place in millions of years. For me, I guess I'm most interested in why the volcano continues to grow, although at a reduced rate now. Of all the theories I've heard thus far, yours makes the most sense to me, although most of your colleagues rebuke it and it goes against the laws of nature," Cole said, hoping to anger Almquist so that he would defend it.

Andres's face reddened, but he kept calm, mostly. "Thank you, Mr. Hollingsworth, I appreciate the vote of confidence. You know how the scientific community operates in general. They can be such an obdurate group. And most don't want to give credit to others, even when credit is due."

Cole noticed the vein in Andres's neck bulging. He had finally rattled the smooth-talking Swede. Cole pressed on. "So, you still believe in your theory that the volcano is recycling its magma through an intense hydra-steaming process and adding mass to itself? It makes sense, when you think about it. But the part I can't seem to understand is how the molten lava cools so quickly in regular ocean water. What is your theory on that?"

Almquist was taken aback. This was the one answer that continued to elude him, and he was not about to give Cole further information that he and his newspaper could announce to the world and take credit for. "My, my, you have studied my work, haven't you? I'm impressed." Almquist paused, eyeing Cole in a peculiar manner. "Well, if there isn't anything else, I really must be going. Back to the shop, as they say." Andres rose to take his leave. Before he opened the door, Cole stunned him with another question.

"Andres, do you happen to know a man by the name of Nikolai Kavrikov?"

Almquist stopped dead in his tracks, his body immediately stiffening.

"A fellow scientist, perhaps?" Cole added.

"Why. . . why do you ask?"

"No reason, really. I just thought the two of you might have met each other, since you both seem to know so much about the ocean."

Kavrikov. Now that was a name Almquist hadn't heard in some time. Once a brilliant Russian oceanographer, Kavrikov had defected near the end of the Cold War and came to Sweden in search of asylum. There, he debunked a number of Almquist's theories, which he had stolen from other scientists' research. Just as Andres was about to be exposed, he had informed the Russian Embassy of Kavrikov's location, and three KGB agents had come in the night to take the highly regarded scientist back to Russia. Almquist had received a hefty reward for the betrayal of a fellow scientist and, at the same time, salvaged his career.

Almquist did not turn to face Cole, fearing his expression might give him away. "No, Mr. Hollingsworth, that name doesn't sound familiar to me. Should I know him?" Andres asked curtly.

"No, I don't suppose you should. I was just wondering, that's all," Cole said. It was obvious by the Swede's reaction that he did know Gamer, but did he know the Russian was on Cole's team? Cole intended to find out.

Almquist hurried away in the mounting darkness, rattled. How would Cole have known that name? No one in the scientific community had heard a word about Kavrikov in years. Most thought him dead or, at a minimum, spending his remaining years in a Russian high security prison for treason.

Cole popped open a bottle of Old Harbor Kofresi Stout, his favorite beer. He had been introduced to the Puerto Rican craft beer during his time here with Lindsay and had developed a fondness for the local brew. Just one more small reminder of the woman he loved so much. He raised the bottle in salute to Lindsay and laughed at the same time. He wondered how Andres was feeling right now. Cole had foiled every attempt by the Swede to learn why Cole was actually here by turning everything around and gleaning valuable information for himself. The scientist wasn't so smart, after all. There were book smarts and then there were street smarts, and Cole was developing the latter.

Reacting to his growling stomach, Cole strolled up to the cantina in search of scotch and some food. He also needed to complete the call to Gamer that Andres had so rudely postponed. The waiter poured Cole a glass of scotch and handed him a menu as Cole dialed Gamer's number. Two rings later, the skipper answered. Before Cole could say hello, the Russian—Cole was beginning to think of him in those terms—spoke immediately, which was out of character for the soft-spoken boatman.

"Cole." He didn't bother calling him sir. "I hear you had a visitor earlier. Mario informed me, so you know I wasn't spying on you. I think I know the man, and if I'm correct, he is bad news." Concern was evident in the Russian's voice, which had suddenly taken on a more pronounced Eastern European accent.

"Yes, I did, and an interesting one at that. You and Mario are quite the tag team down here."

"Just trying to protect you, sir." Evidently, Gamer had either calmed down or had remembered to treat his wealthy client with respect.

"Do you know Andres Almquist, a Swedish oceanographer?" Cole asked, allowing Gamer the courtesy of answering the question himself.

"I knew it. Shit!" Gamer exclaimed. "I think he's been following us. I noticed a reflection off a watch or a piece of jewelry or something near one of the vacated warehouses near the dock yesterday, just as you were leaving. I took off in my boat but circled back after shutting down my engines and heard a car leaving, and it wasn't Mario's van."

"Interesting. Have you noticed anything like this before?" Cole asked.

"Not to my knowledge. Isn't the Swede part of the scientific team being funded by Hollingsworth?" Gamer asked, all business now.

"Yes, he is. He wasn't supposed to know I'm here, but he found out somehow. I think he's in direct contact with our chairman, Bill Gaines, who has a peculiar interest in this project," Cole said, but he wasn't about to elaborate. Cole motioned to the waiter to bring him another scotch. "Gamer, I need to ask you a question, and I need an honest answer. A lot depends on this. Is your real name Nikolai Kavrikov?"

There was dead silence on the line as Cole awaited the boatman's answer.

"How did you find out?"

"I had my people do an identity check on you after you took me out to find the luminescent creatures in the water. You seemed to know a lot more about the ocean than a man in your position would normally know. The search wasn't easy, but money can get you almost anything you need, for the right price. I apologize for going behind your back. When I mentioned your name to Almquist, he looked shell-shocked. His body language alone drew lines off of the seismograph," Cole said half joking.

This elicited a chuckle from the Russian.

"And if I'm right, you might be a person who knows a whole lot about seismographs," Cole said.

"Guilty as charged. In another life, I was a Russian oceanographer of some renown, before defecting to Sweden. Just as I was about to expose Almquist for stealing research from other scientists and taking credit for their discoveries, he ratted me out. That very night, KGB agents abducted me and smuggled me out of the country, taking me back to Russia to face charges of treason. I spent the next eight years in a shithole of a prison, mostly in solitary confinement, until the Russian Institute of Oceanography, known more commonly as UNIRO, needed my assistance to deal with growing pollution in the Ural River, and the lake it flowed into, which was affecting the supply of sturgeon and, consequently, their supply of caviar. Fucking ironic, isn't it?" Nikolai said, his voice laced with sarcasm.

"Let me guess. While studying the Ural, you found an opportunity to escape?" Cole speculated.

"Correct. I had some key assistance from other disgruntled scientists. Without their help, I wouldn't have gotten far. I owe them my freedom."

"Thank you for your honesty, Nikolai. Can I call you Nikolai?" Cole asked.

"I'd prefer Gamer if you don't mind, or Nick, but that is your choice. Even in this part of the world, Russian espionage is rampant."

"Okay, Gamer it is. But what you've just explained leads me to a second, equally important question. Why are you here, and why are you working for me at this precise moment in time?"

"That's actually two questions, sir," Gamer said matter-of-factly.

"Leave it to a scientist to be so exact. Okay, two questions."

"I originally came to the area because of the unusual nature of the Caribbean Sea and to study its tectonic plate system. I couldn't return to a normal job as a published oceanographer, but by being a boat for hire, I could spend time on the water without being suspected of doing research." Gamer went silent, apparently struggling with the second part of the question.

"Okay, I get that. But what about the working for me part?" Cole asked suspiciously.

"I was getting to that. Since I was in the area when the new landmass was formed, naturally, I was interested in learning more. After the news came out about you being the first person to stand on the landmass and the island being named after your family, I hoped to contact you. It was a shot in the dark that you would even believe me or consider hiring me to conduct research, so I bided my time, hoping for another opportunity."

"And that opportunity arose when Art and I came calling? Talk about destiny," Cole said, sighing heavily.

"Due to my, um, less than scrupulous contacts and the line of business I'm in—smuggling is only a small part of it—I heard that someone from Hollingsworth was looking to hire some muscle and some knowledgeable people to keep them out of the limelight. My friend Mario thought I might be a good addition to the team, since he knew I possessed some amount of knowledge about the ocean. He still doesn't know the full truth. So here we are. . . And I guess you have a decision to make, if I'm not mistaken." Gamer paused, awaiting Cole's decision.

"I suppose I do. How can I trust you? I must admit, this seems far too coincidental. You may have a completely different agenda than me. And if it should come to crunch time in a critical situation, how will I know you have my back?"

"You can't, really. Not until you either know me better or we survive a trial by fire together. All I can ask is that you trust me."

Cole's eyes widened. He was stunned. That was the exact same thing, word for word, Lindsay had asked of him before their final, fateful dive to the bottom of the Puerto Rican Trench. Another crossroads? Another point of no return? He had trusted Lindsay, but then, he loved her. This man was a relative stranger, posing as someone he wasn't. Yet, something in his demeanor suggested he could be trusted. But trusted with Cole's life?

"I can find you another boatman if you'd like, sir. It will only take a couple of hours. The underground is quite efficient down here," Gamer said, nonchalantly, as if he truly understood the dilemma facing Cole.

Cole considered the oceanographer for a long moment. Yes, that is who he truly was. And he had defected from the tyranny of Russian autocracy, survived horrible conditions in prison, and was now offering his help in what would be a dangerous mission for himself as well. This guy knew the stakes—he was a survivor.

"Okay, Gamer. You're my man. You and Mario. But if you let me down, I swear on my parents' grave, I'll kick your ass."

"I would expect nothing less, sir." A moment of silence passed between the men, or maybe it was reflection on the pact they had just made. "When do we leave?" Gamer asked.

"Where do you think we're going?" Cole replied.

"I assume I'm taking you to your island."

"In the morning," Cole said, then he filled his skipper in on all the equipment he thought they would need, while the Russian added in additional gear that would be necessary.

Cole ordered dinner and a final scotch before retiring to his bungalow, praying he would find sleep this night.

CHAPTER TWENTY-FOUR

COLE AWOKE AT DAWN, feeling restless, as the all too familiar feeling of apprehension overcame him, mirroring his anxiety before his dives to the bottom of the ocean with Lindsay. It was the unknown that unnerved him. The inside of the volcano seemed as treacherous as the deep ocean caverns had been, perhaps more so. Would he find Lindsay, or would it all be for naught? He had come this far, but now that the moment was at hand, the fear returned. Cole checked his watch. Mario would be arriving in less than thirty minutes. He needed to get ready quickly. His driver would not be late.

Cole stood inside the lobby, looking out a tiny window, when he spotted the lights of the van approaching. He waited until the van pulled up next to the entrance, then quickly entered the back seat, with a grim-faced nod to his driver. They left the relative safety of the Parador in silence and headed toward a new location. Gamer had decided to launch from a spot farther south, hoping to avoid detection.

Almquist had positioned himself in a different car five miles up the road, behind a row of dilapidated buildings but with a view of the road the driver would be traveling on. He spotted the oncoming van and waited a short time before easing the car out onto the road and following. The sky was brightening, and headlights were no longer needed. Almquist assumed they were headed to the previous pier to meet the boat. When he was approaching an intersection, he planned to take another route to avoid detection only to be surprised when the van took an unexpected turn to the right, heading south. Almquist had little choice but to follow or lose them. He turned to the man sitting in his passenger's seat and questioned him about a possible location where the boat could launch undetected. In a gruff voice, the man described two places he thought they might be headed to, seeming familiar with them both.

The man was dressed in army camo garb, looking very military and very hardened. A CheyTac Intervention sniper rifle lay on the floor of the back seat in two pieces. It was rumored to be the most accurate long-distance firearm, with capability of deadly accuracy up to 2300 meters, well over one mile. A pair of military-grade binoculars lay beside it.

Forty-five minutes later, the van came to a stop near a deserted pier jutting out about seventy-five yards into the water. The boat was moored at the end, waiting.

Almquist came to a halt and turned off the road. The other man dialed his cell phone and began giving instructions to another man for where to bring his boat. The plan was to follow Cole out, but not before they had vanished from sight. Andres suspected they were headed directly to the volcano. What he didn't realize was that Art had also rendezvoused with Cole and that Kavrikov was apparently going with them. Andres had not yet connected Kavrikov as the boatman.

"Art?" Cole exclaimed, after he spotted him talking to the skipper. "What are you doing here?"

"Did you actually think I would abandon you? I'm still not climbing inside that cursed volcano, but I thought I could be of use, or at least look after Gamer's boat, while you two are climbing up the side of that mountain."

Cole reached out and hugged his friend. "It's good to have you with us, bro," he whispered. "Where are the twins?"

"I left them in bed at the hotel we stayed in last night. Finally, a little action," Art said, but he didn't seem overly thrilled with his conquest. It was obvious something more concerning was occupying his thoughts.

Cole turned toward his skipper. "Got everything we need?" "I think so. We can review it all if you'd like." "No, that won't be necessary. I trust you," Cole replied.

Mario waited until the three men were inside the boat before leaving. Again, he had been instructed to disappear so there would be no evidence the group had even been here. He acquiesced but would remain close and out of sight, just in case.

Andres and his companion waited and watched until Cole's boat was nearly out of sight. At about three miles out to sea, it vanished over the horizon. It was time to get their own craft ready, which had just appeared on the water, heading down from the north. They didn't want it to be spotted on land by Cole's driver. Almquist didn't know who he was, but had heard rumors that he had impeccable credentials and was not one to mess with. When he eventually learned that Cole's skipper was actually the Russian scientist, it would send him over the edge.

The twosome climbed into their boat, a Magnum 44' Banzai with a top speed of 75 miles per hour—hardly the equal of the 169 mph Eliminator 36 Daytona ahead of them, but it would have to do. At close to full speed, it would take them almost three hours to reach the shoreline of Hollingsworth Island, but they didn't want to arrive too early. Almquist doubted that Cole's skipper would be nearing top speed with him on board. Cruising at high speed was bound to attract attention.

As Cole's group neared fifty miles from the volcano, Gamer dropped his speed from a brisk 75 mph to roughly 15 mph to gain their bearings more accurately. They were approaching from the south, which had extended their trip time, to avoid direct contact with any seafaring vessels that might be shuttling scientists or gear between Puerto Rico and the island.

Almquist had taken the more direct route and arrived shortly after, but in a different location. If Almquist was discovered, any gatekeepers would allow him to pass through, although they might question his dubious-looking companion dressed in camouflage gear. The sniper rifle was in pieces and well hidden in a secret compartment on the Banzai normally utilized for smuggling. It would not be found.

Andres motioned to their captain to shut the boat down as he reached for the binoculars. He scanned the horizon in every direction, but all seemed calm, with the exception of the smoke and ash plumes billowing high above from the volcano's crater. The distinct aroma of sulfur permeated the seascape. The nearer one was to the island, the harder it was to breathe normally. Most people wore some form of face or gas mask while stationed on or nearby the volcano. The atmosphere remained acrid, with a fine mist of steam rising from the ocean's surface. Each time Almquist visited, the scene reminded him more and more of primordial earth—or at least his image of what it would have looked like millions of years ago. The scientist sat back down and waited, contemplating Cole's motive for being here.

Gamer turned their boat northeast, maintaining a wide berth from the shoreline, heading to the back side of the landmass. From intelligence reports the skipper had obtained, with the help of Cole's pocketbook, they had learned this stretch of the island was totally unmanned. The reports said it was far more rugged and uninhabitable, with difficult access to the upper reaches of the towering mountain. So, it had been left unattended, as it slowly morphed into something quite unlike the rest of the island, which was still barren and covered with cooling lava flows, devoid of any sort of vegetation. The east side of the island would not be studied seriously for some time.

All camps had been set up either on the west shore or on floating, pontoon-like platforms at sea, reminding Almquist of oil rigs—unnatural structures created to steal something vital from the living earth. Taking, not giving, as humanity was inclined to do. What would be taken from this natural wonder?

Although Almquist had been transformed from pure scientist to part businessman, part cutthroat opportunist by the ambition of achieving national acclaim, he was once a seeker of truth, much like Lindsay had been.

His naiveté and sense of unadulterated wonder at the natural world had been stripped away piece by piece over the years, until all that remained was his insatiable desire for recognition and money. However, Andres did not yet understand that this path would only lead to ruin, as he fell further and further from grace.

Forty minutes later, Gamer cut the throttle, and the Eliminator coasted to a stop about one hundred yards from the eastern shoreline. What met their collective gazes immobilized the threesome as well. No longer barren, no longer covered with cooling lava flows, the steeply inclined mountainside was covered in thick, lush vegetation. Stunted palm trees sprouted long, misshapen fronds, tossed about by a stiff breeze. Below, gnarly, muscular-looking plants, in a myriad of bright colors, thrived. A thick layer of mist covered the volcano's top two thirds, by Gamer's estimate, having locked in his USCamel military-grade, range-finding binoculars on the mountainside.

What a strange sight, Cole thought. The low-hanging mist seemed to be emanating from the top of the crater, as evidenced by its slow, downward movement, apparent even from this distance. Why did it end precisely where it did, failing to encroach farther? This struck Cole in an odd manner, unnerving him, as the trio continued to stare open-mouthed at the phenomenon. Even Gamer appeared baffled.

"What do you make of that?" Cole said, directing the query to his skipper.

"I'm not sure. . ." Gamer paused, continuing to gaze through his binoculars. "I don't understand why it is in such stark contrast to the western slope. I've been there twice since its formation. I was asked to ferry over government officials on two occasions."

Just as Cole was about to inquire why government officials would hire someone like this boatman, Gamer continued.

"They wanted to remain anonymous. Everyone who is allowed on the island goes through a thorough reference check. It's not easy to get here and. . . and I guess they didn't want anyone knowing their true identities, so they hired me. It was a good payday." Gamer smirked awkwardly.

"Then I guess it makes sense," Cole said, dropping the subject. That was the Russian's business not his. "I've seen a lot of photos of the island—at least the west side—from the early reporting and then later from satellite photos. And you're right. This side is markedly different, from what I can tell. Don't you find it odd that we haven't seen pictures of this side of the island?" Cole questioned.

"Now that you mention it, yes. I do recall in the short time following the island's creation that it pretty much looked the same all around, although I do remember a few photos showing the more dramatically sloped side we're looking at now—also the small amount of shoreline. As you can see, the mountain's dramatic rise starts much closer to the waterline here. It may be the mist covering much of this side that's blocking satellite photos from revealing the differences."

"But what could have happened over the last three or four months to cause such a drastic change, and with no one noticing it?" Cole said.

"Good question," Gamer replied. "Perhaps we are about to find out."

All the while, Art remained quiet, studying the volcano and listening to his companions. There was something very mysterious going on here. Art had no idea exactly what, but he intuitively knew it wasn't good. Just one more reason for him to stay on board.

"So, Cole, if I may ask, why did you choose this side of the island to explore—other than wanting to avoid being recognized?" Gamer said.

Cole knew this question was coming. It had taken longer than he'd expected, but then Gamer was his employee after all, and his job was to transport and protect his employer from detection.

"That's a good question, *comrade*," Cole said, choosing an endearing term the Russian could likely relate to and, at the same time, indicating this was a mission that would not be fully revealed to the boatman at this time. "Yes, one of my primary reasons was to go undetected. But I have come into some very interesting and highly classified information that there may be an entrance to the volcano on this side of the island," Cole replied. *Highly classified* seemed a whole lot better than fantasy fiction and his miraculous underwater discovery of the volcano's secrets.

"I see. Now that is a rather fortuitous bit of information. I would say it borders on *illuminating,* if you ask me. I'm betting that only one or two others share this information with you," Gamer replied, winking at Cole, acknowledging their clandestine encounter with the ocean's incandescence on their first trip together.

"You might say that. Yes, *illuminating* is the perfect description," Cole said, then he turned his gaze toward Art, hinting at him to remain quiet and quickly putting an end to the discussion. Art had heard Cole's explanation of the map and understood why Cole didn't necessarily want to share it with Gamer.

"What's our next move?" Kavrikov asked.

"I think it's about time to get on with it. Do we leave your boat out a ways, or can we take it closer to the shoreline? It seems to have a fairly flat bottom," Cole said.

"I think we can take it closer." The skipper switched on one of his depth finding devices. "Just like the mountain, the shoreline drops off steeply at sea level. We should be safe. We'll proceed slowly to avoid any potential damage and see how far we can go. I brought a heavy-duty inflatable raft in case we need to paddle in and carry some of our extra gear."

"Good thinking," Cole said. "Art, are you okay staying with the boat while we explore? The last thing we need is to lose it," Cole added, letting Art off the hook.

"Yes, I can handle that. Do you have an extra set of binoculars so I can monitor your progress? Preferably one that can see through fog," Art said, half joking.

"Actually, I have a couple, and one has night vision, which may assist with the fog. . . and, I'll leave you with this." Gamer handed Art a Colt pistol. There's also a long-range rifle on board with an enhanced telescope you can use as well," Gamer said, as if this was expected.

Art accepted the handgun warily but said nothing. It appeared the skipper might be expecting visitors. Art was not exactly a marksman or stiff-armed type, preferring to talk his way out of jams rather than shoot his way out. But at this point, anything was better than venturing inside this hellhole of a volcano.

Little did Art know, but his intuition was spot on.

CHAPTER TWENTY-FIVE

G ROWING IMPATIENT, ALMQUIST DIRECTED his skipper to start trolling the nearby ocean for a sign of Cole's boat. He should have appeared by now. Unless. . . unless he was traveling incognito and had switched boats mid-journey. At this point, it was the logical thing for him to do. His entire trip here had been shrouded in secrecy. Why would that change now? Having launched from a more southern location, the scientist assumed Cole was choosing to come onto the island from another angle. But the *why* of this eluded him. *What does Cole want?* Almquist wondered. The more he thought about Cole's motives, the more confused he became. What was his endgame?

The Banzai headed south while moving closer to the shoreline. A sign that read "Gerace Oceanography Exploration Team" hung from either side of the boat, indicating to any interested parties that they had free range of the closed area. If anyone tried to board them, his credentials would do the trick. If not, he had the muscle to back him up.

Within twenty minutes, a security boat approached with increasing speed. Andres ordered his boatman to slow down, although they probably could have outrun them. But why bother? He would dispense with these amateurs posthaste. They waited until the craft came along side. One of three men in uniform leaned against the railing, calling out to them.

"You are being stopped by the Hollingsworth Island security team. Please identify yourselves."

Andres bristled at the mention of the Hollingsworth name, as though the mountain personally belonged to Cole.

"I'm Andres Almquist, head researcher for the Gerace Institute's exploration team. Can't you read the sign attached to our boat?" Andres said disrespectfully. "This is my skipper, and this is my associate." He pointed toward the two men. "We have full rights to be here and to explore every facet of this area." Andres reached into his pocket and flashed his credentials. "If you don't believe me, you can contact Dr. Votelli, the director of the institute."

"That's all very good, Mr. Almquist, but I will need to see your credentials and a photo ID. No exceptions."

"You've got to be joking!" Andres exclaimed, becoming further irritated with this rent-a-cop. The two men glared at each other, neither one willing to back down. If Almquist hadn't been in such a foul mood over Cole's meddling, he would have handled this in a diplomatic manner, but the mention of the name Hollingsworth had sent him over the edge.

"Just do what he says," whispered the man standing next to him. "Then we can be off."

"Okay, here." Almquist tossed his credentials to the man, who fumbled with the catch but managed to not drop anything in the ocean.

The guard scrutinized the document, looked again at Almquist to determine if the photo matched the man, looked back at the credentials.

"Okay, you're free to go. Just so you know, we are required to report this incident along with a photo of the boat." One of the other guards snapped a couple of shots with his digital camera. "Have a good day, gentlemen."

The security boat sped away, while Andres watched, seething. "Idiots!" he shouted after them.

CHAPTER TWENTY-SIX

G AMER SHUT DOWN THE Eliminator about forty yards out, based on his assessment of the encroaching rocks underwater. He dropped a metal anchor overboard while tossing Art the ignition keys. Next, he extracted the compressed raft from the storage area, pulled a cord, and the lifeboat automatically inflated. He tossed that overboard as well and secured a strap to one of the carabiners attached to the upper hull.

"After you, Cole," Gamer said. When Cole was situated inside the inflatable, Gamer began handing gear down to him. Mostly supplies necessary for climbing. Rope, small climbing axes, helmets, additional carabiners, a pair of climbing harnesses, and a backpack that held flashlights and assorted smaller gear, including two handguns. The two men had already changed into hiking boots. Gamer jumped in, and Art untied the rope.

For a moment, Art and Cole stared at each other, something unspoken passing between them, as if to say this might be goodbye. Cole smiled up ruefully at his friend with one of those patented Cole smiles—half-cocky, half-amused. Just another crazy night out on the town raising hell.

How long had it been since the former playboy turned. . . turned what? Cole hadn't been himself since his initial return from the island over six months ago. Partying was nonexistent, as were the bevy of beautiful women that seemed to track him down wherever he went. Even the drinking had seemed to disappear, at least in public. Art didn't know that Cole needed alcohol nearly every night to find sleep. All that Art had witnessed was the occasional beer or glass of red wine with dinner.

Art watched in silence as the skipper rowed the twosome toward the shoreline. It wasn't a long trip, but in Art's mind, it seemed to take an inordinate amount of time, as though he was subconsciously willing Cole to return rather than face the unknown inside of the volcano.

Unbeknownst to Art, a tiny craft appeared on the horizon behind him. They had finally caught up. Almquist directed his boatman to position the Banzai in a straight line between the rising sun to the east and Cole's boat near the shore, in case somebody was still on board. The sun was still low enough in the sky that if someone looked back, it would be a direct hit to the fiery orb, temporarily blinding the onlooker. The Banzai slowed and coasted in until they were in viewing distance of Art, through binoculars. Almquist scanned the shoreline, gradually making his way up the mountainside. He did a double take when he spotted the layer of mist covering a large portion of the surface, and then he spotted two figures advancing up the slope.

"Closer," he instructed the boatman. "I need a better view of what they're up to." The boat moved stealthily forward, while Art continued to watch his companions advance up the mountainside. It was slow going, but they were making progress.

The beach area closest to the water was still quite barren. With rock outcroppings and cooled lava flows, it was devoid of plant life. As the terrain quickly steepened, a myriad of green, brown, and reddish vegetation began to appear. Thick, tubular plants snaked along the surface, combined with large ferns and stunted palm trees. Brilliantly colored flowers dotted the landscape—deformed shapes resembling nothing that had existed on the earth in eons. Art spotted movement in and above the flora. There appeared to be birds of some type, which he confirmed through his high-powered binoculars. Strange birds. He zoomed in on the closest one, shocked to see it resembled more of a reptile with wings than anything. Featherless, its scaled body led to an elongated neck, ending with a small head and protruding beak. Its wings appeared leather-like, at least from this distance. The creature's body was earthy brown, its wings a brilliant blue. It sailed overhead like a kite, occasionally swooping low and disappearing amid the tropical plants. Although Art was no scientist, the scene appeared to him primordial, for lack of a better term. Something about it screamed of a distant past.

Farther back, there was another observer, watching with equal interest through his military-grade binoculars. The unusual terrain had temporarily distracted Almquist from his original targets, Cole and his boatman, as they edged their way steadily up the mountainside. Refocusing his gaze back on the Eliminator, he confirmed that Art Barkley was the man left on the craft, apparently to protect it. He knew Art's background fairly well, and he was no strongman—just another attorney, who was one of Cole's lackeys. Art presented no physical threat, but he was a member of the interview group that had selected Almquist's team and knew him. He was also a very close friend of Cole's and seemed to have his confidence, so Andres would need to be careful about how to deal with him, should something arise.

At approximately five thousand feet, Cole and Gamer took a break. The climb was steep, with the vegetation becoming denser, taking its toll on their energy level. Both men were in good shape, but the trek wasn't easy. The boatman retrieved two bottles of water from his backpack and handed one to Cole. Cole looked back down to the shoreline, which was still visible, and spotted their boat. Although thirty-six feet in length, it looked like a toy from this perspective. The glare of the early morning sun made visibility difficult, so he failed to notice the other boat further out to sea. All appeared normal.

With his binoculars locked on Cole, Almquist continued to ponder the reason Cole was climbing this side of the mountain. Surely with his clout, he could have obtained access to the west side and the abundance of researchers and experts stationed on or nearby the island. What in the world was Cole searching for? It was driving the Swede crazy. It had to be something important.

Cole and the boatman were on the move again, while two sets of binoculars tracked their ascent. Art noticed they were approaching the fog line as their images grew blurred. He felt his heartrate spike as the comrades disappeared into the silent, swirling mist. A moment later, they were gone from sight and there was nothing Art could do to help them. Sighing heavily, he reached for the rifle with the enhanced viewing night scope. For a moment, he thought he spotted movement through the mist, appearing green through the scope. The images reminded him of stickmen—bone-like structures moving jerkily along.

From farther back, Almquist watched the two men disappear, cursing to himself. Where were they headed? He had no idea that an opening might exist. The thought had never occurred to him. Were they intending to climb all the way to the top? That would be impossible, they would never survive. And for what?

The surface temperature had cooled dramatically under the cloak of dense mist. Most of the sunlight had disappeared, and visibility was being affected. Droplets of water formed on the flora. It was as if they had entered a rainforest, which seemed to fascinate the Russian, who had stopped to inspect the changing landscape on numerous occasions, jotting down notes. *Once a scientist, always a scientist*, Cole supposed.

The sound of rustling leaves startled the pair, as something moved nearby. By the volume of the clatter, it didn't appear to be small or one of the reptilian-like birds they had encountered on the ascent. Both men froze. What sort of creature could be lurking on the mountain? The only animals, aside from birds, that would have any sort of contact with the volcano would be ocean dwelling, and there was no way they could survive at this height, even if they had managed to come on shore.

Were they being followed? Cole's thoughts turned to Almquist. Had he tracked them here? That seemed at least somewhat possible.

Gamer retrieved the handguns from his backpack and handed one to Cole. "I don't like the sound of that. Something, or somebody, is up here with us."

"I know, and it might be your scientist friend following us. I know he's been watching our comings and goings. He wants to know what we're doing."

Cole's immediate thought was to contact Art to see if another boat was nearby, but their cell phones didn't work here. He turned to Gamer. "I don't suppose you brought any walkie-talkies or something we could use to communicate with Art?"

Gamer shook his head disparagingly. "I'm sorry, Cole, that little detail slipped my mind."

"You couldn't have known Art would show up at the last moment. Don't beat yourself up over it," Cole said.

"I should have brought something, just in case anything came up. That was a huge oversight on my part."

Cole slapped the skipper on his shoulder. "Let's wait a few more minutes and if everything seems okay, we'll proceed upward," Cole said.

Gamer nodded, continuing to look around and listen. Ten minutes passed without further incident. The twosome moved upward, handguns still clutched and pointing forward.

They were approaching 8000 feet in altitude, if the barometric altimeter they were using was operating normally, and they stopped again for a brief rest. Although Gamer didn't realize it, Cole knew they were getting closer to where he had calculated the entrance to the cave would be, even though it was only approximate. They needed to climb another 3500 feet or so and then they would be in the vicinity, at least height-wise. At 11,500 feet, breathing would be labored, but livable. The *death zone*, as it was known, came at about 26,000 feet, depending on other atmospheric conditions, but it could be lower. Cole had done his homework on this, so he was confident they could make the climb. If the opening was actually higher in altitude, it could present a problem. There was no way they could climb much higher without oxygen, and they hadn't brought any with them.

As the sun continued to rise in the sky, Almquist began to worry that Art might turn around and spot them. The sun's location had lost its ability to protect them from view any longer. Anticipating that Art would turn at some point, he ordered his skipper to retreat until they were just beyond the horizon. They could wait there until something happened that would require their intervention or until Cole returned to his boat. It appeared it would be a long wait.

CHAPTER TWENTY-SEVEN

C OLE AND GAMER WERE on the climb again. The terrain remained fairly constant, even though the air was heavier and the temperature continued to cool. The air should have grown thinner the higher they rose, but like so many other things about this newly formed island, it seemed to contradict nature's laws.

After another hour of climbing, Cole glanced at his altimeter—9300 feet. He wondered how Art was doing below. Was everything okay, or had Almquist snuck up on him, maybe holding him captive. The not knowing was driving Cole crazy.

"What's on your mind, Cole," Gamer said suddenly, as though reading his thoughts.

"I'm just worried about Art. We probably shouldn't have let him come with us. I hate that he's down there alone and out of our sight."

"I don't think you give your friend enough credit. He seems resourceful to me. Besides, I don't think you could have gotten rid of him. He seems quite devoted to you," Gamer replied.

Cole pondered this statement for a moment. Yes, Art had turned out to be a true and steadfast friend, and Cole found himself ever more grateful for this. He hadn't had many true friends in his life, at least the male type.

They were either jealous of his wealth and power, or they wanted something from him. When it came down to it, would anyone else have accompanied him on this quest, as absurd as it was? Lindsay, yes, but she wasn't available at the moment. Cassie might have come along, if she thought there was a chance to find Lindsay again. He doubted Ryan would have agreed, even though he was no coward. Only Art had volunteered to help out, and even after refusing to set foot on the island, he had shown up anyway and offered his assistance. The only reason Gamer and Mario were here with him was because they were being paid a shitload of money.

"You're right, of course. I should give him more credit," Cole said, almost regretfully. Cole quickened his pace, determined to reach the opening as soon as possible, blocking out all other thoughts. Those thoughts, those moments of indecision, were holding him back and delaying his singular goal—to reunite with the only woman he had ever loved.

Gamer recognized his resolve and followed silently in Cole's wake, occasionally looking back to ensure no one was following.

Eleven thousand feet. They were getting close. Still, nothing in sight looked remotely like it was in any way different from the terrain they had been climbing for the past couple of hours. Cole refused to take another rest break, stubbornly ascending the mountainside as if his life depended on it.

"Cole," Gamer called out. "Why don't we take a little break. The mountain isn't going anywhere."

Cole stopped momentarily, looking back at his companion. "If you want to stop, that's fine, but I'm heading forward. You can catch up later. . . if you want."

In Cole's mind, he was now leaving Gamer behind. He wouldn't allow him to follow him inside, if Cole was able to find the secret opening. But Gamer didn't know that yet.

The Russian, who seemed to possess a heightened sense of intuition, perhaps shaped by his years of persecution, realized that Cole's attitude was changing, that he was taking charge. Maybe that's what corporate CEOs did in certain situations, when they needed to rely on their own instincts.

Survival instincts. Something that Gamer knew a great deal about. So, he acquiesced and followed dutifully in Cole's tracks. He still had a job to do—to protect his employer—and he wasn't about to abandon that responsibility.

They continued to climb relentlessly until Cole stopped to check his altimeter. Gamer had brought one along, too, but more for measuring differences in terrain at varying altitudes as they ascended the mountain. He had brought it primarily for scientific reasons. It suddenly dawned on him that Cole must be looking for a very specific altitude or location. That had to be the reason he checked it so frequently. But what was he searching for?

Just like Andres Almquist, Gamer was becoming more curious—or was it suspicious? He wanted to ask Cole what he was searching for but knew he wouldn't get the answer. He'd just have to wait and see.

Cole stopped abruptly, as though he had stepped on a land mine. The sudden change in pace caught Gamer unexpectedly and he almost ran into Cole's back.

"Are you all right, Cole? What did you find?" Gamer asked.

Cole failed to answer, instead staring at a break in the vegetation, which was continuing to grow larger as they rose up the mountainside. Cole spotted an opening of sorts, resembling a tunnel of trees that might line a country road or a long driveway to a chateau. It appeared to lead directly into the mountain, but the end was not visible. Only a swirling mist revolving counterclockwise. And in the middle. . . in the middle, a fire angel suddenly materialized—just like the one that appeared in the luminescence under the ocean. Its black eyes locked on Cole, sending a sudden, searing heat up his spine. The image screamed of evil. Cole became paralyzed in its presence. Unable to move, unable to speak, all he could do was gaze at the apparition before him. The fire angel smiled wickedly back at him, raising one hand that looked more like a vicious claw.

The malevolent claw suddenly jerked, and a bolt of lightning flashed by the side of Cole's face, striking Gamer directly in the chest, knocking him off his feet and down the slope. Cole tried to scream, but barely uttered a squeak.

Slowly, the pressure subsided, and Cole relaxed. His first impulse was to empty his firearm into the creature, but instead he turned to look for his skipper. What he saw enraged him. Lying unconscious about thirty feet below was Gamer, the front of his jacket scorched, his eyes wide open and glazed over. No one could have survived that blast.

"Why?!" Cole screamed. "What purpose did that serve?" He could barely see through the water in his eyes. The fire angel crooked its neck as if it didn't understand the question. There was no remorse in its ebony eyes, only malice.

Cole watched in horror as the abomination turned and floated away, propelled by fiery wings, until it disappeared into darkness. Without warning, a tremendous blast shattered the silence, and the mountain shook as if it was about to implode. A massive fireball shot out of the crater, and the sky turned to ash. Cole was knocked to the ground, going deaf by the ear-shattering explosion that had just ripped the atmosphere apart. Cole lay dazed but was awake enough to feel an intense heat encroaching from above. He flipped over and saw, through the smoke and ash, a red current running down the mountain like a river, decimating everything in its path. And in the distance, he heard a screeching, howl-like voice, like a prehistoric beast writhing in agony, as though being burned alive.

No humans shall pass here, save one. The earth is reclaiming its own.

The voice spoke as if coming from the heavens, echoing in all directions.

And then there was only silence. The violent shaking subsided. The lava flow was quickly cooling. The smoke and ash that had shut out the sunlight dissipated as the sun replaced the sky that had only seconds ago been on fire. Cole watched in utter shock as the landscape changed dramatically, almost as if the eruption hadn't happened.

Rising shakily, Cole stood for a moment before turning and heading back down the mountainside. *Set fire to the rain,* resonated in his head. The same fateful words that Lindsay had uttered seconds before the new landmass had erupted out of the earth's fiery core.

He looked for Gamer as he descended, fully expecting him to be dead or buried in lava, but to his amazement, the boatman was sitting up, looking around as if he had no clue to where he was, with only a child's innocence in his expression. Cole approached cautiously.

"Nicolai," he said tentatively. No response, only a man staring at his feet, oblivious to everything around him.

"Nikolai!" Cole said more insistently. The name seemed to spark some recognition within the crumpled man. He looked up at Cole, not seeming to recognize him. The hardened look of a cagey survivor was gone, replaced with confusion, eyes questioning.

Cole reached down to help him up. Gamer offered no resistance. Cole placed Gamer's left arm over his shoulder and wrapped his right arm around the skipper's back. The twosome began the arduous trek down the mountainside in silence, as the sun continued to move to the west. There would only be four or five more hours of daylight left, barely enough time to reach the base. Cole still had his backpack, so they had at least one flashlight. Where Gamer's backpack was. . . well, at this point it didn't matter. All that mattered was a safe return to their boat, if it was still there and in one piece.

The twosome made much better time climbing down the mountain and reached the shoreline just as twilight was descending. Art had turned on the searchlights mounted on the top of the sea craft, focusing them directly on the shoreline, hoping, but fearing the worst. He had witnessed the explosion in the sky and felt the earth-shattering rumble that sent shockwaves in all directions.

Art had never felt so much relief when he spotted his companions enter the field of light from the Eliminator's powerful lights. It was obvious something was wrong. Cole was holding the boatman upright as they limped along. Art felt an immediate need to jump into the water and go assist, but then he heard Cole's voice shout out across the distance.

"Art, just keep the light shined on us. We'll be there shortly."

CHAPTER TWENTY-EIGHT

C OLE GUIDED THE INFLATABLE back to the Eliminator and threw the rope to Art to secure it. It took both men to lift Gamer back into the craft. Cole handed Art what remained of their gear and clambered on board.

"Art, if you wouldn't mind, please sit with Gamer, and I'll drive us back to Isabella. As soon as we're in range, call Mario and tell him we need a qualified medic, preferably a trauma doctor, waiting for us when we arrive. I don't know what's wrong with our skipper, but I think he's in pretty bad shape."

Art nodded and sat down next to the boatman. He wrapped a blanket around his shoulders and offered bottled water, which Gamer refused with a slight wave of his hand. Art noticed the burnt material on his jacket and smelled a strong sulfur order mixed with the unmistakable scent of burned flesh. That couldn't be a good sign.

Under the cover of night, there weren't many security boats patrolling the area as Cole sped quickly back to safety.

Almquist and his crew had already left the water but had decided to stay on the island to see if they could discover just what happened. Since they had clearance, it wasn't difficult to gain access to the west side of the volcano. From their previous viewpoint earlier in the day, something major had occurred inside the volcano, yet their fellow scientists were barely talking about it, which surprised Andres. He approached a colleague he knew fairly well and questioned him about the eruption. He was told that it had been a minor incident and really nothing to be concerned about. A quick, small eruption, some lava released, but nothing more. Things like this happened frequently.

Almquist couldn't believe what he was hearing. From the opposite side of the island, it had been a major event. How could it not have been noticed on this side? And what did Cole being there have to do with it, if anything. Hadn't they heard a voice—or something resembling a voice—issue a warning of some kind? The voice was indistinct and garbled, but there had been something. The entire sky seemed to catch fire, if only for a few minutes. And then all went calm. Had Cole and his skipper survived? Almquist had lingered for a couple of hours out of sight, but Cole's boat had remained stationary, with no sign of Cole's return.

Andres left the large tent to reunite with his team to discuss what to do next. They decided to head out at dawn to the east side of the island to see if they could discover any more clues. They would sleep on it tonight and start fresh in the morning.

Cole guided the Eliminator deftly next to the pier, tying it off. When they assisted Gamer out of his craft, Mario and a small ambulance were waiting, lights turned off. A medic and someone who looked like a seasoned trauma doctor stood by with a gurney and oxygen. The pair did a quick assessment, loaded Gamer onto the gurney, and attached an oxygen mask over his nose and mouth. Next, they hooked him up to an IV to inject some much-needed fluids, electrolytes, and antibiotics, while Cole and Art looked on, concerned.

The doctor turned to Cole. "He's in pretty bad shape. We need to get him to a hospital. Your driver has filled me in on the sensitive nature of your visit here and the need for discretion. I have arranged to take him to a small, out of the way clinic for the time being. It is well staffed, with good equipment. It exists—how do I say it—for those clients needing to remain anonymous.

There will be no official record of him being there and no way to track him. You have my word," the doctor said, as if he was used to this sort of thing.

Cole stepped forward and offered his hand in appreciation. "Thank you, Doctor. I can't tell you how much we appreciate your quick response and assistance. Here's my cell phone number. Please call me at any time if I can do anything. . . anything at all to help. And please let me know when we can see him."

The doctor nodded, and the two medics loaded Gamer into the ambulance, and Mario drove them away, leaving the van. Art and Cole stared at each other in the darkness—Cole deliberating how much he should tell Art, and Art wondering what the hell had happened up on the mountain.

Just as Art was about to question his friend, a man dressed in what appeared to be a police uniform—it was difficult to tell in the dim light—approached cautiously.

"Gentlemen, Mario asked me to contact you. I'm to watch over your boat tonight. You can take his van back to your lodging. That way, you have transportation should you need to leave. We'll reconnect in the morning for further instructions."

Again, both Cole and Art were impressed with the efficiency of Mario and his network. It seemed nothing was out of his reach. Even with Gamer down, there were no hiccups in their service level. If he survived this trip—though it seemed less likely with each new event—Cole was going to offer both Mario and Gamer steady employment in the States. The two men were becoming indispensable.

Art drove the van back to the Parador Villas. The pair had agreed to delay discussing what had happened until the morning, when they would both have clearer heads. Cole needed sleep desperately but wondered if he would find it tonight.

Art needed to check on the twins, but he was in no mood for a romp in the sack. Things were spiraling quickly out of control, and his concern for the sisters was ratcheting up as well. It was late, so he decided to contact them in the morning. Perhaps it was time to send them home. A strange sense of foreboding had overcome Art throughout the day, and he hadn't even heard Cole's explanation yet. He undressed quietly, slipping into bed, utterly exhausted, and was soon fast asleep. Next door, Cole sat slump shouldered in his chair, nursing a second scotch on the rocks, staring blankly into the darkness.

CHAPTER TWENTY-NINE

C OLE RECEIVED A TEXT from Art the following morning that he was leaving to find the sisters in San Juan. He'd explain later. Cole rolled over in bed, determined to catch some additional sleep. It had been a rough night, and his headache wasn't helping matters.

Art had called a driver so that Cole would have access to the van if he needed. He assumed Cole would want to visit Gamer at the earliest possible time. Something serious had happened up on that mountain, he was sure of it, and Cole was probably feeling responsible, since he had returned to the boat unharmed.

What caused Gamer's unusual condition? Art pondered, as they neared the hotel to pick up the Swanson sisters, who by now were probably at their wits' end. At least they had a nice room to hang out in and a highly rated bistro inside the hotel to enjoy breakfast. He dialed Shelby's cell phone a second time, but there was still no answer. What were they up to? Charging up a storm in one of the nearby boutique stores and using Art's credit card out of spite? Thank God he had given the women his American Express Black Card, otherwise his Visa would probably be over the limit by now. He didn't want to look like a deadbeat, next to one of the richest men in America. He still had his pride left, if not his senses.

He longed for the relative obscurity of the business-oriented courtroom, hostile witnesses, and unsympathetic judges—judges not particularly inclined to support wealthy clients whose businesses were not always principled. At least he knew the rules there. Art stayed clear of the criminal trials for murderers, rapists, and common thieves. That was nasty business—and it didn't always pay well. Contract negotiations, mergers and acquisitions, and the occasional white-collar crime were more to Art's liking. Somehow that felt cleaner and less corrupted. Art had done a good job of convincing himself of that over the years, and he had the reputation to prove it.

Art knocked on the door to one of the three suites on the top floor, anticipating the girls' reaction to his abandonment and return twenty-four hours later. He hadn't had cell access for most of yesterday, so there had been no communication other than a cryptic note he had left for them in the early morning hours explaining that he had a pressing matter to deal with and would try to make it back last night. Well, he hadn't, and he could only imagine their indignation at being deserted as if they were just a pair of high-priced hookers who had served their purpose.

Art knocked again and was met with only silence. He slipped his key card into the electronic lock, attempting to open the door, but was surprised to find it no longer worked. He called out Shelby's name. Nothing. He hadn't bothered checking the front desk. He assumed they would either be inside the room or at breakfast. It was still relatively early. They weren't in the restaurant on the first floor when he passed by heading to the elevators. Where the hell were they?

"*Señor*, may we clean the room?"

Startled by the voice behind him, Art turned quickly to see a room cleaning crew approaching. Art held his ground.

"Did you see the women who were staying here this morning?" he queried the woman who had addressed him.

"No, *señor*. We were just told to clean up. I think they already check out," she replied in broken English. "We have a busy day. May we enter, *por favor*?"

Art stepped aside, confounded by this latest development. He entered the elevator and pushed the button to the first floor. Slowly, the compartment descended, stopping twice along the way, further irritating the attorney. When the doors swished open, he pushed past the other occupants, heading to the front desk for some answers.

"Mateo," he addressed the front desk clerk after checking the name on his badge. "I'm Art Barkley, and I rented room 1101 for two nights. My companions, Sydney and Shelby Swanson were also staying in the suite. Have you seen them this morning?"

Mateo quickly touched a key on his computer, checking the room reservation, then looked up. "Yes, Mr. Barkley. The two women checked out earlier this morning."

"Did they leave a note or message for me?" Art asked impatiently.

Mateo checked his computer again, then looked at the individual room mail boxes. "No, sir, not that I can tell. They left in what seemed like a hurry, with a bellman carting their luggage. I think they hailed a cab, but I can't be sure."

"Shit!" Art exclaimed, then he paused, recalling they hadn't arrived with much luggage, just overnight cases and some clothing. "Just how much luggage?" Art inquired.

The clerk pointed to a large luggage cart nearby. "Besides what they were carrying, a cart like that was full. Looked like mostly packages. Will there be anything else, Mr. Barkley?" Mateo asked politely.

"No, that's it, thank you." Art stepped away from the front desk, moving to a secluded corner in the lobby. He tried Shelby's cell phone again, but it quickly went to voicemail. She obviously didn't want to talk to him. Art headed over to the bell captain's desk.

The man looked up, about to address Art, but couldn't get the first word out.

"*Señor.*" Art didn't bother to look at his name tag. "Did you help two blonde women with their luggage earlier this morning as they were checking out?"

"Yes, sir, if you are referring to the two beautiful American women. Very impressive. They looked to have made quite the run on designer clothing by the look of the packages they had piled on the luggage cart. It was practically overflowing. Are they models?"

Art fumed but held his temper in check. "As a matter of fact, they are both Ralph Lauren models. We were supposed to meet here this morning, but I was delayed. Did they say where they were headed?" Art asked, more politely this time, wanting this man's cooperation. "Did you call them a cab, by chance?"

"No, they said they had already arranged transportation. I walked them to the front entrance, waited until a stretch limo pulled up, then returned inside. That's the last I saw of them."

Art didn't bother with a thank you or goodbye, instead he hurried outside, dialing Cole's cell phone.

When Cole answered, he sounded much more alert than the previous call. Art filled him in on what had transpired at the Vanderbilt Hotel and asked if Cole had heard from either of them or seen them return to the Parador. It was only a ninety-minute drive, and they could have easily arrived by now.

"No, Art. I've been in my room all morning, waiting for Mario's call. Hold on, I'll head over to their rooms." The phone went silent as Cole knocked on each of the bungalow doors.

"It doesn't appear they're here, Art. Each of their rooms is dark and locked. I'll head up to the cantina and call you back in a few," Cole said and then ended the call. *Why would they check out and not contact Art?* Cole wondered. Maybe it had something to do with Art disappearing for twenty-four hours and ignoring them.

As Cole approached the restaurant, his phone buzzed again. Finally, his driver. "Yes, Mario, how is Gamer. Can I see him?"

"I'm afraid he's not doing well. He slipped into a coma during the night. Dr. Morales is perplexed by his condition. He told me it looks like it might be a form of electrocution, but for the life of him, doesn't understand the source. It wasn't severe enough to cause death, but they tell me it affected his central nervous system. They have him hooked up to life support and continue to do tests."

Cole froze in his tracks. What he had seen was real, even though the event was fading quickly from his memory. The fire angel. The bolt of lightning. The rasping voice's warning. What did it all mean?

"Mario, I'm headed over shortly. I need to check on one thing first, and then I'll leave. I have your van. Please email me the address to the clinic. See you in a few."

After checking the cantina and the front office but not finding any trace of the twins, Cole dialed Art.

"No sign of the girls, Art. They haven't been seen since the three of you left the other day. I just spoke with Mario, and Gamer is not faring well. He's in a coma, and I'm headed over there now." Cole hesitated as though he wanted to say more. "I'm sure they'll show up soon. Call me when you know more." Cole clicked off, leaving Art even more conflicted.

CHAPTER THIRTY

COLE ARRIVED AT THE clinic thirty minutes later, entering through the twin glass doors at the rear. What would normally be the front of the building was mostly blank, with the exception of two small windows above eye level, covered with thick shades. Mario was standing inside the lobby. The building was relatively small for a hospital-like setting, but then, there weren't a lot of patients staying here. It was a squarish, cement, nondescript building with a small sign over the entrance that simply stated "Isabella Medical Supply" in Spanish, as if it were a pharmacy or a distributor. Most of the parking was located in the back, out of view from passing traffic. The inside, however, was quite the opposite from the exterior, with state-of-the-art medical equipment well suited for trauma victims and other severe injuries. It wasn't cheap, and it was staffed with excellent health care workers. The patients generally wanted anonymity, and they paid handsomely for it.

After checking in, Dr. Morales ushered Cole into a small but well-equipped private room—all rooms were private—where Gamer was lying unconscious, hooked up to tubes and an oxygen mask. Three monitors were lit with every vital sign that could be monitored. Through an open-vested hospital gown, Cole glanced a large bandage attached to the boatman's chest. Gamer's face was ashen, and his breathing slow. He looked dead, or worse. It seemed to Cole that something vital had been taken from him, although he couldn't say just what. Gone was the confident persona he naturally emanated. He looked like a ghost of his former self. Cole sunk into a nearby chair, crestfallen. This was his fault.

Dr. Morales stood a few feet back, observing Cole's behavior. Naturally, anyone would be upset seeing their friend in a coma, but there was something more here. Not only was Morales a top-notch trauma doctor, he was also a psychiatrist. In his line of work, it was often necessary to heal both the physical and mental states of his patients, so they could remain outside of the state-controlled health system of Puerto Rico.

"Mr. Hollingsworth, what can you tell me about your skipper's injury? This is one of the most mysterious incidents I have ever seen. Quite frankly, I am at a loss for how to properly diagnose his symptoms and, therefore, his best form of treatment. Any information you can provide would be of significant help."

Cole sat silently, as if he were oblivious to the question. After a long moment, he met the doctor's gaze. Cole's eyes were filled with compassion. . . and something else. Was it fear? How could Cole explain it to this man, when he didn't understand what happened himself—and couldn't reveal too much. "Doctor..." Cole hesitated, unsure. "I really can't tell you exactly what happened. I didn't see all of it, but when we were about a third of the way up the side of Hollingsworth Island, there was a sudden eruption that released a fair amount of lava in a short period of time. Something struck my friend, but it all happened so fast, it was a blur. It looked like maybe a flash of lightening or electrical current, but that really doesn't make sense." Cole went quiet again, awaiting the doctor's response.

Morales stood still, considering Cole's explanation. Without a word, he strolled over to his patient, opening Gamer's eyelids and revealing blank, glazed eyes. After checking his vitals, he turned to Cole.

"It does make sense, actually. My initial thought was some sort of electrical shock, but given the circumstances of where his injury occurred, I didn't think that was possible, since there were no storms in the vicinity.

However, the island is so massive it does have the ability to create its own weather patterns, especially at the upper levels. Perhaps. . . " The doctor's voice trailed off. "Is there anything else you can tell me, Mr. Hollingsworth?"

Cole shook his head. He wasn't about to tell him about the fire angel. Hell, he almost didn't believe it, and he knew Dr. Morales wouldn't buy it either.

"Is there anything I can do, Doctor? Fly in another specialist from the States? Money is no object here. I want you to know that," Cole said, unashamed.

"No, but you have given me something to think about. I have some ideas. If I feel the need for further assistance, you'll be the first person I contact. I sense this man means a great deal to you. You have my word on that."

"Yes, he does. He saved my life. I don't forget things like that. I'm counting on you to fix him. Are we clear on that?" Cole demanded.

"Yes, I am clear on your meaning."

With that, Cole rose and walked over to his friend. Leaning low over the railing, he stroked Gamer's forehead, whispering something to him. A moment later, Cole strode past the doctor and out the door, leaving little doubt that he expected results.

CHAPTER THIRTY-ONE

"**M**ARIO, I NEED TO get back to the Parador. Did you drive over here in another car?" Cole said.

"No, I took a taxi, since you were driving the van. Hop in, and I'll take you back."

Cole climbed into the back seat rather than sitting next to his driver. It seemed to Mario that Cole wanted to be alone with his thoughts. He would not push his employer to reveal what had transpired with the doctor, although he desperately wanted to know more about the boatman's condition.

The trip back was a silent one, both men deliberating what the next move would be. By the time they reached the Parador Villas, Cole was in a dreadful disposition. Sometimes silence spoke much louder than words. It didn't take a genius to see what Cole was feeling; his anger bubbled just below the surface, as if it, too, was about to erupt.

Cole didn't bother to thank his driver for the ride. He stepped outside, then hesitated.

"Mario, can you handle Gamer's boat? It could be a rough ride, especially if that asshole, Andres Almquist, attempts to follow us," Cole said, each word dripping with disdain.

A hint of a smile crossed the driver's face. Finally, some action. "Yes, sir. I'm no Gamer, but I'm pretty adept at handling water vehicles. I'll get you to wherever you want to go. And if you need me to, I'll handle that arrogant son of a bitch for you."

"I'll see you at six in the morning, outside the lobby. Until then." Cole strode purposely toward his bungalow, determined to find the entrance to the volcano and to confront the fire angel or whatever it was. This time, he would make the climb by himself.

Art was sitting in the wicker chair on his front porch, obviously waiting for Cole's return. He was twin-less. Not a good sign.

"Any news, Art?" Cole asked, dispensing with any attempt at small talk.

"Not a word. They've disappeared without a trace." Art handed Cole a bottle of beer. It was obvious he had been imbibing for a while. Four empty bottles stood haphazardly beside his chair, a fresh one in his hand.

"I'm sorry, Art. Maybe it would have been better to leave them home. Do you think that's where they went?"

"At first, I did. But the more I've thought about it, the more I believe they would have said something or at least texted me. It's not like them to go missing like this. They won't answer my calls. I checked with the major limousine services that operate in the area. None of them had been called to the Vanderbilt. But the bell captain told me he saw them get into a black stretch limo when they left early this morning. Don't you think that's odd?"

Cole sat down in the adjacent chair and considered Art's statement. It did seem odd. If the sisters were upset, they would have complained about it. They were not ones to remain quiet.

"Why don't we give them a little more time. If we don't hear anything by tonight, I'll ask Mario for a lead on a good PI who can keep his mouth shut," Cole said.

Art raised his bottle in a mock salute, but just what he was saluting escaped Cole. He wasn't looking at his friend. He wasn't looking at anything at all. He rose, wobbling for a moment, then stepped in front of Cole—just as a shot rang out, like thunder. Alerted by the sudden sound, Cole watched in horror as a crimson swath of blood spread across Art's chest. Art's mouth dropped open, his eyes went blank. . . and he crumbled to the ground, like a robe after the body inside had just evaporated, lifeless.

CHAPTER THIRTY-TWO

F OR A MOMENT, COLE sat paralyzed, as though he was the one that had taken the bullet. Then he grappled in his pocket for his phone. He punched in Mario's number, praying the driver was nearby. It was his only hope. The phone had barely rung twice when the driver appeared, running down the path, having heard the shot as well. Cole dropped to his knees and began to apply CPR, as Mario dialed his own phone, but not 911. There wasn't time for that.

"Cole. Cole, let me see him," Mario exclaimed, leaning down next to the limp Art. Cole was shaking violently now, and the driver had to pry him off his friend to get a look. It took less than five seconds for Mario to assess that Art was gone, but he couldn't tell Cole, not yet.

Within minutes, the sound of powerful rotors sounded above them, and a strong downdraft buffeted the area. A helicopter touched down, and two medics jumped out of the open side with a variety of medical gear, followed by a stretcher being pulled over by another attendant.

"Cole, let the medics through!" Mario screamed over the din of the rotating blades, but Cole wouldn't budge, holding Art's hand as if releasing him would drain the last bit of his life force.

Reluctantly, Cole finally stepped away and watched in terror as the medics loaded Art into the chopper and streaked away into the gathering darkness.

"Come on, Cole, I'll drive you to the clinic. Dr. Morales and his team are standing by. If anyone can save your friend, it's them."

Cole followed dutifully, like a dog would follow its master. They climbed into the van, and the driver sped away, but not before putting a flashing red light on top of his vehicle. They arrived in half the normal time. The helicopter pilots were standing nearby, awaiting further instructions. The two men nodded to Cole as he passed by them and went through the glass doors. They looked grim. Cole's heart sank.

He and Mario had said little on the ride over. Cole had regained some control of his emotions and assumed that prolonging bad news might provide a ray of hope. But it hadn't looked good. Art had lost a lot of blood in a very short time. The sound of the gunshot had been earsplitting and had shattered the stillness. It had to have been a high-powered rifle. Something suddenly occurred to Cole—had the bullet been meant for him? Where Art had taken the hit—chest high—was even with Cole's head while he was still sitting in his wicker chair. His thoughts were becoming so jumbled he couldn't think straight.

Once inside, Cole was guided to a waiting room and offered fresh, hot coffee. He accepted but immediately put it down on a table next to his chair. Mario stood by Cole's side, like a secret service agent, protecting his employer against any unwanted intrusion.

The pair waited in silence, fearing the worse. It wasn't a long wait, however. Dr. Morales emerged from the operating room; his surgical scrubs covered in blood. Art's blood. The look on his face was all it took. Art hadn't survived. He approached Cole guardedly.

"Mr. Hollingsworth, I am so very sorry. We did everything we could to revive him, but he was gone before he arrived. I am. . . so very sorry."

Cole stared up at the doctor as if he wasn't there, as if by denying his presence he could escape the truth. The awful truth that his best friend was dead.

"Do you need some time, Mr. Hollingsworth? Nurse Fletcher is at your disposal." He indicated a woman standing nearby.

Cole rose, meeting the doctor eye to eye. "What I need is my friend back!" He pushed by Morales with a searing glare of anger. Cole walked out the glass doors, followed closely by his driver. Cole stood alone, looking up to the stars just beginning to form, wondering what the hell was happening.

Minutes passed while Cole stood motionless, peering into the darkness, against a backdrop of slowly whirling rotor blades and diffused light emanating from the clinic.

Mario approached him. "Mr. Hollingsworth, is there anything I can do for you?" the driver asked compassionately. "The chopper is at your disposal, as am I."

Cole turned slowly. "Tell the pilots they can leave and thank them for their quick response. Let them know a substantial check will be coming their way soon."

"Yes, sir. That is very generous."

"Is it? When all you have left is money, it doesn't mean an awful lot," Cole said, turning away, staring once again into space, as if he was now totally alone in the world.

Cole felt the strong downdraft and heard the high-pitched sound of engines humming as the craft lifted into the night sky. He was going to the mountain tomorrow, but not before leaving explicit instructions with Dr. Morales on what to do with Art's body.

CHAPTER THIRTY-THREE

COLE SAT ALONE IN the darkness of his bungalow after Mario dropped him off. The night was quiet, so quiet, and Cole once again felt as though he were imprisoned in a dream. Nothing seemed real anymore. Nothing made sense. He had surprised his driver when he'd confirmed they were still headed to Hollingsworth Island in the morning. Mario had warned against making impulsive decisions. He was right, Cole knew. He also knew that Mario had taken a risk in contradicting his boss, but in a strange way, he admired that. He knew that meant the driver cared about him. At least someone did.

Cole's thoughts turned to everything that had happened to him over the past year—losing his parents, reconnecting with Lindsay, her father's scam that had worked to perfection, their descent to the bottom of the ocean and discovery of a portal to the afterlife. And finally, Lindsay's heroic attempt at saving Cole from certain death, as they rocketed through crushing layers of the ocean depths, culminating with a new landmass being created, which the world hadn't seen in millions of years. He laughed in disbelief. Things like this just didn't happen to normal people, but he supposed he wasn't normal people.

What lay ahead for him now? As the disturbing thoughts continued to swirl inside his head, his mind's eye suddenly locked in on the Cantina de la Noche. Something about his last encounter there haunted him. It wasn't so much the boxlike object he'd discovered that had led him to a critical clue about an opening on the mountain. No, it was what the gypsy-witch had said that unnerved him most. Her words seemed to float before his eyes.

If you choose to use this key, it will come at a great personal cost to you. So be forewarned.

Hadn't she said something more? And then it hit him like a shockwave.

There is an extraordinary price to be paid for immortality. More than that I cannot say...

Immortality. That was the word that had stayed with him, that had embedded itself deep in his subconscious until the exact moment when it would impact him the most. And now he was standing at the threshold to discovering just what her words foreshadowed. *Did immortality lie within the volcano?* Cole pondered, as exhaustion set in, combined with several glasses of scotch, which were now taking control. Cole fell into a deep but restless sleep, spiraling further inside the raging fire burning within Hollingsworth Island. Lindsay was calling for him.

CHAPTER THIRTY-FOUR

A KNOCK ON HIS BUNGALOW door abruptly awakened Cole. At first, he didn't know where he was. The faint light of early morning filtered through his window, casting shadows across the room. Dust motes floated in the damp air. Cole glanced at his watch—6:00 a.m. Shaking his head in an attempt to regain his bearings, it dawned on him that Mario must be the person knocking. Who else could it be? There was no one left. Art was dead. Gamer was lying in that forsaken clinic, comatose and fighting for his life. The Swanson sisters had gone missing.

Cole pushed himself out of his chair—he hadn't reached the bed last night. "I'll be right there, Mario." Cole flung open the door, gesturing for his driver to enter. The cramped room smelled of sweat and stale booze. Mario noticed the half-emptied quart of scotch next to the chair. A broken glass lay on the hardwood floor below.

"Rough night, Mr. Hollingsworth?" Mario questioned.

"You might say that. Just give me a few minutes to clean up."

Mario handed his boss a Styrofoam cup of steaming coffee, along with a small bottle of aspirin.

"You think of everything, don't you?" Cole said with a half smirk.

"I try, sir. Is there anything else you require before we leave?"

Cole shook his head and headed into the bathroom for a quick shower.

Mario left the room, taking a seat in one of the wicker chairs, envisioning how the killing took place. He knew it was not some random shooting. The bullet had splintered Art's spinal cord before exiting the body and leaving a massive hole. It could only have been a professional armed with a high-powered sniper's rifle. It suddenly occurred to him that the bullet might still be lodged into one of the wooden planks next to the doorway, unless the killer had waited and watched until all was clear, then snuck up in the shadows to extract the evidence. But that would have been risky. The echoing shot would have attracted a lot of attention.

Mario rose to inspect the nearby wall. Sure enough, there was a hole directly behind the chair. Retrieving a ten-inch stiletto from his coat pocket— he preferred concealed weapons, unlike Gamer, who wore his bowie knife on his hip like a sword. Assassins took on many guises. Art had left out this little detail about Cole's companions, ensuring that Cole would get the best protection that money could buy. Something about this trip had seemed unusually dangerous, almost fateful to the attorney, and so he had gone to great lengths and spent considerably more money than the budget had called for to ensure Cole's safety. Would this be Art's parting gift to his friend?

Flicking the lethal knife open, it locked into place. A curved, wicked blade appeared, gleaming in the brightening light. Mario started digging into the wood, which was weathered and beginning to take on dry rot, until he hit something solid. Further cutting revealed the remnants of a slug, which he dug out. He examined the hollow point bullet, or what was left of it. It was a bullet meant to inflict maximum damage to its target. This confirmed they were dealing with a trained killer. He pocketed the slug and sat back down, waiting for Cole. There would be time to discuss this later, but now was not that time.

Mario took the moment to call Dr. Morales and check in on his friend's condition. Nothing had changed, but he was holding his own. During the brief conversation, Dr. Morales questioned the driver about Cole's decision to hold Art's body in the small morgue in the clinic's basement. Cole had been very specific about keeping it a secret. Morales assumed Mario knew about Cole's intent, but it surprised the driver. Cole had not mentioned it to him. Mario played dumb, thanked the doctor for his assistance, and then quickly ended their call.

Cole emerged from the bungalow, looking like he had recovered, at least somewhat. His eyes were still filled with an interminable sadness, but there was also resolve in those deep, brown eyes—the sort of eyes that all leaders possessed. Steely, penetrating eyes. With each new experience, each new tragedy, Cole was developing toughness, like an invisible coat of armor. Something—anything—to cover up the vulnerability.

"You ready, boss?" Mario asked.

"As ready as I can be, I suppose. Sorry I overslept," Cole said.

"No need for an apology, sir. Most people would be incapacitated for days after what you experienced last night. By the way, no change in Gamer's condition. I checked with the staff this morning, but he's holding his own," Mario said, intentionally leaving out the doctor's name. He knew Cole didn't like the man. There was no need to throw fuel on the fire.

Minutes later, they were on the road, heading to the pier where the Eliminator was moored. Again, Mario had selected a different location to launch from. Not that Almquist would be fooled, but a little diversion never hurt.

Cole was riding in the front seat this time and as Mario looked in the side view mirror on the passenger's side, he noticed the Colt pistol attached to Cole's belt. It must have been the one he had received from Gamer. That was a good sign. Cole was preparing himself—but for what?

"Have you heard anything about Almquist's location or what he's doing?" Cole asked. "He seems to have quietly disappeared, or he's keeping his distance."

"I haven't noticed him, but with Gamer out of action for the moment, I have added two more men as security. One to keep an eye out for the scientist, and one to help manage the boat for us. If it's okay with you, he will be accompanying us out to the island."

"That's fine. Where are you finding these extra people on such short notice?" Cole asked, intrigued by his driver's resourcefulness.

"Here and there. We have a pretty tight network of men we can count on down here. We even have a few women who fill in occasionally, depending on the need." Mario looked over, half smiling, then went silent. It appeared that was all Cole was going to get in the way of an explanation.

Cole nodded and went silent, too. He trusted the driver more and more each day. With Gamer going down and Art no longer among the living, he needed to rely on this man even more than before.

It was nearly seven-thirty when the twosome reached the pier. Cole spotted the Eliminator, with a man standing next to it, about fifty yards out to sea. The silhouette reminded Cole of Art standing there just the other day, when he had surprised Cole and shown up to help after all. A jolt of regret struck Cole with such intensity it took his breath away. But he couldn't afford to think like that. He needed to stay focused until he could unleash the plan he had been formulating shortly after his friend's death. A plan that seemed as preposterous as the concept of immortality itself.

CHAPTER THIRTY-FIVE

B ILL GAINES'S CELL PHONED buzzed. Looking down at his phone, he saw the number he had been waiting for flashing on the screen. "Finally," the chairman murmured. Placing his coffee on his desk, he picked up the phone.

"What's the current situation, Andres? Has the job been completed?"

"Not exactly, sir. Things were on schedule, but something unexpected happened—"

Gaines didn't wait to hear the rest, blasting into the scientist. "How could this go wrong? We hired the best marksman money could buy. He's never failed to successfully complete a mission."

"Sir, he had Cole in his sights, dead to rights. At the last second, Art Barkley stood up, just as he was firing the shot, and the bullet struck him in the chest. Cole moved out of position, and a moment later, his driver came running down the path. Our man waited as long as he could but the shot echoed so loudly people were beginning to react and a crowd began to form so, well, he had to leave."

"This is unacceptable," Gaines said, pausing to gather himself. "How is he doing?"

"It appears he didn't make it. At least, that's what our source tells us. He was flown to a clinic, and he never left. By the way, Cole's boatman is apparently there as well, receiving treatment for something serious," Almquist said.

"Good, Barkley was a pain in the ass and loyal to his boss above all else. This means Cole is even more vulnerable now. It should be easier. What about the Swanson sisters?"

"They're tucked safely away, out of sight, as you instructed."

"See to it that they remain there. We can use them as leverage if needed. Report back to me as soon as you have further news." He hung up.

Almquist stood for a while, contemplating just how badly things were spiraling out of control. He hadn't signed up for this, but he was in it so deep now, he couldn't see his way out. Not with Gaines breathing down his neck. Although he didn't know the man well, he knew of his reputation. The fact that he had no qualms about killing the owner of Hollingsworth Enterprises, kidnapping innocent people, or stealing away his company clearly indicated he was not a man to mess with. Speaking of people not to mess with, his thoughts turned to Cole's driver. Andres had done his best to find out more about him. What he had learned so far didn't paint a pretty picture. He was as tough as they came. His background was sketchy, but the terms black ops, assassin, and other unflattering descriptions had surfaced. Almquist shuddered at the thought of running into him in a dark alley. He wouldn't stand a chance.

CHAPTER THIRTY-SIX

MARIO PARKED THE VAN behind a wooden structure so it wouldn't be visible from the street, then strode down the pier alongside Cole. The sun was rising, reflecting its golden hues off of the shimmering Caribbean Sea. Mario knew the day would be hot, probably in more ways than one. They needed to depart quickly.

The driver introduced the new man to Cole as simply Rico. Rico and Cole shook hands but did little else. Mario had already informed his assistant of what Cole had experienced the night before and told him to speak only when spoken to.

Rico looked fit—over six feet tall, with shortly cropped black hair, and muscular, with a 9mm Colt hanging on one hip and a wicked-looking machete on the other. *What is it about knives down here*? Cole wondered. Suddenly, he wished he had one.

Rico stood aside, allowing Cole to step onto the boat. He remained stationary as Mario stepped on board, then untied the rope that held the Eliminator tethered to the wooden pier. Mario fired up the engines, and the threesome headed out to sea. About a mile out, Mario pushed down hard on the throttle, and the boat practically flew out of the ocean, as a massive plume of water spread out behind them.

After reaching ninety miles per hour, he settled into a constant speed. Mario was aware of the boat Almquist was using and at a top speed of seventy-five miles per hour, he would quickly put distance between Cole and anyone attempting to follow. He had directed Rico to scan around them for any sign of intrusion. They were basically taking the same route as before, in a wide sweep from the south to the back side of the island. They wouldn't be noticed, and if they were, they'd simply outrace the intruders—or shoot them. After Art's murder, Mario had decided it was time to play hardball. No one was going to threaten his boss again.

Cole sat next to his new skipper, in a somber mood, contemplating his ascent up the side of the volcano and what he might experience this time. Would he be able to find the entrance? Would he be able to enter safely? And would he find Lindsay? If so, what would she reveal to him?

Cole continued to sit pensively as his driver guided the Eliminator skillfully atop the ocean's surface, as if this was child's play. He had been rather modest when Cole asked him if he was capable of handling a boat like this. Cole doubted Mario was incapable when it came to handling anything. For a moment, Cole was distracted from thoughts of the volcano, until Mario shouted out above the din of the twin Mercury racing engines.

"We're being followed! Buckle up," Mario said, then he turned to Rico. "What do you see?"

Rico focused military grade binoculars at an object approaching swiftly from the north. Mario slowed the craft temporarily so that Rico could focus in on the intruders.

"Looks like three men in a go-fast boat. I can't make out their faces yet. No official signage on the hull, so it probably isn't security," Rico replied.

"It has to be Almquist. But it's who he's with that worries me," the driver said, with a hint of concern.

"Who could possibly be with Almquist who would be a concern to us?" Cole asked. "He just wants to see what I'm up to—why we're making trips to the far side of the island. He's a scientist, for God's sake."

"Are you sure about that, sir? Think about all that's happened in the past forty-eight hours. The twins are missing, Gamer is in a coma, and your friend. . ." Mario hesitated, becoming emotional. A first for this man, at least that Cole had seen. "Someone, or a group of people, are working against you, Mr. Hollingsworth. I'd bet my last dollar that the sniper who shot Mr. Barkley is on that boat, and the fact they've traded in the Bonzi for a craft that is almost as fast as Gamer's boat means their plans have changed. That is not a boat for observation. It's meant for attack," Mario said grimly, refocusing his attention on his assistant. "Rico, any more to report?"

"They've definitely spotted us, and they're headed directly at us."

Mario scanned the skyline and the surrounding horizons. "It just might work," he muttered to himself. Without warning, he turned their craft due east and punched it. The intruder's boat changed direction immediately, veering sharply to its left, pursuing. When Mario had maneuvered the boat directly in line with the rising sun and the oncoming boat, he did a move that stunned Cole. Working the throttle and the steering wheel in unison, he spun the Eliminator around in a single move, like a race car driver might change directions on a dime. Burying the twin throttles, the Eliminator sped directly at the oncoming boat like a torpedo, with the scorching sun still low in the eastern sky and blinding the intruder's vision. Cole had no idea how fast they were going, only that they were closing the gap in a matter of seconds.

The impending collision appeared unavoidable, but then something happened that Cole had not anticipated. Mario turned the boat again in a hard left, only feet from the intruders, swamping the oncoming craft with a huge wave of water. Mario completed the 360-degree turn, coming alongside the waterlogged craft. In one fluid motion, he retrieved his stiletto from a side pocket and thrust it forward with incredible speed, burying it deep into the sniper's chest just as he was raising his rifle to fire. The sniper was still for a moment before falling backward, overboard, as both Almquist and Cole watched in utter shock. Rico had his own high-powered rifle aimed at Andres's head, just waiting for Mario's order to shoot the son of a bitch.

Almquist's hands rose quickly above his head in a sign of surrender. "Please! Please don't kill me!" he screamed. "I didn't want to—it wasn't me. I—" His words came fast and short, as though he had lost his ability to form them.

"Tell me one good reason why we shouldn't put you down," Mario said, sounding more like he was talking about a rabid dog.

"I … I know who is behind this—who shot your friend, Mr. Hollingsworth," Almquist stuttered.

"We know who shot Mr. Barkley, Almquist, and he's shark bait now." Mario motioned to where the sniper had fallen into the water and sunk.

"Yes … yes, it was him. He pulled the trigger. But the man you're looking for is the one who ordered the hit. I'll tell you if you'll let me live. And I promise that it will shock you," Andres said, looking directly at Cole.

This time, it was Cole's turn to speak. "You have exactly thirty seconds to tell us, unless you want to join your friend at the bottom of the ocean. Then we'll decide if you live or die," Cole said, recalling the look on Art's face seconds after being shot. An expression he'd never forget.

"Okay … okay," Andres hesitated, taking a deep breath. "It was your chairman of the board, William Gaines."

At first, the confession seemed not to register with Cole, as though Almquist was answering a totally different question or speaking in a foreign tongue. When it finally sank in, Cole stepped forward.

"That's preposterous. Gaines would never have ordered Art's murder. He may not be the most ethical person around, but he's no murderer."

Slowly regaining his wits, Almquist considered his next words carefully. He knew it was the difference between life and death.

"Mr. Hollingsworth, it wasn't Art Barkley the contract was put out on. It … it was you. Had your loyal friend not stood up at the precise moment he did, you would be the one lying in the morgue, not him." Almquist went silent. Cole's mouth fell open.

"We have the information we need, Mr. Hollingsworth. I say shoot Almquist and his boatman, tie them to their boat, and sink it. No one will ever find them out here," Mario said, spitting on the floorboard, disgusted.

Cole continued to stare at the scientist, as if in denial.

Rico appeared ready, if not eager, to finish the job.

Cole raised his hand. "Hold on a minute." Cole turned to his driver, whispering, "We need to figure out how we can use this information to our advantage. Almquist is obviously working with Gaines, so they are probably communicating regularly. If we can turn Almquist, we can influence Gaines without his suspecting it. We now know our upstanding chairman is not above anything—and he has a totally different agenda then Art and I originally thought. This is serious shit."

"Are you sure, Mr. Hollingsworth?" Mario whispered back.

"Yes. It's my only chance to get to the truth," Cole said. His driver nodded.

Cole turned back to Almquist. "We've decided to let you live, Andres, but under one condition. You are working for us now. We'll feed you the information we want you to pass along to Bill Gaines. If you fail to do this, you're done." Cole hesitated, reflecting. "And I think the scientific world would be a lot better off without you, if you get my drift."

Andres Almquist, now a thoroughly defeated man, had little choice but to comply. He nodded his agreement. "I'll do what you ask. You've won." *At least for now*, he thought.

Mario turned to Rico. "Kill the driver, then sink their boat."

As Cole was about to object vehemently, Rico dropped his rifle, stepped up, and practically flew into the other craft, unleashing his machete in midair rather than causing a loud shot to echo for miles. Upon landing, one swift move was all it took, the gleaming blade slicing deeply into the man's neck, nearly severing his head, splattering blood on Almquist's shirt. The scientist recoiled in horror.

Mario turned to Cole. "Sometimes, you just need to make an example. You'll have no further trouble with that scientist." Cole stared at his driver, flabbergasted. Back in the US, the man would have been arrested, tried as an accomplice to Art's murder, and most likely served some jail time, depending on his level of cooperation in the case. Down here they obviously had their own method of justice. Cole had to admit it was effective, as he unconsciously stroked his neck with his right hand.

It was over—all except the cleanup, which was carried out with efficiency. While Almquist sat slump-shouldered nearby, Cole watched as the
intruder's boat filled with water and began to sink, the driver tied securely
to the steering wheel. The blood would eventually lure the sharks that in-
fested this area of ocean, and the bodies would be gone, just another craft
lying in silence at the bottom of the ocean—its secrets protected within a
watery grave.

CHAPTER THIRTY-SEVEN

N OW THAT ALMQUIST WAS an unintended member of the crew, Cole could not complete his initial objective. They had little choice but to return to Isabella. Cole supposed he could wait one more day, but time was of the essence now, due to their new predicament—how to deal with Bill Gaines in a way that would somehow keep him placated for a few days. That would take some consideration.

Rico was at the helm now, guiding them back to shore. The pace was considerably slower than the trip out. Mario sat directly facing Almquist, glaring at him as though the slightest misstep and Andres's body would be separated from his head, too.

The wound created by Art's death was still far too raw for Cole to concentrate effectively on anything but finding Lindsay, so he decided not to interrogate Almquist just yet. That could wait until later, with Mario's assistance.

As the Eliminator skipped across the gentle waves, Cole stared back at the majestic volcano, which was quickly disappearing beyond the horizon. When it disappeared completely, so too did his connection with the fire angel. The closer he came to the island, the more he felt its pull. And now. . . now it was only the memory of Lindsay's final act that propelled him to take action. Action only he knew about now, due to Art's death. It was a burden that he had finally shared with his friend, and it felt like the weight of the world had partially been lifted, even if Art hadn't completely believed his story. Who could he lean on now?

After reaching the launch pier and tying off the boat, some last-minute instructions were given to Almquist, which included phone silence with Gaines until further notice. Cole needed time to formulate a plan of action. He needed to keep the chairman distracted and off guard—at least until he could ascend the mountain and find the secret entrance, an entrance that might not even exist.

Mario dropped Cole off near the cantina so he could order food to take to his room. The driver stayed in the van for now, at the ready, while Rico patrolled the grounds of the Parador Villas, against the manager's bitter objections. He didn't want his guests scared. It was bad for business. When Rico placed his hand on the handle of his machete, staring the man down, the manager shut up, reentering the lobby while cursing in Spanish. The machete seemed even more intimidating than the pistol hanging on his other hip. In this part of the world, machetes and other wicked-looking knives spoke more of assassins and brutal killings than a handgun might. It brought to mind severed body parts—and that was not an image anyone wanted to think about.

Cole entered his bungalow with a meal of grilled jerk chicken, Spanish rice, and fruit salad, along with a fifth of scotch. He had apparently forgotten about the half-full bottle sitting on his nightstand. He had some serious thinking to do. As much as he tried to concentrate on how to handle Gaines, his thoughts turned to Art, and he immediately lost his appetite—for food, that is. The scotch went down easily.

Shoving the Styrofoam container of food away, he clutched the glass of liquor in both hands and lowered his head, overwhelmed with grief. He had just lost his closest friend, and now he knew it was because of his chairman of the board. Cole cursed loudly, slamming his right fist hard against the desk. So hard, in fact, the impact sent a stinger up through his elbow and into his shoulder. Somehow, the physical pain that followed felt far less painful than the heartache. Slowly, the realization that the kill shot had been meant for him inundated his mind, making him dizzy. How could Gaines have betrayed him so?

Cole's thoughts turned to the Swanson sisters. He still hadn't heard from them, even after repeated attempts to contact the twins. Something was definitely wrong. Picking up his cell phone, he dialed his driver. Mario answered immediately.

"Yes, boss, what do you need?"

"I'm worried about the Swanson sisters. They won't answer or return my calls. I had some people in Newport check, and they have not returned to Rhode Island nor have they bought any airline tickets or scheduled a private flight. Is there anything you can do to help locate them?" Cole said tiredly. He didn't need more to worry about.

"I'm on it. As soon as I have anything, I'll let you know." The line went dead.

Cole sat alone, bathed in lambent sunlight filtering in through the shutters of his room, as the sun continued to set in the west, casting its fading light at angles and creating pockets of shadows. He seemed oblivious to the passing of time, as though it no longer existed, reminding him of being at the bottom of the ocean with Lindsay. That incorporeal state—separating the body from the spirit. And what about Art's body? Lying in a morgue, spiritless.

Cole dialed the clinic to check on Gamer, hoping for some good news. Dr. Morales was paged. A few minutes later, he answered.

"Mr. Hollingsworth. I assume you are calling for an update on your friend?"

Friend? The word struck Cole as anomalous. Art was his friend. He had only known the boatman for a couple of days—and yet, he had become a friend, too, a trusted companion. The mad Russian scientist, masquerading as a boat for hire. Cole let loose a muted laugh at the thought of him but quickly sobered up. This man had also been willing to risk his life for Cole.

How many more sacrifices would be made for the billionaire as he selfishly pursued his own personal agenda?

"Yes, Doctor. Is he any better?" Cole asked.

"He is holding his own. He's still in a coma. He's a fighter, though. Most people would be gone by now. We are doing everything we can for him. I had a specialist in electrically inflicted wounds flown in. Your friend shows all the signs of electrocution, but there's something different. I'm hoping the specialist can shed some light on his condition and provide an alternate form of treatment. I have your number, and I will contact you with any news, day or night."

"Okay. Thank you," Cole said, then he abruptly ended the call. What had he expected? Gamer's condition was dire. Cole didn't think he could stand another death on his behalf, and one so soon. He swallowed the rest of his drink, refilling it without even thinking about it, as though it was a habituated response.

The bungalow was mostly dark now, and Cole was no closer to a solution regarding Gaines then he had been after returning to the Parador. The quiet was unnerving. Cole needed time, a commodity that now seemed far more precious than money. Time to think. Time to get his head together. Tomorrow would be arriving early. Mario would be coming for him at six-thirty. They would be going back to the mysterious island. And this time, Cole would not accept anything short of success—or he'd die trying.

CHAPTER THIRTY-EIGHT

C OLE'S CELL PHONE BUZZED, waking the billionaire abruptly. He had once again failed to make it from the chair to the bed. His back ached, and his neck was cramped from sleeping at a bad angle. He grasped at the phone, and it fell to the floor. Looking at his watch, he saw that six had arrived, though it felt as if he had not slept more than an hour or two.

Retrieving the phone, he recognized the caller. Mario was calling earlier this morning, obviously to allow Cole time to shower, sober up, and leave at the predetermined time. "Damn driver!" Cole muttered to himself, before answering the call.

"I'll see you in the lobby in thirty minutes," Cole said brusquely, then ending the call. He stumbled into the shower, allowing the jets of tepid water to hit his neck and upper back as he braced himself against the tiled walls with both arms.

Gathering his things, Cole walked the dirt path up to the lobby, preparing himself to call Almquist. First, he needed to confer with his driver to confirm they were in agreement.

Mario was leaning against his van, arms crossed. Standing next to him, Rico held coffee and a container that could only be breakfast. The handgun and machete hanging from both hips reminded Cole of a scene from a western movie. Even Mario was sporting a gun on his hip now. Cole's eyes widened at the sight of the sawed-off double barrel shotgun—the type of weapon used only for close quarters fighting. Both men were stubble-faced, muscular, intimidating. *Is there going to be a gunfight today*? Cole wondered. Neither man was smiling.

"What?" Cole asked, unsure how else to greet his companions.

"Bad news, boss," Mario said. Rico looked on, expressionless.

"What sort of bad news?" Cole asked tentatively, thoughts of Gamer's demise conjured in his head.

"The twins. I. . . I'm afraid they've been kidnapped. The limo that picked them up the other day from the Vanderbilt Hotel wasn't from a legit service. It took a little muscle and some cash, but we discovered it was sent by a notorious group, often called the *Crucibles*. The gang is basically for hire and wouldn't have initiated this on their own. We have yet to establish a contact, but rest assured we will." Mario went silent, allowing Cole time to absorb this next calamity.

Cole stood frozen in the pale morning light, trying to fathom this series of events. He was trapped in a murder mystery beyond description, sinking deeper and deeper into a quagmire of deception. What next? Only his entry into the fiery, raging hellhole that awaited inside the towering volcano. Why the word *hellhole* suddenly occurred to him, he could not say. Perhaps a reference to Dante's *Inferno*, which he and Lindsay had discussed on several occasions. Was that ultimately where Cole was headed, destined to experience it firsthand? Was that the path that led to immortality? Cole shuddered at the thought, endeavoring to wipe it from his mind.

Cole recovered from his momentary paralysis, focusing back on the current situation.

"Any idea where they're being held?" Cole said.

"Not yet, but my men are working on it. It's only a matter of time. Someone will crack. We just have to apply the right pressure points."

Cole didn't really need to know just what pressure points were going to be applied, only that they would be applied, and soon. Cole nodded his agreement, as if to say, *do whatever it takes, I'm getting tired of this shit.*

"Do you think Bill Gaines could be behind this?" Cole asked Mario.

"Maybe. He has certainly demonstrated his willingness to do just about anything. But my question is why. What does he gain from this action? There will be ramifications for this, and he will become more exposed, if his involvement can be traced back."

Cole contemplated his driver's explanation for a long moment. "Leverage!" he blurted out. "He's using this as leverage against me, if he needs it. What other reason would he have?"

"You're probably right, boss. It's the only thing that makes sense."

"Do whatever you need to do to find them. Spare no expense. I want them back—and alive," Cole said with renewed conviction, as though he had become totally engaged again.

A hint of a smile crossed the driver's face. Turning to face Rico, he issued a directive in Spanish. Rico nodded, then he quickly disappeared out of sight.

"He'll be back shortly. He just needs to make, um, a few last-minute phone calls before we leave. Are you ready, boss?"

Ready as I'll ever be, given the circumstances, Cole thought, but he simply nodded.

Mario understood, not just the intent of Cole's nod, but what this man must be feeling. For so many years, Mario had worked for wealthy men, most up to no good, and he couldn't have cared less who they were. What mattered was the paycheck. He did have limits to just how far he would go, but for the most part, the actions demanded of him came from bad people and went to bad people. In the end, they got what they deserved. But something was very different about Cole's situation. He seemed more *human*, for lack of a better description. He found he cared for the billionaire more each day. Or was it respect? He would not let this man down.

Rico returned ten minutes later, and the threesome climbed into the van. They hit the road just as the sun fully emerged from the horizon, painting its glorious portrait onto an expansive ocean canvas. Just another idyllic day in the tropics—or so it would seem.

CHAPTER THIRTY-NINE

H AVING FORGOTTEN TEMPORARILY ABOUT Andres Almquist, due to the news of the Swanson sisters' abduction, Cole's thoughts now turned to Gaines. Bill Gaines the chairman of his company. Gaines the puppet master, who liked controlling the strings of everyone around him, apparently even his boss.

"Mario, we need to call Almquist. This can't wait much longer. I'm sure Bill Gaines is anxiously awaiting an update from him, and knowing Gaines, he won't wait long. Any delay will only make him more suspicious."

"Yes, I agree. What did you have in mind?"

"It won't take long until Gaines learns about the disappearance of his assassin, if he hasn't already heard. I'm assuming an intermediary brokered the hit, and that person would maintain close contact with the sniper, right?"

"You are correct. There were probably a couple of intermediaries involved. One or more down here, and one in the United States. There's no way someone like Bill Gaines would have direct contact. It would be suicide," Mario said.

"That being said, we need to distract Gaines for a few days, with something believable. Something that will keep him at bay. I need time before he continues to hunt me. . ." Cole hesitated at the vociferous grunt from his driver, as if he was grossly offended that Cole had become the hunted and not the other way around.

"As I was saying, we need Almquist to contact Gaines right away. I think he should say that I've disappeared for the time being, discontinued my trips to the Island, out of grief for Art. That Almquist doesn't know where I am, and maybe I've returned to the States to arrange for the funeral. Under no circumstances should he say anything about the twins. Hell, Almquist doesn't even know that we know," Cole said. "So that shouldn't be an issue as long as we keep that a secret. Can all of your men be trusted to keep their mouths shut about the twins? I know it's a tight network down here, and, well, people have a tendency to talk."

"My men are as trustworthy as they come. They know the rules. If anyone steps out of line,"—Mario patted Rico's machete—"they'll never step out of line again. Everyone understands this. We share a bond that few others do." The driver's eyebrows rose, indicating there was no need to further question his men's loyalty.

Brothers to the end, Cole mused. That kind of loyalty was indeed rare. Cole nodded, then he punched in Almquist's cell number. Even though it was still early in the morning, the scientist seemed awake and alert. Perhaps he was expecting Cole's call.

"Yes, Mr. Hollingsworth, what can I do for you?" Almquist said with forced sincerity, which did not go unnoticed by Cole. Just a further reminder that this man could not be trusted either. *Rico might impart a little additional loyalty to the scientist, if need be,* Cole thought.

"It's time to contact Bill Gaines. I assume you do this by phone and not email, right?"

"That is correct, sir. We normally have a call every day or two."

"Okay, this is what we want you to tell him," Cole said, filling Almquist in on the details. "Oh yeah, I almost forgot—if we see you anywhere near a boat or any more of your dubious looking companions attempting to launch one, you can consider our agreement null and void. Rico will contact you immediately with the official termination papers, if you get my drift."

This response elicited a smirk from Rico, as if he would like nothing better than a contract termination.

"I understand, Mr. Hollingsworth. You can count on me," Almquist said.

"Good. We'll contact you tonight for a follow-up. In the meantime, if Gaines suggests any immediate action that would be detrimental to our plans or indicates he intends to pay us a visit, text the word *eruption* to this number immediately." Cole rattled off his burner cell phone number. Then he ended the call and turned to Mario.

"Do you think he got the message?" Cole asked.

"I think he did. I especially liked your reference to *contract termination*. If he misunderstood that, he's lamer than I thought," Mario said, almost good-naturedly, as if they were simply discussing a minor piece of business and the boilerplate script at the end of any legal contract. However, it would be stretching it to suggest that this contract was legal. But Cole no longer cared. He had reviewed hundreds of contracts in his lifetime, and none were more important than this one.

Cole dialed Dr. Morales's cell phone, in the unlikely chance there would be any improvement in his boatman's condition. After a lengthy medical diatribe, most of which passed right over Cole's head, it seemed that Gamer was improving, if only slightly. His vitals were finally getting stronger. Morales explained that the specialist was treating him with mild forms of electric shock—which at first horrified Cole—in order to stabilize the arrythmia the initial injury had caused. Like using fire to fight fire, according to the doctor's nontechnical explanation. Stabilizing the boatman's heartbeat was key to his recovery.

At last, a little good news. Cole shared the update with his companions, which brought a wave of relief, however tenuous it might be.

Nearing their destination, Mario eased the van into a secluded parking space, and the threesome hopped out and headed for the pier. The uniformed guard was standing by, at the ready. He appeared to be the same man as before. Cole wondered if he'd spent the night or if he had been given some relief.

"Have you seen any suspicious-looking characters in the vicinity since we left yesterday?" Mario asked the security guard. "Any boats coming by for a quick glance at what we're doing?"

"No, *señor*. I haven't seen anything suspicious."

Mario patted the man on the shoulder. "We will be departing shortly. Please hang around for an hour or so and alert us if you notice anything unusual. You have my number."

"Of course, *señor*." The guard stepped to the side so the crew could come aboard. Then he walked away, stationing himself near the shoreline and seeming to melt instantly into the landscape.

"We got everything?" Cole asked.

Mario glanced at Rico, who nodded. "We're good, Cole," the driver confirmed.

Mario fired up the twin turbo engines and eased away from the pier. It was only a minute until he pushed down on the throttle, and the Eliminator felt like it had just taken flight, only this time, Cole had complete confidence in his driver's boating skills. He had proven that without a doubt yesterday. With the belief that no one was following this time, Mario opened up the engines, and the go-fast boat was soon skimming across the ocean at over one hundred miles an hour, a fine spray of warm, tropical water stinging Cole's face and neck.

Is this fast pace really necessary, or is the driver just having a little fun? Cole wondered. His mind turned to Serena—the world-class, super sports car disguised as a Maserati, a street legal automobile, sitting in his garage in Newport. Cole liked speed as much as anybody and decided just to enjoy the ride.

The companions reached the eastern shoreline of Hollingsworth Island in record time. Cole didn't know it, but Mario had arranged for a second boat to join their mission to keep a watch on their progress. His team had hastily painted the Gerace Institute logo on the side so it would look like a security boat. It worked to perfection. No one seemed to notice the Eliminator racing across the nearby waters, or if they did, they paid no attention to it.

Mario shut down the engines at about one hundred yards out to sea, and the craft drifted in closer before coming to a halt. Cole glanced at his watch—9:15 a.m. Still plenty of time to reach the hidden entrance, especially without interruptions. Rico tossed the anchor out of the boat, then grabbed the inflatable raft from its storage compartment. After inflating the rubber raft, it too was tossed overboard and tethered to a carabiner. Mario and Rico began loading gear, which appeared to be far more than Cole needed. Obviously, someone was planning on accompanying him up the mountain. It was time for Cole to set things straight.

"Gentlemen, thank you for getting me here safely and for the outstanding job you and your team have done in protecting me in this. . ." Cole paused as a wave of emotion swept over him. "For protecting me in this difficult time. I couldn't have come this far without you and. . . and I will always be grateful and in your debt."

Both men gazed back at Cole, confused. What was their boss inferring? Surely, he wasn't considering going it alone from here. Mario stepped forward.

"If you think I'm going to allow you to climb that mountain alone, you better think twice," Mario said, all pretense of boss and employee vaporizing on the spot.

Cole stared back at his driver for a long moment, his expression implacable. He patted his driver on the back smiling wryly, as if to say, *you have no authority to question my behavior beyond this point.*

"Mario, my friend, this is where we part ways. We may, or may not, ever see one another again. The fates hold different futures for us both. Again, please accept my sincerest thanks for everything you've done for me. If I fail to return by nightfall, you are to leave immediately and report nothing to the authorities. I only ask that you follow up on the twins and rescue them if at all possible. You can do with Almquist what you want, it is of no concern to me. If Gaines causes you or your people any pain, you have my permission, along with my blessing, to terminate his contract as well," Cole said, with a hint of a smile crossing his face. "Furthermore, I have set up a fund for you to access to complete the tasks I've assigned to you. . . and to help Gamer recover." Cole handed Mario an envelope he produced from his backpack. "All the details are articulated inside, and there is a contact person for you in Newport. I have also set up a fund that only you can access with final payment for your services. I trust you will find it sufficient."

Both Mario and Rico stared open-mouthed at their boss, deeply conflicted as how to respond. Mario continued to stare, shaking his head in disbelief. He just couldn't allow his boss, now his friend, to go onto that mountain so vulnerable.

"Mr. Hollingsworth, please allow me to accompany you to the shore. At least I can ensure you arrive safely, and I can stand guard should something unexpected happen."

Cole considered his request thoughtfully. "Okay, but under one condition. If you hear or see something up on the mountain during my ascent that you feel is threatening, you give me your solemn promise not to come after me. Short of that, I go alone."

Acquiescing, Mario reluctantly agreed, and the two men shook hands. The deal was done. The contract signed—a contract that could not be broken.

"It's time." Cole turned to Rico. "Thank you, Rico." Cole stepped forward, giving the bodyguard a hug. Rico remained silent during the exchange, whether it was by orders or the inability to express his emotions, Cole couldn't tell.

Just as Cole was about to step into the inflatable, Rico unbuckled his belt and handed Cole his machete. Stunned, Cole initially objected, but Rico didn't take no for an answer. Cole glanced at Mario, who nodded his approval.

"May it protect you as it has protected me. Good luck, Mr. Hollingsworth," Rico said with a heavy Spanish accent, then he stepped away.

"I don't know what to say, Rico, except thank you for this incredible gift. You have no idea what it means to me."

Rico smiled, pleased, and watched silently as Cole and Mario stepped into the raft and set course for the shore. Cole glanced back at Rico one last time, flashing him the thumbs-up sign as if they were equals. *An assassin with a heart*, Cole thought. *They don't make them like that in the States.*

Once on shore, Mario unloaded the gear Cole would need and left the rest in the inflatable.

"I guess it's time, Mario. Again, thank you for everything. May fortune treat you well." The two men hugged, an embrace the driver seemed reluctant to release.

"You don't have to do this alone, boss. Whatever happens up there will go with me to my grave," Mario said, trying in vain with one last, valiant attempt to help his employer.

"I do need to do this alone. I wish there was another way, but unfortunately, there is not. Trust me on this."

Mario lowered his head, as if ashamed he could not do more. When he looked back up, Cole spotted moisture forming in his steely, dark-brown eyes.

"It's okay, Mario. Really. By the way, when Gamer is up and about, I think you should challenge him to a boat race." Cole reached for his wallet, extracting one of the few hundred-dollar bills left, handing it to his driver. "My money is on you!"

The driver stared back, confused, but accepted the bill without comment. Then he broke out laughing, as if this final gesture made sense somehow.

"May fortune treat you well, too, Mr. Hollingsworth. *Vaya con Dios.*"

Cole picked up his gear, turned, and headed up the side of the island that bore his family name. What the future held for him was anyone's guess. Only the fates knew. He would need to let it all play out.

CHAPTER FORTY

T HE ASCENT SEEMED MORE familiar now as Cole made his way up the mountain toward the fog line. Nothing had really changed since his initial trek up, and yet, something was definitely different this time. At first, it felt like a weight had been lifted, but the more he climbed, the more overpowering the feeling became. And then it dawned on him. An inescapable feeling of welcome was beginning to consume him. Like someone—or something—knew he was coming, and in some unfathomable way was reaching out, guiding him.

The thick vegetation seemed less dense, the path wider, as if the mountain was opening up, allowing him to climb unimpeded. His thoughts flashed back to the numerous trips to the bottom of the ocean with Lindsay. *Would he be required to do likewise in his ascents up the volcano until reaching his destination?* he wondered.

Cole paused for a moment to clear his head, just to make sure he wasn't dreaming or being affected by the altitude. He had reached the fog line without sensing the passing of time. Glancing at his watch, he was stunned to see that nearly three hours had passed since he began his ascent. He looked back toward the water, unable to spot Mario, but did see what must have been his boat, a tiny spec in the ocean, barely visible through the mist. He checked his altimeter—9,076 feet. He had only a short distance left until he would be at the spot where he and Gamer were confronted by the fire angel, if indeed that was what they had encountered.

Taking a deep breath, Cole braced himself for the unexpected and continued his climb, but he was quickly distracted by a voice inside his head.

Is that you, Cole?

Cole stopped immediately, thunderstruck. An invisible voice was calling to him again, but this time, it wasn't his mother's melancholy voice calling. Her voice had been replaced with Lindsay's. Immobilized by the haunting sound only he could hear, Cole looked up as the air around him suddenly quivered, like heat waves on an arid desert horizon. Cole stood transfixed as the scene unfolded; an orifice opened amid a swirling circle of shimmering mist as a body began forming within the vacuum.

The eyes became visible first—dark, gleaming orbs of obsidian staring at him like focused lasers. Slowly the rest of the figure materialized, becoming flesh. The body of a female emerged, cloaked in an iridescent black gown that touched the ground while also appearing to extend beyond that space. Lengthy waves of auburn hair hung past her shoulders.

As Cole continued to stand immobilized, the wings formed—long, angular bolts of thick feathers erupting in fire, changing hues from chrome yellow to deep crimson, as if they had the power to liquify metal. A circle of searing flames formed around her legs. The image was complete, at once horrifying and, yet, more mesmerizing than anything Cole had witnessed before.

For a long moment, they gazed at each other like complete strangers, but strangers who were deeply connected in some mysterious manner. Cole endeavored to speak but no words would form. The fire angel floated before him, head tilted inquisitively.

You've come at last. You've come for me. Long have I waited. She reached out a hand, gesturing Cole forward. *Allow me to show you a world unlike any other. . .*

"Lindsay?"

CHAPTER FORTY-ONE

SATISFIED THAT COLE HAD not encountered anything unusual, Mario stepped into the inflatable and rowed himself back to the Eliminator. Rico was at the ready to receive his boss. Little was said while the two men gazed up the steep mountainside, silently considering Cole's plight. Their relationship with the billionaire appeared to be over, at least directly. There were still some loose ends to clean up—rescuing the Swanson sisters, attending to Gamer's recovery, confronting Andres Almquist and, perhaps, Chairman Gaines himself. Mario had no intentions of skipping out on his obligations, with or without Cole present.

The twosome watched the island darken as the waters around them changed hues with the setting sun. It was time to go home. Yet, something unspoken would not allow the driver to abandon his post. What was Cole searching for? Mario pulled out his high-powered night binoculars, scanning the mountain one last time. Nothing. No movement. It was as if Cole had disappeared into the mountain, leaving no trace. For a moment, Mario considered spending the night and searching for his boss in the morning, but he recalled his promise—the promise Cole forced him to make. He couldn't break that either.

"Boss?" Rico questioned, as though he had just read Mario's mind. "Shouldn't we leave?"

The driver nodded reluctantly. Rico took a seat in front of the controls, firing up the twin engines. He waited for a moment, waiting for Mario to take a seat next to him. When he didn't, Rico turned the boat and headed away from the shoreline, while Mario continued to gaze up at the foreboding mountain, searching.

The return trip to Isabella took a little over three hours and seemed more like a funeral procession than a trip over the ocean in a world-class speed boat. The uniformed man greeted them at the dock but immediately went silent at the expressions on his companions' faces. Mario stood stone-faced, while Rico simply shrugged his shoulders before throwing a rope to the uniformed man to tie them off.

Where is Mr. Hollingsworth? the guard thought, but he decided not to ask for fear that something bad had happened during their trip. It was not his place to intrude or to know. He had been assigned one job, and one job only, to look after Gamer's boat.

Mario gave the guard some last-minute instructions to wait for two men in his employ who would be by shortly to take the Eliminator to safety. He handed the guard an envelope containing payment, thanked him for his service, then strode determinedly toward his van, with Rico following close behind. The uniformed man watched the van drive away until the taillights were no longer visible.

CHAPTER FORTY-TWO

STILL DAZED FROM THEIR initial encounter, Cole followed in the angel's wake. Yes, she must be an angel, not a demon, although it was difficult to completely expunge that thought. The fire burning on and around her lit the way through the darkness, but to where? It could only be inside. What awaited him there?

Suddenly, a second orifice opened in midair, quivering and expanding at the same time. *Another portal?* Cole wondered. *An entrance inside the volcano or a gateway to another dimension?* Indistinct images flashed in Cole's head, momentarily overwhelming him, while his mind conjured thoughts of deep ocean trenches. They had no submersible this time to protect him. All he possessed was faith—faith that this was really Lindsay, that she was leading him to a new point of discovery, rather than to his death. Perhaps she wanted him to see something first, so he would understand the profound transformation that had taken place with her.

Doubt crept in as Cole began to suspect that this creature was not the Lindsay he knew and had come to love. But if not Lindsay, then who?

The apparition stood aside and pointed to the opening, indicating that Cole was to enter first. The angel's expression gave little away, appearing neither deceitful nor hopeful, only determined to get on with it. Another point of no return, no doubt. He supposed the time was now or never.

As he stepped inside, the sensation was immediate, as if a hook had abruptly gutted him, transporting his body through a field of blinding light, as a scorching wind howled around him. Cole screamed, his body suspended in a raging inferno of agony. Intense pain followed, pain he had not thought possible. Had Lindsay cast him into a fire pit, into the first level of Dante's *Inferno* to commence his journey through hell? Was this the price to be paid for his offensive wealth, his arrogance, his ignorance? Was this the price to be paid for immortality?

These questions and more raced through Cole's mind, as he endured his torturous bondage, mired in a living nightmare of unbearable pain. Had he come this far, witnessed so many tragedies, only to be incinerated inside the natural wonder he and Lindsay had created.

Gradually, all feeling and thought faded, until there was nothing left except oblivion. Cole's vision constricted—all he could see was a dazzling wall of white light before him, beckoning him to enter, and in doing so, allow the end of himself. There was really no choice at this point—death was his only hope for escape. He welcomed it now, and a moment later, he passed through.

CHAPTER FORTY-THREE

SUNRISE DAWNED AND WITH it, a mammoth explosion shattered the mountain top. Massive fireballs filled the sky with burning ash, blocking out the emerging light. Night had seemingly returned, and the sky felt broken. Thunderclaps echoed across the expanse as streaks of deadly lightning zigzagged across the horizon in all directions. The island shook with unimaginable intensity, as though releasing the full power of the earth's core into the heavens. But this was not a heavenly sight. Hell was being unleashed on the natural world, demonic and punishing.

Scientific teams and security personnel scrambled to get off the island as massive rivers of lava flowed down the mountain, unrelenting, devouring everything in their path. Few made it to their watercrafts, and those who did either suffocated in ponderous layers of deadly sulfur or were boiled to death by the scorching waters that had suddenly caught fire. Farther out to sea, the scientific, oil-like rigs melted, collapsing into the depths of the ocean, never to be seen again.

Mayhem and destruction ruled the day, and still Hollingsworth Island spewed out its malice, as though sending the world a message to take notice. But just what that message was had yet to be heard.

By midday, a military-grade cruiser had arrived on the scene. National guards were being deployed from nearby countries. A nuclear equipped submarine had been dispatched, and more warships were being sent from Naval Station Mayport in Jacksonville, Florida. No aircrafts were allowed in the area due to the heavy debris and lethal gases still permeating the atmosphere. Satellite photos were worthless. The world had indeed taken notice, watching breathlessly as the destruction unfolded, a grave acknowledgement to the power of nature.

Mario and Rico had defied maritime warnings, racing the Eliminator to within viewing distance of the island while donning oxygen masks. The intense heat rising off the ocean would not allow them too close, though. Mario maneuvered the boat to the eastern side of the island where few others had visited. Most of the damage and death had occurred on the west side and, as usual, all efforts were focused there.

Rico anchored their craft, while Mario focused his high-powered binoculars on the middle and upper regions of the volcano. The mist has evaporated, revealing more lush vegetation with very little damage. There existed a few trickles of lava flow that had not yet reached the water. Marine birds sailed overhead, as the sky slowly began to clear.

It was the stark contrast of the opposing shores that first caught Mario's attention. The east side remained calm, vegetation flourishing, birds in flight, like nature was meant to be. The west side, on the other hand, was desolate, with utter destruction of nearly everything that had recently existed. Burned, scarred land, torched vegetation, the ocean on fire, with death and destruction everywhere. *What could explain such a stark transformation?* he wondered.

It seemed as if there were two faces to the mountain, inexplicably fashioned. There had to be a reason, but what defined these two disparate landscapes? Gradually, the answer came to the driver. People. The west side was being impinged upon, while the human race squabbled over territorial rights and who might benefit financially. The east side stood unfettered by human intrusion, healthy and thriving. For someone like Mario, who had spent most of his life in the shadow of felonious activities, this newfound knowledge was like an epiphany. Could a balance be struck by these opposing forces? The driver couldn't see how this might be possible, the concept so abstruse, so turned his thoughts to less philosophical musings.

Neither man wanted to utter the words, but both knew that Cole could not have possibly survived the calamity. No one could have. But they had to see for themselves. Mario dropped his hands, allowing the binoculars to fall to the bottom of the boat. This endeavor was fruitless. What had started out as a serious, clandestine expedition had gone south quickly, and now most participants were either dead, disappeared, fighting for their lives, or kidnapped. What else could go wrong?

As the sun grew higher, more ships arrived, including a medical frigate and a transport ship of marines. Mario had repositioned the Eliminator with a good view of the western shore to better monitor the situation. It appeared that amphibious landing crafts would be deployed as soon as it was safe. Evidently, the Western world was treating this natural disaster more like a military threat than a humanitarian crisis, at least in Mario's opinion.

Wasn't that just like the West? To deal with a natural phenomenon from a purely defensive position, as if being attacked. As if some foreign adversary was causing it and looking to point a finger at someone. Hollingsworth Island had quickly morphed from a scientific endeavor of great importance to a political one.

What are the authorities planning to do, blow the island up? Mario thought, as he watched in growing dismay. His thoughts returned to Cole. Where had he gone . . . and why? Was there the slightest chance he had somehow survived? He needed to know.

Turning to Rico, he said, "We are not giving up until we learn what actually happened to Cole. He seemed to know what he was doing when he climbed that mountain. Maybe he had discovered an entrance or a secure spot to stay while he searched. . . for whatever he was looking for." Rico nodded.

Mario turned his gaze from Rico to the mountain, staring intently at it as if he was attempting to figure out a bizarre puzzle. For a long moment, he studied the landmass thoughtfully.

"Gamer," he muttered to himself. "We need to contact Gamer. He might be the one person, aside from Mr. Barkley, who knew why it was so important for Cole to gain access to the island."

"But he's in a coma, right?" Rico questioned. "How can he help us?"

"Cole said he was improving. We need to contact Dr. Morales immediately. Let's head back until we are within cell phone range and call him. Gamer may be awake now."

Without delay, the go-fast boat sped away, maintaining a wide birth from the collection of ships anchored nearby. No one seemed to notice their departure; everyone was too focused on the volcano and the rivers of lava still pouring out from the crater high above. An hour later, Mario's phone showed service, and he punched in the doctor's number. Morales answered immediately.

"Hello, this is Dr. Morales. Who am I speaking to?" He didn't recognize the number at first.

"This is Mario Hernandez, Mr. Hollingsworth's driver. I'm calling to see how Gamer is doing. It is imperative that I speak with him immediately."

"Where are you, and why isn't Mr. Hollingsworth calling?" the doctor replied tersely.

"Where I am is of no significance. Just answer the question, Doctor."

"As I told Mr. Hollingsworth yesterday, the patient is improving, although not yet fully awake. He has shown signs of movement, made a few sounds like he is attempting to speak, but he is still in critical condition."

"We'll be there in a little over an hour. Can you give Gamer a stimulant or something to accelerate his waking? I wouldn't ask if it wasn't of the utmost importance," Mario replied.

"That would be extremely risky. I don't think I can authorize it. I—"

"Then I'll authorize it or find someone who will. I suggest you start considering what the best option is before we get there. Do I make myself clear, Doctor?"

Morales hesitated before replying. He didn't like the sound of this, but he was aware of the driver's reputation. Say no to this man and you might find yourself lying at the bottom of the ocean in a body bag, your only companion an assortment of used bricks.

"Okay. . . okay. We'll be ready for your arrival, but I warn you—" Before he could complete his sentence, the phone went dead.

CHAPTER FORTY-FOUR

FROM SOMEWHERE DEEP WITHIN his subconscious mind, Cole Hollingsworth drifted in a weightless state, gliding inside deep shadows pierced by streaks of dazzling white light, moving up and down rhythmically. There was no sense of being inside a body, only a sense of infinite thought. Images began to appear, darting in and out of focus. Images that seemed familiar somehow, like they might be connected to a former reality.

Had Cole once again entered the portal to the afterlife? Had Lindsay taken him there so that he too might cross over? Something was very familiar about this space, like an altered dimension, where only thought and knowledge existed. Slowly, Cole regained a modicum of his senses, bringing with it a measure of sagacity. Yes, he must be in the space he and Lindsay had explored together—that incorporeal state where the deceased resided until their greatest need had been answered. And what was Cole's greatest need? To reconnect with Lindsay, the only woman he had ever loved.

Cole, you've come at last. Long have I waited.

Hadn't he just heard these same words spoken telepathically? Or had he heard these words in another lifetime? It might have been hours—it might have been years. The time continuum no longer functioned normally here.

Cole continued to float in this ethereal dimension, oblivious to worldly matters and finally released from all responsibilities.

And then, it happened. Cole began to transform into a human-shaped body of pure light, as a shimmering figure formed before him. Diamond-studded wings spread out as a silver-scaled, luminous body took shape, blinding in its intensity. The angel smiled like a sunrise at daybreak, and Cole knew at once. Lindsay had returned to him. She was not the fire angel after all; that apparition had been his guide, or maybe his executioner, but it no longer mattered. The sphere that had only moments earlier been a void of blackness with thin strands of glistening light was now lit up like a supernova exploding in deep space, revealing galactic secrets.

Lindsay hovered before Cole, lighting up the world from within, discharging silver shards of cosmic fire in all directions. Gradually, she floated toward him, and Cole was again consumed with love beyond description. An internal flame reignited, burning inside his heart, melting it until it became one with hers. Like conjoined infants born of the womb, there was no separating them now. Their souls had become fused together, entwined in an eternal bond, transcending life itself. A world without end.

For a long moment, the pair luxuriated in a state of unadulterated bliss. A primordial state that harkened back to the creation of life itself. Lindsay's theory on abiogenesis—a theory that won her national acclaim as a human scientist—was, in truth, the theory of evolution. Inert compounds, no matter how complex, could not have created a creature like the angel who embraced him now. She could only have been created by a higher power. A power that created all life—the Architect of the Universe.

Too soon, Lindsay released Cole, forming a space between them. Suddenly, Cole felt afraid, fearful that he might lose her again. Her gaze mesmerized him momentarily, and then she spoke.

What is it you want, Cole? Why did you come for me?

It was a simple question, really. Yet, Cole found he could not answer it outright. He had spent the last six months thinking about what reconnecting with Lindsay would mean to him. These thoughts, these emotions, were never far from his mind, day or night. And now. . . now that he had found her, he was rendered speechless.

It didn't matter that he was dead—or maybe he wasn't—he didn't fully comprehend his situation. He flashed back to his experience with his parents before they had passed on. Their greatest need was to see their son one last time. Was this Cole's one last chance to see Lindsay? Was what he was about to say to her the most important thing he would ever say, thus sealing his fate for eternity? The finality of the situation paralyzed Cole in a state of abstract confusion. Cole continued to gaze at the angel indecisively, unable to verbalize his thoughts—too afraid to utter them for fear of losing her.

She seemed to sense his ambivalence, reaching out her hands in a gesture of contrition as if to say, *It's okay, speak from your heart. For only there will you find the truth you are seeking.*

"Lindsay. . . I came back to find you, against staggering odds. My life means nothing without you. I have no purpose, no joy, only a daily routine of mediocrity. Ever since my return to Newport, I've thought of nothing but you. I sensed you calling me from across an ocean. Whether that ocean was real or imagined, I cannot say. But I knew I would not stop until I found you—or found the truth." Cole went silent, ashamed that his explanation wasn't more profound somehow. He was speaking to an angel, a deity, and he sounded like a lovesick teenager unable to communicate his feelings. What did she think of him now?

Lindsay drew near again, hesitating before wrapping her wings around Cole protectively, like she had done at the bottom of the ocean. Was she attempting to save him again or simply quell his pain?

That's enough for now, Cole. This is the start of your journey to find your true purpose in life. Allow me to be your guide. There are two choices before you. You can embark on the test of fire, which, if successful, will eventually lead you to immortality. But the risks are grave. You need to be fully committed, or you will be consumed by eternal flame, destined to wander the underworld without purpose. Lindsay paused to give Cole a moment to consider her words. When he asked no further questions, she continued.

Or you can return to human form, just as you were before entering this space. You'll be like you were before, however, you will retain this experience, which will make you wiser. From there, you can take on the task of making a difference in this world with your newfound knowledge. You can also return to Newport and run your company as you see fit. The choice is yours.

Cole stared at the angel incredulously, as neither choice was to his liking. Would the journey to immorality include Lindsay? And at what cost? Would the choice to return to human form exclude her? That was simply not acceptable. His head was spinning, wrapped up in delusions. Could this be a dream? It seemed to make more sense. Cole fought to regain focus, attempting to ascertain answers that would make things clearer, then addressed the angel again.

"I assume if I seek immortality, I will be with you? You probably already know I encountered the bar mistress of the Cantina de la Noche again, and it was she who first mentioned to me that the cost of immortality would be grave," Cole said. "I've already lost my best friend, my parents. I'm totally alone in this world. What more could I lose?"

Your future. That is a momentous thing to lose. Please consider this carefully. But to answer your question—yes, we will be together.

"And what if I choose the mortal life and return to human form, will I lose you then?"

A human cannot survive in my world. You've already experienced what it cost you to reconnect with me. The torture you endured to reach this place. We exist in different realities, in different dimensions, yet remain connected only through our everlasting love.

"Not the best of choices, wouldn't you say? All I want is to love you," Cole said, hesitating, as a new thought occurred to him. "If I am able to survive the test of fire and gain immortality, can I bring Art back to life? Also, what would our roles be together, I don't understand that yet."

Lindsay paused. It was now or never. Cole needed to know what was at stake. She would not keep him in the dark as she had done before, leading him along slowly to the bottom of the ocean and the portal to the afterlife.

As to your first question—no, you cannot resurrect your friend. What is done is done. I am sorry. As far as our roles as angels, we. . . she paused. *We will rule this world together. We will possess the power to reshape it in a consecrated vision, the divine vision our creator imagined it to be, which humans have desecrated.*

As if Cole's present condition wasn't unfathomable enough, this explanation pushed him to a new level of confusion. Could the two of them actually reshape this world? Hadn't they already done that with the creation of Hollingsworth Island?

However, if you choose to return to the mortal world, you may be able to save Art. I can transport you back to a time before his death. But in doing so, you will pass beyond this encounter and it will fade from memory. We may be able to reconnect at a different time, depending on the mortal path you follow. More than that I cannot say.

Cole was dumfounded at the choices—or lack of them, that is. Why couldn't this be easier? They had cohabited well enough during their search for his dead parents. Why was that no longer possible?

"Lindsay, I don't understand. When we were together the last time, we were fine. You appeared to me as human, even though you possessed powers no other human could have possessed. Why can't we return to that state?"

It is no longer possible, Cole. An angel is only allowed to reanimate once, and I chose you. I died a second death as a human being during the creation of this mountain, and I will remain in this form forever. I'm—

"How do you expect me to make a decision!" Cole exclaimed, interrupting. "How can I choose between you and Art? And how can someone like me become a moral compass to the rest of the world, when all I've known in my life is wealth and privilege?"

Oh, Cole, you are so much more than you realize. Few have experienced your lifestyle. Few know how to operate in your world. That experience alone is priceless. It is the people in your world that most affect the state of this planet and of humanity itself. Through their greed and lust for power, they are the reasons our living earth is being defiled and the human race in most parts of the world suffers. You are the puppet masters. Don't you think it's about time you got to know the rest of the world?

She was sounding more like Lindsay now, at least, the Lindsay he had come to know. Confident, argumentative, caring. She had never looked more beautiful than at this precise moment. Lost in her allure, all Cole could do was stare at her in bewilderment.

Now, what do you say to returning inside the mountain and allowing me to show you a world unlike any other?

CHAPTER FORTY-FIVE

B Y THE TIME MARIO and Rico reached the clinic and entered Gamer's room, the boatman was awake, but he was still looking pale and weak. He sat propped up against a mound of pillows, with Dr. Morales and one of the nurse specialists standing next to him. The two men approached cautiously and were greeted with a faint smile.

"I'm sorry I can't shake your hands, but I am glad to see you. Please come closer," Gamer said in a rasping voice.

"How are you feeling, *mi amigo*?" Mario asked.

"Like I've been struck by lightning," Gamer replied, choking out a feeble laugh.

Mario turned his gaze to Morales, indicating the remainder of this conversation was off-limits to the medical staff. The doctor caught his meaning and gestured for the nurse to depart. As he followed her, he spoke to Mario in a hushed tone. "You don't have much time. The stimulant will only last a short while before he relapses into sleep. I hope this was worth it," Morales said spitefully. Mario turned his attention to Gamer.

"We wouldn't have come unless it was vital, and I promise we won't keep you long. You need your beauty sleep," the driver said, winking as his companion. "This concerns Cole. He instructed us to take him back to the island yesterday and insisted on making the climb alone, no matter how strongly I objected. We stood guard until he had disappeared. I considered staying the night, but he made me promise not to follow him. By the way he talked, it didn't seem he would be returning. Can you tell us what he was looking for?"

The boatman took a deep breath. It was obviously difficult for him to talk. But like Mario, the Russian was tough as nails, and he was just as committed to Cole as the driver was.

"I don't know all of the details, but from what little I do know and from what I learned from his friend, Art Barkley, I think Cole was looking for a woman, an American oceanographer of some fame. . ." Gamer paused, taking another deep breath while reaching for his oxygen mask.

"Apparently, she had commanded a submersible to help Cole search for his parents, who had recently been killed in a major storm off the coast of San Salvador. According to Mr. Barkley, the two had fallen in love and were nearby when the volcano erupted. Cole was reported to be the first person to set foot on the newly formed island. Barkley was hesitant to tell me much more. I'm not even sure he knew the full story, but he did offer one last bit of information so someone other than himself would know. Mr. Hollingsworth believed the woman somehow survived and, um, exists inside of the mountain." Gamer went silent, succumbing to exhaustion quickly.

"That's ridiculous. No one could survive inside that hellhole of a volcano," Mario exclaimed. "It must be something else." He was about to question his friend again when he noticed that Gamer's eyes had closed and his head had slumped back against the pillows. He fastened the oxygen mask over Gamer's face while instructing Rico to call the medical staff back immediately.

On their way out, Mario thanked the doctor for his service, before leaving through the back doors.

"Now that we know what Mr. Hollingsworth was searching for, we need to formulate a plan. Personally, I don't believe the woman is alive, but apparently our boss does," Mario said, now reengaged in their mission.

"But, boss, Mr. Hollingsworth made us promise not to interfere. And he's paid us a great deal of money to follow his orders," Rico replied.

"Damn the money! I'll pay it back. I'm not leaving that man alone on that accursed mountain. If he still lives, we'll find him. He can't do this alone," Mario said.

"So, what's the plan?" Rico asked, not particularly keen on returning to the island.

"I don't have a plan yet, but we'll figure it out as we go. Call the guard and have Gamer's boat ready to launch within the hour."

CHAPTER FORTY-SIX

P ENETRATING THE WALL OF living light, Cole and the angel passed through unfazed, leaving the portal to the afterlife behind. What presented itself next stopped Cole in his tracks, the landscape so overpowering it took his breath away. It reminded Cole of a scene from *Star Trek III: The Search for Spock*, when Dr. Carol Marcus takes Admiral James Kirk inside the newly formed planet, revealing life reformed and reimagined—the Genesis Effect on full display, creating life from proto-matter combined with other, powerful inert compounds.

Inside of the volcano was unlike anything Cole had ever seen or imagined possible. An immense, hollowed-out crater spanned for miles in all directions. And in the center, a massive tube that appeared to be shimmering crystal, funneling an ocean of molten lava from the earth's core to the upper rim, pouring its deadly contents down the mountainside. Everywhere else, outlandish, lush vegetation grew in a myriad of colors defying description. Strange, winged creatures sailed the open spaces. Larger creatures too distant to distinguish roamed the lower levels. Approximately halfway up, the fire angel hovered in space, malevolent in stature. It seemed to be controlling the lava flow somehow.

Moments after Cole's arrival, the fire angel waved its wicked, claw-like hand toward the funnel and the lava flow stopped, frozen in place. Cole couldn't believe what he was seeing. He had passed from the afterlife to another altered dimension, in the blink of an eye. Was this Lindsay's creation or that of a higher power? What was its intent? A hundred questions filled his head as he gazed out in utter astonishment at what could only be called a miracle. The miracle of life reborn. And there he stood on its threshold, viewing what might be a new race of living beings, with angels as its shepherds.

Cole's thoughts harkened back to the *Star Trek* movie, which seemed less like science fiction than what he was now witnessing. Something about that movie bothered him, but exactly what it was eluded him. Was it something about the Genesis Effect itself—a flaw perhaps?

Cole turned toward Lindsay, who had remained silent while the immensity of what lay before him gradually took root. "So, is this real, or are you showing me a glimpse of immortality?" Cole asked matter-of-factly, as though they were discussing plans for a new real estate venture.

Oh, this is very real. If you were to leave the confines of the mountain, you would see the Caribbean Sea sparkling before you, adorned with ships surveying the recent destruction created by the latest eruption. Beyond, the island of Puerto Rico looms.

"Destruction? What happened? When I was climbing the mountain, before I was abducted, everything was fine," Cole said, using the word *abduction* to indicate that this had not been all his idea.

Cole, you were not abducted, but never mind that. Immortality spells the difference between you being an intimate part of all that you see before you or not. If you choose the mortal life, you will be outside looking in. But that doesn't mean you cannot impact what happens here. Our enduring connection will allow you some amount of passage back and forth so that you can make the human race aware of its impending doom. And as I told you, the choice is yours.

Cole gazed back, flabbergasted. Lindsay was again speaking to him in riddles. He should have been accustomed to that by now, based on previous experiences with Lindsay, the oceanographer, but that was then. He needed to release her from her past and accept her for what she was now—an ethereal being with unearthly powers. The power of life and death, or so it seemed. The power to alter Cole's life irrevocably, passing him through death to immortality, or returning him to the world of the living. God, what a decision to make. Cole suddenly felt ill-suited to make such a momentous choice. In his mind, he lacked the courage and desperately wanted Lindsay to make the decision for him. Intuitively though, he knew she would not do this for him. It had to be his choice—a choice he would either live with the rest of his natural life or be tethered to for eternity.

Cole turned away, unable to look Lindsay in the eye, ashamed of his weakness. He was being given an indescribable opportunity to do things few others could. How many had faced this dilemma before him? How many angels existed to serve the all-powerful being, fulfilling destinies unknown? Did he possess a heart pure enough to change the world in positive ways? Or would he fall from grace, distracted by human frailties and temptations?

The questions continued to come hard at him, as he stood on the precipice between the life he knew—of precious, human life—and the bondage of immortality. Why the word *bondage* came to mind, he could not say exactly. Wasn't immortality the ultimate freedom from the struggles that life often presented? Cole hadn't faced many of those struggles in his short life, other than the tragedy of losing his parents and his best friend, but he now held the power to fix the latter. And in the middle of it all stood Lindsay, beckoning him to join in her quest—a quest he did not fully understand. The love they shared could no longer be the natural love between two human beings, quite possibly the greatest gift humans could experience. Their love would either be consecrated by an eternal union, burning like stars in a spiritual world of space and time, or lost to him if he chose the mortal life. They would never have children. Cole would not have an heir. Hollingsworth Enterprises would be overrun with infighting until eventually being sold off in pieces, while the legacy his father so wanted vanished under Cole's watch.

Cole hadn't really thought these things through during his search to reconnect with Lindsay. *What did I expect to find?* he wondered, as he stared down at a new world being created before his very eyes. Lindsay could not be human again. What had made him think she could? Now, she had revealed to him that she could no longer morph back into the woman he loved, that she would remain an angel forever. The sudden revelation broke Cole's heart. Falling to his knees, he broke out in convulsive sobs, as the bittersweet realization took hold. He felt his heart melting again, separating from hers, and with it, the promise of a future with the one person who completed him.

Gathering every ounce of courage he could muster, Cole stood and faced what might have been his savior. The pleading in his eyes could not have been more regretful.

Lindsay smiled ruefully back, but with the compassion that only she could emanate. She knew the outcome.

She stroked the side of Cole's face with a featherlight touch. The orifice reopened beside him, quivering with iridescent light. Cole walked through it, feeling as broken as he ever had, but with a newfound conviction to make a difference.

The decision had been made.

CHAPTER FORTY-SEVEN

"**H**EY, BRO, WHERE THE hell have you been? The twins are on a rampage and are actually threatening me. They want out of this shithole immediately," Art said.

Cole stood in stunned silence for a long moment.

"Art. . . is that really you? I . . .I can't believe it. I—"

"You hooked up with some *señorita*, didn't you? I don't blame you. It's about time." Art laughed and handed Cole an ice-cold beer.

A moment later, Gamer and Mario came down the path to their bungalows.

"Are you ready to depart to the island? The boat is loaded and ready to go, boss," Gamer said, looking revitalized, as though he was the poster child for healthful living. He had even shaved, which really didn't suit him in Cole's mind. He preferred the rugged, swashbuckling character he had come to like and respect.

Cole turned his gaze toward Mario, who had become almost like a brother to him. These men who had risked their lives for him. And Art Barkley, who had actually died for him. Could a man have better friends in life? Cole doubted it, and he fought back the sudden urge to hug each one of them.

His thoughts turned to Lindsay. She had kept her promise—had transported Cole back to the past—and, in the process, had given him a future worth living for. In his mind's eye, her visage suddenly appeared as she reached out to him again.

Remember always, my love, we are only an ocean apart. . .

Cole smiled a sad smile, then he addressed his companions, who were eagerly awaiting his instructions.

"Gentlemen, we won't be going to the island, at least not now. I have other plans, and they include each of you. That is, if you are willing to hang with me?" Cole asked, rather than demanding.

Art stared at his friend incredulously, as if to say, *are you fucking crazy? Why did we come all this way, spend all this money, to give up now?* Though he didn't verbalize his thoughts, the expression on Art's face gave him away.

"It's okay, Art. I found what I needed to find. My work is done here, at least for the present. It's time to head home."

The sudden shock of Cole's abrupt change of plans left all three companions more than a little perplexed. What had Cole found, and when? He had only been to the island twice, and both visits were short-lived.

"Mario, have there been any eruptions from the volcano lately? Any change of scene on the western shore?" Cole asked.

"Not to my knowledge, sir," Mario replied, confused by the question.

So, the major eruption and destruction of everything near the island has been wiped clean, as if it never happened, Cole thought to himself.

"There will be no more calling me *sir*, understand? My name is Cole, and I'd appreciate it if you would call me by that name. Each of you, in your own way, have become my closest and most trusted advisers. Together, we passed a test of fire, so to speak. While you may not fully understand yet, someday the complete story will come out. For now, we forge ahead as brothers, or not at all."

Cole could not help but laugh at the timid expressions on the faces of Mario and Gamer, two of the toughest and most highly skilled men he had ever met. They appeared less willing to call their boss by his first name than to enter into a battle with life-threatening consequences. But they had already done that.

Art stood back, staring at Cole with his patented *now what* look that he was accustomed to making when dealing with his boss. He simply shook his head in disbelief, remaining silent.

"So, what's the plan, boss—um, I mean, Cole?" Mario asked, awkwardly. Some habits were hard to break.

"How fast can you be ready to leave. We need to fly to Mexico. From there, we'll take my private jet to Newport, Rhode Island. There are some people I want you to meet there. I'd also like to offer you official positions in our company, so you both have access to information that would otherwise be deemed confidential. I'll fill you in with more detail on the way there. Do we have a deal?" Cole said expectantly, as if they couldn't refuse. He was still the CEO of Hollingsworth Enterprises, after all.

Both men nodded. There were a few last-minute details to take care of, so it was agreed they would all meet at seven in the morning. Art made a few phone calls to arrange for airplane tickets, then he hurried off to inform the Swanson sisters that their ordeal was over. They would soon be living the life of luxury they were accustomed to, and rightfully deserved, in their minds. Their modeling careers awaited them. This news would only make them more grateful. Art was counting on that. Apparently, Art hadn't learned much humility during his brief stay in the morgue.

The mention of the Swanson sisters stopped Cole in his tracks. Had he arrived back at a point in time before they were kidnapped? How ironic. At least this was good news. Mario didn't seem to be affected by the mention of the twins, either. It appeared everything was back to normal—or at least as normal as it could get considering where they were.

CHAPTER FORTY-EIGHT

SEVEN ARRIVED, AND WHEN Cole exited his bungalow, the entire group was waiting for him, looking anxious—well, all except the twins, who were beaming. Both women approached Cole and hugged him tightly.

"Thank you, kind sir," Shelby exclaimed.

"You've saved us," Sydney echoed.

Art had a satisfied expression on his face, as though they were all just one big, happy family again.

Mario and Gamer stood at attention, neither man appearing relaxed. They were leaving their home environment, where they felt relatively in control. But what would they face in the corporate world? How would they adapt? It would be frowned upon if they were to start slashing people's throats if they got out of line. They had spent a long night talking about the possibilities and in the end, they decided just to trust Cole and Art. What other choice did they have?

"Thank you for being on time. Is everyone ready to leave?" Cole asked, his remarks directed more at the driver and the boatman. He wanted them to have one last chance to say no. What he intended to ask them to do in the future might be their most dangerous challenges to date. They needed to be fully committed—or stay home.

Both men nodded, understanding Cole's intent. The six companions strolled up the path, toward the front office lot, where a stretch limo waited. They no longer needed to travel incognito, and Cole felt they had earned it.

Art settled up at the front desk amid a fair amount of grumbling. Rico stood nearby, sporting a new machete and looking grim. The hotel manager wished them all good luck in the future, along with a stern warning never to return. As he passed by Rico, he cursed at him in Spanish, which elicited a wry smile. The assassin took a quick step toward the manager, hastening his retreat into the back office.

The group was still laughing when they entered the limo. Rico stood alongside the automobile, shaking hands with Cole and wishing the group good fortune. He would not be going with them. Mario had given him instructions as to his role. He would be keeping watch on the island and on Andres Almquist, paying the scientist regular visits to keep him in line. Evidently, Almquist couldn't get the throat cutting incident on the boat out of his mind. Every time he came into contact with Rico, he seemed to shrink in stature. Fear was after all, a great motivator.

It was time to say goodbye to Isabella and all they had experienced here. For some, it was time to return home. For others, it was perhaps the start of a new life. Neither Mario nor Gamer had sent much time in the States. To them, America was a shining beacon of freedom and wealth that existed beyond their reach. They failed to understand that America was as much an illusion as it was real. The puppet masters hard at work behind the scenes vying for power and, in the process, defiling the environment. Polluting the oceans, shrinking the ice caps, depleting the ozone, exposing planet earth to deadly ultraviolet light from the sun. Sucking natural resources from the planet until, someday, they would not be replenishable. And still the puppet masters toiled unwaveringly for power and riches, while holding the rest of the world hostage.

While this might be a severe condemnation of the greatest country in the world, it could not be ignored. Recent changes in America's governance in the nation's capital was unwittingly exposing these things that occurred behind closed doors, in corporate board rooms, in clandestine meetings. Even as the leader of the free world espoused ideas to make America great again, the disparity between the *haves* and the *have nots* continued to grow in unprecedented numbers. Homelessness in the great urban areas of the country abounded. Instead of building bridges to unite humanity for the good of all, walls were being constructed to keep out the riffraff from third world shitholes. To many, it seemed like the country that was built on immigrants and ingenuity had achieved what was needed and it was now time to keep the rest of the world outside its boundaries and the power structure in place.

Cole was beginning to understand this, however subconsciously. While the recent experiences with Lindsay were slowly fading from memory, some things lingered, fueling Cole's imagination for a better world. A world of respect, of dignity, one where the Bill of Rights and the Constitution really meant what was penned in those iconic documents, during a simpler age. But the question remained—how in the world could Cole do anything about it?

CHAPTER FORTY-NINE

THE LIMO ARRIVED AT Rafael Hernandez Airport, leaving behind events that had been impossible to foresee upon their arrival in Puerto Rico. Rafael Hernandez stood in stark contrast to the desolate airstrip that had launched their initial flight to Isabella. They would now be flying in a private chartered jet to Mexico's General Mariano Matamoros Airport, where Cole's Dassault Falcon 7X superjet waited to whisk them off to Rhode Island.

The companions had heard some of Cole's plans during the limo ride. Something was different about the CEO that Art couldn't identify. Cole had again changed during his second visit to the massive volcano in the Caribbean. Had he actually encountered Lindsay while on that mountain? Or had he come away empty-handed? And finally, why the abrupt departure? Cole seemed determined to pursue a change of plans, a different path going forward, but those plans were once again being closely guarded by his good friend. Art could do little but acquiesce. It would unfold eventually. For now, it was enough that he was going home and in good graces with the twins again.

Once airborne, Hollingsworth Island became visible on the starboard side, towering over the oceanscape, intimidating as ever. As Cole gazed out one of the side portholes, a strange sensation overcame him, as though he was leaving something priceless behind, something that could not be replaced. A longing crept into his heart, a feeling of love unrequited. He was leaving Lindsay behind. Had this been his choice? Had she forced him to leave? The events were becoming more and more convoluted as time slipped by, leaving only emptiness and questions that seemed destined to haunt Cole forever.

Drinks and food were offered, and most partook. Only Cole had no appetite and settled for a scotch on the rocks. Too soon, the majestic mountain disappeared beyond the horizon, and Lindsay's pull began to dissipate.

The flight from Puerto Rico to Mexico was relatively short. The chartered jet had taken off immediately, and with clear skies ahead, the landing was unhindered.

Cole's trusty pilots were at the ready, standing in front of the Falcon, dressed in official pilot suits. Art had contacted them the day before, and the crew had hastily left Newport in the middle of the night to reach the Mexican airport. Cole greeted the men warmly and introduced everyone. Head pilot Frank Martin was back in action, recovered from his previous heart attack. The heart attack that had occurred while flying Cole and Lindsay to San Salvador during their initial search for answers to Cole's parents' mysterious deaths. Bill was also part of the crew. Bill, the less experienced copilot, who had valiantly landed the Falcon amid a brutal storm while Frank lay unconscious in the pilot's seat next to him. The crew had reunited, and somehow, it felt right.

The party of companions was growing. They were now eight in number. It suddenly struck Cole as symbolic, reminding him of the nine comrades in Tolkien's *Fellowship of the Ring*. Were they actually becoming like the Company of the Ring? All during this trip, Cole had been reminded of the fantasy masterpiece that had been one of his favorite stories while growing up. It had started with his discovery of the mysterious, boxlike object appearing during his encounter with the Cantina de la Noche, followed by the water runes and the map that led him to an opening high up on

Hollingsworth Island. The similarities were astonishing. A modern-day trek through Middle Earth? It couldn't be. Cole shook the puerile thought out of his head. But still, all they needed was one more companion and they would become the Nine Walkers.

What they really needed was a wizard. But where to find one of those?

CHAPTER FIFTY

A LTHOUGH THE FALCON WAS loaded to capacity with passengers, Cole kept to himself. The others did their utmost to entertain one another but couldn't help but notice the brooding CEO, surrounded by a shroud of impenetrable isolation. Deep in thought, Cole failed to notice the passing of time or the fact they were now circling Green Airport, awaiting landing instructions. This would not be like their last landing, when Cole had returned to a media firestorm. Then, the world was waiting with baited breath to see the billionaire who'd risked everything to discover the truth about his parents' disappearance and, in the process, was the first human to set foot on the newly formed volcano in the Caribbean. That landing also launched the Ralph Lauren modeling careers for the Swanson sisters.

What a homecoming it had been. Cole had temporarily become the poster child for survival magazines worldwide. The fifty-million-dollar scam by Lindsay's father had quickly been forgotten. For the next few months, Cole had been treated like a hero, until the reclusiveness set in. Whispers of uncertainty filled the halls of company headquarters as Cole withdrew further and further inside himself.

William Gaines had taken advantage of Cole's mental absenteeism to form an alliance with key board members. Battle lines had been drawn, and the conflict finally came to a head after the chairman usurped Cole's authority with his own scheme to take media control of news reports emanating from Hollingsworth Island. It was a brilliant plan actually and had caught Cole completely off guard. It was that singular event that had spurred Cole to finally take action. And now he was returning home seemingly empty-handed. No Mexican printer had been acquired. No control had been seized over the new landmass. Just Cole, Art, and the newcomers, who would only be viewed as interlopers by Gaines and his allies.

To many, Cole's excursion to the Caribbean would be seen as a failure. Yes, there had been a scientific team chosen that included Almquist, an informer for the chairman, but even that was changing, becoming less effective with each passing day.

Had Cole managed to uncover the truth? Had he turned the scientist to his advantage? These were the thoughts that occupied Gaines as he awaited Cole's return home.

But there were other things kept secret, events only Cole understood, and these would be Cole's trump cards as his fate unfolded. Gradually, the plan was coming together, and it would be unleashed at precisely the right time and place. If successful, the ramifications would be irrevocable and quite possibly catastrophic.

Lindsay hadn't been completely honest with Cole while they were inside the volcano. She had transported him back in time and wiped some of his memory clean so that he could depart of his own free will. But it was all gradually coming back. It had only been a temporary delay. During the return flight to Newport, she had come to him in a dream state and re-revealed all. The imagery was as clear as the cloudless expanse of blue sky they were floating on while awaiting their descent.

The order was given, and the Falcon dropped out of the sky like an attacking dragon belching fire and brimstone.

And then all hell broke loose.

CHAPTER FIFTY-ONE

A T PRECISELY THE SAME instant Cole's private jet touched down, Hollingsworth Island erupted with such force, it blew the mountain top off, filling the sky with hellfire and suffocating ash. Crimson lava gushed out in rivers of fire, like massive waterfalls. The island shook with such intensity, shockwaves registered on every device capable of measuring such things across the planet. The world had never experienced anything close to the magnitude of the explosion, which made a nuclear detonation seem like a firecracker on the Fourth of July. The scientific teams still on the island stood no chance, incinerated in mere heartbeats. The oil-like scientific rigs out to sea melted like evaporating steam, hissing malevolently, as they dissolved into the ocean below, superheating the water around them. Any seafaring vessel within a mile fell victim to instantaneous combustion.

Hell had just been unleashed on the unsuspecting world, and time itself stood still, paralyzed in the earth's inexorable pain. For a long moment, the planet was incapacitated—nothing moved, no communication was possible. Only the sound of screeching tires could be heard as the Falcon hit the tarmac and succumbed to the physical harnesses that slowed its progress. After the jet taxied to its final destination, the side door flew open, the stairwell touched ground, and Cole deplaned, followed by his companions. What next met their gaze could only be possible in a movie—as if the movie camera had been put on pause.

The airport was eerily silent. Nothing moved. Birds hung motionless in midair. The world as they knew it had come to an utter stop, frozen in place. Intense humidity turned the air intolerable. Humidity that had never been experienced at this level before. The toxic odors of methane and sulfur permeated their surroundings, and Cole knew at once. This was Lindsay's work. She was sending a message, not only to Cole but to all of the world, that the time of reckoning had arrived. It was one hell of an announcement. But wasn't it what Cole had recently experienced? As Cole's group pressed forward, things gradually began to move again. Birds resumed flight, and the scene returned to normal, as if nothing had happened.

Sixteen hundred miles away, the volcano quieted, the lava flows slowed, and the steam surrounding the island dissipated into the troposphere, washing the oceanscape clean of man's intervention. The sky brightened as a strong wind blew away the ash, until all was peaceful again—at least for the time being. But in reality, it was simply the calm before the storm.

CHAPTER FIFTY-TWO

C OLE'S LIMO WAS WAITING when they arrived at the main terminal at Green Airport. Cole decided to take his guests to his house first, before he and Art left for the office. Cole dialed Grace Foster, his executive assistant and personal friend, to let her know he would be arriving at the office within ninety minutes, then abruptly hung up.

Surprised by the sudden announcement that Cole and Art were back, she headed into Cole's office to organize the pile of mail and packages he had received while away. A quick dusting of the furniture and she was satisfied he would find everything in order. She had kept one letter that looked to be of a personal nature locked away in her desk drawer. The letter had no return address, but was postmarked from Australia. She now placed it at the bottom of the stack on his desk and then waited. She decided not to alert Bill Gaines or give him any advance notice of Cole's return. It was better this way.

Gamer and Mario were naturally impressed with Cole's house on the cliffs. He guided them in through the front doors, keeping the Maserati out of sight.

"Everybody, please make yourself at home. There are plenty of bedrooms and bathrooms upstairs if you would like to freshen up. As far as food goes, there probably isn't much other than canned or dry goods. But the liquor cabinet is well stocked!" Cole joked.

Cole addressed the two men from the Caribbean. "Art and I will be leaving for the office soon. I suggest you and Mario stay at the house until I return." Next, he turned to the twins. "You are also welcome to stay, but my driver is at your disposal. You're probably eager to return to your homes."

The women nodded, smiling.

"But all of you please keep what we experienced to yourselves. It's crucial. Frank, Bill, here are the keys to the silver SUV in the garage." Cole handed Frank the key fob hanging on the nearby wall. "No need to return it. We'll all talk again soon."

That piece of business concluded, Cole and Art disappeared through the service doors. A few moments later, the sound of a high-revving engine pierced the silence, as the pair drove away in the Audi R8 Spyder, an able substitute for the Maserati.

The twins lingered for a while, making small talk with Gamer and Mario until it began to feel uncomfortable. No one mentioned how time had apparently stood still when they'd landed at the airport. Perhaps because no one believed it to be possible, just an aftereffect of too much jet lag and too little sleep. The women excused themselves and were soon traveling in the back seat of the limo down the switchback driveway, away from Cole's house.

Bill and Frank said their goodbyes as well, leaving the two men sitting alone and staring out of the expansive windows to the vast ocean beyond. The Russian and the Spaniard had traded one ocean for another with no idea of what lay ahead for them.

Forty minutes later, Cole and Art entered corporate headquarters, to the astonishment of numerous employees. Hushed conversations followed as people speculated on where the pair had been and what they had been up to. Something about a printing company for sale? Their departure had been so abrupt and secretive that no one was sure.

Grace was standing in front of Cole's office, as though guarding it until he arrived. Cole gave her a bear hug and a warm hello. Art hugged her as well, but his embrace was quick and unemotional.

"Where is Gaines?" Cole asked gruffly, getting straight to the point. When Lindsay had appeared to him in the dream on their flight home, she had given him back the memory of the chairman's assassination attempt and Art's death. Art didn't know, and probably never would, but this truth was shattering. Gaines had actually tried to kill Cole. Cole's blood pressure spiked at the thought of seeing Gaines again.

"I believe he's in his office. I didn't tell him you were back. I hope that was okay," Grace said, tentatively.

"That's perfect. Thank you." Cole nodded at Art to follow him. The two men headed to the chairman's office in high anticipation of his reaction.

Cole didn't bother knocking on the door, instead shoving it open and entering. Gaines did a double-take, looking stunned to see the CEO with Art Barkley standing beside him. His gaze fell directly on Art as his eyes widened. Gaines struggled to find the words that would not give him away.

A curious, enigmatic event was taking place. Unknown to each, the men were living in altered realities. For Gaines, time had passed normally. For Cole, time had reversed itself. And Art stood somewhere in between, oblivious to his previous fate, supposedly dead.

Cole, when did—when did you get back? Why didn't you let me know you were coming? I—I could have called in the available directors to meet you. . . and to discuss your trip," Gaines said, flustered. Normally a calm, collected man under pressure, the sight of a dead man unnerved him. *Had Almquist lied about that?* he wondered. The scientist had sounded so convincing, and his contact in the Bahamas had confirmed it, but this was the only thing that made sense. People didn't come back from the dead. Gaines slowly regained his composure. He would deal with Almquist later.

"So, you're surprised to see us?" Cole asked, patting Art on the shoulder and sending a subtle message to the chairman that maybe Art shouldn't be here.

"Well, yes, but I'm glad you're back. With all the carnage taking place on the island, we were concerned you might have been caught up in it all," Gaines said, attempting to divert attention from himself and back to the volcano.

It was too soon for Gaines to have learned the facts about the massive eruption that had just occurred a little over an hour ago. He must have heard from Almquist. Few knew the details of the event yet, but Cole had seen it in his mind's eye. This catastrophic event was similar to the one that had taken place while he had spent time with Lindsay and the fire angel, only this one was far more violent.

Was time catching up to itself? Was the world morphing forward into real time? And what does that mean for me? These and other thoughts occupied Cole as he stood staring at the man who had become his mortal enemy.

CHAPTER FIFTY-THREE

"WHERE TO START?" COLE mused, taking a seat in front of the chairman's desk. Art took a seat beside his boss but remained silent. This was Cole's show. He was there for backup and to be a witness should the truth need fixing. Gaines could spin things as well as anyone could.

"Just so you know, Bill, we chose not to invest in the Mexican printer. It became too messy with the drug cartel group involved. The corruption down there is so mired in the political system that we couldn't associate our name with it. It's really too bad, though. Had they not been involved, it had great potential for us." Cole paused to watch the chairman's reaction.

Gaines nodded. "Makes sense. It was bound to come out, and we don't need that kind of publicity."

"Glad you agree, Bill. As to the island itself, well, our scientific team may still be able to monitor it, that is if they can get close enough—or are still among the living," Cole interjected, hoping for a reaction from Gaines. "As for creating a new publishing division to focus on science and, in particular, Hollingsworth Island, we are going to shelve that idea for now. I'm sure you understand," Cole said.

Gaines was slow to nod his agreement this time, frowning. "Are you sure that's a good idea, Cole? The island is still very active and even dangerous, but that will only fuel the public's need for more news about it. It is still a great opportunity for us to take advantage of," Gaines said guardedly.

"Perhaps for you, Bill, but no longer for me. Indeed, Hollingsworth Island may be about to take advantage of us."

Gaines stared back at his boss as if he was speaking in riddles or a language he didn't understand. "Cole, with all due respect, you're not making sense. I don't understand," Gaines said.

"Oh, but you will. . . you will," Cole said. Then he abruptly rose, exiting the chairman's office without another word.

Art rose as well, hesitating briefly. He continued to gaze at Gaines, scrutinizing him with disdain, as if the man's days were numbered. He walked out, leaving the chairman totally confounded as to what had just taken place.

Art caught up to Cole as he was entering his office. "Cole, are you going to tell me what the hell is going on? That little exchange with Gaines was bizarre. I'm as confused as I think he was," Art said.

"In time, bro. Let's just let things play out for now," Cole replied, not looking at his friend.

"Don't tell me we're going through this shit again!" Art said angrily.

Cole tossed Art the key to the Audi. "I need some time to catch up," Cole said, pointing to the stack of mail occupying a corner of his desk. At this rate, Cole would be carless within twenty-four hours. "I'll call you later."

Art was about to come back hard but caught himself in midsentence. "Damn you, Cole. . ." Turning, Art marched out of Cole's office, cursing to himself.

Cole pressed his intercom. "Grace, please hold my calls, and if anyone asks, I'm not available for the remainder of the day."

"Yes, sir." Grace pushed the button, silencing the intercom. At the same time, she wondered what the future would bring. One thing she was sure about: it was bringing with it a changed Cole Hollingsworth—again.

Forty minutes later, Cole had dispensed with the majority of his mail, having saved the few that required action. After tossing the last magazine into the trash, he noticed the envelope lying at the bottom of the pile. It was hand addressed to him, but with no return address. Failing to notice the postmark, Cole slid his letter opener smoothly through the top flap, extracting a handwritten letter penned in impeccable cursive. He hadn't seen longhand like this since his school days and English teachers. *Who wrote like this anymore?* Cole wondered. His curiosity piqued, Cole stared at the letter for a moment before reading it.

The words flowed like a gentle stream in a timeless valley.

> *Dearest Cole,*
>
> *I hope this letter finds you well, but I suspect otherwise. For months now, I have lived mostly undetected in the deep bush of Australia, among nature in all of its splendor. The quiet and the solitude have restored me and have filled my senses with renewed hope. I was broken when you left—we all were. I will forever be grateful to both you and Art for what you did for me and for Ryan. Although Ryan and I are no longer together, he is pursuing his own method of healing, and I can only pray that he finds peace as I have.*
>
> *You made all of this possible. I could not have healed without this time alone. I have come to terms with Lindsay's death, and I hope you have found some measure of peace in the ultimate sacrifice she made for you. Hers was a gift beyond measure. She loved you so much, and although it was incredibly painful, as least you had time with her. The two of you shared an everlasting love in the blink of an eye. How many people can say that?*

Cassie Thomas's letter dropped involuntarily from Cole's hand as the grief came flooding back. Tears formed and began streaming down his cheeks. Their brief time together in human form had changed him forever. Lindsay's smile that had lit the surroundings like a sunrise. Her touch that sent shivers throughout his body. The sound of her lilting voice challenging him to be a better man, a better human being.

Cole picked up the letter and continued reading.

I just arrived in Rhode Island after spending a few days in San Salvador. I needed to see it again and to remember. To confirm it was all real. While away, the experiences we all shared faded like one of those illusive dreams that holds us in its clutches and slowly lets us go but refuses to leave altogether. While I was in San Salvador, I heard rumors, whispers of your presence, of your return. Perhaps you were there for the same reason I was. To find closure. Or perhaps you were there for another reason?

What I discovered astonished me. The changes, the island. The series of events that have led us all to this moment in time. Lindsay came to me three times in dreams while I was in Australia, and in each dream, she revealed to me visions that were beyond description. In her final appearance, she instructed me to find you again. Although I don't understand the whys of it all, she convinced me to try. And so, I am here, waiting and hoping you will reach out. Although I don't fully understand why Lindsay wants us to reconnect, my love and respect for her has motivated me to try. Please contact me at the number below. I wait for your call.

Love always, Cassie

Cole sat alone in his office, the letter still clutched in his hand, speechless. Time seemed to slow down again, as if he was morphing back to an out of sync reality. But this time, Lindsay was not calling him; Cassie Thomas was. The affable, Australian beauty who happened to be a world-class diver and Lindsay's closest and most trusted friend.

And now, they were nine companions.

CHAPTER FIFTY-FOUR

C OLE NEEDED FRESH AIR. His office seemed to be closing in around him, like his first descent inside the *Harbinger II*—suffocating. He opened his office door to a darkened hallway. Glancing at his watch, he was staring at 7:14 p.m. It was growing dark outside, and Cole had failed to notice the passing of light to darkness. On his way down the elevator to the parking garage, it occurred to him he no longer had a car. He had given the Audi to Art. There was Uber, of course, but Cole detested riding in one of those cramped vehicles while the driver's forced conversation, which he had no desire of engaging in.

Stepping outside and into the fresh air, he was about to call Art, when he noticed a man across the street standing next to a Maserati. His Maserati. *What the hell?*

"Looks like you could use a lift, boss," Mario said.

Cole stared at his driver in disbelief. Gamer was sitting in the cramped back seat, reading a newspaper. Cole's newspaper.

"What. . .how did you get here in that car?" Cole demanded.

"Art called us a few hours ago to see if you had returned. He said you were acting strangely, and he was concerned about you. He told us to go into your garage, find this car, start it up, and talk to it," Mario said, shaking his head as if Art had gone loco. "We thought maybe Art was the one acting strangely. But then this voice—this woman—began talking. We told her who we were, and she started barking out orders. She made some kind of phone call from within the car and apparently checked with security at your offices. Next, she told us to hold on and then raced out of the garage and down the driveway. I didn't think we stood a chance of making it to the bottom, but we did. Next thing we knew, we ended up here."

"That voice you heard is Serena. She is the bane of my existence. I swear I'm gonna drive her off a cliff someday."

Now, Cole, we were only trying to help. And by the way, welcome back. Did you miss me? Serena cooed.

Mario broke out laughing. "She's quite the car. I've never seen anything like it. I could have used her—I mean, it—a hundred times," Mario said.

"Don't get me started, you won't like what you hear, I promise," Cole said.

"I know, that's what she told us," Mario replied, unable to suppress a grin.

"God damn car!" Cole cursed.

Gamer remained uncharacteristically silent. Whether he wanted to avoid the fray, or he was just having too much fun listening, it was difficult to say.

Mario stepped aside, allowing Cole to enter the driver's seat. He took the seat opposite Cole, strapping on the seat belt.

"Where to now, boss?" Mario asked.

Before Cole could answer, Serena spoke up. *Am I grounded again, Cole? We haven't even had a chance to catch up.*

Fuming, Cole slammed the gearshift into first and rocketed out of the parking space, tires screeching, leaving a billow of smoke in his wake.

This time, both comrades laughed. Cole cursed again.

"Let's grab something to eat, and then I'm taking you back to my house. There is someone else I need to reconnect with," Cole said. A few minutes passed before Cole found a restaurant he liked. South Border Bar & Grill. He thought his friends might like some cooking more reminiscent of their part of the world. Maybe a couple of shots of tequila to calm the nerves. The food was good, the liquor better. The restaurant had a tropical feel, including a group of scantily clad, Hispanic waitresses who had taken a special interest in Cole's companions.

An hour later, Cole had to practically drag his mates out of the restaurant, promising they would return soon. That seemed to placate the men, and they all climbed into the Maserati. Serena quizzed the men all the way home. Cole dropped off his companions in front of his house. However, he did not join them, instead wishing them a good night before he drove away into the darkness.

"Serena, please dial Cassie Thomas." The phone rang five times before a woman answered. The sound of her voice temporarily stunned Cole, as more memories flashed back. The Australian accent, which had only become more pronounced during her time back in her homeland, brought with it a new sense of melancholy that swept over Cole like a crashing wave.

"Cassie?"

"Cole?"

"It really is you. I got your letter, but I wasn't sure if you had written it or if someone else was messing with me. It is so good to hear your voice. . . I can't even begin to tell you. How are you?" Cole asked, as if he had just discovered a long-lost friend he'd never expected seeing again.

"It's me, Cole, and I am so glad to hear your voice, too. I have missed you terribly. I've often wondered what you were doing, how things were going. . . and how Lindsay's absence was affecting you. Night after night, I lay alone in the bush, looking up at the stars, thinking. I never expected to be back here. I never expected to find you again. We live in such different worlds." Cassie pulled the phone away from her cheek, becoming emotional. "By the way, how is your attorney friend, Art Barkley, doing? Up to his usual shenanigans?" Cassie asked, attempting to lighten the mood.

"You might say that. You were only around Art for a short time, but you seem to know him pretty well," Cole replied.

"Before I left for Australia, I watched the news and read the papers, trying to keep track of the two of you. Those Swanson sisters are really something. Lindsay told me a bit about them when you were on the frigate. And now they're famous Ralph Lauren fashion models," Cassie said.

"I can't seem to get away from them. It's all Art's doing," Cole replied adamantly, as if he was being accused of something. "But they have been supportive. They've led a rather privileged life, and I think they were just bored. They accompanied us on our recent trip back, but again that was all Art's idea. I swear," Cole said.

"You don't need to apologize, Cole, really. They are beautiful women who run in the circles of your world. I understand. And speaking of privileged lives—"

Before Cassie could complete the sentence, Serena interrupted. *Cole is not like that any longer. He doesn't care about being rich. He's changed, so don't make him out to be something he's not!* Serena exclaimed protectively.

"And who might you be, miss, if I may ask?" Cassie asked haughtily.

I'm Serena, Cole's driver, um, his advisor, um, his car!

Cole rolled his eyes, thinking this was about to get ugly.

"His car? Oh, I remember now. You must be the cryptic voice of Cole's infamous Maserati. Lindsay told me all about you. Sounds like you and Cole are back on speaking terms, again." Cassie could not help herself and broke out laughing.

I beg your pardon! There's no reason to insult me, Serena said indignantly.

"Now, now, ladies. Let's all calm down. No need to be argumentative. We're all on the same team," Cole said, now the peacekeeper.

I'm on your side, Cole, no matter who this hussy from the outback thinks she is, Serena said.

"I think you're about to be grounded again, Serena. Just saying," Cassie replied, beginning to enjoy the encounter. Serena was everything Lindsay had said she was and more. Cassie recalled how Lindsay had mentioned she thought Serena was in love with Cole, if indeed a car could fall in love. And with all of the AI loaded into this supercar, maybe it could.

"I apologize, Serena. I know how much Cole favors you. It's an honor to meet you," Cassie said, attempting to defuse the situation.

Finally, some respect. I accept your apology, Ms. Thomas.

"Thank you, Serena, that was magnanimous of you," Cole said.

Serena snorted, but otherwise remained silent.

"So, back to our previous conversation, Cassie. Where are you staying? When can we meet?" Cole said.

"I'm staying at the Newporter Hotel, close to the marina. Do you know it?" Cassie said.

"Yes, I know exactly where it is. My yacht is anchored at the marina. . ." Cole hesitated, immediately wanting to take his statement back. Just another indication of *his* privileged life.

Do you still own that tugboat? I thought you donated it to that recent charitable auction, Serena said.

"What auction?" Cole whispered. "Cassie, I still own it. I'm not sure why Serena said that."

"She's just being protective. I get it," Cassie said.

Cole glanced at his watch. It was nearly ten in the evening. "You're probably pretty tired, but do you want to meet tonight, or would tomorrow morning be better?" Cole asked.

"It's not too late for me, if it's okay with you?" Cassie replied, her tone brightening.

"There's a quiet bar in the back corner of your hotel. It should be mostly deserted by now. We'll see you in twenty," Cole said. Serena snorted again.

As promised, the Maserati pulled up in front of the hotel twenty minutes later, stopping under the awning to the front entrance. The Newporter was one of those quaint but classy hotels that catered to higher-end clientele. Small, stylish, and with an impeccable reputation. Cassie was standing outside, waiting. She was determined to see this so-called supercar of Cole's and to personally say hello to Serena. Cole stepped out of the driver's side, running a hand through his thick, black hair, appearing like a celebrity under the diffused lighting. A valet attendant quickly approached.

"Welcome back, Mr. Hollingsworth. Nice to see you again. Will you be spending the night?"

Cassie watched from the shadows as Cole handed the young man some cash. He pointed to an empty spot, and the valet nodded. Cole closed the car door, and the Maserati drove itself to the parking space and turned off its lights, but it didn't quite blend in with the surroundings.

Cassie approached. The two eyed each other for a long moment, and the world seemed to time lapse in reverse again. She was even more beautiful than Cole remembered, as he'd been so enamored with Lindsay at the time. Cassie was tall, lean, and muscular, with thick brown hair naturally streaked with gold. Deeply tanned. High cheekbones that spoke of good breeding. Her smile was nearly as spellbinding as Lindsay's. After a moment, Cassie practically flew over, flinging her arms around Cole's neck and embracing him. Then, she started to cry.

Cole held on tightly, attempting to quell her pain. And in between them stood the image of Lindsay and all the memories they had shared. Alone in the stillness, they stood, joined together.

And then something happened neither one expected.

CHAPTER FIFTY-FIVE

A SHIMMERING LIGHT ENGULFED THE pair, surrounding them with the same feeling of love they both held for Lindsay. Breathless, they stood in a cocoon of what resembled shimmering angel's wings, protected for a moment against the cruelties of a harsh world.

Like a whisper riding on the breeze, Lindsay's voice resonated inside their heads. *Remember, we are only an ocean apart.*

But this time, she seemed to be speaking to them both. A moment later, the ethereal experience that bordered on the sublime faded away. The pair stood awkwardly, facing one another and still clinging to each other, as if a line had been crossed that should not have been traversed. They both loved Lindsay, but for different reasons. For a fleeting instant, their mutual love for her had fused Cole and Cassie together, as if an angel had passed on something indiscernible, joining the pair as one.

Cole cleared his throat, gesturing for Cassie to head inside. Cole led her to the corner bar, an intimate lounge that was dimly lit. Plush, burgundy chairs faced black granite tables. Fresh flowers and a short candle burned, giving off a mildly spicy fragrance. Cole held out a chair for the diver, and they sat facing one another. Cassie's deeply tanned face glowed in the candlelight.

For a moment, they simply stared at each other, a hint of the previous awkwardness still lingering. The silence was broken by the cocktail waitress approaching. Dressed in an impeccable white blouse, black vest, and tight black pants, she smiled genuinely at the pair.

"Nice to see you, Mr. Hollingsworth. Welcome back to the Newporter. We've missed you," she said.

Cole smiled, a bit embarrassed, and nodded. "It's nice to see you, too, Carla. I'd like to introduce you to my close friend, Cassie Thomas. Cassie, this is Carla."

The two women forced a smile at each other. Cassie extended her hand. Carla took it but appeared surprised it had been offered.

"Nice to meet you, Ms. Thomas," Carla said.

"It's my pleasure, Carla. Any friend of Cole's is a friend of mine," Cassie replied, her strong accent temporarily distracting the waitress while adding a measure of intrigue to the situation.

"What can I offer you two?" She handed them a pair of menus featuring house specialty after dinner drinks and liqueurs.

Cassie didn't bother to look. "Do you offer Foster's beer?"

"Yes, we do. And Cole, what sounds good to you?" Carla tilted her head in his direction. "Your usual scotch on the rocks?"

"No thanks, I'm off the hard stuff. I'd like a glass of merlot. Something from California. Surprise me."

Carla padded away. Cole turned his gaze back to Cassie only to find her staring at him with an inquiring expression, as if to say, *You and this woman have a connection, don't you?*

Cole immediately caught her drift. He'd seen that look before on many of the women he'd dated in the past. Always suspicious, always wanting to know if Cole had a past with the multitude of women he knew. Cole was so well-known in Newport that it was difficult for him to go anywhere and not be recognized. The fact that the majority of people recognizing him just happened to be beautiful women might have been the key.

"It's not what you think, Cassie. I've been here a lot since it's close to the marina. Been here with coworkers, business associates, friends, and. . ."

"And women? It's really okay, Cole. Lindsay struggled a bit with the same thing, but then, you and Lindsay were in love. You and I are just friends, right?" Cassie said, yet her alluring gaze suggested things may be changing.

"You're right, we are friends, and very good friends at that. I'm not proud of my past, Cassie. I took advantage of women. But I can honestly say those wild and woolly days are behind me." Cole smiled contritely.

"We've all changed, Cole. We have Lindsay to thank for that. God, I still miss her so. What I'd give to see her one more time. . ." Cassie's voice trailed off, a melancholy expression crossing her face.

Instead of responding immediately with comforting words, Cole gazed at this woman curiously, pondering the events that had led them back to each other. She was still a relative stranger, but at the same time, she had begun to feel like a sister to him. He trusted her explicitly. He respected her even more. *Should I tell her the truth or is it too early for that?* Cole wondered.

"Be careful what you wish for, Cassie, you just may get it," Cole said, immediately regretting uttering those words.

Cassie's eyes widened. "What did you say?"

"I was—"

Fortunately for Cole, Carla returned just then with their drinks. She placed the chilled glass of Foster's in front of Cassie. Then she uncorked a bottle of Duckhorn Vineyards Estate Grown Napa Valley Merlot and poured Cole a taste. Cole lifted the glass to his nose, then nodded without tasting it. She poured the deep-burgundy wine into the exquisite, crystal wine glass.

"Enjoy!" Carla said, then she disappeared into the backdrop, leaving the couple to contemplate Cole's statement—a statement that was beginning to cause Cassie a great deal of distress.

"Did you just say what I think you said?" Cassie implored, her voice filled with trepidation.

The cat was out of the bag now. Cole had little choice but to be honest with her if he wanted her trust and if he wanted her to be by his side while he faced the greatest challenge of his life. Although he had made the decision to live the mortal life, deep inside, he believed he still possessed a path to immortality.

"I wasn't quite prepared to tell you yet, but somehow it just sort of slipped out. I guess because it's you sitting there. If I had been having this conversation with anyone else but Lindsay's closest and most trusted friend, I would never have mentioned it." Cole paused to gather his thoughts.

Cassie looked on in shock as the magnitude of what Cole's words meant began to take root. Speechless, she averted her gaze from Cole's, staring off into space in what could only be a state of utter astonishment.

Cole took a long pull of his wine, waiting for Cassie to come back to earth. She had momentarily left it, he was sure.

"So, Cole, when did you last see Lindsay?" Cassie asked bluntly. Gone was the affable Australian who had seemed so glad to reconnect with Cole. She was turning hostile, like Cole was hiding a secret so insidious he could not be forgiven. It didn't matter that Cole hadn't known where Cassie had been these past six months, because Art could have found out for him if he had wanted to see Cassie again. To tell her the truth.

"I'm sorry, but Lindsay and our reconnection just happened two days ago. I'm still reeling from the experience. For a while, I thought it might have been a dream, like you described in your letter. But with the recent devastation on the island, I knew it was real," Cole said.

"Okay, Cole, I forgive you. . . and I understand, I think. Please tell me what actually happened. How did she appear to you and where?" Cassie hesitated. "I don't know, it just seems impossible—but just about everything else we've recently experienced feels the same."

"I know, it is surreal." Cole replied. "I'm not quite sure where to begin, but I'll do my best to describe it to you."

What followed held Cassie in rapt fascination well into the early hours of morning. Sometime during the night, the bar had closed, but Cole had been allowed to stay because of who he was. He told Cassie everything, from the time he and Art arrived in Isabella, to the discovery of the mysterious box at

the Cantina de la Noche and what it had revealed. He described Art's murder, the shot that had been intended for him. He described his two climbs up
the mountainside, what happened when he met the fire angel, and Gamer's
near-death experience. He told her how he believed he had experienced his
own death before being resurrected by Lindsay. Lindsay, the angel who
would remain in that state forever. Next, he told Cassie about being inside
the volcano and what he had seen there. And finally, he told her about the
choice he was given between living a mortal life or one of immortality and
what his decision had been.

Cassie remained silent throughout the entire explanation, taking in one
improbable event after the other, each one more implausible than the one
before it.

They had spent the night together talking, while Cole poured out his
soul to the Aussie. Daylight arrived, and if it hadn't been for the servers
who worked the early shifts, neither Cassie nor Cole would have noticed.

Exhausted, Cole glanced at his watch, stunned to see it was 6:20 a.m. He
flashed back to the all-night talks he and Lindsay had shared. Cole smiled
ruefully at Cassie, those memories now bringing mostly pain.

Cassie rose, walked around the table, and sat in Cole's lap. She wrapped
her arms around the billionaire, like Lindsay had done so many times, and
whispered something in his ear that seemed to sooth him. Cole closed his
eyes and drifted away to another place, while Cassie continued holding him.

CHAPTER FIFTY-SIX

"SO, WHAT DO YOU say to some breakfast? There's a nice bistro just down the street. Good pastries, even better coffee," Cole said.

Cassie released Cole. "That sounds great. I'm famished. Let's get the hell out of here," she replied enthusiastically.

The pair walked arm in arm down the street, which was just coming to life. Restaurants were opening. Shopkeepers were cleaning off the sidewalks, preparing for a day of business. The sun had risen, revealing a beautiful Rhode Island morning. A salt-tinged sea breeze gently stirred the many leaves that had fallen to the ground during the night, rustling the ones still attached to trees.

They ordered breakfast and sipped espresso, saying little to each other. What was left to say after a full night of talking? Only questions remained, although Cassie was unsure of what questions to ask. Cole was hesitant to say more. The pair seemed content to eat, occasionally stealing a glance at one another. Each time Cole gazed at Cassie, she blushed, like a schoolgirl on a first date, captivated by the boy facing her, fidgeting with her food.

"Don't you like your breakfast?" Cole asked. "We can order something else, if you'd like."

"No, the food is fine, really. I just can't get Lindsay and what you said out of my mind."

"You need to eat, Cassie. Let's finish up, and we can drive over to my house. I don't know about you, but I'm beat. A nap sounds pretty good to me."

"Sounds like a plan," Cassie said, and she quickly devoured the rest of the omelet on her plate. Emptying her cup of coffee, she rose, yawned, and stretched, revealing an area of her midsection—muscled, tan, with an emerald-shaped jewel the color of her eyes embedded in her belly button.

Cole didn't recall seeing that before, on those times she'd worn a two-piece bathing suit. While on the frigate, she had mostly been dressed in wetsuits or casual pants and tops.

Cassie noticed Cole staring at her stomach and smiled. "Just a little something I had done while in Australia. It was either this or a tattoo of a submersible," she laughed.

"Good choice, I'd say." Cole paid the check, and the pair left to rejoin Serena. Cole wasn't looking forward to what she had to say about being left alone all night in a parking lot. It was not something she was accustomed to experiencing. Cole warned Cassie they may be receiving an earful when they entered the car. Cassie replied she was up to the task. No automobile, even one costing over two million dollars, was going to intimidate her.

Serena started in on Cole the moment he entered. Cassie remained silent until Cole settled Serena down, at least enough for the drive home to be bearable.

They reached Cole's house, and the far garage door automatically opened. Cole guided the Maserati into its slot and wished Serena a pleasant day. Cassie did likewise. Serena said nothing.

Once inside, they headed into the main living room area and were greeted by Mario, Gamer, and the twins. Cole had called them on the drive home and asked the women to come over to meet Cassie. Art was also in attendance, but he seemed preoccupied, viewing something out of Cole's Meade MAX telescope. Only Bill and Frank were absent.

"Everybody, this is Cassie Thomas, Lindsay's closet friend and a fellow diver who worked at the Gerace Institute in San Salvador. She commanded the frigate while Lindsay and I searched for my parents," Cole said.

Art turned abruptly at the sound of her name. "Well, well, Ms. Thomas, what a surprise! I thought you were still hiding out in Australia. It is great to see you. Welcome to Cole's humble abode." Art strolled over and hugged the diver. "Really, it is so nice to see you. I'm assuming things have returned to normal?" Art whispered.

Cassie embraced the attorney, thanking him again for his help with her disappearance. She pulled back. "I wish I could say everything is normal, but I think you know that's not true. And that's the reason I'm here."

"Cole told you. . . everything?" Art asked in a hushed voice. Cassie nodded.

"Cassie, I'd like to introduce you to Sydney and Shelby Swanson. You never actually met them, but they've been with us all the way," Cole said.

The women exchanged pleasantries. The twins gave her a good once-over, appearing a bit astonished by the sheer beauty of the Aussie. They had heard she was a world-class scuba diver and oceanographer but had no idea she possessed high-fashion model looks. Shelby glanced over at Cole only to catch him staring at Cassie as though mesmerized by her presence. Now this was interesting.

Next, Cole introduced Cassie to his newest associates, Gamer and Mario, describing what they had done for him in Puerto Rico and on Hollingsworth Island, leaving out the assassin part. That would remain secret—or perhaps surface on its own in the coming days and weeks.

"Nice to meet you, Ms. Thomas," Gamer said. Mario echoed Gamer's statement, and the three shook hands.

"Thank you both for helping Cole. He told me about you last night and how much he values your friendship."

Both men bowed their heads in response. At least they weren't wearing machetes or guns, appearing somewhat normal, if men like them could do so. It was a challenge to camouflage the gritty toughness they wore like armor, the deep lines cut into their faces, the steely looks of determination in their eyes from years of clandestine operations facing danger. Innocence that had been washed away so many years ago.

For a long moment, everyone stood in anticipation, awaiting Cole's instructions, until the silence became awkward. Cole cleared his throat.

"Thank you all for being here. What I'm about to say must remain just between us. No one else can know. We've got a big problem with Bill Gaines, the chairman of the board, who will not give up his hold on Hollingsworth Island. He has contacts in Puerto Rico and is continuing to build a network down there for his own personal interests. Andres Almquist, one of the primary scientists on our research team, is a paid informant for him. He has others, including some pretty shady characters." Cole paused to let this information sink in to the few who didn't already know.

Satisfied that no questions would be forthcoming about Gaines, Cole continued.

"Art and I met with him yesterday in an effort to set the record straight, but it was obvious to me that he is not about to give in, even though I gave him a direct order." Cole turned to Art for confirmation. Art nodded his agreement.

"We'll assign someone within the company to keep an eye on him after we leave. I'm thinking about Grace Foster, my long-time executive assistant. She is completely trustworthy and seems to get along with Gaines okay. He'll hesitate to cross her because of me. We have someone keeping an eye on Almquist. He's a, um, an associate of Mario's and very reliable."

"Hold on, Cole. Did you just say we're about to leave again? We just got back," Art said brusquely.

"I was about to get to that. Cassie's appearance has. . . well, it has changed things. I can't go into all of the details now, but trust me, it's important." Cole said, not revealing his plans and what he had learned from Lindsay in a dream. Cole turned to the twins. "You don't need to come with us. In fact, it may be better for you to remain here. If too many people leave, it might make Gaines even more suspicious."

Sydney and Shelby turned away, speaking to each other in hushed tones. For a moment, they seemed indecisive. Then they turned back toward Cole, and Shelby spoke for both of them.

"We agree with you, Cole. We would like to stay home, but if something comes up that you feel we might be of assistance with, all you need to do is contact us and we'll be there."

"Thank you, both. It's great to know you are there for us," Cole said.

Art looked unhappy, but there was little he could do about it.

"Art?" Cole questioned, unsure of what his friend's response might be.

Art turned and strode back toward the wall of glass, peering out to the ocean beyond. He didn't want this, at least not so soon. Even though he was Cole's closest friend, he suddenly felt like an outsider. Cole had Gamer, Mario, and now Cassie, along with Rico, the blade-wielding assassin watching over Almquist. What could Art possibly add? He wasn't licensed to practice law in that part of the world. He certainly wasn't the strong-armed type. Then it occurred to him that he still held the title of president at Hollingsworth Enterprises, at least in name. Maybe he would be the best person to keep an eye on Gaines. If he stayed in Newport, that might send a less threatening message to the chairman. The decision was made.

Art turned to face Cole, his expression resolute. "Not this time, bro."

Art took a tentative first step, then picked up his pace, walking toward the front door, stopping only for a second to pat Cole on the shoulder. "I'll call you later," he said, leaving the entire room in stunned silence as he disappeared out the door.

CHAPTER FIFTY-SEVEN

AFTER THE SHOCK OF Art's sudden exit had subsided, the twins said their goodbyes, leaving a blindsided Cole to address the remaining people in the room.

"I respect Art's decision. He may yet change his mind, but for now, we should not count on that. But I know Art; he will be at the ready if we need him. He will not abandon us." Cole paused, as though Art's decision had caused him great pain.

"Cassie and I were up all night and are both extremely tired. We need to catch some sleep. I'll send out a text later this afternoon for our next meeting, when we can begin planning our trip. Gamer, Mario, my driver is available to you, or you're welcome to stay here. Until then," Cole said, then he walked toward the elevator to the upper levels. A moment later, Cassie left the room as well.

Cole waited outside the elevator on the third-floor landing until Cassie arrived. "My bedroom is on the far right. There is a nice guest room on the left with its own bathroom. You'll find a robe in the closet. The other bedrooms are on the second floor. Sleep well," Cole said, then walked away. Cassie stared after him until he was no longer visible.

Cassie entered the guest room and did an immediate double take. It was beautifully decorated, with expensive, original art hanging on the walls, and a large window overlooking the cliff and ocean beyond. A fireplace occupied one corner, and a sitting area with a couch and two chairs faced it on the right. The room looked like a luxury suite in a resort hotel. A door led to a large bathroom containing double sinks, a separate shower, bathtub, and a wet bar. She could only imagine what Cole's master suite looked like. How many women had succumbed to the bachelor's charms on this floor? She laughed at the thought.

Cassie placed the robe on the edge of the bed, stripping down to her panties, and entered the bathroom. A hot bath seemed in order. She turned on the double faucets and eyed the bath products lined up on a glass shelf. Mineral salts, tangerine bubble bath, and a variety of aromatherapy products and candles. She lit a vanilla-scented candle and poured in a couple of ounces of the bubble bath, watching as the tub filled and bubbles formed on the water's surface. Sliding off her last garment of clothing, she stepped into the bath and slipped beneath the warm water. The soothing sensation was immediate. For twenty minutes, she luxuriated in the warmth and solitude of the dimly lit room, the candle casting shadows on the walls as it flickered, reminding her of shadows cast in the ocean.

She rose and dried herself. Passing through to the bedroom, she slipped in between the silk sheets, like a hand into a velvet glove. The blinds on the large, plate glass window suddenly closed on their own, casting the room into dark shadows. New age music played softly in the background. Moments later, she was fast asleep.

In the room down the hall, Cole wasn't so fortunate. He needed a stiff drink to relax, as wild thoughts of Lindsay the angel, swept through his mind. Cassie's image would suddenly appear, blurring the scene, as Cole struggled to find the sleep he so desperately needed. Finally, exhaustion overcame him, and he drifted off. Time passed slowly, and the sun rose gradually in the sky. Morning faded to afternoon. Nothing stirred while they slept.

Hours later, a knock on Cole's door awakened him. The room was dark and the visibility low. A figure appeared to be approaching—or was this another dream?

"Cole, are you awake? I can't sleep. Can I lie down beside you?" Cassie asked.

Still half-asleep, Cole was confused at first. He shook his head, attempting to regain his bearings. For a moment, he had no idea where he was. He felt his bed shift slightly as Cassie sat beside him. She was wearing the robe.

"Cassie, I don't think this is a good idea. I'm sorry, but I'm just not ready for anything like this. I hope you understand."

"Of course, I understand. . . and it's not what you're thinking. I've been alone for so long, I just wanted to feel a body next to me, to have some sort of human contact. That is, if it's okay with you. Then we can sleep." The yearning in Cassie's voice was undeniable.

Cole didn't have the heart to say no. He lifted up the bedspread, welcoming the diver into his bed. The robe slipped to the floor, and in the darkness, Cassie took her place next to him, wrapping her right arm around Cole's bare chest. He felt warm to the touch and protective. At first Cole hadn't noticed, but they were skin to skin. He felt her firm breasts against his back, and something stirred inside him.

True to her word, she made no further advances, and the pair fell back to sleep for the remainder of the afternoon. Sometime during their slumber, their positions had changed, and when they awoke, Cole was holding her in his arms, facing the opposite direction.

"Cassie?" Cole exclaimed, at first failing to recall her intrusion into his bed. Cassie stretched and yawned, totally unashamed by their nakedness together. Cole wasn't so calm and tried to cover up while endeavoring to look the other way as she sat up in bed, smoothing out her long, luxuriant hair.

Cassie gazed back at Cole, watching as he tried to cover up. She smiled fetchingly and laughed. "Oh, Cole, don't be so modest. One would think you'd never seen a woman in the buff before. And we both know that isn't true!"

"Well, no, of course not, but it's you. . . I mean. . . how did you get here?" Cole was obviously flustered.

"Don't you remember when I asked to lie beside you so I could go back to sleep? You seemed okay with it then."

Cole was fighting to keep his eyes locked onto Cassie's face but wasn't having much success. It had been a long time after all, and here was this incredibly sexy woman sitting naked in his bed.

Cassie raised Cole's sheets and slid in next to him, rolling him over onto his back. "It's okay, Cole. We're just two healthy adults in need of each other. It's basic biology. Nothing to be ashamed of." She lowered her face to his, softly kissing him on the mouth.

Cole hesitated, allowing her touch to captivate him, but then quickly pushed her away. "Cassie, no, this isn't right. I'm sorry, I just can't. I'm still in love with Lindsay."

"I know. You will always love her. But unless you choose the path to immortality, providing that's even possible, you will never be with her again. The two of you cannot coexist in alternate realities. Now that we have reconnected, I see more clearly why Lindsay sent me to find you. I believe she wants us to be together. There is really no other reasonable explanation."

Cole was stunned by Cassie's directness, but even though he didn't want to admit it, somehow it began to make sense. There was no denying his attraction to Cassie. It had been immediate when he spotted her standing in front of the Newporter Hotel. When they embraced, something had passed between them, and Lindsay had spoken to them both. It felt like he was seeing Cassie for the first time, and he was captivated by her. He suddenly realized there was no one else he wanted by his side as he faced a future so unpredictable, it defied description.

Cassie's eyes shown like starlight, her lips moist like dew on a morning flower, opening up to him as if rose petals were blossoming. He drew her close again and, just before he kissed her, her smile melted his heart. He was lost in her embrace. She pressed her body firmly down on his, feeling his erection growing. She slid his boxer shorts down his legs, kissing his thighs and moving slowly back up to his mouth. Their kisses were long and deep. Finally, she guided him inside of her, and they moved rhythmically to a form of music that only they understood. With each thrust, waves of euphoria swept through Cassie's body, like surf crashing on the shoreline. Their breath came quick and labored, as if staying connected was the only way they could become whole again. With final thrusts and shuddering ecstasy, they climaxed together, before lying back on the bed, breathless.

Cole clung to Cassie as if letting her go would be the end of him. Cassie restricted her pelvis muscles, keeping him inside of her. For the rest of the afternoon, they lay together, joined, in an eternal embrace.

Suddenly, Cassie bit Cole's ear, like a lioness might do to her mate.

"Ouch!" Cole exclaimed, awakening from their dreamlike state. "What did you do that for?"

"Just a little love bite, my dear," Cassie chortled. "I think we need to get up and get dressed. In case you've forgotten, you promised to text the others with your plans. It's getting dark outside."

"My plans have changed," Cole said.

"How so?" Cassie replied.

"We're staying in bed for the next week. Then we'll figure out what to do," Cole said, almost sounding serious.

"You think you can handle that? I'm in a lot better shape than you are. You may not be able to survive the Aussie stranglehold," Cassie said, laughing seductively.

"What was that we just went through? That felt like a stranglehold to me."

"Cole, that was just foreplay. You haven't seen the best of me yet. Not by a long shot."

"If that was foreplay, I'm a dead man!"

"Enter at your own risk, no pun intended." Cassie broke out laughing, adding, "Oh, I see you've already done that."

Cole flipped Cassie onto her back, and soon the pair was lost again in their lovemaking, as if nothing else in the world mattered.

CHAPTER FIFTY-EIGHT

I T WASN'T UNTIL EIGHT in the evening that Cole sent out the texts he had promised earlier. He copied Art Barkley, just in case.

We leave in two days. We're headed back to Isabella. My executive assistant has made all the arrangements. We'll fly out of Green Airport on the Falcon. Pack lightly, we can get what we need while there. Meet at my house at 6:30 a.m. Friday morning, and we'll head out at 7:00 a.m. More to come later. Enjoy your time in Newport, it could be rough going after that. - Cole

The cryptic message was simple, to the point, and ominous. These same words portrayed Cole more and more, as his mission in life seemed to change with each passing day. His companions were becoming accustomed to his evolving moods, yet it didn't make things easier.

Cassie was in the kitchen, attempting to put some sort of acceptable meal together. They hadn't eaten since breakfast, and the workout that followed had drained a good deal of energy from them both.

Cole was in the shower, allowing the double-spray heads to rain down pulsating streams of hot water, relaxing his back muscles. The shower stall was large, beautifully tiled, and obviously built for more than one person. Cole's cell phone buzzed. Turning the spigots off, Cole dried quickly and reached for his phone. A text from Cassie.

He opened it and was greeted with a photo of a steaming bowl of wide noodle pasta, mixed with diced tomatoes, what looked to be sliced zucchini, basil leaves, and large, grilled gulf prawns. Sitting next to the bowl was a large hunk of parmesan cheese, a crusty French baguette, and a glass of white wine. It could have been a photo from one of Newport's Michelin-starred seafood restaurants. Cole needed little coaxing and, instead of taking the time to dress, donned a thick, wool robe before heading down to the first level of the house. On the way down, he pictured Cassie in his bed, the time they spent together in the heat of passion. And now this woman could cook! Then he remembered the wonderful food she and Ryan had prepared while on the *USS Truett*, the frigate that had been his temporary home while he and Lindsay searched for his dead parents. A shot of guilt gripped him as the thought of Lindsay flashed through his mind. The mortal Lindsay, the woman he would never again see or touch.

It should have been no surprise—the cooking, that is. *What other abilities does Cassie possess?* Cole wondered, as the elevator stopped and the doors swished open.

Cassie was standing casually next to the countertop where the food had been placed, sipping a glass of wine. She was dressed in tight, forest green slacks and a loosely fitting ivory, silk top that appeared semi-transparent, her long, luxuriant hair tousled and falling down her shoulders. All of the sudden, food seemed secondary.

Cassie looked up, catching Cole standing solitary and gazing at her, like he was admiring a rare portrait in an elite art gallery. The look on his face gave him away immediately, like a little boy with his hand in the proverbial cookie jar—awaiting either a scolding from his mother or a reward for a job well done. She smiled alluringly back at him, allowing their gaze to linger. Her cheeks turned a pale shade of pink, as though she was embarrassed by the attention.

Is her blushing real or contrived? Cole mused. He hoped it was real. It meant she was modest and genuine and, in a sense, still possessed a degree of innocence, reluctant to accept her place beside Cole, where Lindsay should have been.

Cole approached, their eyes still locked intently, until he was standing inches away. She cocked her head as if to ask a question but instead kissed him softly on the lips, and the world seemed to slip away again.

Cassie broke their embrace, although it took some effort. "Cole, I think we need to eat before the food gets cold."

Cole released her, but he continued staring at this amazing woman, the only person who had made him feel hope since losing Lindsay in the mountain. She handed him the wine, and they sat on the high chairs and began to devour the food.

The meal was exquisite, and Cole complimented her over and over. She smiled and blushed again. Their hunger satisfied, the conversation turned to Hollingsworth Island and the upcoming trip. She was as confused as the others as to what Cole was planning, but she also knew the truth about Lindsay—a truth that had not been fully revealed to the other companions.

Cole struggled to communicate exactly what those plans were, or what he expected to find upon their return. He only knew that they would be entering the mountain, if indeed that was still possible. He needed to learn more and to understand the mysterious messages the mountain was attempting to communicate—as if the mountain actually could communicate. Something he still did not understand. It had to be Lindsay's doing. And just what was her plan? Intuitively, Cole believed it was monumental, with the potential to change the natural world she so loved. But, in the process, how would her plan affect the human race? Too many questions remained unanswered, and Cole was determined to find the answers, even if it was the last thing he would ever do. Only then could he continue to make a difference.

The couple moved to the living room, taking seats in the white leather chairs facing the darkening ocean roiling beyond the glass façade. The first evening stars were sparkling in the distance, like jewels spun into a majestic tapestry spanning the heavens.

A shooting star suddenly flashed across the night sky, illuminating the darkness. Cassie gasped. The phenomenon never ceased to thrill her, harkening back to her childhood days when her mother would tell her they were really star-crossed lovers searching for each other across the universe until they could become connected again. And when that happened, a new sun was formed, giving birth to planets as if they were its children. It was a fairytale only a child could believe in, but one that Cassie somehow carried with her to this day. She turned to look at Cole, who appeared starstruck himself as he gazed upward, lost in deep thought. *Could Cole be my star-crossed lover?* Cassie wondered. Only time would tell. But in the presence of angels, perhaps anything was possible.

They continued to sit silently as the night grew darker and the silence became oppressive, each wrapped up in their own troubled thoughts of what was yet to come. Finally, Cassie rose and offered her hand to Cole, as if to say, *enough for one night, it's time to find sleep again.*

Cole smiled but refused her invitation. He needed time alone. It was difficult to think clearly with Cassie so close. She was beginning to color his thoughts. It wasn't a bad thing, but he could not allow himself to become overly distracted. Something inside him said this moment in time was too important. This might be the defining point in his life—a life thus far squandered away by excessive wealth without repercussions.

"I'll be up later," Cole said, returning to his musings. Or was it brooding? Cassie was uncertain which.

Cole was hard to read. When they were all together on the *Truett*, Cassie's role was one of support, and she'd been far secondary to Lindsay. At times, she'd felt that Cole had barely noticed her. She had Ryan, and Cole had Lindsay, the apparent love of his life. But things had changed, hadn't they? She climbed the stairs and entered the guestroom. She would let Cole make the decision to join her or to be alone. There was no need to pressure him.

Many hours later, as the sun broke the darkness with its glorious light, emerging out of the ocean to the east, Cassie awoke. She had slept well. Sleep she desperately needed. She rolled over to touch Cole only to find her bed empty. For a split second, her heart was empty, too. He had not come to find her—or maybe he had but then left for the solitude of his own space.

Wrapping a robe around herself, she glanced at the clock on the far wall—9:20 a.m. She had slept for almost eleven hours. As she paced the room, indecision overtook her. Should she go to Cole's room? Should she just go downstairs in search of coffee and casually run into him? Seesawing back and forth, she finally found resolve. It wasn't like they were married or even a couple. So much had happened in the last thirty-six hours, it had basically overwhelmed her. Then the terrible thought that she was merely Cole's latest conquest crept in. Cole was, after all, a master of seduction. But he had been so believable, and she had fallen for it hook, line, and sinker. She shuddered at the thought. It was obvious. Cole hadn't had good sex in a long time. Hadn't she suggested in the middle of the night that they were just two healthy adults with normal needs—and he had acted on that information.

"Damn it!" she cursed. She was allowing herself to become too vulnerable to him. Just like Lindsay had confessed to her about her feelings for Cole. What hypnotic-like control did Cole possess that made women fall into his bed? It couldn't have anything to do with his vast wealth, his one-of-a-kind house, over-the-top sports cars, his Hollywood good looks. What woman would fall for that? Had she too been a victim of the charms he wielded in a most surreptitious manner? The bastard!

Cassie tossed the robe on the bed and quickly dressed, intent on confronting the playboy that was the real Cole. The man who wore many masks. It was time to peel them all away.

She didn't bother knocking on his bedroom door, forcing herself inside, only to be shocked. The bed was made, and nothing was out of place. It was as if no one had slept there during the night. Next, she practically sprinted down the two flights of stairs to the kitchen. It was empty as well. She peeked into the living room, with the same result. Where the hell was Cole?

The scent of freshly brewed coffee wafting out of the kitchen lured her back. Next to the coffee machine, a canister of coffee was being kept warm in a thermos. A plate of fresh fruit and pastries lay nearby, along with a handwritten note.

She picked it up, expecting a hastily contrived excuse that was little more than a lie.

Dearest Cassie,

I apologize that my penmanship is a sorry example of cursive, especially compared to yours. I hope you will forgive me. I never took the necessary time in school to learn it properly. You'll probably understand. My interests lay elsewhere. I am so sorry about last night. I wanted to be with you, but I just needed some space, and I hope you can understand that as well. I left for the office to tie up some loose ends and to pay a visit to Bill Gaines. I should be done around 1:00. What do you say to some lunch? I reserved a table at the marina restaurant for 1:30. Great views of the ocean and the pretty sail boats. I'm thinking you might like that? It's very relaxing. And while you are gazing out on the ocean, I can stare at you. I owe you a good meal after the feast you prepared for us last night. My driver can pick you up, or if you're feeling especially adventurous today, you might be able to convince Serena to bring you.

Hope to see you then?

Cole

Cassie's heart melted, as she once again fell under Cole's spell. This was either the best attempt at an apology she'd seen or the biggest load of BS a man had ever delivered to her. After a moment of indecision, she chose the former, and her heart immediately flooded with elation. Cole really did care, and at this time in her life, that was mostly what mattered. Her mind was made up. She would follow him on his journey, to the end, no matter the cost. She filled a mug with hot coffee and headed outside to the deck. The ocean shimmered all the way to the horizon, as the sun arced higher in the midmorning sky. Her hair fluttered in the strong salt breeze gusting off the ocean.

Australia no longer called to her. Cassie Thomas was exactly where she needed to be.

CHAPTER FIFTY-NINE

AGAINST HER BETTER JUDGEMENT, Cassie practically flung herself at Cole when he entered the restaurant. She didn't care what other people thought, even after noticing a number of people staring at her unexpected greeting. Just about everyone inside knew or recognized Cole. If she was in this thing with Cole, she was all the way in. No regrets.

Cole appeared somewhat startled but didn't hesitate to hug her back, and then he walked hand in hand with her as the maitre d' led them to a table for two tucked in the corner and facing the bay. It was a glorious day; the sail boats were out in mass. Apparently, a lot of people in Newport didn't work on Thursdays.

Cassie beamed as she stared at Cole in anticipation of news from the office.

Cole looked back curiously, confused and amused by Cassie's reaction upon seeing him. "So, what's up? That was quite the greeting, if I do say so. You have something to tell me?" Cole asked.

"Nothing in particular. Just happy to see you, I guess. And thanks for the note."

"Of course. I didn't want to wake you. I was up early, and I checked on you, but you looked dead to the world. And, I must say, pretty comfy, all tucked into the covers—and cute, too."

"Cute? I didn't think that word existed in your vocabulary, at least where women are concerned. Puppies, yes. Maybe even little children. But women?" Cassie let out a snort of laughter, as if there was no way the great Cole Hollingsworth could be guilty of such a portrayal.

"Hey, give me a break. I'm not that callous. . . am I?" Cole hesitated as he contemplated Cassie's statement—or was it an indictment?

Just as Cassie was about to reply, the waiter arrived and offered menus. "Good afternoon, Mr. Hollingsworth, and to you, Miss. Will there be anything required from the bar?"

Cassie ordered a Foster's and Cole a glass of chardonnay. The efficient waiter turned as if he was part of a castle guard, spinning on one foot and walking stiffly away.

"He's from England, a little on the formal side," Cole said matter-of-factly, as if it was of no consequence.

"Do you know everyone in Newport?" Cassie asked, the debate about the word *cute* forgotten. Just as well. She hadn't come here today to challenge Cole.

"No, I don't know everyone—far from it. One of the major reasons is my father. He was so well-known here, almost a legend, you might say. He also donated a great deal of money to rebuild this place. It was antiquated and falling out of favor with the well-to-do locals, so he came to its rescue. Things like that aren't easily forgotten."

"No, I don't suppose they are. I can only imagine what it was like for you growing up in such a wealthy and prominent family, especially as an only son," Cassie said wistfully.

"It had its ups and downs. There were definitely benefits, but at the same time, it could be tough. Hard to know who your true friends really were, or who was just after the money. My life did open a lot of doors, but many of those doors weren't especially nice." Cole hesitated, a remorseful expression crossing his face. "But it's the life you're dealt, and in the end, it's what you choose to do with it that matters."

This was the correct answer, of course, but did he really mean it? Cassie gazed deeply into Cole's eyes, searching for a sign of humility. This was the one area she was still unsure about. She wanted so much for it to be there. She had glimpsed it when he was with Lindsay, at least toward the end. But would it be there for her?

Their drinks arrived, along with mineral water and a selection of artisan breads. Cole thanked the server. "Please give us a few minutes, then we'll order."

The waiter clicked his heels together, nodded, and stepped away to attend to other guests.

Cassie suppressed a laugh. Cole's eyebrows rose. "What's so funny," he asked.

"You don't even know, do you?" Cassie replied.

"Don't know what?" Cole asked, with a hint of irritability in his voice.

"This. . . all of this. Waiters imported from England. Pretty faces everywhere. Service that borders on royal treatment. The affluence of it all. It just washes off of you like water on a duck. You're oblivious to it. This is your world, and I get that, but the rest of us live in. . . well, we live in other worlds, that's all. I grew up in an economically challenged home, but with parents and a sister who loved me and sacrificed so much for me so I could follow my dreams to become an oceanographer and deep-sea diver. I didn't have money, but I turned out okay, didn't I?" The pleading in Cassie's eyes was undeniable.

Stunned by Cassie's remarks, Cole had no comeback and was instantly rendered speechless. Was this Cassie or Lindsay speaking to him? Or was Lindsay speaking through her most trusted friend, controlling her every thought? All of the sudden, he was transported back to the *Truett*, where the threesome of Lindsay, Cassie, and Ryan deconstructed the billionaire until he was stripped of his pride. Lindsay had forced Cole to face the question of faith and his lack of it, his belief that God didn't exist. It had been the low point of their journey together, perhaps the low point of his entire life. Yet, he had somehow survived it, seeing himself for what he truly was—broken, but with the ability to start fresh. And then Lindsay was taken from him and he was no longer the same man.

Had he forgotten all of that in the aftermath of his desperation? Had it vanished as suddenly as the only woman he had ever loved? It was all coming back, pulling Cole into suffocating darkness. He felt like he was inside the submersible again, over five miles underwater in a cavern so dark, there could be no salvation.

The couple stared at each other. Cassie shrunk back in her chair. She had not intended their time together to be a debate. She didn't even know why she had said those things, only that they came out of their own volition. Moisture filled her eyes, and she desperately wanted to turn back the clock.

Cole stood shakily, staring at Cassie with deadened eyes. "Excuse me, please. I need some fresh air." He walked toward the nearest exit and, a moment later, disappeared, leaving Cassie sitting alone, tears streaming down her cheeks.

She had challenged him, after all. She couldn't help herself. Not unlike Lindsay, she had fallen hard for this man, but the wealth, the privilege, stood between them like an impenetrable wall. How could a little-known girl from halfway around the world change a man like Cole Hollingsworth? Was it even possible?

Some time passed—Cassie had no idea how much—before she rose to find Cole. Once outside, she scanned the deck to her right and left. Nothing. Looking down to the lower deck in front of the pier, Cole was not there either. Had he left the premises? She steadied herself on the railing, staring out to sea as if looking at something only she could see.

Her heart felt as empty as the distant horizon.

CHAPTER SIXTY

COLE WANDERED OFF TO a deserted area of beach a few hundred yards off the beaten path to reflect on the things Cassie had said, or perhaps had accused him of. That seemed closer to the truth. He stared out at the pounding surf, seeing nothing in particular. Cassie was different than Lindsay in many ways, and yet, her message was the same. He recalled the unabashed manner in which she had spoken to him before his final, critical dive, when Cole was getting ready to leave the *Truett* and everyone else aboard. He'd had enough after finding out that Lindsay's father, Jacob Featherstone, had swindled his company out of fifty million dollars.

He was packed up and waiting for the helicopter to arrive to take him back to Gerace Institute of Oceanography. Cassie confronted him only moments before he was about to leave and let him have it with both barrels. Cole recalled her fateful words—words that had kept him from leaving.

If you leave now, Cole, you'll never know the truth. Run back to your precious company and live out your life in ignorance. But when you're old and lonely and the only thing you'll have to keep you company is your money and a whore, the truth will haunt you to your grave.

These words still burned indelibly inside his mind. These words that had convinced him to stay and trust Lindsay one last time. One last dive. And yet, had he left, maybe Lindsay would still be mortal. He couldn't afford to think like that any longer. And now, Cassie was telling him the same thing, in essence. How did she know him so well?

Lost in thought, Cole failed to notice the apparition forming in the water only yards away. Something faint glimmered underwater, and a rush of bubbles hissed to the surface, followed by a howling wind, jarring Cole out of his meditative state.

The first thing he noticed were wings emerging from the rising tide—wings studded with diamond-like jewels that shimmered with a brilliance so luminous the emerging sight temporarily blinded him. Slowly, the apparition rose from the ocean's depths, then stopped, suspended in midair. All else around Cole faded until the only thing he could see was the angel before him.

"Lindsay?" Cole could barely get the words to form. "Is that really you?"

Lindsay's smile answered his question immediately. Emotion flooded Cole until his body began to tremble involuntarily. She had come back to him at precisely the moment he needed her to be there.

Cole, don't agonize so. Cassie was just reminding you of the man you really are. A man now free from the chains of power and wealth, which are now simply tools you can use for humanity's benefit, and free from all bonds that stand in your way. Have you forgotten our time together so quickly?

"But—"

No buts. And don't blame Cassie; I had a little something to do with it. Cast off your anger and feel the truth. You're a better man than that, right?

Lindsay's eyes shown with the power of sunlight, her expression so enduring, as if she held the key to life itself.

Again, Cole felt like he was caught up in a dream, an endless dream of he and Lindsay together for eternity. Had he made the wrong decision? Should he have chosen immortality? What a monumental decision he had been presented with. How could a man decide rationally? This was a dilemma that defied rational thought. In fact, it may defy thought altogether. It needed to happen on its own, like it had for Lindsay. She hadn't chosen a life of immortality—she had drowned trying to find his parents at the bottom of the ocean. Somehow, she had willed herself back, as though she had made a deal with. . . with God—or was it the devil? What other deity held the power to restore life, to shape the future? Only Lindsay knew the answer to that. Perhaps she would reveal it to him someday, so he could truly believe and find the faith that had eluded him his entire life.

The angel spoke again, and Cole was transported back to reality. She hovered, a mystical being against the backdrop of an expansive oceanscape.

It's time for you to return, Cole. The mountain—your mountain—is changing, and we need you. Now that Cassie has joined your group of companions, you are ready.

Cole hesitated. "You called it my mountain. How can that be? It's no one's mountain. . . well, except maybe yours," Cole said.

You are its father, Cole, and I am its mother. Together, we birthed a phenomenon that hasn't happened in millions of years. The volcano would not have been possible without you. You need to understand that. It's crucial.

Cole stood dumbfounded, oblivious to everything around him. He failed to notice Cassie approaching from the north, about one hundred yards away.

"How can humans be parents to inert materials, like a mountain? This makes no sense to me."

Cole, you are missing the point. As I've told you before, the planet and everything on it are living organisms. Some things appear different, of course, but living they are. We are killing mother earth by defiling her. She sends us signs, such as global warming, rising oceans, and changing weather patterns. Or like the Ice Age that needed to take place for the advancement of civilization, cleansing the earth of the great dinosaurs, giving way to warm-blooded mammals that would eventually usher in the human race. But those were natural occurrences that renewed our planet over eons of time.

It wasn't until the dawning of the human race that the true destruction began. Slowly—but, in the perspective of Earth's timeline, taking only a moment—humans have seized from the earth its very lifeblood by ravaging

it of non-renewable resources, sucking out oil and other precious minerals
selfishly. And, in the process, creating great strife among nations. And now,
our watchwords are sustainable, renewable, and such, but little is being
done other than talk. The advocates are in a minority and are being quashed
by the powerful. And the puppet masters are hard at work, ensuring the
continuing destruction of this precious sphere that hangs in space, the only
outpost for human life in the galaxy.

Lyndsay paused, allowing Cole a moment to reflect on her words, as
Cassie grew nearer.

I must go now. But remember my words. And finally, consider this:
would you allow the evil in men to destroy your very own child? Think of it
that way. We await your coming.

There was a flash of brilliant light, a sudden howling of wind, and then
the apparition vanished into the water, at the same time Cassie placed her
hand on Cole's shoulder. Cassie brushed back the hair the icy ocean breeze
caused to sweep across her face.

"Cole, I'm so glad I found you. I was really worried. Please accept my
apology for being so insensitive."

Cole turned toward her but said nothing. His eyes possessed a far
away and deeply troubled look as he gazed at the diver—or perhaps, gazed
through her. Then he reached over, drawing Cassie into his arms. For a long
time, they stood motionless on the deserted stretch of beach, clinging to
each other as if they were the only two people left on the planet.

CHAPTER SIXTY-ONE

B ACK IN THE SAFE confines of Cole's house on the cliffs, the companions gathered, at least those who would be going back to the island. Cole, Cassie, Gamer, Mario, and the pilots were all there, but the conspicuous absence of Art Barkley hung over them like a dark cloud. Less so was the non-appearance of the Swanson sisters, but that was expected. Art had played a pivotal role from the very beginning, and Cole felt a sense of abandonment, even though they had spoken by phone about it after Art returned to his condo. At least Cole had a better understanding of Art's motives now, but it didn't make things any easier. Cole addressed the group. "Thank you for being here. We will be leaving tomorrow morning at nine. My driver will take us to Green Airport, where the Falcon is stationed. Frank and Bill will be flying us directly to Isabella this time. No need to stop in Mexico. Your bedrooms upstairs are made ready. Dinner will be served in an hour. I've arranged for a caterer to handle that, although I would have liked to treat you to Cassie's cooking." Cole looked over at Cassie, giving her a wink. Cassie blushed.

"I promise to treat you to a gourmet meal when we return." Cassie said, but the wavering in her voice hinted that could be a long time away—or maybe never.

"Make yourself at home, everyone. I need to do a little paperwork, but I'll be back down for dinner," Cole said, then he turned away and headed for his office on the second tier.

Cassie stood awkwardly, unsure what to do. Should she join Cole, or should she stay and try to get to know everyone better? That was probably the better course of action, but she and Cole had said so little to each other since she challenged him at the marina restaurant. She desperately needed to talk to him. Sighing, she supposed that could wait until later—that is, if he allowed her in his bedroom.

Dinner was actually quite good. Naturally, with Cole doing the ordering, it was first-rate. Tender jerk chicken, spicy fajitas, grilled prawns, along with a variety of salads and sides. Even a couple of pitchers of margaritas, which quickly disappeared well before the food. Cassie returned to the refrigerator on more than one occasion for cold beer and chilled white wine. When Cole finally poured himself a scotch, she knew things were weighing heavily on his mind.

It was getting late, as the sky continued to grow dark and the fog rolled in, cloaking the ocean in its slow-moving mist. Everyone was stuffed and a little inebriated, but that was to be expected. They faced an uncertain future, and Cole was again becoming his reclusive self.

Cassie looked over at Cole, trying to get his attention, and their eyes met. An understanding smile appeared briefly on her face. Cole nodded. Soon after, one by one, the companions made their way to their rooms. Sleep would not come easy tonight, but the liquor would help.

Cassie and Cole reached the top level, having said nothing to each other in the elevator. Cassie exited first and paused. Cole followed and immediately did a right turn toward his bedroom. Filled with anxiety, Cassie hesitated as she contemplated her next move.

"Cole, can we talk? I don't think I can sleep if we don't," she said.

Cole stopped but failed to turn around. "Okay, if that's what you want."

"I was going to take a quick bath, but if you would prefer, we can talk now."

"Take your bath. I need to send out some emails. I'll be in my room. See you in a few," Cole said.

Cassie agreed, but she wondered if that meant she would be spending the night with him or if he would only allow a short talk after he finished his business. She wasn't sure if she should be happy or feel rejected.

Cassie didn't spend much time in the bathroom, just enough to wash her body and refresh herself. She dabbed on a bit of perfume, dressed in a sexy nightgown, and then wrapped herself up in the thick, wool robe, adding a pair of slippers so she wouldn't look like she was trying to seduce him. But if the mood hit Cole, she would be ready.

Twenty minutes later, Cassie knocked on Cole's bedroom door.

"Come in, it's unlocked."

Cassie entered to find Cole lying on his bed propped up against a couple of overstuffed pillows, dressed in navy blue shorts and a Harvard T-shirt. His legs and feet were bare. He was studying his cell phone, or maybe he wasn't but wanted Cassie to think he was doing something, anything but waiting for her.

"Hello, Cole. Do you need a little more time to finish up?" Cassie asked before taking a seat on a leather chair next to the fireplace. No fire was burning, no candles, nothing—just a brightly lit room. It appeared Cole was all business tonight.

"I'm done," Cole said good-naturedly. "What's on your mind?"

"I'm still upset about how I treated you at lunch today. And when I finally found you alone on that beach, it seemed like you were in another world. I hate to say goodnight to you before I find out what you're feeling." Cassie paused, gathering the strength to get to the heart of the matter. "So much has happened between us in a very short time, never mind the shock of us reconnecting. I think we may have moved too fast. . ." She allowed her last words to linger, hoping to elicit a response.

Cole remained silent for a time. She could see the gears grinding in his head as he considered what to tell her. Was he thinking of a way to put an end to their romantic relationship without hurting her? Was he just confused as to her motives? What the hell was Cole Hollingsworth thinking?

Cole cleared his throat. "Actually, I was contemplating how to explain to you what I experienced while on that beach. At first, I decided not to tell you. But the more I thought about it, the more I felt I should. After all, you know my secrets. . . about Lindsay, that is. And our bodies know each other now." Cole flashed her a smile, replete with mischief, as if the best was yet to come. "So, here it goes."

Cassie sighed with relief. He was opening up to her; it almost didn't matter what she was about to learn.

"What you said to me today was absolutely true. You have nothing to apologize for. Your directness startled me though, and it took me back to our time on the *Truett*. For a moment, I thought it was Lindsay speaking to me again. Your words reminded me of everything she tried to convey to me in her attempt to make me a better man and find a purpose in life. I think I had mostly forgotten about that, or at least suppressed it, so I wouldn't have to face my personal failures. After losing Lindsay so abruptly, I went into a fog and couldn't tell up from down. All I cared about was returning to the mountain in an attempt to find her. . . to reconnect."

Cassie rose, walked over to the bed, and sat on a corner, to be closer to him and to show her support.

"I couldn't just sit there at the restaurant and hear those things again. It was too painful. I needed to get away, and I left to find somewhere private, so I had time to think. You'll never believe what happened. An apparition appeared out of the ocean and morphed into Lindsay. Lindsay the angel, in all of her glory. She was as bright as the sun as she hovered only feet above the water—"

Cassie gasped, interrupting Cole midsentence. "So, she is still in contact with you? It must have been important."

"Yes, she has contacted me, but only in dreams or when she somehow puts me in a trance or something. I can't explain it. But this was the first time she has appeared to me in the flesh since I left the island. She wanted to remind me that what you told me was true and that I shouldn't be upset with you. She must have known what you were saying. She even told me she had something to do with it but would not elaborate further. Then she told me it was critical to return—return with you—and that the island was changing. I think she left prematurely when she discovered you were near."

Cassie sat wide-eyed, intent on understanding every word Cole was saying. It now made more sense. Perhaps Lindsay had guided her to say those things to Cole, to challenge him, even though she had planned not to, at least not today.

"I did kind of feel like Lindsay was speaking through me. As I was accusing you of all those things, I felt strange saying them. I had not intended to go there, but it just sort of happened. Maybe it was all of the wealth and power that the marina represents that got me started. I didn't mean to hurt your feelings."

"You didn't hurt my feelings. You just made me see my shortcomings again, and, as I think you'll remember on the *Truett*, the three of you did a pretty good job of that!" Cole exclaimed.

"I suppose we did," Cassie laughed, recalling the hard time they had given the billionaire, the same man who had donated so much money to fund their research. She had felt guilty about it then, but Lindsay had reminded her over and over that it was something that needed to be done.

"Well. . . how can I make it up to you?" Cassie said, and for the first time all evening, she smiled seductively. The mood changed instantly.

"For one thing, you can lose those slippers and come closer," Cole said.

"I can do one better than that." Cassie slipped off the robe, revealing a forest green negligee that might have been the showpiece at Victoria's Secret.

At least it doesn't have wings, Cole thought, recalling an ad he had once seen with the model sporting the wings.

Cole grappled for the room controller. Finding it, he pushed a button, and the lights grew dimmer, a fire sprung up behind the grate, and the shades closed automatically.

Cassie performed a slow twirl, modeling the sexy lingerie, then traveled the length of the bed on all fours, like a lioness approaching.

"We don't have all night, so let's skip the Aussie stranglehold tonight." These were the last words Cole uttered until the couple collapsed hours later on the bed, exhausted, quickly falling asleep.

CHAPTER SIXTY-TWO

MORNING DAWNED FAR TOO early for Cole and Cassie. They lingered in bed for a while, knowing it might be their last respite for a long time. What lay ahead could not be predicted or measured in any way. It would just have to run its course.

The others had gathered downstairs hours earlier, unable to sleep and growing more anxious with every passing minute. The not knowing was the worst part. Hyped up on strong coffee, they greeted the couple warily as they entered the kitchen. The fact that Cassie and Cole were becoming a couple had not gone unnoticed.

Cole was immediately struck by the tension hanging in the air. He supposed he should have expected that. Again, he had been reluctant to tell them why they were returning. Had he been in their shoes, he would have felt the same way. Much like Lindsay had done after she convinced Cole to travel to the Caribbean to search for his dead parents, if she had told him the truth then, he wouldn't have believed her. He needed to play this situation the same way, even though he would have preferred not to. They wouldn't believe him if he told them the truth—how could anyone? Only Cassie was capable of understanding, and even she didn't know the entire story. He couldn't afford to lose any of them. They were all about to face the shock of their lives . . . at least for those who survived. It was something so far beyond their comprehension that it would change them forever.

Cole broke the silence, and Cassie stood to the side, awaiting the outcome. She too had felt the mounting tension. These loyal companions deserved more than Cole was giving them. They either already had or would be risking their lives for this man who seemingly had everything in life. And for what? Money? There was plenty of that to spread around. It had to be something else. But what? The answer eluded Cassie and grated on her. She hoped that Cole was about to explain.

"Sorry to have kept you waiting. This is a big day, and I apologize for keeping all of you in the dark. We are about to embark on a journey that could play a vital role in the future of humanity. I cannot predict with any certainty what is yet to unfold, but I can promise you it will be the greatest challenge that any of you have ever faced. Some of us may not survive this trip, and I want to give you one last chance to bow out. There is no shame in it. You will be well compensated for what you have done for me so far. Money will no longer be an issue for you." Cole paused, steeling himself for what he had yet to reveal while giving everyone a moment to consider his offer. When no questions surfaced, he continued.

"Hollingsworth Island is controlled by angels, and what is happening inside of it is nothing short of a miracle. A new species is being created. The mountain contains the power to change the course of the human race, unless we change our ways first." Cole stopped abruptly at the looks of bewilderment on his companion's faces—or was it disbelief? To them, it was as though he was speaking to them in an alien tongue.

Bill's coffee cup slipped from his hand, shattering on the tile floor, the contents pooling like blood after a gunshot felled its victim. No one spoke. All eyes were on Cole, even Cassie appeared somewhat stunned. Time suddenly slowed down, as if allowing Cole's comments to catch up in everyone's minds. And still no one uttered a word. Had Cole finally gone mad?

Mario was the first to speak. "Is that what you found out on your trips to the island? It sounds like you made it inside the volcano."

Cole nodded but remained silent, awaiting further questions.

"I thought you were searching to find Lindsay Featherstone," Gamer said.

Cole nodded again. "Yes, that was my intent, in fact, it was the sole reason I returned to the island. But what I ultimately found inside is nearly impossible to describe. What I'm about to say will be equally difficult for you to comprehend. I believe I experienced my own death there, descended into a purgatory of sorts, for lack of a better description, and was reborn. Then I was led to the heart of the volcano, where I witnessed it all. Lindsay was my spirit guide. She revealed to me things to come, along with the consequences of our actions, of what the human race is doing to our planet—the planet that sustains us all. And now. . . now we must return to try and set things right." Cole stopped, awaiting further reactions. Had he said too much? The next few minutes would supply the answer.

The companions glanced at each other as though communicating their concerns silently. Cole waited patiently.

"I say, let's get on with it. I'm getting bored sitting around here and looking at the ocean all day," Gamer said.

"I'm game—no pun intended—if the rest of you are," Mario said.

All the pilots could do was nod in agreement, as though saying yes would make it more real.

Cassie moved forward, standing in front of the men, opposite Cole, to show solidarity. "Yes, Cole, we will accompany you." She turned to the companions. "Lindsay has also come to me in dreams, spoken to me about some of the things Cole just told you about. She's also the reason I'm here today. To reconnect with Cole, and with you. For some reason, we have been given an opportunity to speak for the planet. Don't ask me how I know this, but I know it to be true. We stand on a precipice, a great crossroads. For whatever reason, we are joined together in a quest to save planet Earth. This opportunity may never come again. I'm just as scared as all of you, but I would gladly sacrifice my own life if we can make a difference. I believe in Cole, just as I believed in Lindsay—and I believe in all of you. So also, I say, let's get on with it!"

Cole stood in awe, watching as the companions slowly joined hands, swearing to each other to fight to the end. Cole could not have hoped for more.

CHAPTER SIXTY-THREE

NOW AIRBORNE, THE GROUP settled in for the four-hour flight to Puerto Rico. The brilliant white paint of the Falcon shimmered in the cloudless sky as they approached thirty thousand feet in altitude. No one spoke; each one trying to absorb the enormity of what Cole and Cassie had just told them. It was one thing to get all pumped up in the thought of a potential hero's journey. It was quite another thing to actually be doing it.

Cole supposed they needed time to process everything. He sat silently, staring out of a porthole into what looked like infinity—an endless sky leading to a universe dominated only by questions. He had never felt so small, so insignificant. Why him? Why had he been singled out from a collection of far more qualified individuals who could have been chosen for this task? His only qualification was his money. But it was Lindsay who chose him, perhaps guided by a higher power. She apparently saw something in him that others didn't see, including himself.

The turbo engines hummed as they rocketed toward Isabella and the destiny that awaited. Cole hoped his explanation earlier had answered some of the questions weighing heavily on his friends. He wasn't sure if what he had said was actually the truth or if he had misrepresented that, too. In reality, he didn't have a clue what they would face or be asked to do, only that they were returning to an island that grew more mysterious with every passing day.

Cole hadn't told his friends that the recent destruction caused by the violent volcanic eruption was intentional. Although he couldn't prove it, he knew it to be true. It was a warning, a shot across the bow, intended to make the world to take notice. But had it? Probably not. What would it take to achieve global attention? Cole shuddered at the thought, wondering what the true nature of the mountain would soon reveal. Did it really possess the power to shape the natural world and, in the process, change the human race? There were mysterious forces at work there, forces he could not fully understand. Again, the doubt and insecurity crept in. Cole was not up to this task, no matter what Lindsay said. Even with his wealth, Cole didn't have enough money to change the world. What was it he possessed that could make a difference? These thoughts and more occupied his mind until Frank's voice sounded through the cabin speakers.

"Please prepare for arrival. We have started our descent and should be landing in twenty minutes." The seatbelt signs flashed on.

Cole looked around, emerging from his dazed condition. Again, all eyes were on him. Gamer, Mario, and Cassie were staring in his direction as if endeavoring to read his mind.

"You're back among the living, Cole," Cassie said, eying him thoughtfully.

"Sorry, didn't mean to zone out on all of you. Just have a lot on my mind," Cole said. That was the understatement of a lifetime.

"Don't we all," Cassie replied.

Gamer and Mario remained silent. It wasn't their place to question their boss, no matter how hard Cole tried to make them equals. They had spent most of their professional lives serving the wishes of others, whether governments or the powerful. Certainly, Cole qualified for this group.

"What's next, boss?" Gamer asked.

Cole frowned at the use of the word *boss*, yet he understood that this was a tough habit to break for these men.

"We'll grab a limo to our lodging and settle in. We're renting a house outside of Isabella, close to the water. We can have a little more privacy there," Cole said.

The three companions nodded their agreement. Privacy was something they definitely needed.

"Would you like us to make contact with Rico? It might be good to get an update as to what Andres Almquist has been up to," Mario said.

"Excellent idea. After you finish with him, let's meet back at the house for dinner to review plans for tomorrow."

Ten minutes later, the familiar sensation of screeching tires hitting the asphalt and reverse thrusters being engaged signaled their arrival. Just as predicted, the nondescript Lincoln town car was waiting for them at the airport. Frank and Bill would stay to take care of the Falcon and would join them later.

Soon, they were traveling on a narrow, two-lane road to the coast and a remote house nestled above a cove. The closest building appeared to be at least a mile away. There were a scattering of houses, shacks, and abandoned warehouses dotting the windswept landscape, but the area remained mostly remote, to their liking.

The driver came to a stop on the gravel driveway in front of a carport, where a Jeep Cherokee was parked. He unloaded their luggage and toted it up three steps, through the front door, and positioned it near the hallway leading to the bedrooms. Cole thanked the chauffeur and handed him three one-hundred-dollar bills for a ride that should have cost less than fifty US dollars. The driver thanked Cole more than once and handed him his card in case he could be of further assistance.

The house was a stucco affair, with a rust-colored tiled roof. Four bedrooms and three bathrooms were to the right. To the left was a large sitting room with a fireplace and area rugs scattered about, leading to a dining area and kitchen that faced the ocean. The house was in need of repairs and fresh paint, but it would do.

A pair of sliding glass doors led to a large deck, which was definitely the house's best feature. It had a stunning view of the cove and the ocean beyond. Though still too far away to see the island, when Cole stepped outside, the acrid scent of sulfur and methane hit him like a sucker's punch. He hadn't expected it, or at least for it to be so strong. Intuitively, he knew it was Lindsay's way of welcoming Cole and his companions back—a subtle reminder that at any time, the volcano could unleash its fury on an unsuspecting world.

Quite surprisingly, Cole raised his outstretched arms toward the ocean, as though challenging Lindsay to appear. "I'm here, now come see me," he whispered. His voice was carried straight to the island by a sudden breeze, like a formal invitation.

While the others were busy unpacking, using the facilities, and generally freshening up, Cole stood on the deck resolutely, challenging Lindsay to appear.

A voice sounded in his head.

Yes, I see you, Cole. You have arrived. Sounding a little cocky, aren't we? The voice was firm but contained a hint of humor. *The great Cole Hollingsworth has returned to save the day.*

Was that a compliment or a condemnation? Cole wondered.

The island has changed since you were last here. The dense vegetation that covered the east side has encroached to the western shore, so no more scientists will set up camp. Another change you'll notice when you approach is a heavy blanket of mist that now surrounds the mountain in its entirety to just below the summit. The fog is toxic. Either you or Cassie will need to be aboard your vessel to gain entry and safe passage to the island. Make sure your companions are aware of this. Should one of them become overly curious, their lives will not be spared if they try to breach the barrier on their own.

"Understood. Have there been many attempts to come on shore?" Cole said.

A few, but the sudden disappearance of all intruders and their boats sent a strong message. As you will see, there is a military-grade battle cruiser stationed about three miles off of the western shore. News travels quickly around here, but you would know about such things, being in the news publishing business, right? Lindsay had just dropped her first hint, but would Cole understand?

Cole thought this an odd comment, but he quickly dismissed it. "Yeah, I suppose I do, but I haven't been very involved with our publishing these days. I've pretty much left that up to others," Cole said.

Like Bill Gaines, for instance?

"Yes, him, among others. Art Barkley is still acting president and is keeping me up to date on the comings and goings back home."

*Yes, and I might say that is one of your worst decisions. By the way, why isn't Art with you? He's your righthand man—*Lindsay abruptly cut short her sentence, as Cassie, Mario, and Gamer stepped onto the deck. Not that they could hear inside of Cole's head, but there would be time to connect later. Lindsay had imparted the important news before they attempted to gain access to the island.

Cassie stared at Cole, who looked as if he had been talking to an invisible friend. His right hand was raised, palm facing the ocean, moving like he'd been talking with both voice and hand gestures, as people often do.

"Were you talking to someone, Cole?" Cassie asked as she approached.

"Now, who would I be talking to?" Cole said, half joking.

"Oh, I don't know. An angel perhaps?"

Cole scoffed at the inference. Cassie smiled furtively.

"Hey, boss, we're off to see Rico. Okay if we take the Jeep?" Mario asked.

"She's all yours. Look forward to hearing back," Cole replied.

"Call us on your way back, okay?" Cassie said, then she winked at Cole.

The two men left, leaving Cole and Cassie alone. Cassie padded over to the kitchen and opened the refrigerator. As luck would have it, there were a couple of bottles of white wine chilling, along with a selection of craft beers. She opened a bottle of chardonnay and filled two glasses. Returning to the deck, she handed Cole one and then took a seat in one of the lounge chairs facing the ocean.

Cassie raised her glass toward Cole. "Cheers, we've made it back. This time, together. May we find good fortune." The pair clinked glasses.

Cole turned back toward the water and walked closer. For a long moment, he stared out, scanning the horizon. Cassie watched until she could no longer stand the silence. Cole could only be thinking about one thing. Lindsay.

"What troubles you so, Cole?" Cassie asked.

Cole was caught off guard by the question, and his body jerked involuntarily. Lindsay had asked him the exact same question on more than one occasion. Were they really the same woman after all? Was Cassie just a reincarnation of Lindsay, who'd come back to guide him—or to haunt him? To keep him in stasis, stranded between one dimension and another, until he finally made up his mind? Was he being played again?

"Why don't we take our wine into your bedroom? It was a long flight, and you seem stressed. Maybe a little exercise is just what the doctor ordered," Cassie said fetchingly.

Although Cole was tempted, he couldn't get the image of Lindsay out of his head. Now that they were so close, it almost seemed like cheating, going to bed with Cassie.

"Thanks, Cassie, it's a tough offer to refuse, but refuse I must, at least for now. I have a lot of thinking to do, and I need my mind clear. . . and sharp. I hope you aren't upset with me."

"No, of course not. Another time, then," Cassie replied, but she seemed annoyed, like she knew what—who—Cole was thinking about. Just another reminder of the similarities between Lindsay and Cassie. Both women could read Cole's mind!

Cassie departed, leaving her half-empty wine glass on the kitchen counter on her way. Cole continued to stand, gazing out to sea, hoping Lindsay would reengage in their earlier conversation. No voices sounded inside his head, though. It appeared Lindsay had vanished just like Cassie.

Cole was dozing on an outside lounge chair when the men returned.

"Cole, are you here?" Cole heard his name being called from a distance. Just a dream. He turned over on the chair.

"Cole?"

The second calling woke him more fully. He shook his head. He had fallen into a deep sleep, traveling to far off places, filled with disturbing images. He recalled encountering a weathered, stone bridge leading into a swirling mist, beckoning him to cross over. The river below the bridge was stagnant with thick, green algae, bubbling, releasing bursts of steam. There seemed to be movement, like giant slugs were feeding on the toxic, putrid waste. The stench was nearly unbearable. The sky above was broken, littered with cracks, radiating streaks of ultraviolet light that had torched the nearby landscape, leaving it charred and barren. Cole attempted to shake the disturbing images from his mind—yet the stench of sulfur lingered.

Cole rose to greet Mario, Gamer, and Rico, who were standing before him like the three musketeers. "Good to see you, Rico. Been behaving yourself?" Cole asked.

"Don't I always?" the machete-wielding, one-man wrecking crew replied, smiling irreverently.

Cole didn't bother replying, as there was no reason to. In their short time together, they had come to understand one another. Two disparate souls so unlike each other but at the same time connected in order to achieve a goal neither could accomplish alone. A symbiotic joining at the hips—one sporting a high-tech cell phone, the other an old-school weapon deadly in its simplicity. Each device as effective as the other.

"So, Rico, what can you tell me about our friend, Andres? Has he been behaving?" Cole asked.

"More or less. I know he has been communicating with the outside world, and I can only assume it is with your chairman, Mr. Gaines. But we assumed he would be doing that. I've paid him a little visit every day. I've followed him but allowed him to observe me doing so. He seems to be keeping a pretty low profile. With all that's happened on the island, he doesn't have much choice. My money says he's just biding his time," Rico said, then he spat some tobacco onto the deck, as though repulsed by the scientist.

"Very good, my friend. Have you noticed anyone suspicious coming to his hotel?" Cole said.

Rico shook his head. "If I had seen anyone, we would have had a. . . a little meeting to set things straight," Rico said, smiling again, as if he wished someone had shown up just to give him something to do. "I have an associate keeping watch on him while I'm not there. He did report seeing a few hookers, each one different, stopping by every other day."

"That figures," Cole said, then abruptly changed the subject. "What can you tell us about the island? I hear it has been unusually active and undergoing some sort of change." Cole stopped short of telling Rico what he already knew.

"Yeah, strange things. Just after you left, there was this gigantic eruption, like the mountain blew its top off. It destroyed everything around it. Shit just vanished into thin air. I was staying in Isabella when it happened. The earth around me shook like nothing I've ever felt before," Rico said, using his hands and arms to indicate a massive explosion. "Then a few days later, a thick, green fog began to form around the island until it became invisible, everything except the very top. You can still barely see it. I think it's grown in height, but no one really knows. They can't get near it anymore."

"I heard that there's a military cruiser stationed a couple of miles away. Have you seen it?" Cole asked.

"Yeah, it's a big motherfucker. I'm told it's a Zumwalt-class destroyer. It stopped for a short time not far off of Puerto Rico. Me and a friend took a boat as close as we could get. It's loaded with big guns and missile silos. It's one mean-looking SOB," Rico said.

An apt description, Cole thought. Leave it to a high school dropout and an assassin to put it into perspective. A Navy commander couldn't have explained its purpose any better. *Why such an advanced warship?* Cole wondered. This was the best the Navy had to offer, with electronic surveillance equipment second to none.

"So, the US Navy is involved now," Cole said, but he appeared to be speaking to no one in particular.

Rico nodded his head. "You couldn't miss it. Stealthy looking. I also heard rumors there's a nuclear-powered submarine hanging out nearby, but I haven't seen one yet."

Well, it didn't take long for our illustrious military to come calling, Cole mused. Poised to destroy the island rather than to understand it—to understand one of the greatest phenomena to emerge in over a million years. If they thought they could take down this island, they had another thing coming. Cole almost wished they would try, except for the loss of innocent lives and the crew members forced on this mission, forced to follow orders without question. He supposed that was the way it had to be.

A couple of warships were no match for the wrath of a planet, or the wrath of a higher power. An idea suddenly flashed into Cole's mind. This was newsworthy, especially if a covert submarine was patrolling the area and toting nuclear missiles.

"Thank you for the update, Rico. Very helpful. Excuse me gentlemen, I need to make a phone call," Cole said. Instead of expecting his companions to leave, Cole strode by them and headed to the privacy of another room.

"There's some cold beer in the fridge if anyone's interested," Cole said as he passed by.

On his way to his bedroom, Cole glanced into Cassie's room. She was lying on her side on the bed, apparently asleep. He would catch up with her later. He shut his door, pulled out his cell phone, and dialed Art Barkley with his latest idea.

CHAPTER SIXTY-FOUR

ART ANSWERED IMMEDIATELY, AS if he'd been awaiting Cole's call. "So, you made it safely?" Art asked.

"Yeah, the flight was smooth. We're at our house. You should have its location. I just met with Rico for an update on Almquist. Not much to report there. He seems to be minding his manners with an occasional prod from our companion. He's been in contact with Gaines, though. Have you heard anything?"

"No. Gaines has been quiet. He seems to be content spending most of his time either in his office or out of the building. I wonder if he's losing interest?"

"Listen, Art, Rico believes there's a nuclear-powered submarine in stealth mode patrolling the waters near the island, along with a badass Zumwalt-class destroyer that is stationed nearby. But the sub is not showing itself. Both are US warships. If they are carrying nuclear weapons with the intent of destroying the island, I think the public ought to know. There's a story here. It's very hush-hush. Can you get our best and most loyal reporter on it? I'd suggest Russ Adderley. Use some of our influence to quietly snoop around about the sub. If we can confirm its presence, then we go to press. I want it on the front page of all our newspapers."

"You really think that's a good idea, Cole? Going up against the Pentagon is never a great thing, especially if they're trying to hide something. National security, and all that shit."

"I think it's a great idea. There's a lot more going on down here than meets the eye, and. . . well, there's much you don't know yet. When the time is right, I'll explain. We on the same page, Art?" Cole said, as if Art had a choice.

"I'm on it. Talk to you soon." With that, Art ended the conversation, again wondering what the hell Cole was up to. He sent a quick text to Russ Adderley.

Cole sat on his bed alone as the minutes ticked by, drawing ever deeper inside of himself. There was still so much to be done, but exactly what eluded him for the time being. Even though he had the support of a small band of fiercely loyal companions, he still felt mostly alone in this journey. He silently cursed Art for not being with him. He picked up his cell phone, intent on calling him again and convincing him he needed to be at his side, but then quickly put it down. Art had not come for a reason—a reason important enough to abandon his best friend. Perhaps Art intuitively knew Cole needed someone he could trust back at headquarters, at least that's why he told Cole he wasn't making the trip. To keep an eye on Gaines, to connect the dots, to act as a trustworthy intermediary that had Cole's best interests at heart. It could only be that. Surely, it wasn't just the allure of the Swanson sisters, as powerful as that was. Cole knew Art still had a significant role to play. Cole just needed to trust him.

When Cole finally rejoined his team, the pilots had arrived, and everyone was gathered on the deck, drinking beer and watching the sunset turn daylight into twilight, as if this had become a vacation. Cole gazed at the scene for a long moment. All seemed so calm, but what lay just a few miles off the shore could erupt at any minute, creating a global catastrophe. Was he the only person who understood that? It was time to fully engage his crew. They had to know what they were about to face. But most importantly, he and Cassie needed to visit the island to confirm his suspicions before he could reveal all.

CHAPTER SIXTY-FIVE

DINNER HAD ARRIVED AND been consumed by the time Cole received his first text message from Art. He excused himself while the others cleaned up. Art hadn't let him down. In fact, Cole was shocked at the news as he read Art's message. How Art had garnered this information in a matter of hours was astonishing. Cole stared at the message, needing to read it a second time to fully grasp its gravity.

Cole, you were right to bring in Adderley. This guy is really connected. He has a close friend working at the Pentagon and learned there is a Trident-armed Ohio- class submarine, in addition to the Zumwalt, stationed near the island. And both are loaded for bear with nuclear weapons. It's highly classified, but he thinks they intend to demolish the island if there are any more unusual eruptions or if the mysterious fog continues to linger. He was told it's toxic. His Pentagon contact must remain anonymous. More later...

Cole sat indecisively, wondering if he should tell his companions about this unexpected threat. This added an entirely new perspective to their situation and was something no one had foreseen. Battle lines were quickly being drawn. And caught in the middle of it all were Cole, Cassie... and an angel.

Cole cleared his throat to announce his arrival as he reentered the kitchen area. The others turned in unison to see a stone-faced man staring at them as if something terrible had just occurred. Cole's expression spoke volumes as confusion swept over the companions. He didn't speak, he didn't move. He simply stared at each individual as though evaluating their readiness to accept bad news. Cole cleared his throat again.

"I just spoke to Art Barkley. He has an anonymous contact at the Pentagon who informed him that in addition to the Zumwalt-class destroyer stationed near the island, the US Navy has deployed an Ohio-class stealth submarine, carrying Trident ballistic missiles with nuclear warheads, that has yet to reveal itself."

At first it seemed not to have registered with the group. Gradually, the specter of nuclear weapons being launched took hold. Was the United States actually prepared to annihilate the island without regard to the environment or the nearby islands? What had caused so much concern that the Navy's most powerful attack vessels had arrived on the scene? The radius of a nuclear explosion powerful enough to demolish the island would spread significantly onto the neighboring islands. Many lives would be lost unless massive evacuation plans were implemented first.

The companions appeared momentarily paralyzed, awaiting Cole's next words and what that would mean for them.

"I can see by your expressions that you are as surprised and concerned as I am. After Rico told us he had heard rumors of a submarine in the area, I called Art to follow up on it. He contacted our top military correspondent at Hollingsworth to snoop around. The fact that he was able to obtain this highly classified information so quickly is nothing short of remarkable." Cole paused for a moment at the looks of astonishment on everyone's faces. Even Cassie seemed shocked.

"I can tell you that something is changing inside of the volcano, and military intelligence must be aware of something as well, but I'm betting they don't know what. A dense fog has formed around the island, and it is reported to be toxic. In my mind, it can only be hiding something. There may also be some unusual seismographic activity taking place inside and being picked up by the scientific community. Add the two things together and our Navy gets involved—more threatened than interested in understanding. This changes our timetable. Our military must not be allowed to destroy the island. Therefore, we must act faster than previously thought. Cassie and I leave for the island at dawn tomorrow. We need to see exactly what is going on inside. We'll report back as soon as possible. In anticipation of a potential military strike, I've directed Art to run this story on the front page of every Hollingsworth newspaper in our system. It will appear in tomorrow's editions. This may give us much needed time to figure it all out." Again, Cole paused to allow this information to sink in.

"Are there any questions?" Cole asked.

Silence hung heavy in the room as these new revelations were processed by each member of the group. Things had escalated at an alarming rate, catching everyone off guard. Gamer was the first to speak.

"I'm assuming you'll want me to get you there. What time do I need the boat ready?" It was a simple question, really, but also carried with it a heavy weight, as this action would set in motion a series of events that could change the world remarkably, yet only Cole was vaguely cognizant of this fact. Perhaps Cassie would soon be as well.

"At first light. Mario, Rico, are you with us?"

Both men nodded but said nothing further.

"Okay, then. Let's turn in early. We'll need to be well rested in the morning." With this final comment, Cole turned and headed away. The companions watched as he disappeared out of sight, awash in questions that could not be answered. It would all just have to play out.

CHAPTER SIXTY-SIX

MORNING DAWNED, WITH A shuddering cold wind blowing off the ocean. The weather had changed dramatically in a matter of hours. The tropics had lost their luster. The sky was ominously dark, with pinpricks of sunlight piercing through slits in the cloud cover like focused laser beams. Dawn also marked the distribution of the morning newspapers to newsstands and houses across the United States. The headlines appeared as threatening as the weather. A huge photo of Hollingsworth Island— the photo taken before the fog had encroached—dominated the majority of the front pages, while the headlines simply read:

Hollingsworth Island: A Threat or Our Salvation?

For no apparent reason or explanation, the US Navy has deployed its deadliest attack vessels off the coast of Puerto Rico in the form of a Zumwalt-class guided missile destroyer and an Ohio-class nuclear submarine. Both vessels are armed with nuclear weapons and are trolling the waters around the newly formed island. The submarine has not yet surfaced and is in complete stealth mode. This information has been confirmed by an anonymous, high-ranking source inside the Pentagon. These ships are clearly hunt-and-destroy killers whose sole purpose is destruction. What would motivate the US military to deploy such weapons? Numerous scientific teams have confirmed that the island contains a treasure chest of information regarding the earth's early formation and the evolutionary process that has taken place on the planet since prehistoric times. Some scientists have formulated that the island holds vital clues to the global warming of recent years, which is perhaps the most profound challenge the human race now faces.

It has been speculated that the current Republican administration, in conjunction with the most powerful oil and energy lobbyists, are dead set against revealing any information that would deter further drilling for oil, mining for coal, and harvesting other fossil fuels, which would slash corporate profits and adversely affect the economy and the Republican's hold on the capitol.

It has become obvious this administration has little regard for the environment and the long-term effects of climate change, even though the scientific evidence is overwhelming and universal. The potential destruction of Hollingsworth Island is simply another example of the shortsightedness of an administration casting a blind eye to the real challenges facing humanity, all for the sake of profit taking.

What would the effects of nuclear detonations be on the surrounding islands, its people, and the ocean itself? These questions and more need to be addressed by the administration.

(Article continued on page A-4, along with additional photos)

Within hours, the Twitter rampage began, as the president raged against the "fake news" and other media, which had picked up on the story. Hollingsworth Enterprises website and phone lines and were lit up like a Christmas tree, as nearly every news source outside of the organization scrambled to get an explanation. Who was this mysterious Pentagon official who had leaked highly classified information? A whistleblower? Who had ordered the deployment of deadly attack vessels? And, almost as importantly, where was Cole Hollingsworth hiding as the media storm picked up velocity? Foreign governments were calling the White House—governments that had not been consulted about such a drastic measure taken by the United States Navy on its own.

In a word, a shitstorm had overtaken the White House. The fact that the president was vacationing at his golf resort didn't help matters. Top Navy officials were fending off media questions left and right. In less than twenty-four hours, Hollingsworth Island had become the biggest story on the planet. . . again.

Meanwhile, the major environmental agencies and activists were remaining unusually calm. This may have been the most curious aspect of all. It almost seemed as if they had been warned to hold back and let the firestorm play out while they formulated a strategy. In reality, Art Barkley and a few loyal employees had sent an advance copy of the article and forewarned as many of the top environmentalists as possible that their best strategy would be to wait until public support for action had grown to feverish pitch. By all accounts, that was already taking place.

Standing near the pier while Gamer made final preparations for departure, Cole smirked as he read the news article on his cell phone. "God damn, Art," Cole whispered to himself, marveling at his friend's ingenuity. Maybe it was best he had stayed behind to cover Cole's ass, although he would have liked him here by his side. They were becoming quite a team.

Cassie had just finished reading the article as well. "Way to go, Cole!" she exclaimed, slapping him on the back. "That was brilliant. I just hope the Navy doesn't know where we are. They might send out drones to blow us up, too!"

Cole laughed, but there was a degree of trepidation in his voice, as though Cassie's remarks might contain a modicum of truth. Anything was possible with this administration.

The companions boarded the Eliminator, and Gamer fired up the twin engines to a loud roar. He punched down the throttle, and the go-fast boat nearly leapt out of the water like it had wings, too.

"Now, Gamer, please tone it down a bit," Cole said, halfheartedly.

"Sorry, boss. It's been a while, so I was just stretching my legs a bit. All that sitting around was making me crazy," Gamer said.

Cole nodded and looked at Mario and Rico. They appeared equally restless, as though they were just itching for a fight. Cole had yet to tell them they would not be accompanying him onto the island, at least not this time. He suspected they would not take kindly to the news but ultimately would not question his decision. It was critical that he and Cassie assess the current state of things inside the volcano first before charting a course of action. But what that course would be was yet to be discovered.

Gamer settled into a less aggressive pace as they approached the island, maintaining a wide berth from the Zumwalt destroyer. Even though they would not be spotted by the vessel due to their angle of approach, Cole was quite sure the high-tech gear on the ship would detect their presence in the area and track them. Hopefully, the military wouldn't act on it, in light of the media frenzy taking place. They just needed to enter the fog zone before being stopped. Once inside, the Navy could do little about it but risk the ship and the safety of its crew. However, it suddenly struck Cole that a submarine might be able to breach the toxic barrier if the water was sufficiently deep enough to allow passage. Perhaps that was the real reason it was here. The destroyer contained enough firepower to wreak havoc on the island on its own. Then there was the fact that the top rim of the volcano was exposed, and armed drones might be able to gain access. If that were to happen, could the fire angel bring the fury of the earth's magma to bear in time? These and other questions occupied Cole's thoughts as they sped closer to their destination.

Passing over the horizon, the island came into view—only there was no island, just an enormous cloud of greenish fog appearing like a massive tornado of smoke spiraling into the stratosphere. Cole didn't think he had ever seen anything quite so intimidating. Gamer shut down the engines almost as if it was an anatomic response, while the group gazed out in wonder. From deep within the spiraling mist, bolts of lightning could be seen flashing angrily, as if about to emerge and torch everything in their path. A storm within a storm? How much energy was being unleashed inside, and what was keeping it contained?

Mario turned to Cole. "How in heaven's name are we going to enter that?"

All eyes turned to Cole. And in those eyes, Cole spotted only fear, as if his companions were staring at the end of the world. Even Cassie could not disguise her distress.

An acrid wind hit them next, awash in strong odors of sulfur and methane that nearly choked them—like the island was sending out an advance party to evaluate who was knocking on its door.

It was time for Cole to take action. Cole stood and resolutely faced the spectacle—there was really no other word for it—while instructing Gamer to proceed.

Gamer tentatively pushed down on the throttle, guiding the Eliminator forward against his better judgement. He glanced at his boss as if questioning his instructions. Cole turned, nodding. The order had been given.

As they approached, visibility became diminished, as the atmosphere around them turned gray. The air grew even hotter. Still, Gamer held his course, heading into what could only be considered their impending demise. Cole placed his hand on the boatman's shoulder for reassurance, steeling the man. Gamer had promised his boss to follow him to his death, and he would not abandon his promise. Nor would the others. They were a fellowship now, one for all and all for one, united in a cause they did not yet fully understand, but they somehow knew nothing could be more important. They trusted Cole with their lives, and there was nothing more Cole could ask of them.

The days ahead would test them all to the breaking point and beyond.

CHAPTER SIXTY-SEVEN

THE GROUP SLOWLY ENTERED the mist and silently disappeared from sight, surrounded by a murky green fog that stung their eyes and choked their nostrils with its acrid smell. Approaching the island cautiously, Gamer turned to Cole.

"I thought this was supposed to be toxic," the skipper said. "It's rank for sure, but I don't feel like we're going to be poisoned or anything. I thought you said—"

"It is toxic, and if anybody but us entered, it would be deadly," Cole interrupted, stopping short of telling them it was really just he and Cassie who guaranteed safe passage. He would get to that part later.

Gamer dropped the subject; it was enough they had passed through unharmed.

Within minutes, a dark shape began to form in front of them as they drew closer to shore. The fog was still too dense to make out much, but they could see something horrific materializing. It appeared to be pulsating, like it was alive. Bolts of lightning crackled and danced with each other, while the shrill sound of hurricane-force winds filled the air. And still they ventured steadfastly forward, determined to reach landfall.

Suddenly, the mist evaporated, and all cleared. What they next saw took their collective breath away. Before them, the mammoth volcano was engulfed in raging fire. The entire mountain appeared to be burning, blinding them temporarily as if they'd stared at the sun with no eye protection.

They could only have entered hell; everything spoke of death and decay. There existed no redeeming qualities any longer, only misery and impending oblivion, as though the island was writhing in intolerable pain. Gamer shut down the engines and the Eliminator coasted to a stop, dead in the water—water unlike anything they had seen before. It shimmered in a dazzling, gilded hue, like liquid gold. Flat, motionless, and brilliant, it released metallic-looking bubbles that drifted slowly into the atmosphere above.

For a long moment, the companions gazed up at the towering inferno, wondering what was to come and what had guided them here. They must be the first humans to lay eyes on this phenomenon. How could things have changed so drastically in such a short time? Only a few weeks ago, the island had appeared almost normal, its west shore populated by scientists studying its mysteries. Only, those scientists no longer existed. The oil-like platforms offshore that served as laboratories and sleeping quarters had all melted into the sea during the last eruption—the mountain cleansing the area of any human interference, like it was fighting off a disease.

Suddenly, a far-off voice echoed.

Welcome, companions. You are now a fellowship—the fellowship of the flame, the enduring fire that fuels this planet's life force. You have done well to come this far. You are safe within our confines. But be warned—a difficult road lies ahead.

Where the voice came from was difficult to tell. The sound filled the space like it was being broadcast by an ethereal, surround sound system—in front, in back, from the sides. It resonated from everywhere like a chorus of sound, yet singular in nature.

Their questions were quickly answered. Three bodies—bodies with wings—emerged from within the flames, drifting closer until they were almost within touching distance. They could only be described as angels.

Heavenly beings. Magnificent. Two appeared to be fire angels, floating beside the most beautiful creature imaginable. Diamond-studded wings shimmering with the power of a sun, only silver in color. Long, flowing, auburn hair and slate gray eyes. A figure wrapped up in a highly embroidered, scarlet gown, glowing iridescently. The foremost angel smiled, and it felt as if a burden of immense weight had just been lifted. Cole smiled back.

"Hello, Lindsay."

The gaze between the two was so intense that time seemed to stand still, as though nothing else mattered. There was only the love between them. And finally, Cassie understood.

The group continued to gaze in wonder as the luminous bodies floated before them against a backdrop of crimson flames. All but Cole gawked, unable to express what they were witnessing firsthand. This was no fantasy movie, no theme park special effects ride. This was actually happening. How does one describe, let alone understand, such an event? And still they watched, mesmerized and unable to speak. This was nothing short of a miracle. Were they staring at the threshold to God's Kingdom? Were they truly in the presence of angels? No other explanation made sense.

CHAPTER SIXTY-EIGHT

BILL GAINES SUMMONED ART Barkley to his office, something that had not happened since Cole had left the country. Art entered, knowing full well why he was being asked to Bill's office. It could only be the article that had appeared in the morning edition of every paper in the Hollingsworth network.

"Close the door, Art," Gaines directed, failing to say hello or offer any form of greeting.

Art complied, then took a seat in front of the imposing wood desk and large leather chair. Art suddenly felt like a convicted criminal facing a federal judge, awaiting sentencing. And the judge looked none too happy. Art remained silent, allowing Gaines the opportunity to speak first.

"Art, I don't think I need to tell you why you're here. I received a call earlier this morning from the vice president of the United States. He was in an uproar over the article we published today about the island. I only got wind of it moments before distribution. The government is accusing us of espionage—even treason—saying that, somehow, we bribed a high-level official in the Pentagon for top secret information about the Navy's involvement in the area. How could you have allowed such a story to go public without out my permission?" The chairman was glowering, his face turning scarlet.

Art cleared his throat. "Bill, I didn't seek your permission because it was not required. I was directed by the majority owner and CEO of this company to publish it. As acting president, I simply followed orders. I—"

Gaines lashed out. "This is an outrage! I'm still the chairman of the board, and while Cole is off doing whatever the hell he's doing, I do have a say as to how this company is managed. Where did you get this information and how was Russ Adderley involved? He couldn't have acted alone on something this big. The military brass is all over my ass to give them answers."

"First of all, Bill, we don't give up our sources, especially credible ones. The story is true, and you know it. The only thing that could make us reveal where this information came from would be a direct presidential order, and even that may not be enough. It could potentially be tied up for weeks, if not longer, and the story would be ancient history by then." Art paused. "Next subject?" he said, condescendingly.

"You're actually not going to tell me what's going on?" Gaines asked incredulously.

"No, Bill, I'm not. You can always try calling Cole. I believe you still have his cell number."

"God damn it, Art. This is insubordination, and it could cost you your job. I will call an emergency board meeting, and you'll be out on your ass if you don't cooperate," Gaines threatened.

"Give it your best shot, Bill. Unless there is other business to discuss, I have more important things to attend to." Art rose, opened the door, and disappeared down the hallway, leaving a stunned and defeated man in his wake. Art smiled as he strode away. He had always wanted to do that, and it felt damn good.

Art attempted to call Cole. But one ring and the cell phone went dead. No automated message, nothing. That was strange. Normally, they had good cell coverage. It could only mean one thing. Either something bad had happened to his friend or he was out of range or without a phone, which could only mean Cole was on the island.

Next, he dialed Mario, then Gamer, then Cassie. Same response. They must have all passed beyond a barrier, now totally on their own. Art slumped down in his chair, troubled. There was little more he could do than wait. . . and hope. He dialed Russ Adderley to see if there was any further news from the Pentagon.

CHAPTER SIXTY-NINE

L INDSAY MOTIONED THE COMPANIONS forward. Gamer restarted the Eliminator, easing the speedboat forward. What a photo this would have made. A boat full of humans being led by a trio of angels toward an island on fire.

Apparently, Rico thought the same thing. Retrieving his cell phone, he pointed it at the angels and tried snapping a photo. He heard the familiar click just as the phone burst into a cloud of shimmering dust, glittering and falling to the floorboard, staining his boots metallic green. Rico cursed to himself but otherwise remained silent.

The angels slowed to a halt. Gamer did likewise. The shore was only yards away now. The flames vanished before them, revealing something resembling a doorway, only the metal door appeared to be made of solid gold. Strange glyphs ran the length of the façade, reminding Cole again of runes. There was no door handle, just a symbol—a golden eye encased in a circle of fire, staring ominously back at them. Cole instinctively knew no one would pass through without the angel's consent. He stood at the bow of the boat, hands crossed before him reverently, awaiting instructions.

Lindsay smiled again. Cole had changed somehow. He no longer appeared to be the overbearing rogue, no longer seemed to want the world to revolve around him. He had grown, she thought. But would it be enough?

She extended her arms toward the group, just as a bridge materialized between the bow of the boat and the shoreline. Fashioned out of pure light, the bridge arced to its apex halfway to the shore and then fell gently away until touching land.

Cole stepped forward without hesitation, his faith in Lindsay unquestioning. Cassie followed behind him. The others hesitated, wondering if a plank of light could support them, too.

Mario took a tentative step forward, touching the edge of the bridge just as one of the fire angels descended, immediately blocking his path. Her black eyes shown like glistening obsidian, her wings tinged with flames. Mario stiffened, reaching out his arm to Cole for help.

Cole shook his head grimly. "Not this time, my friend. Wait here. You'll be safe." These were the last words the remaining companions heard as the mysterious door slid up. Cole, Cassie, Lindsay, and one of the fire angels slipped through the opening and into darkness. The door slid down, melting back into a wall of flame. One fire angel remained, stationed outside like a sentry. Only, no one had ever seen a sentry quite like this one. She hovered in the air, nearly motionless, encased in a sphere of incandescent light, watching.

There was little they could do about it. Mario took a seat reluctantly. He gazed at his companions with searching eyes. Rico shrugged his shoulders, as though he was used to waiting. Gamer shut the engines down, sighing heavily. All three stared at the remaining angel, willing her to do something—but what?

Their only other choice was to turn around and head back to the house, and they began to debate its merits. There was general disagreement on the matter. Mario reminded his friends that they were in it for the long haul and they could not abandon Cole.

Gamer, on the other hand, wanted to leave. He predicted that Cole and Cassie would be gone a long time, perhaps days, and if they stayed until their return, they would eventually run out of drinkable water and food.

Rico leaned against a railing at the stern of the boat, his machete drawn, sliding a whetstone slowly up and down its length, as if it needed further sharpening. "Whatever you guys want to do is fine with me. But I say we wait until it gets dark, and if Cole isn't back by then, we head out. I think Cole will give us a sign when he needs us. . . or maybe that angel with her head on fire will," Rico remarked, as though her presence meant little to him.

The figure hovering above them glowed brightly for an instant, as if insulted by the assassin's remark.

Gamer and Mario glanced at each other, nodding their concurrence. The decision was made. They would wait until nightfall.

Minutes passed slowly, as the sun arced its way across the sky. Still no Cole or Cassie. Both Mario and Gamer had tried using their cell phones, but without luck. The phones seemed as dead as their surroundings. Nothing moved. The acrid air surrounding them was stifling. By midday, they had nearly run out of water. Could it get any worse?

CHAPTER SEVENTY

C OLE AND CASSIE FOLLOWED Lindsay in silence as they moved slowly
through a darkened tunnel, lit only by the angel's luminescence. They
seemed to be moving upward, but it was difficult to tell exactly. Surrounded
by dense vegetation, the humidity was beginning to take its toll. Beads of
sweat formed on their brows. Still, they carried on dutifully, unsure what
they would find at the tunnel's ending, knowing only that it would most
likely be another startling revelation. One shock seemed to follow another.
This alien world they had been invited to grew more enigmatic with each
new encounter.

Cassie's breathing became labored, Cole's less so, but he too was suffer-
ing from the excursion. "How much longer, Lindsay?" Cole asked.

"Not far, we are nearing our destination. Would you like to stop
and rest?"

"No, we're fine. No need to stop for us," exclaimed Cassie, obviously
insulted by Lindsay's insinuation that they were weak somehow.

"Very well, we'll push on," Lindsay said with a hint of humor, as if she
had just read Cassie's mind.

Long, strenuous minutes passed, as the group made its way into what
could only be the center of the volcano. Steam issued from small cracks in

the walls, bringing with it a pungent odor of sulfur. The tunnel seemed to be growing wider, and a faint halo of light appeared in the distance.

The light grew gradually brighter, and the air seemed somehow lighter. A moment later, they were standing on a ledge, having reached the tunnel's end. Spread out before them, a cavernous chamber revealed itself. Cole and Cassie stopped dead in their tracks, too stunned to utter a word. Something like a squeak escaped from Cassie's mouth involuntarily.

A world so unfamiliar and strange greeted them, as if a new planet had been created. Colors were more intense; the landscape painted with hues that didn't exist previously. The sky was transparent, without a hint of color, as if it had never been tainted with impurities. Mountains rose from the mist below, towering above with snowcapped peaks speckled with shimmering ice crystals. What looked like enormous white eagles soared effortlessly on the breeze, their wings tipped with gold.

Cole breathed in the air and was instantly renewed, as if his lungs had been suddenly purified. Cassie was experiencing the same sensations. Both stood on the precipice, gawking. It was almost too much to take in. An environment so pure, so uncontaminated, it defied description. How could such a place exist, surrounded by a polluted planet that was now covered in toxic, green mist? It occurred to Cole that the scene had changed remarkably in the week he had been gone. How could such a drastic alteration have taken place?

"What do you think, Cole?" Lindsay asked in a voice that seemed to echo across the expanse, neither close nor far away.

Cole looked over and was once again consumed by the angel's smile. *Is this heaven?* Cole wondered. It would certainly fit the description so often associated with it. Had the golden door they'd recently entered actually been an opening to the pearly gates? Had he and Cassie crossed over?

Lindsay allowed the couple to linger in sheer amazement as the scenery drew them in more fully, until recognition began to form in their eyes. This was nature in its purest form. This was nature as it was meant to be, free of man's interference and indifference.

You're beginning to understand, aren't you? Lindsay asked. *Just after the planet and atmosphere fully formed, before human life appeared, this was what the earth looked like. It had transformed from its primeval landscape into a state of grace. It was pure; it was alive; it was vibrant with possibilities. It truly was the Garden of Eden. This was the gift the architect of the universe had prepared for our coming. And look what we've done with it,"* Lindsay added sternly.

The impact of Lindsay's words hit like a landslide, burying them in an avalanche of regret. Tears of remorse rolled down Cassie's checks, unconstrained. Cole stood speechless. There were no words to describe the agony of what they were witnessing. Gradually, their sorrow turned to anger until it morphed into unadulterated rage—rage against the human race for being so shortsighted.

A long silence followed, and it seemed as though time stood still again as a sense of helplessness overwhelmed the pair. An understanding that the planet could never be fully repaired, could never return to this state of grace, washed over them, crushing any hope for a better world.

Eons ago, the universe was created by an omnipotent power—I suppose you could say it was God—and it truly was the Garden of Eden. Time passed slowly, awaiting the first signs of human life. And not unlike the Bible states, at the dawn of creation, a situation occurred that allowed sin to enter, unbridled, a disease infecting everything in its path. This was the start of a long decay that lasted millions of years.

Slowly, the existing universe evolved into a giant black hole, collapsing in on itself, in defense against the infection raging in the natural world. Like all black holes, the hyperintense gravity pulled everything inward, reducing its size, growing smaller and smaller, until the pressure and mass were so extreme it imploded. This is what modern-day scientists refer to as the big bang theory that created the current universe, and to a large extent, they're correct. There are a few contemporary astrophysicists who began to understand this—at least to understand the true nature of black holes. One such visionary was Stephen Hawking. His work continues to fuel the research that will someday solve the greatest mystery of all: how the present universe was created. The rest is history. Lindsay paused at the looks of utter astonishment on her guests' faces. Rather than wait for their questions, which might have taken hours, she continued.

So, if you look beyond this simplistic explanation, you will see that faith and science do go hand in hand. The original universe was created by an omnipotent power, only to be destroyed by its own imperfection, then recreated in an incredible fashion based on the immutable laws of nature. The presence of a higher power was linked into the very fabric of the expanding universe, creating what humans have come to categorize as religion—beliefs based on faith. And they were right, just as the scientists are right in their support of the big bang theory. For lack of a better description, it's like a world within a world. Two worlds existing, without end. Hopefully, someday humanity will understand this. . . before it's too late.

Too stunned to react, Cole and Cassie clung together as if connecting was the only way they could keep from collapsing. Lindsay wrapped her wings around the pair, quelling their anxiety. Gradually, they realized what she had said was true. They believed. The human mind struggles to comprehend the nature of the larger concepts in the universe, and the concept of infinite space, but Lindsay had provided them with renewed hope that maybe, just maybe, they had a chance to make a difference.

For long minutes, they lingered in her embrace, until their strength returned and they were filled with a new sense of resolve. Lindsay released the pair, and the threesome gazed out onto a scene so spectacular that words could not adequately describe it.

"Why are you showing this to us now?" Cassie asked.

So, you will remember. In the darkest hours that will follow, you must remember all of this. It will be the one thing that can guide you through. You are the only two living humans to ever have witnessed this phenomenon. It is a gift I have given you. . . and a curse, Lindsay replied. *Go forth; your journey is just beginning.*

With a stroke of her wing, the glorious scene before them began to fade from vibrant color to black and white, like the ending of an old movie, until all that remained was a sea of green, putrefying mist. In the haze, a silhouette formed, revealing a dark, stone bridge.

Was this their path forward? Looking back, the opening behind them had closed without them realizing. There seemed to be no other way out. They took their first tentative steps walking hand in hand, not knowing where they were headed or what they might encounter on the other side.

Out of nowhere, a discordant guitar chord was struck, badly distorted, and rose in volume as they pressed forward. Then, someone began to sing. But this was no angel's voice. It sounded more like the voice of a tortured soul, lamenting in the distance to a melancholy refrain. Lyrics that were familiar but remorseful as though being judged somehow.

Robin Trower's hauntingly somber *Bridge of Sighs* echoed across the expanse, serenading the pair as they crossed over from a heavenly scene to something that could only be described as a paradox.

The song faded, and they came to an abrupt stop. They had arrived at the end of the bridge, only there was nothing between it and what appeared to be a rocky ledge in the distance. There was only an expanse of empty space, as if a section of the stone crossing had been cut away, separating them from a fall into a deep crevasse below. How were they supposed to cross over?

Cole cursed. This journey was already as challenging as it could be without being faced with nearly impossible obstacles. Was this another one of Lindsay's riddles?

Cassie turned to Cole.

"We need to have faith, Cole. I don't believe Lindsay would lead us to our deaths unknowingly. These obstacles might be here for others, but I don't believe they will spell our ending. Will you trust me?"

Cole hesitated, but he eventually nodded. What choice did he have, really?

"Take my hand," Cassie said, extending her arm.

Cole grasped it, and together they took a step forward, into the abyss. And just like before, when they disembarked from the boat onto shore, a pathway of light materialized, a second bridge—although this one was remarkably different than the one they had previously navigated. Ethereal, shimmering, golden light lit the way out of the green mist. When they at last reached the ledge, what met their eyes could not have been more shocking.

Before them, a dystopian landscape unfolded. Skyscrapers reduced to rubble. Roads cracked, with the fissures steaming. Scorched earth everywhere. The sky was a mix of charcoal gray and lavender, fractured and emitting bolts of electrical charges crisscrossing a broken horizon. Nothing moved except a hot wind that blew dust and ash in little circles like miniature cyclones. Nothing lived, and the stench of death permeated everything. Burned-out cars and buses littered the roadways. An overhead railway system lay crumbled atop smaller buildings. Something about this place seemed familiar to Cole, if not to Cassie.

Cole's gaze shifted to an office complex to his left that still appeared somewhat intact, although heavily damaged. Something drew him to it until he was standing at the entrance to Hollingsworth Enterprises. The sign above the shattered, plate glass windows was still legible. Stunned, Cole suddenly fell to his knees, weeping. They were back in Newport, Rhode Island, a city that had once been so vibrant. The city that had been his only home was now dead and decaying. How had it come to this?

CHAPTER SEVENTY-ONE

CASSIE WATCHED COLE FROM a distance, unsure what he was experiencing. Why had he fallen to his knees so abruptly? She hesitated a moment before joining him, only to discover the reason immediately as she too stared at the burned-out sign bearing his family name. She knelt beside him in silence, wrapping her arms around his shoulders.

Even her tender embrace could not begin to quell his pain. They had been transported into the future—a future so bleak, it defied description. A dead world. What had caused such destruction? Nuclear war. . . or something else?

Cole's body continued trembling as he remained in his prone position, as though he lacked the strength to rise up.

Cassie reluctantly stood, having noticed a newsstand nearby that appeared relatively intact. *Curious,* she thought. She approached cautiously, as if it might implode at any moment. In stark contrast to everything else surrounding them, a fresh-looking pile of newspapers was neatly stacked on top of the stand.

Gingerly, she reached out, retrieving the top copy. In her outstretched hand, she held a copy of the *Newport Daily News*, a branch of Hollingsworth Enterprises. The headline simply read:

The End Is Near: Shelter Underground If Possible.

May God Save the Human Race

There was no story, no explanation, just a large photo of searing, ultra-violet rays scorching the earth. She guessed all of the stories, the explanations, the excuses, had already been written. There was no need to repeat it all. The planet had been overcome with pollution, had been drained of natural resources, and had finally been brought down by extreme global warming and the toxic burning of fossil fuels, destroying the ozone. Then she noticed the date of publication—December 24, 2033. The enormity of the date stunned her. Just thirteen years into the future. How could this have happened so quickly? It didn't seem possible.

As Cassie stood mesmerized, staring at the headlines, she felt a hand touch her shoulder. At first, she lacked the courage to turn and face him. Any hope she'd possessed at the start of this journey had been shattered, washed away by an ocean of despair. They were witnessing the end of humanity. Was anyone left alive amid all of this destruction? Would this ruined land be their final destination to wander until the toxicity overwhelmed them, too? Were they the last living humans left on the planet?

Cassie began trembling with uncontrollable sobs as the stark realization took hold. They were too late to save it. Had Lindsay just shown them a world free of man's interference, a glimpse of heaven, so at least they had something to look forward to in the end?

The newspaper slipped from her hands as she turned to embrace Cole, if for no other reason than to keep from collapsing. Cole grabbed Cassie, steadying her.

"I know. . . I know," Cole said softly. What else could he say? No words could soothe the pain or wash away the images surrounding them.

Cassie looked up at Cole, her eyes filled with tears. Cole didn't think he had ever witnessed such anguish in another person's face. He so wanted to ease her pain. He cursed at Lindsay for making them face this on their own. And for what?

Gradually, they regained control of their emotions, at least enough to converse. They were here for a reason—and they were alive. Lindsay had led them to this place, to this moment, and it was up to them to figure out why.

"So, what do we do next?" Cassie asked, desperately hoping Cole was formulating a plan.

Cole's initial plan was simply to shrug his shoulders in denial. But something in his eyes let Cassie know he was deep in thought. Cole released Cassie and took a few steps forward, surveying the landscape. Now over the initial shock of the devastation, he placed his hands on his hips, assessing their situation.

Cassie watched the man she was falling deeply in love with in fascination. Fortified with the newfound knowledge Lindsay had bestowed on them, a heartrending sense of faith overwhelmed her. There was a higher power after all. With renewed courage, she suddenly felt they could make a difference. They just couldn't allow themselves to fall victim to despair.

For what seemed like hours, the couple walked together along the dusty road that would lead them to the ocean. Perhaps there they could find a clue or, at least, some inspiration. They talked little along the way, both consumed by their own thoughts, endeavoring with everything they were made of to figure out a plan to fix this.

The first thing to come into view was the marina—or at least what used to be the marina. The elegant clubhouse lay in piles of rubble, the grand clock over the portico flattened, its large glass shield shattered. Farther out, the pier consisted of mostly partial wooden posts of uneven heights, dotting the area like torched fenceposts missing their railings. The elegant sailboats and grand yachts that used to grace the shoreline, were little more than ghost ships now—hollow skeletons, like giant dinosaur bones rising out of a quarry. And that's when it hit them.

There was no water to be seen, only a gradually sloping canyon that spread to the horizon like the Dead Sea. Scattered sea life lay everywhere amid salt-crusted shorelines, rotting in the humidity and the toxic air.

Cassie's hand covered her mouth, unconsciously. The ocean—her ocean—the place she loved most and had dedicated her life to understanding, had vanished.

Cole was too stunned to react. All he could do was stare and try to remember what it had been like before, conjuring images of a far better time. He gazed over to where his yacht had been moored only to see it in tatters. It wasn't the loss of money or the one-of-a-kind ship that broke his heart; it was its destruction, along with the destruction of everything around him. He was immediately reminded of his privileged life—his upbringing, the Ivy League education, the over-the-top sports cars, and the bevy of gorgeous women he'd used like playthings.

He suddenly wondered how Serena—his wisecracking Maserati—had fared. Had she made it? Was she driving herself around, looking for him? If anyone could survive, it would be her. This one thought made him smile, until it was overtaken by the image of the car on the side of the road, out of gas, running the battery out of power as she desperately tried to call Cole's cell phone from her in-dash phone system. He could almost see the glowing green light that indicated her Artificial Intelligence systems were engaged flickering to red, until the car was dead, too.

Now, here he was, standing alone with probably the only other living person on the planet, viewing the final destruction of the human race—and he hadn't done a damn thing to prevent it. What a wasted life; one caught up in an endless party of excessive self-indulgence. He, along with other influential people who had turned a blind eye when they could have done something, deserved this. But what about the billions of innocent people who had fallen prey to the whims of the powerful? What were their sins? Believing in their leaders? Suddenly feeling nauseous, Cole leaned over and retched on the spot.

Cassie looked over and instantly knew what he was feeling. Remorse. Regret for his failings. She and Lindsay had spent long hours discussing Cole, the man, and what they knew he was capable of, fearing he would never reach that potential, would never discover his true purpose in life.

Lindsay had sacrificed her life so he could live to see the light and finally understand. And now, they were witnessing the world's end and he still hadn't grasped what that was.

It was about time she took charge.

CHAPTER SEVENTY-TWO

NIGHTFALL WAS DESCENDING, ALL water and food had been consumed, and the time had come to fire up the Eliminator and head back to Isabella. Although reluctant to leave Cole and Cassie, the threesome knew it was necessary. Gamer turned on the ignition, switched on the lights, and headed back to their temporary home in the forming twilight.

Rico watched in fascination as the fire angel hovered in midair, emitting a corona of crimson flame like it was her personal armor, until she disappeared into the distance like a bad dream. There was something about her that intrigued the assassin, even though he was a self-proclaimed atheist. She was sexy.

Ruggedly handsome, Rico had experienced many women, some quite beautiful. But he had never been with an angel, if that was what she really was. Perhaps she was just an apparition, conjured in his head by mind-altering powers beyond his comprehension. *That's possible,* he thought, as he listened to the throaty roar of the Eliminator's powerful engines, propelling them back to land.

Gamer tied off the boat on the dock below their rented house, securing it with steel ropes and locks. They couldn't afford to lose this baby, probably the hottest go-fast boat in the area. It would be highly coveted by drug smugglers and the like. He thought about hiring a guard to watch it through the night, but it had gone untouched the previous evening, so he decided to wait one more day before calling a friend who could discreetly connect him with the right person.

As the threesome walked up the flight of wooden stairs to higher ground, Gamer noticed that a thin layer of green mist was just beginning to intrude onto landfall. Previously, it had merely surrounded the island. Now, it appeared to be encroaching inland. Gamer commented on it, and his two companions, who had not noticed it, became concerned. What was causing this transformation? Cole and Cassie had told them it was toxic. Since neither Cole nor Cassie were here, what would that mean for them?

Entering the house, they spotted Frank and Bill sipping beers outside on the deck. At first, this was a welcome sight. Mario grabbed a six-pack of Corona from the fridge, and the three musketeers headed out to join their companions. The name for the infamous, swashbuckling heroes was beginning to stick with them. And why not? They didn't come much tougher than this group. Besides, they had taken a liking to the moniker. All for one, and one for all! It fit. And somehow it bound them together even more closely.

Their appearance without Cole and Cassie immediately drew concern from the pilots. They turned to face the men, and everything froze in place. Frank's and Bill's faces had turned a putrid shade of gray, with small boils forming on their skin. The stench was evident from a distance. The toxic mist appeared to be consuming them. Yet, they didn't seem to be overly affected by it. The five men stared at one another, until Frank finally spoke.

"What's the matter with you guys? You look like you've just seen a ghost," Frank said, unaware of what had caused the concerned looks on their companions' faces.

Never the shy or socially correct one, Rico stepped forward. "Have you seen yourselves lately? You might want to take a look in a mirror," he said bluntly.

Frank and Bill looked at each other like Rico had gone loco, but they didn't move. Rico left for the nearest bathroom, returning with a hand mirror, which he handed it to Frank. "Here," he said.

Tentatively, Frank raised the mirror to his face. His mouth fell open. He gasped, continuing to stare at himself for a long moment before handing the mirror to Bill.

Bill accepted the looking glass reluctantly, unsure of what he would find, since Frank appeared normal to him. Bill's reaction was nearly identical. The expression of utter confusion on his face did not go unnoticed by the others. He was staring at a corpse—his corpse—or at least that was what appeared in the mirror. His arm dropped to his side, still clutching the mirror.

"What's happened to us?" Bill exclaimed. "Before you three arrived, we were feeling fine. We were sharing a few beers and watching the horizon growing dark, waiting for your return."

Frank suddenly noticed the eerie mist intruding onto the deck, surrounding them. "What did you bring with you? The sky was clear before your return and now everything is being covered by this. . . this green fog. What does it mean?" Frank asked disbelievingly.

Bill swiped his hand through the air, as though he could grab a handful of the stuff and inspect it, then turned to Gamer. "Why aren't you guys affected. You look totally normal to me. I don't understand."

A sudden flood of guilt overcame the boatman. These two brave pilots were here to help but were being kept at arm's length as if they didn't really matter. They had no idea what existed on Hollingsworth Island or what this green mist really was. And unlike the three musketeers, they were being adversely affected. Gamer grabbed the mirror from Bill's hand just to confirm he wasn't transforming, too. As he suspected, his skin remained unchanged. Apparently, they were still under Lindsay's protection.

"Where's Cole?" Frank asked, concerned.

"And Cassie?" Bill echoed.

"They stayed on the island. They're with—" Mario stopped midsentence, unsure if revealing the truth, at least as much as they understood, would be in everyone's best interest. "Um, they are safe."

Frank, the more aggressive of the two, stepped forward. "What aren't you telling us? You were about to say they were with someone. Please don't keep us in the dark. We're part of the team, aren't we?" Frank's tone was insistent.

Mario really couldn't argue the point. Not only were they fellow companions, they were also Cole's employees, and they wouldn't be here if Cole didn't trust them implicitly. He glanced over at Gamer for support.

Gamer nodded and edged closer, although he was equally as uncomfortable as Mario. How did one explain the presence of angels to people who hadn't actually seen them? He started out low-key and noncommittal to see how it would go first.

"They are with Lindsay Featherstone. She took them inside the mountain to explore. Um, she suddenly appeared to us and, well. . . she's back!" So much for low-key.

Both Frank's and Bill's mouths fell open at the same instant. They had spent quite a lot of time with Lindsay during their first trip to the Caribbean to search for Cole's dead parents. They were also keenly aware of Lindsay's disappearance after the final dive that ended with the creation of the massive volcano. They wouldn't be fooled that easily.

"What do you mean, Lindsay's back?" Frank exclaimed. A lengthy silence followed.

Gamer took a deep breath, continuing. "She first appeared to both Cassie and Cole in dreams. Later, she materialized out of the water to Cole, on a beach in Newport. We were not aware of any of this at the time. All we could do was take them at their word, no matter how preposterous it sounded. Apparently, Lindsay warned Cole of major changes taking place inside of the island and convinced him to return again." Gamer paused to ensure the pilots understood. It seemed by their expressions they did, so he continued.

"You already know some of this from our meeting with Cole. Next thing we know, we end up here and on our way to the island this morning. We were pretty much in the dark as you about what we would find there. And let me tell you, what we encountered is still almost too strange to be believable. About one hundred yards out from the shoreline, the green mist appeared, completely surrounding the island. Only the very top was visible.

We were told the fog was toxic, but as long as we were with Cole and Cassie, we would be protected. After penetrating the mist, we reached the island, and that's when it happened. . ."

"What happened?" Bill exclaimed, sounding unconvinced, as if they were being led astray again.

"*She* happened. Lindsay appeared to us as an angel, coming out of a ring of fire. And, if you can believe it, two other angels appeared with her—"

"Fire angels," Mario interjected, taking over for Gamer. "Lindsay opened some kind of magical door or portal, and Cole and Cassie were led inside. We tried to follow, but one of the fire angels blocked our path. Next thing we know, the passageway collapsed, and they were gone. We waited for Cole until it was almost dark, but we had exhausted all of our water due to the intense humidity, so we returned here. That's all we know. Honestly," Mario confided. He stepped back hoping they had been convincing. And they had been—until Rico spoke up.

"It's true, and one of the fire angels was hot! I think she likes me. I'm just biding my time. She'll come over to my side, eventually."

"Yeah, right, and I'm fucking Santa Claus," Frank said, growing more distrustful.

"Frank, don't put any stock in what Rico just said. He's being delusional." Gamer flashed Rico a disparaging look. "But what we just told you is the truth. I swear on our friendship. You have to trust us," Gamer said.

What choice did they have? After further contemplation, the two pilots acquiesced and nodded.

Assured no further convincing was required, Gamer approached Frank to examine his facial skin. "Let me take a closer look at you," the former oceanographer said. Like Lindsay, he had the title of *Dr.* attached to his name, too.

He touched Frank's face and looked into his eyes, spreading his lids apart. "Do you feel pain, any sort of burning sensation?"

"Now that you mention it, yeah, I feel like I am developing a fever, and my vision is slightly blurred," Frank said, growing alarmed.

Gamer turned his attention to Bill. "And you, Bill?"

Bill nodded his head.

"I think it's time we get you some professional help. Mario, can you please contact Dr. Morales and let him know we will be arriving with two patients in about an hour. We'll explain in more detail when we arrive. I want this thing kept under wraps."

Mario dialed his cell phone. Not unsurprisingly, Dr. Morales answered on the second ring. He had learned his lesson while taking care of Gamer after he was almost killed on the mountain during his first climb with Cole. He knew these men were not ones who took kindly to disappointment.

They quickly packed a few necessary items and were in the Jeep within minutes traveling to the clinic. The place didn't advertise itself as a clinic, but it was second to none in terms of equipment and capabilities. Rico remained at the house in case Cole and Cassie returned.

Dr. Morales himself, along with two staff members, personally greeted the companions at the back of the building. Initially, the doctor appeared startled at the pilots' appearances, but he said little until he could get them into an exam room. No need to stir things up right off the bat. He had come to expect unusual injuries with this group. . . and no excuses.

CHAPTER SEVENTY-THREE

Wiping his mouth with his shirt sleeve, Cole stood up. Another glance across the landscape seemed to renew whatever senses he still possessed. Cassie approached.

"Cole, please tell me what you're feeling? I sense it's mostly regret. Regret for the sins of the powerful. Your sins. That maybe you could have done more to help the less fortunate. And I'm not referring to money or handouts. You now see yourself and others like you as the primary cause for the misery we are witnessing. Am I correct?"

Cassie's words instantly rendered Cole defenseless and guilt-ridden. Just like on the *Truett*, when she'd told him not to leave Lindsay prior to the last dive in the *Harbinger II*. A dive that would change everything. A dive that had now changed the natural world as well.

"Yes!" Cole shouted, his voice cracking. "Are you happy now? Once again, you have cut me down to size. You and Lindsay—it seems like that has become your life's work. What is it you want from me?" Cole said, his gaze penetrating like laser beams all the way through Cassie's heart.

Cassie's eyes welled with tears again. "You don't know? You still don't know?" She paused, becoming even more emotional. "I want you. . . Lindsay wants you. . . the world wants you to make a difference. Go back and use your influence and all the resources at your command to let the human race know what their indifference has done to our planet. Convince them there is still time to save it. Just like you did with the article in your newspaper about the Navy and nuclear weapons."

"And how am I supposed to that, trapped in the future with no apparent way back?" Cole asked mockingly. "Snap my fingers and rub my ruby slippers together and recite, *There's no place like home, there's no place like home?*" Cole's temper began to flare, and he was becoming more belligerent by the second.

Finally, some emotion, some sense of purpose, Cassie thought. "Yes, something like that. You hold the key to our return. Just believe in yourself and, after you have reached that state of grace, take the first step backward and allow Lindsay to once again be your spirit guide," Cassie said confidently. "We can return."

Cole appeared as if he was about to rebuke Cassie's comments, when he stopped himself. Instead, he simply stared at her. She saw conviction growing in those deep, dark eyes, until a light sparked.

"Well then, what are we waiting for!" Cole exclaimed abruptly.

Cassie smiled and followed Cole as he turned around and headed back to the point where they had entered. After they reached the area where they had first encountered this dystopian world, Cassie tugged on Cole's arm.

"Let's grab some of these, just in case we can take them back successfully." She grabbed a handful of the newly printed newspapers still piled on the stand and handed them to Cole. "If nothing else, they will become collector's items, but we may be able to use them to our advantage."

Cole didn't immediately see the advantage but took hold of them anyway. Cassie was usually right about things, and the more time he spent with the Aussie, the more he came to believe it. She wasn't Lindsay, but she was still an amazing woman.

They reached the abyss, noticing the section of the stone bridge was still conspicuously missing. Cole did not hesitate this time. Taking Cassie's hand, he led them over the edge as a ramp of pure light materialized, supporting their collective weight until they stepped again onto the cold, decaying stone.

Gradually, they climbed the gentle slope toward its apex, where Cassie tugged on Cole's hand, stopping him. He turned to face her. There was something mysterious in her gaze, otherworldly. She smiled wistfully, just as they heard music beginning to play softly in the background.

"Cole, if we listen with our hearts, we can hear the earth singing."

A moment later, the pair was serenaded by the lilting lyrics to Secret Garden's Sleepsong.

Cole listened in silence as the song foretold that there would always be angels to look over him.

On and on it serenaded the pair until Cole's eyes became heavy. Just before he fell prey to a dreamworld, Cassie released his hands, vanishing in a cloud of shimmering dust, blown away by a warm breeze.

CHAPTER SEVENTY-FOUR

COLE AWOKE SOMETIME LATER from a dreamless state, lying on the beach below their rented house, newspapers still clutched under his arm. It appeared to be early morning. A hazy sun hung low in the eastern sky. He rose groggily, staring at familiar sights but not realizing exactly where he was. Slowly, he came to his senses and looked around for Cassie. Where had she gone?

Cole clung to the uneven railing as he climbed the two flights of wooden stairs to the ledge above the sand. Still feeling queasy, he walked gingerly through the house to the outside deck, which was empty. He called out to his companions. A single voice responded.

"Hey, boss, where the hell have you been?" Rico asked as he stepped onto the deck. "And where's that gorgeous girlfriend of yours?"

Cole winced at this description. But then, Rico called it like he saw it. It didn't really matter after what he and Cassie had just experienced.

"She should be around somewhere. Maybe she's in her bedroom," Cole said.

"I don't think so. I've been here the whole time, and you're the first person I've seen come back."

Momentarily distracted from Cassie's absence, Cole wondered what had transpired here since they entered the volcano. "How long have I been gone, and where are the others?"

"It's been a little over twenty-four hours," Rico said, hesitating. "You aren't going to like this, boss. Frank and Bill are sick. Gamer and Mario took them to see Dr. Morales. They didn't look so good when they left a couple of hours ago. I haven't heard back from them."

"Sick? What's wrong with them?" Cole asked, confused.

"Haven't you noticed the mist covering this place. Looks like we brought it back with us. It's hard for us to see, but it turned the pilots' skin gray, and boils appeared on their faces—"

"What!" Cole exclaimed, having failed to notice the dull green fog surrounding the house, as if it had become a part of them now—cloaked in toxic air but not realizing it. "You're not making sense, Rico."

"I know. It doesn't make sense to me, either. But I'm just a hired hand."

"You're far more than that, my friend," Cole said, reaching for his cell phone. It had disappeared as well. "Can I borrow your phone, Rico?"

"Sure." Rico handed a spare phone to Cole, since his previous one had been destroyed, too. Cole quickly dialed Gamer.

Gamer answered immediately. "Hey, Cole, you're back. Thank God. How are you two doing?" the boatman asked.

"We're. . . um, I'm fine. We just got back, but I can't find Cassie. I'm sure she'll show up soon. How are Frank and Bill doing?"

"Too early to tell. It seems they've been exposed to some form of toxic material. Morales thinks it's an airborne substance but hasn't identified its source yet. They're in isolation, hooked up to ventilators as a precaution. We decided not to tell the doctor too much until we heard from you. How would you like us to proceed?" the boatman said, pausing to consider just how Cole had made it back without a boat.

Cole looked out in the general direction of the island. The horizon was indeed shrouded in a sickening, greenish haze. Not nearly as dense as they had experienced near the volcano, but undeniably present. It was true then.

But why had it affected the pilots and not them? Rico appeared normal. His skin color hadn't changed—deeply tanned, with a scruffy beard that could use a little trimming.

"Hey, Gamer, I'm noticing the mist on the water but less so on land. My guess is that it's slowly moving inland. Has it reached the clinic yet?" Cole asked.

"Not that I can tell. Within a couple of minutes after we left the house, it cleared up. Nothing but sunshine now. Strange, don't you think?"

"That's an understatement. Hey, I don't have a car, but I'll call a driver if you think I need to be there," Cole said.

"No, I think you should stay put. Now that you're safely back, I'll ask Mario to secure another vehicle so we have more mobility. One car isn't cutting it. Give me a shout when Cassie shows up."

"Will do. Talk to you soon," Cole said, then added, "While you're in town, please pick up another cell phone for me. A burner is fine. I seemed to have left mine on the island."

"Copy that."

Cole handed the cell phone back to Rico, troubled. The pilots sick. Cassie missing. What was happening? It didn't feel right.

"Boss, you hungry? There are leftovers in the fridge, or I can whip you up some eggs and tortillas," Rico offered.

"Maybe later, thanks." Cole had lost his appetite. He needed to get to the bottom of things. Heading to his bedroom, he powered on his laptop. Maybe there was something in the news about this mysterious fog. And what was the crew on the Zumwalt destroyer thinking? Surely, they were aware of it.

Oddly, there was no mention of the encroaching mist on any news website Cole could find. There were still lots of articles questioning the Navy vessels in the area, but that too seemed to be diminishing. The folks in Washington were obviously playing it down and focusing elsewhere. The White House was spreading stories about imminent attacks Iran's religious fanatics were planning against US targets. The president and his advisors were considering deploying more forces in the area, not long after they'd committed to taking troops out. In Cole's mind, they were fabricating stories to deflect criticism over their handling of Hollingsworth Island and the presence of nuclear weapons.

Key environmentalists around the world were beginning to speak out about the potential harm that would be done to the area post nuclear detonations, should those occur. It seemed the articles published by Hollingsworth's newspapers were paying off. According to one article, the Zumwalt destroyer had moved farther out to sea but, reportedly, was still in the vicinity.

It was time to call Art. Four rings later, the attorney answered. "Who's this?" Art asked impatiently, as if he was expecting someone else.

"Art, it's Cole. I'm using Rico's phone. I left mine on the island. It's a long story. How are things back at the office? Gaines under control?"

"As much as can be expected, considering he's still up to his ears with the White House over our publishing those defamatory articles about the Navy deployment—or at least that's what they're calling them. Now that some of the environmental agencies are weighing in, they've been threatening Gaines if Hollingsworth continues to criticize the White House. I'm not sure what the government can do, but it's got Bill rattled. Everyone's asking where you are in all of this turmoil. I think your absence may be the bigger story," Art said.

"Good, let's keep them guessing. By the way, we've got a strange situation going on down here. In the last day or so, the mist that had recently been directly surrounding the island has thinned out but appears to be moving inland, and it has hit landfall, at least on the eastern shoreline of Puerto Rico. It appears to be toxic in some shape or form. It's affected Frank and Bill, and they are now in the clinic with Dr. Morales, in isolation. I don't know how serious their condition is yet, but I should hear soon. The strange thing is that it hasn't affected any of us who went to the island. It's like we have some kind of immunity from it," Cole said, not wanting to fully reveal yet how they'd come to be immune.

Art remained silent for a long moment, contemplating what Cole had said. He was aware of the fog surrounding the island, as that had just appeared on the *National Newsline*, but there'd been nothing about it spreading.

"We've heard nothing about it spreading inland up here. That seems really strange. I wonder what could be causing it?" Art mused, puzzled. His absence from the area was definitely making it more difficult to understand what was happening to his friends, and he was becoming more alarmed with each passing day. What the hell was going on down there? And he hadn't even heard about Cole's latest trip to the island yet. "Maybe I should head down there. I'm not sure I can add anything more up here. I'll stay in contact with Adderley in case we need him again. Now that environmental groups are taking up the call, we may not need to continue publishing our op-eds. What do you say, Cole?"

"I'd say that's a damn good idea. It's about time! But let's not let the pressure off too much. Keep the articles coming when we learn something new," Cole added, half mocking.

"I'll make the arrangements and let you know when I'll be arriving. In the meantime, text me if you hear anything more on the pilots' condition. I don't like the sound of that." Art disconnected, feeling that the situation was starting to unravel. He needed to be by Cole's side now that things were ratcheting up and the White House was involved. This was no longer a personal excursion of Cole's to reconnect with Lindsay or an opportunity to advance scientific research in the area. It seemed to Art that it was becoming a global event with far-reaching consequences—consequences that had the potential to be catastrophic.

CHAPTER SEVENTY-FIVE

WITH NO TRANSPORTATION AND still waiting to hear back on Frank's and Bill's conditions, Cole headed out to the deck to wait for Cassie's return. He sat alone, gazing out to sea, peering through the haze that was dulling the shimmering tropical waters beyond. The more he sat alone, the more worried he became, straining to remember just what had happened when they attempted to leave the futuristic dystopian landscape they had experienced together. They had arrived at the Bridge of Sighs together after grabbing a stack of newspapers that had been published by the *Newport Daily News*. Published in the year 2033. But it all became blurred after that. He recalled crossing the mysterious bridge of light, leading them onto the decaying stone bridge. But then. . . what happened next?

Hadn't they heard a song resonating from a distance as they climbed upward? Something about angels? Yes, about angels watching over him. As they reached the apex of the bridge, Cole recalled becoming suddenly sleepy. Cassie had turned him around and kissed him, leaving him temporarily paralyzed. She had whispered something, perhaps. It was all so muddled in his head. Something about a price to pay. Or was it a *toll* to pay? A toll so they could cross over and back to the present? Yes, that was it. And then she had vanished into thin air, just as he was overcome with sleep, falling to the stone path below. Next thing he knew, he had somehow washed up on the beach beneath this very house.

Cole stood abruptly, panic racing through his body. "Cassie!" he screamed as the sudden realization overwhelmed him. "Cassie?" he called out again. Cole's voice echoed across the expanse of ocean, guided by a mysterious power, until it reached the island.

And then it happened. Lindsay, the angel, appeared, hovering in the distance, lighting up the sky as if the heavens were opening up just for Cole, while the rest of the space turned dark. And by her side, Cassie suddenly materialized, adorned with massive, gray wings tinged in scarlet, more warrior-like than angelic. A wicked-looking sword hung from one hip, shimmering like it was on fire. In her right hand, she clenched a jewel-studded, devilish dagger, reminding Cole of Elvish death blades fashioned in the underground forges of Rivendell in Middle Earth. Her chest plate was a combination of gold and white armor, revealing a bare waist. Below that, similar armor covered a part of her midsection before leading to exposed legs and knee-high boots of brilliant red material adorned with gilded symbols. Her hair had turned completely golden, no longer a blend of colors. *Fierce* was the word that came to Cole's mind.

For a moment, Cole stood mesmerized by her presence, until he realized what was happening. It was Cassie who had paid the toll, so Cole could cross over safely.

"Cassie!" he screamed again, as he dropped to his knees in anguish. "Not you, too!"

Cassie—or the ethereal being she had become—floated toward Cole, and the world around him seemed to freeze, as though mesmerized, too.

Do not lament, Cole. I am now the Light Warrior, here to protect you while Lindsay guides you. Do you not recall the words of Sleepsong from when we crossed over the Bridge of Sighs? There will always be angels to watch over you. Your work is only just beginning. All that you need to move forward, we witnessed on the other side. Allow that broken planet to be your ring bearer—to be your inspiration. It will show you the way. You possess the power to alter humanity. Do not allow the naysayers or heretics to block your path. Planet Earth has selected you to champion her cause. What greater honor can there be?

Through tear-drenched eyes, Cole gazed up at the Australian beauty who had transformed into a celestial being. It appeared she had been the one to choose immortality. *How ironic,* he thought. Speechless, he remained on his knees, unable to rise up as their images gradually faded away. Just before she disappeared completely, Cassie released her dagger. Cole watched in amazement as the object magically floated in his direction, coming to rest two feet away. It glimmered as though it possessed the power of a star. The emerald gemstone that Cassie wore in her belly button, which Cole had noticed when they reconnected in Newport, was embedded in its hilt, along with the words: *We will always be connected.*

Cole gingerly took hold of the weapon. It fit him like a glove, as though it was an extension of his own hand. For a very long time, Cole stood at the edge of the deck, fondling the dagger and looking out toward the island, until darkness no longer allowed a view.

Like Rico the assassin, Gamer the boatman, and Mario the driver, Cole had earned his own form of a deadly blade, although he suspected this one was unlike any other that existed in the ordinary world. And now. . . now they had become the four musketeers.

CHAPTER SEVENTY-SIX

THE FOLLOWING MORNING, COLE was abruptly awakened by a stout pull on his shoulder. Someone was calling to him from a distant place. Somewhere between slumber and wakefulness, he heard his name being called again.

"Cole."

Gradually, Rico's face came into focus as Cole regained his senses. His first thought was of the dagger he'd obtained the previous night. It felt as if it was still in his grasp, but when he looked down at his hand, it was gone. The weight seemed to be there still, but nothing was visible. He glanced around, then looked over at Rico, thinking he may have grabbed it to inspect. Nothing.

Cole rose gingerly from the chaise lounge he had been sleeping on.

"Are you okay, boss? You look like you've been through a battle or something. Can I get you anything?" Rico asked, concerned.

"I'm fine, just tired. . . and a little stressed. I'm worried about Cassie. Have you seen her yet," Cole asked. Then the image of Cassie, the warrior angel, came flooding back. Once again, Cole seemed to be caught between a dreamworld and reality, as the line between the two continued to blur. Most humans would have gone mad by now, but it was only his undying love for

Lindsay that had kept him sane. And then there was Cassie, the mortal, who Lindsay had apparently sent him as her surrogate. Just when he thought he was falling in love with her, she chose to join Lindsay, the angel, and the two were now immortal.

Rico shook Cole's shoulder again. "Are you sure you're okay? You look like you're in another world."

"Sorry, Rico. Just got a lot on my mind. Have you heard anything from the clinic? How are the pilots doing?" Cole asked, attempting to divert Rico's attention away from his current state of mind.

"About the same, I guess. Gamer called earlier and said nothing much has changed. He asked about you, and I told him you were asleep outside."

"I need to head over there. Have we secured another vehicle yet?"

"Yeah, Mario has it and is heading back to the house. He should be here in about thirty minutes. Why don't you catch a shower, and I'll make you some breakfast," Rico said.

"Thanks, I'll be back shortly." Cole paused. "Have you seen a knife—actually it's more like a dagger—lying around anywhere?"

This elicited a confused expression from Rico as he cast a quick glance around the deck. "No, boss, ain't seen nothing like that." He patted the machete hanging from his hip as though that was the only blade worth mentioning, then added, "I can get you one in town real quick."

"No, that's all right, but thanks." Cole turned and headed inside to shower and clean up. It had been a while. Standing in the shower, with streams of hot water pelting his cramped neck and back muscles, he searched his mind for a clearer picture of what really happened last night. Two angels had appeared before him. Cassie had transformed into an astonishing, warrior-like angel who initially struck fear into Cole, but she'd later calmed him with her words. She had given him her dagger; he was sure of it. Had she taken it back while he slept? Was it only a metaphor to convey her message of protection? Was it another dream?

Frustrated by the contradictory events and his inability to remember correctly, Cole swore loudly and slammed his right hand hard against the tiled wall. He immediately felt a sharp pain and a searing heat shoot up his arm, as the dagger materialized in his hand, back in his control. Cole's mouth dropped open as he stared at the magnificent weapon. He twisted his hand around, gazing at the instrument. Had the blade become a part of him? Like it was a part of his body that he could control? He slashed at the washcloth hanging from the spigot. It separated the cloth into two strips like a hot knife through melting butter. He watched the two halves fall silently to the tiled floor. He hadn't even felt the cut. The only sensation was one of passing something through thin air. No impact, no resistance—only a clean cut. *How sharp is this thing?* Cole wondered.

In his minds' eye, Cassie's visage appeared, and she was smiling. And then Cole finally realized this was no dream. He was now ninety percent human and ten percent. . . what? Ten percent angel? Was this his first step toward immortality? Would he be required to earn it in chunks?

Suddenly, he realized he'd need to find a way to hide the dagger. He couldn't just walk around with this thing tethered to his hand. Gradually, he relaxed his body and willed the knife to disappear, imagining it gone. No sooner had he done so than the deadly blade vanished, leaving only his normal hand. A devilish smile spread across his face. A magical weapon couldn't be all bad.

He dried quickly, slipping into clean khakis and a green, nondescript T-shirt, then strapped on some leather sandals. He entered the main living room just as he heard the gravel outside crunching under car tires. Mario had arrived.

Opening the door, he greeted the driver warmly. Mario handed Cole his new phone. He hadn't forgotten. He was also apparently back to driving his old, weather-beaten, white van. Cole wondered what the attraction was. He guessed they'd seen a lot of action together and that his driver just couldn't give it up.

"Good to see you back, boss. We were getting worried about you," Mario said.

"Good to see you, too. How's Gamer?" Cole asked.

"As ornery as ever. I don't think he likes being in that clinic much. Or maybe it's Dr. Morales. Hard to say. By the way, how's Cassie?"

Just the question Cole was hoping to avoid, or at least delay. But that would be impossible. She was a vital part of their mission, and her absence could not be denied. But how to tell them? Cole hesitated, uncertain. He owed these comrades an honest explanation, but he'd prefer to tell them all at once.

"She's back on—"

"Hey, boss, breakfast is ready," Rico shouted from the kitchen, providing Cole with a brief respite.

"You hungry, Mario?" Cole asked.

"I could eat. I'll be right there."

Cole entered the dining area to see the table filled with dishes of hot food, with steam rising up from the plates. The table had been set for three. Scrambled eggs with fried chorizo and green peppers, flour tortillas, shredded chicken, salsa, and some sort of bean concoction topped with melting cheese. Hot coffee and cold orange juice completed the meal.

"I hope you like it," Rico said, with a half-smile. He was obviously proud of his work but wanted to remain humble, which was not something he was accustomed to doing. He was all macho—the alpha male—and cooking seemed like women's work, at least to him.

"What's not to like, Rico? You've outdone yourself," Cole said, taking a seat. He was suddenly overcome with hunger. He hadn't eaten in a long time.

Mario appeared. "Nice spread, amigo. I think you should exchange that machete of yours for a chef's knife and go into business," the driver teased.

Rico frowned. "There's no need to insult me, Mario. What do you think I used to cut up all this stuff!"

Cole choked on a mouthful of eggs, imagining where the lethal blade had been prior to chopping up their breakfast.

"Not to worry, boss. I sterilized the blade before using it." The assassin grinned, but it was less than convincing.

"Don't mind him, Cole. He's just being his usual, annoying self," Mario said. In a blinding move of speed, he drew his stiletto and threw it at Rico.

It passed within an inch of Rico's left ear, embedding into the wall directly behind him.

"Nice shot. Is that all you got?" Rico said, taking a step forward.

"Now, now, gentlemen. How do you expect me to eat with all of this commotion?" Cole said, though he considered revealing his own dagger, that is, if he could conjure it in time. It might be the best way to start the conversation about Cassie. At least it would grab their attention. First things first, though. He needed to eat.

Cole's intervention seemed to do the trick. The comrades appeared to calm down and began eating their food in strained silence. Something was obviously bothering them, but what?

After satisfying his hunger, Cole pushed his plate forward, sighing. The time had come to fess up. Gamer would just have to wait. Remaining silent until he had his friends' full attention, Cole closed his eyes and seemed to be calling on something inside of himself. While the two comrades watched in rapt fascination, he held up his right hand, and the brilliant, jewel-studded dagger materialized out of thin air. The handle appeared to be attached to his hand in some inexplicable manner. Cole uncoiled his fingers, and the knife remained stationary. The wickedly curved blade was approximately twelve inches long, and the guard extended three inches to either side. The edge of the blade gleamed, honed to a sharpness that startled even Rico, who maintained his machete to razor-like standards as if his life depended on its ability to cut through anything.

"Holy shit!" Rico exclaimed. "Where the hell did you get that?"

Mario gazed at his boss in silence, as though too stunned to speak—or was it that he already knew something? A wry smile formed on the driver's face. "It was a gift, if I'm not mistaken? And a very special one at that."

Cole returned the driver's smile. "How did you know?"

"I've heard rumors a weapon like that exists, one that is not of this earth. It's bestowed on only a select few deemed worthy of such a blade. No human could have forged it. I've never seen one before, but the myths have been passed down from the days of the Inca's, whose connections to the ancient gods are legendary," Mario said reverently, as though Cole had been touched by the gods. "Did you receive it from Lindsay?"

"Actually, my friends, it was a gift from Cassie. I was waiting for the right time to tell you, and I hoped that Gamer would be present—"

"Cassie?" Rico interrupted. "How could that be possible? She's not a—" Rico suddenly went silent as the realization of what Cole was telling them begin to sink in.

"It's a long story, and one that I want to share with you, but our boat-man needs to hear it at the same time. What do you say to a quick trip to the clinic? I think he would appreciate being rescued, at least until he hears what I'm going to say," Cole said, with a hint of sarcasm.

Both men nodded, apprehension etched on their faces.

CHAPTER SEVENTY-SEVEN

MARIO DROVE THE VAN into town, while his two passengers remained quiet. Cole was lost in thought, a state he seemed to be spending more time in lately. Rico was apparently still in shock over the sudden appearance of the magical blade. The trip over seemed to take longer than usual.

The driver steered the van to the rear of the clinic, and the threesome exited. Gamer was waiting for them in the lobby after being alerted of their impending arrival. His first impulse was to hug Cole, but he decided shaking hands would be the best move. "I was wondering when I'd see you again, boss. Thank God, you made it back safely. Cassie back at the house?"

Cole's harsh expression startled the boatman. "Before we discuss my experiences on the island, I'd like to check on Frank and Bill, okay?"

Gamer nodded, then he glared at his two companions as if they'd been hiding something from him. He didn't like secrets, especially from these men.

Dr. Morales appeared out of nowhere and not a minute too soon. Tension was again mounting among the three musketeers. Cole sensed it again and was determined to get to the bottom of it, but first he wanted an update on the pilots' condition.

"Cole, will you please accompany me to my office?" Morales asked. Apparently, the others weren't being invited.

Cole gestured to his companions to follow, but the doctor intervened. "Just you, Mr. Hollingsworth, please. You friends already know how they are doing."

Cole looked at his men to see how this would affect their moods. They shrugged their shoulders but looked further irritated at being left out. Cole followed Morales to his office, and the doctor closed the door after Cole was seated.

"It's not good, Mr. Hollingsworth. Your pilots are weakening by the hour. We've completed every test we had at our disposal and have no identifiable cause. If I were to guess, I would say it's a rare, airborne pathogen of some sort. Under an electron microscope, the virus looks unlike anything I have ever seen before. It's attacking their lungs and respiratory systems. At first, we thought it was a new, stronger flu strain, but the fact that their skin has changed color and is forming boils makes it all the more difficult to understand." Morales paused for a moment. "Is there anything you can tell me that might have caused or contributed to their infections?" He asked this in a controlled manner, not wanting to offend, but it still came off like an accusation.

Morales was aware of Cole's close connection with the island—and he had heard things. Every patient Cole had brought to him so far was as unique a case as he had seen. He still didn't know what happened to Art Barkley, after he suddenly disappeared from the basement morgue. What he didn't know was that Art's murder had been wiped clean from the memory of others. Time had been reversed as if it had never happened, and Art was back in Newport, alive and well. Why he still believed Art had been murdered was curios, since no one else even suspected it had happened. Did Lindsay have a reason to allow his memory to live on? What role did Morales have in the future that meant he needed to still believe Art had been shot? With Art due to arrive shortly, it would most likely be the shock of the doctor's life.

Cole sensed Morales was leading him into a corner and that the doctor believed, in some way, that he was responsible for what was happening. And in a way, he was. He cleared his throat.

"Doctor, you may know about the unusual mist that has been cloaking the volcano recently?" Cole paused in anticipation of a reaction, but Morales only nodded as if he was aware of the phenomenon. "Well, it seems to be encroaching inland. We noticed it about twenty-four hours ago. When it first hit landfall, it hit the house we're staying at. As it juts out on a cliff, its location was one of the first to be exposed. Since then, it has thinned out significantly. It has not yet reached Isabella. Apparently, Frank and Bill were exposed to it at its full intensity, and I suspect the mist has somehow caused their current condition."

This was all the doctor was going to get from Cole. There would be no mention of his trip inside the mountain or the angels' existence. That would all have to come out in due time, if it ever did.

"I see..." Morales stroked his chin with his right hand. "That at least makes some sense. Was there anyone else in the house at the time?"

"No. My men were elsewhere and arrived later. In fact, they were the ones to discover the pilots' condition. Neither Frank nor Bill had any idea at first."

"Now that's interesting. They didn't realize they had any symptoms?"

"Apparently not," Cole replied.

"When did you become aware of their condition, if I may ask?"

"I never saw them. I returned to the house after they were sent here," Cole said.

"And none of you have any symptoms? You must have been exposed to it, also. This seems odd to me."

"Just lucky, I guess. What can I say?" Cole replied, shifting in his chair uneasily. Morales was smart and very experienced, but he could not know that Lindsay had granted the companions immunity—at least those who had ventured to the island. No one would believe that. He could only hope this little secret would remain a secret, especially if the mist continued to spread.

"I'm calling in a virologist to take a look at your pilots, Mr. Hollingsworth. Based on what you've just told me, if this thing begins to spread, it could become a pandemic. If so, we'll need to inform the neighboring countries and the World Health Organization. We'll need to set up a tight lockdown to help prevent the spread."

This had not occurred to Cole, as his attention had been focused elsewhere. But the doctor was right, of course. This could become a national crisis if it wasn't handled correctly, with the potential to morph into a global one.

"If there is nothing else, Doctor, I'd like to see my pilots," Cole said.

"Of course. But you'll need to wear a mask and gloves and keep your distance. We can only assume they are contagious. Nurse Agular will fix you up with the necessary PPE. Please follow me."

Cole followed Morales, secured the necessary safety equipment, and tailed the nurse into the pilots' room. They were staying together; Cole could only assume to keep the virus contained. As he approached, Cole stopped abruptly. His companions were wearing protective masks, and an oxygen tube covered their mouth and nostrils. But even behind all the protective gear, deathly pale faces stared back at him. He hadn't known what to expect, but nothing quite like this. His companions appeared more like zombies than living humans. His heart sank as he gazed back at his trusted employees, unable to speak. For a long moment, he simply stood in silence, until the guilt overwhelmed him.

He should have been more protective of these men. He knew that only under his and Cassie's watch could his companions avoid the toxic effects of the mist. By excluding the pilots from traveling to the island, he'd also excluded them from protection. They had wanted to come, to be a part of this journey, and he had let them down. Cole cursed. Then he asked the nurse to leave the room. He needed some time alone with his friends.

CHAPTER SEVENTY-EIGHT

C OLE ENTERED THE LOBBY, where his three companions were standing around awaiting instructions and looking concerned. Clearly, they weren't speaking with one another, and once more, Cole felt the tension lacing between the men.

"Come on, we're headed back to the house. I'm with you, Gamer," Cole said, stomping out the back doors.

Cole slipped into the passenger's seat of the Jeep as Gamer started the engine and headed out of the parking lot, followed closely by Mario and Rico in the van.

Cole turned to his boatman. "What do you make of this? You're a scientist. You must have some idea."

The boatman hesitated, knowing what Cole was asking of him–a more educated opinion. Gamer had the uneasy feeling that what he said next would directly influence his boss's next moves.

"Well, if I didn't know better, I would say the power within the mountain—whatever that power is—has begun to exert its will on the planet. I believe it created the mist and is now spreading it outward to get humanity's attention. To wake them up, so to speak. It's a warning." Gamer looked over at his boss for his reaction. He knew his theory sounded preposterous. Yet, he knew Cole had experienced events that few, if any, humans had been privy to. He might just understand.

Initially, Cole appeared thunderstruck; his mouth dropped open, and his face turned white. But rather than blowing this explanation off or chastising his boatman for even suggesting such a thing, Cole appeared to consider what he'd said.

"What would make you say such a thing? Are you saying you believe the volcano—or the creatures inhabiting it—possess the power to infect the world, and not just with volcanic eruptions?" Cole asked, wondering how this Russian scientist could have guessed what he was beginning to suspect as well. Gamer had no firsthand experience with the angels and had never been inside the mountain. It could only be pure speculation on his part. But then, he was a brilliant oceanographer himself, even though he routinely disguised this aspect of his persona in favor of the tough-guy act.

"I think you know why I said what I did. I think you know much more than you're telling us, and I'm hoping you will take me into your confidence so I can help you. There is something very strange going on inside that mountain, and I believe you've seen it. Every time you return, you seemed to have changed in some way."

"You're very observant, my friend. How you came to this conclusion with so little firsthand knowledge is remarkable. And yes, this is what I believe, too. On my last visit, Cassie and I crossed over. . . um. . . I mean, Lindsay revealed the future, and it wasn't pretty. Due to man's abuse, this planet is declining rapidly, and we need to do something about it—before the mountain takes measures into its own hands. There has been lots of talk about global warming and pollution but little is being done about it. Mostly partisan bullshit. But the real question is, what can we do to make a difference?" Cole replied.

"You know, Cole, if you look back at the history of the earth, at least as much as we are confident about, you'll see patterns. From the comet that hit the Mexico area that triggered the end of the dinosaurs, to the great ice age, to pandemics and other natural disasters. They all have had a cleansing effect, so the planet could change and renew itself. I believe the climate change and global warming currently taking place is leading up to the next great cleansing. I also believe that, in some miraculous way, Lindsay is giving us clues and warnings this time so that humanity might survive. That is, if we can see past our own folly and shortsightedness before it's too late."

Again, Cole considered Gamer's explanation carefully. Were the angels sent to give them that warning? Had the creation of Hollingsworth Island been the trigger for the next calamitous evolution of the planet? It somehow made sense. And isn't this what Lindsay had been trying to convey to him all along? Just last night, when Cassie came to him as a supernatural being, she told him that he had been chosen to lead the fight to save the planet. She had sacrificed her mortal life to protect him as well. The signs were all there. He couldn't ignore them much longer.

"After we return to the house, I'll fill you and the others in about what I experienced on the island. And then, you and I will return and enter the mountain. We can only find the answers we seek inside."

Twenty minutes later, the four men clambered into the house and headed out to the deck, but not before grabbing a small ice chest filled with cold beer. Cole stood, while the others popped open the bottles and took seats facing their boss and the ocean beyond. The faint, green mist hovered over the water, turning it a soiled, grayish color. No sea birds sailed the sky as they normally would. The area was eerily quiet and seemed to be moving in slow motion. A faint smell of decay permeated the air.

"The time has come, my friends, for me to reveal more to you. I do appreciate your patience and loyalty without the need to know everything—or the need to ask me the questions I'm sure you have all been harboring. I think that may be what I respect most about each of you—your steadfastness during the entire journey so far." Cole paused for a moment to gauge his companions' expressions. Were they finally ready to hear the truth and yet remain willing to stay the course? Cole found no immediate answer in their eyes.

"When Cassie and I entered the mountain with Lindsay, after you first experienced the angels, that was just the beginning. What is going on inside is nothing short of miraculous. A new environment is being created, and possibly new life forms. After witnessing this, Lindsay guided us to an ancient, stone bridge and bid us to pass over. When we arrived at the other side, we were transported to a futuristic world, a broken planet. Our planet. It had been destroyed, stripped of natural resources, and no human life could be found. We witnessed firsthand what our disregard for the environment had caused and what our future looked like if we didn't do something drastic to reverse its course. We were heartbroken. I was led to Hollingsworth headquarters, or what was left of it. A once vibrant building reduced to rubble. And it was there that we found these recently published newspapers." Cole reached over to a table and handed out three copies of the *Newport Daily News* to the men, as they stared at their boss as if he was speaking to them in an unfamiliar foreign language.

The headline was all it took, along with the date of publication. The photos spoke for themselves. A dystopian world, beyond salvation. Gamer seemed to be affected most, probably due to his connection to the natural world through science. But all three men were visibly distraught as they silently contemplated what this meant. It was nearly incomprehensible. What stood out most was the publication date. 2033. Just thirteen short years into the future. How could it have happened so fast?

All three men looked up at Cole at the same time with searching eyes and questioning expressions. Little hope existed in their faces.

"We. . . I mean, I, brought the papers back so you could see them. Cassie didn't make it back. There was a price to be paid for such a discovery. The toll to cross over to the future and back to the present is tremendous. For me to return safely, it cost Cassie her mortal life. And she gave it willingly. . ." Cole paused as a wave of emotion ripped through him. He wiped his eyes on his sleeve before continuing.

"She is now among the angels and by Lindsay's side. She came to me last night as a celestial being to share the message that the fate of the planet somehow rests in our hands—and that she is here to protect us. At first, I thought it was just a dream, but I know now that it was not."

Cole raised his right hand and, just as before, the magical dagger formed in his palm. Though Mario and Rico had already experienced this conjuring, they were still startled by its appearance. Gamer, on the other hand, appeared shell-shocked as he gazed at the glimmering blade that could not have been of this earth.

"This was her parting gift to me. What it means exactly eludes me, but it may yet have a purpose to fulfill. I believe the toxic mist we experienced when we first arrived at the island is thinning and spreading inland to infect humans, like a warning. A warning that we must change our ways as a human race or face the fate that Cassie and I witnessed. But I still need answers. That is why I must return. Are you with me?" Cole asked grimly, fully aware of what he was asking of his companions. He supposed they had all reached another point of no return. But with each new, profound experience, more questions arose and even more danger loomed.

Gradually, each man nodded.

"I'll ready the Eliminator," Gamer said, rising immediately. "I'll see you down at the dock." He left without further comment.

The others rose to gather some things, mostly water and food, remembering their last trip and the stifling humidity they had experienced. Half an hour later, the companions gathered at the small wooden dock. Gamer was already on the boat and at the controls. The threesome stepped in, and the boatman fired up the twin engines, heading out to sea and the fate that awaited there.

Gamer guided the boat skillfully over the choppy water. Too soon, the mountain's silhouette materialized over the horizon. Shrouded partially in mist, it had never looked more ominous, as though expecting their arrival with nothing but bad news to bear. Cole wondered what they would find this time. Would they even be allowed inside? Would they find answers—or just more questions?

The companions remained unusually quiet as the go-fast boat skimmed the water's surface, the only noise the loud humming of the engines and the sound of the hull battering the waves like drumbeats leading them into battle.

The boatman shut off the twin engines. The boat decelerated rapidly and then leveled out. They would coast their way in. As the shoreline became visible, all eyes were focused on the twin fire angels hovering in the air a mere fifty yards away. Flames shot from their wings in uneven bursts. No sign of welcome here. Cole sensed their ambivalence, as if they were questioning the need for the comrades' return.

The apparitions remained silent as the companions passed slowly by, their deadly obsidian eyes glued to the men as though any hint of aggression would be dealt with swiftly and without mercy. Mario shuddered as they slipped on by. Rico didn't seem quite so enamored with them this time, having thought he might get to hook up with one previously. These weren't exactly the Swanson sisters.

Gamer throttled back a bit and threw an anchor overboard just feet short of the shore, making the boat come to a full stop.

And then they waited.

CHAPTER SEVENTY-NINE

THE VOLCANO WAS NO longer on fire, though the acrid smell of sulfur and scorched earth still permeated the surroundings. Billows of steam hissed from nearby fissures that had not yet healed. From high atop the mountain, the shrill squawk of a winged reptile echoed across the expanse, bringing with it, images of a prehistoric world. And these four men were the intruders. What malice awaited inside?

An iridescent orifice appeared, surrounded by a swirling mist. Two luminescent bodies floated forward. Lindsay was the first to fully take shape. The men gazed awestruck as the second body fully formed. Cassie Thomas, the Light Warrior, materialized in all her grandeur. The men bowed to their knees, all except Cole. Was she an angel or a demon? Her shimmering visage dominated the landscape as she looked down on the mortals. Never had they seen anything quite like her, not even in fantasy movies. She looked like a goddess who could instantly crush anything in her path. Now, in daylight, even Cole was taken aback. She had not appeared quite this intimidating—or malevolent—in the darkness. Neither deity was smiling.

Lindsay glided forward, while Cassie remained stationary. *What brings you back to us, Cole?* Lindsay asked. *What is it you seek?*

Cole responded immediately. "What are you doing to us, Lindsay? Your mist is spreading and making people deathly sick. We just came from the clinic, where my pilots are fighting for their lives. Dr. Morales has called in specialists. If they can't quickly discover a cure or a treatment, this will turn into a local crisis with implications far wider," Cole said, deciding not to pull any punches. He needed answers, and he didn't intend to leave without them.

Lindsay eyed Cole disdainfully, like she could crush him any minute for his insubordinate questioning of her.

This is not my mist. I am only its guardian. Mother Earth created it and allowed the winds to spread the toxicity across the waters for one intended reason: to infect humans until they realize what they are doing to her. Eventually, a pandemic will occur, and it can only be averted when the world's powers come together and enact sweeping environment changes. As you and your boatman recently discussed, you are on the threshold of a great cleansing overtaking the globe. The warning has been given. Unless behaviors change drastically, the human race will be wiped out, the life forms now evolving inside your mountain will take seed outside, and a rebirth of Earth's inhabitants will dawn.

Too shocked to respond, Cole stared back at Lindsay, a being he no longer recognized. This was not Lindsay the mortal, nor was it Lindsay the benevolent angel he had come to love unconditionally. This was an otherworldly creature with the power to extinguish all of humanity while she stood back watching. What had happened to change her so drastically? Where were the angels to watch over him? He turned toward Cassie for support but was met with similar indifference. Her expression remained implacable, derisive even.

Cole spread out his arms as if surrendering—or was it desperate pleading? His companions remained speechless, frozen in place.

Long moments passed as Cole gazed at the angels reticently.

"So, this is the message you want me to leave with? To spread the word that the end is coming. To expect an unprecedented pandemic to take hold, one that has no cure? And that all we need to do is stop polluting the earth and stripping it of its natural resources? And if we are obedient little men and women, we can continue to live, by your good graces? Otherwise, we will all suffer horrible deaths?"

All except you four. You will be left unaffected by the virus, to your dying days, as living examples of what might have been. And I promise each of you extended lifetimes. It will also remind you for eternity of your inability to act. That you irrevocably failed your fellow human beings.

Cole couldn't believe his ears. For a moment, he thought he had descended into hell. . . again. There could be no other explanation. The two women that had meant the most to him in life—other than his mother—were now judging and rejecting him like he was the enemy.

"Do you think world powers will just stand idly by? Especially the United States? They are already suspicious of this island and will shortly know of the toxic scourge emanating from this cursed mountain. They will bring the full weight of their military power down on you, and this volcano will be obliterated. They have two nuclear attack vessels in the area just waiting for the order."

Let them bring their insignificant weapons. They are nothing compared to the power of the universe. I welcome the challenge. Now go! Lindsay said. Just as suddenly as they had appeared, the angels vanished.

The gauntlet had been thrown down. It was time for action, but Cole had no clue what to do next. He motioned for Gamer to start the engines. His eyes—eyes that burned—remained transfixed on the spot of the confrontation. He now appeared alone in this celestial battle, in this battle for the planet. Had Lindsay finally deserted him, disgusted with his lack of action? Had she lost faith after extolling his virtues.

The foursome sped atop the waves, heading back to Isabella. Cole was determined to do something. But what? He felt like he was sinking into a bottomless abyss. He would have been better off dying in the trenches at the bottom of the ocean. Hollingsworth Island would just have been a dream. It wouldn't exist today. Damn Lindsay!

CHAPTER EIGHTY

T HE FOURSOME ARRIVED AT their dock. Gamer tied off the boat, and the men climbed their way up the wooden steps to the house on the cliff. As they entered from the rear, they found Art sitting on the deck, sipping a beer and waiting. Somehow, he had managed to find his way here. He appeared to be sniffing at the air for something.

"Rico, would you please grab one of the masks out of the van for Art. He should not be breathing this air without some sort of protection," Cole said.

Rico hurried to the van out front to get one of the specialized breathing masks they had obtained at the clinic. Returning quickly, he handed it to Art.

"Please just put it on, Art. The air around here is not safe to breathe any longer," Cole said. Art looked confused but complied. "It's a long story, my friend," Cole added, praying that Lindsay had extended Art temporary immunity from infection. No doubt she was aware of his arrival.

The high-tech mask did allow for communication, but the sound was muffled. Art stood to face his companions, about to question them, when Cole spoke first.

"You're wondering why we aren't wearing them, right? That's also part of the story. Have a seat. And you might need another beer," Cole said, indicating to Rico to bring more bottles.

After everyone had settled in and taken a few sips, Cole started his tale, leaving out nothing. Art listened patiently as the story unfolded—a story too extraordinary to be true. By the time Cole finished, Art's beer was empty. He rose, placed the empty bottle on a nearby table, and then stared at his best friend as if he had finally lost it.

"You actually expect me to believe this shit, Cole? Angels, toxic mist, a plague about to wipe out the human race, and a global cleansing with new life forms appearing from. . . um, how did you put it, *your* mountain? Is that all, or did I miss something?" Art said, incredulously. He raised his right hand to pull off the mask but was caught off guard by Mario's lightning-fast reaction.

"Please keep it on, Mr. Barkley," Mario said. "This is no joke." Art tried to twist out of the driver's grasp, with zero success. Reluctantly, Art nodded, and the driver relaxed his grip.

Cole tossed the attorney another bottle. Art swiped it out of the air and sat back down, as conflicted as he had ever been. With each passing day, each new experience, the group was rapidly descending into a quagmire of implausibility—or was it denial? The scenario made *The Twilight Zone* seemed more like *Mister Rogers' Neighborhood*. This couldn't be happening. Maybe this faint mist was affecting everyone's mind, resulting in hallucinations. There had to be some other explanation—something that made more sense.

"So, gentlemen, what is it you want of me?" Art asked matter-of-factly, rather than engaging in a tirade.

"To believe. Art, it's the only way you can help us. . . or help me. Perhaps one more trip to the island will make you a believer. Even though I just told you we were basically rejected only hours ago, Lindsay and Cassie may make an exception for you, especially since you were so helpful in getting Cassie back to Australia and out of the media's reach after the island's formation."

Art agreed, although he secretly thought it fruitless. But maybe Cole needed to see it through someone else's eyes in order to return to his senses. That alone was worth the effort.

"Let me change, and then we can leave." Art walked through the sliding glass doors and into a nearby bedroom after picking up his duffle bag.

Twenty minutes later, Art, Cole, and Gamer left the dock in a roar, speeding out to sea on a mission to convince the attorney that what they said was true. A lot depended on this.

"Explain to me again, why the four of you are basically unaffected by this so-called toxic mist, while others are getting sick?" Art said, as the Eliminator skimmed across the water at a rapid pace.

"On our first visit to the island since our return, the mist was much thicker and —including Cassie at the time—basically remained close to the volcano. When we approached, we were granted some kind of protection from it so we could enter safely. This immunity remains with us. Frank and Bill did not accompany us on that first trip. So, when the mist initially reached landfall, they were the first people to become infected. I'm not sure if you are immune, having been in the States," Cole said.

Art nodded, as if he understood, but the look in his eyes suggested he still did not believe, though he continued to wear his mask. Without further questions, the threesome sped toward the island in silence until the mammoth volcano came into full view. Although Art had been near the island previously, it had been a while since he'd seen it up close. The spectacle shocked him with its sheer enormity. It was nearly impossible to comprehend its girth on television or in a photograph. You needed to see it in person to understand. It did indeed appear otherworldly. There really was no other description that came to mind. The more Art gazed at the mountain, the more it seemed to be pulsating as if it was breathing. Art shook his head, trying to clear up fuzzy vision, but still the mountain pulsated, unnerving the attorney.

Gamer guided them to the location where they had encountered the fire angels on previous trips. In the distance, something red-hot glowed, hovering in midair. Although they were too far away to discern exactly what the object was, it did capture Art's attention, as the Eliminator did a beeline straight at it. Gamer failed to slow his boat's speed in order to give Art the full effect. And it seemed to be working.

Soon a body became apparent, enveloped in searing flames. Art's mouth dropped open. Gamer slowed the craft, pulling up alongside the creature. Art continued to gawk as the angel gazed down at this stranger. Its obsidian eyes sent shivers up the attorney's back. The specter bowed its head slightly in Cole's direction, and Gamer passed by cautiously. So far so good.

Art was about to turn around to continue staring at the Angel but he was immediately reprimanded by Cole. "That's not a good idea, bro," Cole said sternly. Art caught his drift and turned back, still dazed.

The Eliminator eased in the rest of the way, stopping just yards short of the shoreline. Too stunned to ask questions, Art stood shakily in the craft, not knowing what to expect next. Whatever questions he may have had swirling inside his head were quickly answered.

A shimmering ball of iridescent light began to unravel, enlarging until sufficient enough in circumference to allow a body to materialize from deep shadow. Spellbound, Art watched in horror as the celestial body emerged and floated toward him, nearly blinding him with its intensity.

"Lind–Lindsay?" Art stuttered.

This time, the angel smiled, as if welcoming a long-lost friend. Before Art could stammer further, Cassie—the Light Warrior—emerged, as if about to unleash the fury of an exploding sun. Art's knees buckled, and he collapsed on the spot. The sky around the angel crackled with electrical charges, silver and gold shards crisscrossing, blinding the companions temporarily.

Oh my, Cassie muttered, as if still getting used to the effect she had on mortals. From somewhere within, she dialed back the sheer luminosity that naturally poured out from her armor-clad body. She clutched deadly blades in both hands, like intensified light sabers, that contained the power to slice up a planet.

As the light faded, vision returned to Cole and Gamer. Art was still on his back, but slowly recovering. Cole helped his friend stand up and held on to steady him. Cassie floated toward the attorney warily, stopping at a safe distance to avoid scorching the shaken man. Art cleared his throat.

"Well, I don't think you'll need my help anymore with avoiding the media!" Art exclaimed, half joking. This elicited a laugh from Lindsay and a smile from Cassie.

I'd give you a hug, Art, but I'm afraid you might burn up, Cassie retorted. *And by the way, welcome.*

Art didn't know whether to laugh, cry, or collapse again, the encounter was so overwhelming.

It is good of you to come, Art. Your presence here is much needed. Cole has missed you terribly. Even though the chain of the nine companions has been broken, you complete the circle of five, and this group shall be the ring bearers going forward, Lindsay said with conviction. *Trust each other and do not falter in your faith—or there will become a betrayer among you.*

Art nodded as if he understood, which of course, he didn't. Little had managed to sink in at this point, other than the fact that he'd just experienced his first encounter with angels.

I go to prepare your way, Cassie said, and she suddenly burst into a fireball of golden flame, taking flight like a ballistic missile. Rising into the sky like a shooting star, she rocketed up the mountainside in a blur of blinding light before disappearing into the troposphere.

Welcome to Hollingsworth Island, Art Barkley, Lindsay said, motioning the two men forward. Gamer would again be left behind to guard his boat. His obvious frustration did not go unnoticed by Cole.

The two companions entered the darkened tunnel, following the shimmering light cast by the angel, as she guided them deeper and deeper into the mountain. Art remained speechless, which was unusual for the attorney, who normally had something to say about everything. He was never shy about expressing his opinions—or his condemnations.

Lindsay's light dimmed as an opening at the tunnel's end came into view, emitting its own form of light, white-hot. A cool wind swept by as the two men arrived at the precipice, revealing the cavernous mountain hall. Cole should have been sufficiently familiar with it by now, but still its grandeur astounded him. Much like his deep-sea dives to the trenches at the bottom of the Atlantic Ocean with Lindsay, the landscape continued to unnerve the billionaire.

How it affected Art was anybody's guess, as he gazed out in wonder at a site that simply defied words. The creation of a new world. A pristine environment so pure and free from contaminants that only a cosmic power could have created the biosphere. Cole looked on silently, as tears streaked down Art's face, unconstrained. And for the first time, Art understood. He understood Cole's compulsion to find the truth and complete a mission unlike any other undertaken by a single human being. There would be no more doubt. All that remained was for Art to find the courage to be at Cole's side, standing resolutely against the powerful and the bureaucracy that allowed the defiling of their precious planet in the name of profits.

CHAPTER EIGHTY-ONE

ART QUICKLY BECAME MESMERIZED by the birdlike reptiles floating high in the sky, the movement of life forms below, and, in the middle, the crystal-clear tube filtering molten lava up to the crater beyond, tended to by two fire angels hovering in the open spaces. In disbelief, Art turned to Cole.

"Can these beings actually control the lava flow? If so, that would explain a lot. It would also give them immense power. A power I suspect cannot be challenged," Art said.

"Yes. Although I didn't believe it at first, I witnessed it firsthand. It seems they can call on it at will," Cole said.

"My God. It appears they have the power to back up their threats to spread a pandemic, and no one expects that. And this is the source of the virus, right?" Art said, solemnly.

"Exactly. I believe this is our biggest challenge. To inform world leaders of what lies ahead if we don't change our ways. We have the power to report this through our vast news networks, but I also believe that is not sufficient. I fear that certain governments, probably most, will discount our warnings—at least until the angels strike back. I have come to believe this is sort of a two-tiered plan. First, Lindsay unleashes the virus and waits for a response. That has already happened, but it's moving slowly. As it worsens,

I think the military response will be fast, especially from the United States. As you know, we've already got powerful attack vessels in the area. The sort of destruction the military can cause to the island will be critical. However, if the island can fend off a nuclear attack, which I now think is possible, the balance of power will switch to the angels."

"Do you really think the island can withstand a nuclear attack?" Art asked disbelievingly.

"I'm really not sure, but I still don't understand the full nature of its power. I don't think we should underestimate the power of the planet or the resourcefulness of otherworldly beings. This could be child's play for them. I just don't know."

Just as the conversation was becoming more focused, Cassie appeared inside the mountain. Below her, a pathway formed, leading to another opening in a stone wall below. Lindsay waved her hands and the two men floated down, landing softly at its entrance. Staring at the Bridge of Sighs, Cole became emotional, recalling the trip he and Cassie had recently made together—and how it had ended.

Are you ready to see our future, Art? Cassie asked, her voice ominous.

"As ready as I'll ever be, I guess. Lead on."

The angel gestured, and the two companions moved forward warily, anticipation building with every step. For Cole, this trip would be a sobering reminder of his recent experience and the mortal woman who slipped through his arms. For Art, it would be a revelation that would affect the rest of his life, changing him forever. For any human, no trip across the bridge could leave a person unchanged.

When they finally reached the other side, the missing section that would normally materialize as a path of light was already in place. It no longer needed to be conjured after its travelers were judged worthy of crossing over. It was open to the companions free of restrictions. The angels had willingly accepted Art as a warrior in the fight to save the planet. Cole was filled with pride. Art was becoming more like the brother Cole had never had, and he liked the feeling. Just as in the *Lord of the Rings*,

Art was to Cole as Samwise Gamgee was to Frodo Baggins. Frodo could not have destroyed the ring of power without Sam's help. But at what cost? Would it be the same for Cole and Art? These thoughts occupied Cole as they crossed over.

The dystopian world abruptly presented itself, stopping Art in his tracks. As if the presence of angels had not been enough, this morbid scene elicited an entirely new confluence of emotions. He had never witnessed such an atrocity outside of science fiction or fantasy movies, and those were just the musings of writers brought to the silver screen by filmmakers. They always seemed like make believe, no matter how good the special effects were. However, this was so much more. It was as real as anything Art had experienced thus far. Just as real as the two of them standing on the rotting, pestilent landscape. Yet, there was something familiar about it. It took a while to sink in. Art suddenly realized they were standing in the area formerly known as Newport, Rhode Island. But it bore little resemblance to their home now.

Art and Cole walked for a time along the desolate road that had led Cole and Cassie to the ocean—only there was no ocean left. An arid wind blew dust and ash in their faces. The stench was almost unbearable. It didn't take long until Art had seen enough. Cole warned him where they were headed, and Art didn't have the stomach to face it. He knew these images would remain with him forever, and he wanted to minimize any further effects. He had already seen enough to haunt his dreams for a lifetime.

The two men turned and headed back, silence their only companion. There wasn't much to say. The landscape had said it all. Cole guided his friend on a short detour to the building that was once Hollingsworth Enterprises. He handed Art the freshly printed newspaper, presenting a stark contrast of color against a scorched and broken cityscape. Art stared at the headline, noticing the date. This final revelation was too much for him to bear. Art dropped the paper and began to run—to be gone from this accursed place. There existed no hope here, no promise of a future, only death and destruction.

As Art ran, his only thought was that he should have stayed away. That had been his initial decision when originally asked to make the trip. He had his reasons for staying behind. Why hadn't he maintained the good sense to stay put? And now... now he could never go home again, knowing what he knew, seeing what he had seen. He could never look his colleagues or clients in the eyes again without regret, possessing such knowledge. He was dead to that world now.

Arriving at an obstruction, Art stopped, while Cole caught up. Cassie was standing in his path, surrounded by a halo of brilliant light, the air around her quivering. There appeared to be no way out. *Is there more I need to see?* Art wondered. He didn't think he could take any more.

Have you seen enough? the angel asked.

Art nodded, still too stunned to speak. It took all of his strength not to collapse again. He hadn't asked for this. He had been thrust into this living nightmare against his will. As he was not one to hide his head in the sand, sometimes the naïveté of not knowing was far better. This experience was bringing new meaning to the phrase *ignorance is bliss.* Witnessing the fate of the human race in finite terms brought with it an entirely new perspective—a burden so heavy he didn't believe he could shoulder it. *Leave it to others*, he thought to himself, as the Warrior of Light gazed at him pensively, seemingly able to read his mind.

"What?" Art shouted. "What do you want from me?"

Haven't you already asked that question of your companions, if I'm not mistaken? What was it they asked of you?

"To believe," Art replied, more calmly this time.

Well, Art, do you now believe? Cassie asked.

"I believe you and your fellow angels are threatening to destroy the human race unless—" Art cut his accusation short, as if by completing it, he would lend credibility to their cause.

I believe you and your fellow humans are doing a good enough job of that on your own. We are only the guardians of this place, sending out a dire warning of consequences, should humanity fail to act. Your group of five holds the key that can ignite it all—if you would just believe!

With her parting comment, Cassie faded into a shimmering ghost of herself, but not before passing on the permanent immunity Art needed to survive, while breathing the toxic air. Then, the orifice reopened, leading the way back.

The two companions entered and were immediately transported back to Gamer and his boat. Apparently, there would be no more revelations on this day. They had seen, and they had been given their marching orders. All that remained for them to do was to take action.

CHAPTER EIGHTY-TWO

"**W**ELL, THAT DIDN'T TAKE long," Gamer remarked.

"How long were we gone?" Art asked.

"Less than an hour. There must not have been much to see," the boatman replied indifferently, obviously still riled about not being included.

Art looked at Cole sideways. To him, it seemed like they'd been gone for many hours, if not days. How such an experience could be absorbed in less than an hour confounded the attorney.

"Time passes in different intervals on the other side, Art. Spatial relationships are altered, too," Cole said. "Trust me on this one."

What could Art do but take Cole at his word? He was having serious problems understanding anything that had happened to him since he'd arrived back in the tropics. Come to think of it, things had stopped making sense the moment he'd touched down on Gerace Institute's frigate in search of Cole over six months ago.

Art still had no idea he had been shot and killed. This was the one piece of information Cole had not passed on for fear of losing Art for good.

On the boat ride back, Art contemplated Cole's explanation about how time worked differently on the other side and what that might mean for him. Could he somehow return to the past through a magical gateway? Could the angels grant him this wish? But hadn't he already done that, though he just didn't know it? Art was so grounded in the incontrovertible laws of nature—as least his understanding of them—that such a thought seemed preposterous. But if he was to regain his sanity, along with some sense of normalcy, wasn't it worth a try?

"Cole, can I ask you a question? It's important."

"Of course, what's on your mind?" Cole paused at his lame response. There must have been a million things on Art's mind after what he'd just experienced. "Go ahead, shoot," Cole added.

"With all that we're experiencing, I was wondering if there's a way to travel back in time. . . um, to return to a point where one could escape a present reality?" Art whispered, stuttering.

Cole gazed at his friend, immediately understanding the question. There it was—an admission. Or was it a confession? Art clearly wanted out. Even after all he had seen and the many discussions the two of them had over the past six months, it appeared Art's heart wasn't in this. Cole couldn't blame him. He really didn't have any skin in the game—unless one considered, on a higher level, the salvation of the human race to be a relevant and achievable goal. A concept so abstruse, it was nearly impossible to comprehend. How could a couple of disparate men save the world, when the world apparently didn't want saving?

Cole stared deeply into Art's questioning eyes. He needed to take this request seriously—and he needed to be honest, if he was to be believed. No short, bullshit answer would appease this man.

"Can an answer wait a bit, Art?" Cole replied, as the shoreline of Isabella came into view in the distance. "Let's dock, grab a beer, and then we can talk."

The boatman suddenly slammed down the throttle, and the Eliminator practically leapt out of the water.

"Hey, what's going on, Gamer?" Cole exclaimed.

"Wouldn't want Art's answer to get delayed. Christ, why am I even here? If all you want is someone to drive you back and forth to the island, there are plenty of skippers who will do that and keep their mouths shut, especially with the money you pay—sir!" He was beginning to feel more like a low-level hired hand, waiting around while the big boys conducted their own form of business behind closed doors. But then, he was used to that action. "So, all that talk about one for all and all for one, that was just bullshit, right? What about all that trust the angels spoke about?"

Cole was stunned by Gamer's accusations. He did have a point, though. Was the circle of five already breaking up, before getting started? Cole suddenly felt sick to his stomach. He had asked so much of these men and was now treating them like servants with an inferior social status. Was the wealth and influence men like he and Art possessed finally raising its ugly head, separating the haves from the have nots? Were different classes of people, and the divide between them, unavoidable? In his world, of course they were.

Cole knew these men could never fully grasp the concept of privilege and affluence that had defined Cole his entire life, but the real question was, could Cole navigate to their level, to relate and treat them as equals?

Gamer, once a highly respected scientist, might have related, although he had not been a member of the Russian aristocracy. But then he'd fallen from grace after his defection and subsequent imprisonment.

Mario, a black ops badass, hadn't graduated from a prestigious military academy or been awarded any medals of honor. He had risen to the top of his craft by sheer determination and toughness, and his successes were normally kept under wraps. Killing people wasn't exactly conversation de rigueur at highbrow cocktail parties.

And then there was Rico, raised in the worst of ghettos, where drugs, prostitution, and child trafficking was the norm rather than the exception. He never had a chance to experience the good life. He had to fight every day just to survive.

Yet, all three of these men were here, willing to risk their lives for Cole, more out of respect than for the money they were receiving, which had become secondary now. Cole cursed to himself. He'd better start trying to relate, if he didn't want to lose them. He also knew he could not complete this journey without these companions.

Gamer guided his boat in and tied off at the dock. The threesome strode quietly up the steps toward the house, where Mario and Rico were eagerly awaiting their return. Cole turned to the boatman.

"You are more than welcome to join us, Gamer, if you'd like. But this decision is really up to Art, not me. It may be of a personal nature, and I would only ask that you respect Art's privacy."

"Yes, of course. Please excuse my outburst. I don't know what got into me."

"No apology required, my friend. It is I who should apologize to you. I don't know how I could be so insensitive. You, along with the others, are essential to our success. There is no way I can do this alone," Cole said.

This explanation appeared to placate the man, at least temporarily. He left to join the others on the back deck, while Cole accompanied Art to the living room. They took a seat facing one another, without the benefit of grabbing a drink first. Art just wanted to get this over with.

Art remained silent for a few minutes, contemplating how to start the conversation. He was still very conflicted and hadn't fully made up his mind either way. More than anything, he wanted to understand Cole's expectations and what they meant for him. Art cleared his throat.

"You know I didn't believe you at first, Cole. About the angels and everything. I was wrong, obviously. The experience was too much for me to take in. I'm not even sure I have a role here, at least one that can make a difference. I mean, I'm all for saving humanity, but you have the most at stake here, with Lindsay and all. You control the money and, to a lesser extent, the press. The others are the muscle you'll need to protect you while you're down here."

Cole nodded but remained silent, allowing Art all the time he needed to get his thoughts out.

"What you've been trying to tell me all along didn't feel real on some level, but I tried to go along because of who you are. I realize that an event as monumental as the forming of a giant landmass is a significant natural event and would likely have environmental consequences, but never in my wildest imagination could I have envisioned this. The enormity of it all has literally blown my mind. I. . . I really don't know what else to say." Art hesitated, realizing his next words would probably break Cole's heart. They had been joined together by a series of events of such enormity, they had both been irrevocably changed. They could never return to their former lives as if nothing had happened—that is, if anyone survived this ordeal.

"Cole, I don't think I can continue on this road with you any longer. I'm not strong enough. It seems the powers the angels possess can accomplish almost anything. I'm hoping they can transport me back in time, at least to a place before I came back here. Then I can put the scenes of our destroyed planet out of my mind. I know I'm grasping at straws here, but I don't know what else to do."

Cole had suspected this, or something similar, would be Art's request, based on the question Art had asked on the boat, but the shock of hearing it out loud crushed him. He stood and walked over to the open space between the living room and the kitchen, gazing out beyond the deck to the ocean. He saw the three musketeers standing and talking, each with a bottle of beer in their hand. *What were they discussing?* Cole wondered. How to bow out gracefully? How they were sick of being treated like second-class citizens? Cole was quickly losing control of the companions, which would only spell failure. He couldn't start over.

Cole stood for a long moment, frozen with indecision. Images flashed in his head. Should he have chosen immortality? That way he wouldn't have let these men down. But then Art would be dead. There would not have been the reversal of time he had chosen over immortality, to save his friend from that fate. And what about Gamer? Would he have avoided injury? Cole and Lindsay would have been joined forever. Was that option still available to him? Especially since Cassie had crossed over. Or had she taken his place? The questions came hard and fast.

And now Art was asking the same thing—to be cast back in time. Not to save Cole, but rather to save himself from horrific memories he could not live with. How ironic. Should he confess to Art what had actually happened?

Art was lost so deep in thought that he failed to notice Cole standing next to him.

"Art, I believe Lindsay has the power to grant your wish, but I also believe there will be a heavy price to pay for that. I cannot tell you what that price will be, but I do know it will change you beyond what you can now imagine. The question you must answer is, are you prepared for the outcome? Once made, there will be no turning back." Cole's words contained such finality that Art seemed to morph into an altered state as he considered his words.

"I also believe there is a role for you in all of this, that there always has been. My advice would be to sleep on it and make your decision tomorrow. Things may be clearer to you then," Cole said, then he walked out of the room.

CHAPTER EIGHTY-THREE

COLE AWOKE EARLY THE next morning to the high-pitched screeching of seagulls flying overhead. Having failed to eat dinner, the aftereffects of excessive alcohol only made matters worse. He donned a robe and headed to the kitchen in search of cold water. As he approached, he spotted Art eating breakfast alone. No sign of the others. Cole grabbed a bottle of water from the refrigerator and took a seat opposite his friend.

"Sleep well?" Cole asked.

"I've slept better," Art said, without looking up. "You know, Rico is a pretty good cook," Art added, making small talk.

"Have you made your decision?" Cole asked, unwilling to delay the conversation.

This time Art looked up at Cole, gazing at his friend with sheer determination, having steeled himself to deliver the answer he knew Cole would not want to hear. Art had spent most of the night on the deck, looking out to sea, searching for answers.

"Yes, Cole, I have. I want you to know this was one of the most difficult choices I've ever had to make, possibly the most difficult. I love you like a brother, man, but I must leave. That is, if the angels will grant my wish.

I asked Gamer if he would ferry me out to the island one more time, if it's okay with you."

Cole's expression remained unreadable. He had expected this, had even written his friend a letter during the night that he would send with him back to the States, hidden away in Art's travel bag. If Lindsay wiped Art's memory clean of the last thirty-six hours, the note might seem cryptic, but Cole hoped it would be enough to keep the attorney away. He could not be allowed to return here.

"You have my blessing, Art. Leave with Gamer whenever you want," Cole said.

"Aren't you coming with us?" Art asked, confused.

"No, sorry. You're on your own for this one. This should be between you and Lindsay." Cole finished the last of his water, stood, and walked back to his room to shower and dress, leaving Art sitting at the table with his fork in hand, speechless.

Art cleared his plate and headed outside to find the boatman sitting beside Rico, the assassin sharpening his machete. Art supposed cutting bacon with it must have dulled the blade somehow.

"When can you leave, Gamer? I just spoke with Cole, and he agreed to it. I'm ready anytime you are," Art said.

"Meet me down at the dock in twenty, and I'll be ready," Gamer said curtly. He had spoken to Art earlier about his plans to leave but still had no idea why he needed to return to the volcano. But it must be important if Cole approved it.

Art headed straight to the boat, wanting to avoid contact with the others. He felt horrible about his decision; he could only imagine how the other men felt. Art was sitting in the passenger's side of the Eliminator when Gamer stepped in.

"Ready?" the boatman asked.

"Yes."

"Are you sure you want to do this?"

"Do what? What do you think I'm intending to do?" Art asked acrimoniously.

"Deserting your best friend when he needs you the most. Or is there something else you are planning to do that takes you out to the island?" Gamer said.

The boatman had just dealt Art another crushing blow. As if his own guilt wasn't bad enough, now he had to hear it from the men brave enough to see it through no matter how much danger they faced. If it wasn't essential that he meet with Lindsay, he would have jumped out of the damn boat and headed straight to the airport. This promised to be a torturous trip across the water.

Two hours later, the volcano came into full view. Gamer had wasted little time getting here, speeding over the water's surface like an ocean racer. There had been almost no conversation along the way, other than Art asking to slow down. The boatman refused Art's request, increasing his speed whenever the attorney suggested it. It didn't take for Art long to stop asking.

They passed by the guardian fire angel, who sent shivers up Art's spine. He tried not to look at her, which was nearly impossible to do. He didn't want to close his eyes. That would only make him appear weaker to the Russian.

Gamer pulled up close to the shore and shut down the engines. They coasted to a stop and waited. Their wait was short-lived. The shimmering orifice opened almost immediately, as Art gazed at it in wonder. The attorney could come here every day for a month and still the spectacle would be no less daunting.

Lindsay glided out but seemed less ominous somehow. She hovered for a moment, looking down at Art with a compassionate expression, apparently waiting for Cassie to materialize. But Cassie didn't show. Art supposed it was now or never. He stood unsteadily.

"May I come onshore, Lindsay?" Art asked warily.

Gamer didn't object, he had no interest in hearing their conversation or getting more involved. Disgusted by the situation, he pulled his cap over his eyes and pretended to take a nap.

Lindsay waved her hand, and the bridge of light appeared, arcing its way over to the shore. Art walked tentatively across, following the angel into the darkened tunnel.

Why have you come to me alone, Art?

"I've come to a decision. A decision I had hoped I would never have to make, but in my mind and heart, I know it's the right one, at least for me," Art said, lowering his head in shame.

I know what it is you seek, Art. Do not hang your head in humiliation. Each person has their own limitations. But what you ask of me has consequences some more profound than others, but each will exact a price. Just ask Cole. His sacrifice was a monumental one.

Art was stunned. *Just what did Cole sacrifice?* Art wondered. He recalled their conversation yesterday, when Cole had basically told him the same thing about a price to pay, but he had not mentioned he'd faced a similar dilemma.

"What was Cole's sacrifice?" Art asked disbelievingly.

That I cannot say. It is up to Cole to tell you, if he will. And for you to ask him.

"I cannot get the images of what you and Cassie showed us yesterday, or the oncoming pandemic, out of my mind. After talking with Cole, I'm certain there will be nuclear attacks on your island from our overzealous military. Are you prepared for that? Nothing good is going to come of this. And unless humanity makes drastic changes overnight, it appears the wrath of the angels will come down hard. I can't stay here and watch it all unfold. Even if I were to leave now, I know this knowledge would torture me forever—that is, if any of us survive. I am asking you to wipe my memory clean of the last thirty-six hours, so I can return home without these visions. . ." Art stopped, beginning to lose it emotionally. He was tortured between staying and facing these atrocities or leaving and betraying his best friend. The only cure would be to forget. Forget it all.

As he stood in the presence of an angel, he began to feel helplessness overtake him, like he could no longer make the decision himself. "Please, Lindsay, help me, I beg of you," Art pleaded.

Here stood a broken man. It must have been mortifying to come face to face with one's own weaknesses.

I will grant your wish, Art. In doing so, your and Cole's relationship will never be the same, nor can you ever resurrect it. You will recognize him, of course, and you may even interact again, but not like brothers. Cole will know what you've done, since he was a part of it, but you will not. Yours will be the only memory altered.

You will also lose the immunity from the virus you were granted yesterday. In return, your memory of these past events will be washed clean when you land in Newport. Once decided, you cannot reverse its course. All that is left for you to do now is choose.

Art's heart sank. He struggled for breath. Everything seemed to be closing in around him. How could he make this decision? Again, Art flashed back to Lindsay's words that Cole had faced a similar predicament. If only he knew what that was and what Cole had given up, it might help him make his own decision. Cole hadn't seemed that different when Art returned to Isabella the other day. And yet, Lindsay was indicating that Cole's sacrifice had been monumental. More monumental than his? *My God, what had Cole given up?* Art wondered.

"How long do I have to make my decision?" Art asked, uncertain he wanted to actually hear the answer.

There really isn't a hard and fast timeline, but I must warn you, events that have yet to take place could adversely affect your ability to make the decision for yourself. I suggest you decide soon.

Art stared at the angel as a sense of finality swept over him. The time for further questions had passed. The time for action was upon him. Inhaling deeply, he closed his eyes and for a brief moment, attempted to visualize life without his best friend. Life without the knowledge that Cassie had become a fierce guardian angel entrusted to protect them all. That Cole's pilots were at the clinic, fighting for their lives. And finally, that there was a nuclear attack looming on the horizon that could destroy them all. In the blink of an eye, it could all be wiped clean. Opening his eyes, Art nodded at the angel, too distraught to speak the words. Then he turned and walked away.

It was done.

CHAPTER EIGHTY-FOUR

GAMER DROPPED ART OFF at the dock. They exchanged a brief goodbye, and Art thanked the boatman, wishing him well. Gamer sped back out to sea. Art wasn't sure if he had another mission or if he just needed to get away. He watched for a moment as the rooster tail following the boat rose high up, until the Eliminator seemed to disappear into heatwaves on the horizon.

The climb up the wooden stairs was laborious. Art felt the weight of the world on his shoulders. There would be a quick farewell to Rico, a heartfelt, emotional goodbye to Cole, a final ride with Mario to the airport, and then. . . then it would be over. What would it feel like to lose one's memory, even if for a short time? Would he be haunted by unidentifiable echoes of a shadowy past until the end of his days? When he stepped off the airplane in Newport, would it seem as if he'd just stepped out of his office to use the men's room? Would he even know he had left in the first place?

Art encountered Rico first, sitting on the back deck, humming a tune. Mario sat nearby, reading a book—both men looking inconspicuous. The scene appeared as casual as it could get, as if nothing was about to change. Just another lazy day in the tropics, whiling the time away. But it was anything but that. It was a time of reckoning, unlike any Art had ever faced. He didn't see Cole, so this was the opportune time to say goodbye. Only, these companions did not know what was actually happening.

During the boat ride back, Art had considered various scenarios of what to tell these men. The truth could not be told, nor believed. It was best just to tell them he was going back to manage the dissemination of environmental news articles and editorials to inform the world of the impending doom.

"Gentlemen, I'm glad I found you," Art said in as cheerful a voice as he could muster. "I wanted to say goodbye. I'm on my way back to Newport and Hollingsworth headquarters to help spread the word through all of our news channels about what we're facing down here. This needs to take top priority if we have any chance of influencing world powers. I'm going to miss you guys."

"Cole told us a little while ago about your plans. We're all for it and know you'll do a great job," Mario said, almost sounding sincere. "I will drive you to the airport whenever you're ready."

"Thank you, Mario. I really appreciate it." Art hesitated as if he wanted to say something more, then thought the better of it. "I'm just going to say goodbye to Cole, and then I'll be ready. Take good care of him. . . promise?" Art said, his voice cracking midsentence. Both men nodded.

Art found Cole in the living room, sitting in the same seat as when they had faced off in the previous evening. He was obviously waiting for him. He had what appeared to be a double scotch on the rocks in his left hand, but it was still full. Perhaps he was saving that until after Art walked out the door.

"Cole. . . Lindsay granted my request, and I leave immediately. I have to ask, but I'll understand if you won't answer. What dilemma did you face, and what sacrifice did you make when you confronted Lindsay before? She wouldn't share it with me, but she said it was a monumental decision for you to make."

Although Cole wanted to tell Art everything, it could quite possibly force Art to stay out of sheer humiliation and guilt. Art had made his decision. *Let it be*, Cole admonished himself. Let the fates prevail.

"I'm sorry, Art, but I can't tell you. The decision needed to be made, and I believe it was the right one, but only time will tell." Cole rose and put the glass down on the table next to him. He approached Art, wrapping his arms around his friend. "I'm going to miss you, bro. Give them hell in the newsroom. I'll be looking for great articles showing up soon. And be sure to say hello to the Swanson sisters for me," Cole said, half joking. Although Cole didn't know the final details of the deal Art had struck with Lindsay, he had a pretty good idea. The cost would be their friendship, along with Art's recent memories.

Art clung to his friend as if he couldn't let go. This was it. What else could he say? Unbeknownst to Cole, Art had written him a letter during the night as well. He only hoped it would help Cole to understand his decision.

Art picked up his bag at the front of the room and opened the door, stopping briefly. It was all he could do not to turn around to face Cole—the man he had come to love and respect—for one last goodbye. A second later, Art vanished outside and into the running van Mario had waiting for him. They sped off on the gravel road, heading to a future Art could no longer envision.

The two companions said little on their drive. Some small talk about what the newspaper's strategy would be, who they would contact first, and how much they would be focusing their attention on the upcoming pandemic. Art did his best to answer the driver's questions but struggled to concentrate on anything but Cole's look of disbelief when they'd said goodbye. Although Art suspected Cole tried to hide it, there was no mistaking the look of betrayal in those dark, searching eyes.

Mario pulled up to the regular terminal. Art would be taking a commercial flight rather than Cole's Falcon 7X. Cole's pilots were unavailable anyway. Cole had offered to find substitute pilots, but Art had refused. He couldn't bear the thought of flying in Cole's personal jet for almost four hours. He couldn't stand reliving the memories of he and Cole together in that plane over the years. He needed to be surrounded by strangers to ease his pain.

Mario retrieved Art's luggage and gave the attorney a hug. "Don't worry, amigo, you'll see each other again. Keep us posted on your progress, and we'll do the same."

Art was startled by the driver's parting words. Did he know? Had Cole taken him into his confidence so that someone else would know what to do if something bad happened to their boss?

"You got it, Mario. Thank you for everything you've done and risked for Cole. He couldn't have a better friend. And take care of him. He'll need you now more than ever."

Art walked away. The driver watched until Art had passed through the barrier, wondering if he would ever see the attorney again. They lived in such different worlds.

After Art passed through security and customs, he boarded the Boeing 737 and settled in. He suddenly wondered exactly when the transition would take hold. His memory was still intact. The horrific scene of a dystopian landscape raised its ugly head, the specter of death as real as it had been before. Cole still felt like his best friend. All the memories were present. Hadn't Lindsay said something about how it would happen when he touched down in Newport? Their conversation was becoming more tangled in his head with every passing minute.

After three inflight cocktails and a nap, the captain's voice shocked Art out of a restless sleep. They had started the descent and would be landing at Green Airport in twenty minutes. Feeling muddled, Art searched his mind for recent events. They instantly flashed back, as though he had just turned a TV on to a rerun of his life. Nothing had changed yet. He cleared his head and prepared for something dramatic to happen.

Since the plane was landing at Green Airport, he would be deplaning from portable stairs directly onto the tarmac. It would be a short walk to the terminal and parking spaces. He grabbed his bag from the upper storage compartment and waited as the passengers before him moved like a herd of cattle toward the two exits. Art would be using the rear exit.

He took his first tentative steps down the stairs. The second his foot hit the ground, everything went fuzzy. Before him, a long, darkened tunnel materialized. It felt like he was floating through it. Time seemed to grind to a halt, and bright lights flashed in his head. A moment later, Art emerged from the other side, oblivious to his surroundings. For a long moment, he stood shakily, while an odd sense of time rewinding itself took hold. The next thing he knew, he was standing alone in the middle of the tarmac with no idea what to do next. In fact, he couldn't remember why he was here or even how he had come to this place. He had no recollection of the four-hour flight he had just drank and slept his way through. No memory of his being away. Nothing.

He did recognize his surroundings. He was at Green Airport in Rhode Island. Was he here to pick up someone, or had he just dropped someone off for their upcoming flight? What the hell was wrong with him? After excruciating minutes of indecision and confusion, he regained some control of his senses and decided to head in the direction of the terminal. Perhaps someone was waiting for him there.

As he was about to go through the glass sliding doors, he noticed a man in a chauffeur's suit holding a sign. A sign with his name on it. He approached warily. Why would someone in his hometown be holding up a sign with his name like he was a total stranger?

"I'm Art Barkley. Are you looking for me?"

The chauffeur gave Art a quick once-over, comparing a photo he was holding to the man facing him. "Yes, sir, Mr. Barkley. Please follow me, and I'll take you to your office."

Too stunned to respond, Art followed the man dutifully to a black limo parked in a reserved spot. Art climbed in the back, and he was soon on his way to downtown Newport. What Art didn't know was that Cole had arranged for an anonymous driver to pick him up and discreetly drive him to his law offices. He thought the shock of Art arriving at Hollingsworth headquarters unaware he had just spent the past forty-eight hours in Puerto Rico and traveling on planes might be too harsh a homecoming. Surely there would be questions. Others had to know he'd been gone.

CHAPTER EIGHTY-FIVE

C OLE'S CELL PHONE RANG. It was Dr. Morales. Cole answered warily. He wasn't in the mood to hear more bad news.

"Yes, Doctor, what news do you have?"

"Your friends are about the same—no worse, no better. They're fighters. We've completed further diagnostic tests on them and it appears there is a high concentration of microplastics in their lungs and blood system. We've never seen anything like it. How Dr. Connors even suspected this enough to request the tests is quite remarkable, but then, he is one of the top men in his field. He also concluded this condition—which is not really a virus in his mind—is being spread by the mist emanating from the island. It's affecting their respiratory systems and slowing damaging other key organs—"

"Are you telling me they're infected with small particles of plastic? That seems impossible," Cole interjected. "It has to be something else. Where could the plastic have even come from? It must be a virus."

"We think it is modeling a virus. The pilots' temperatures have returned closer to normal, but there is no real improvement in their conditions, so we have to look elsewhere for answers."

"Have you heard of other people being infected?" Cole asked.

"Yes, reports are coming in from farther inland. It's becoming more serious. I have no idea how many cases yet, but local hospitals are beginning to fill up."

"What sort of treatment can be used to extract microplastics from a human body?" Cole asked.

"That's the million-dollar question isn't it, Mr. Hollingsworth?" Morales responded evasively. It occurred to Cole the doctor was holding back information. "What's even more bizarre is that the condition doesn't appear to be contagious between humans, like a virus most certainly would be. We discovered this completely by accident. It will take more testing, of course, but if this proves to be the case, it can only mean one thing. It is being spread solely by the mist, and it may be intentional."

The angels. . . of course, Cole thought. "Is there anything I can do to help? I can arrange for more doctors and researchers to be flown in, at my cost. Anything to assist," Cole said.

"That's very generous of you, and we will certainly take you up on your offer. May I also suggest a concurrent course of action, Mr. Hollingsworth?" Morales asked, then he awaited Cole's response. Based on past history, he knew Cole could become suddenly antagonistic at suggestions that affronted him. But then, most men of his wealth and influence did.

"What exactly are you suggesting, Doctor?" Cole asked suspiciously.

"Please take no offense, but there is a prominent scientist who was researching the island before it became off-limits. I think you may know him. Andres Almquist? After he heard of a similar diagnosis from a local hospital, he recently told a reporter he believes Hollingsworth Enterprises is conducting secret tests inside the mountain, since you are currently the only private entity with access to it. People have seen your boat coming and going. I—"

"Hold on just one damn minute, Doctor! I am very familiar with Almquist and his rantings. You can't believe a thing that man says. And besides, what he's accusing me of is complete, unadulterated bullshit. He's as ambitious as they come and offers his services for sale to the highest bidder." Cole momentarily pulled his cell phone away from his ear to cool down.

That son of a bitch. It's time we have Rico pay him a little visit, Cole thought to himself. They had basically left him alone, but obviously he had been working behind the scenes.

"So, Doctor, what is this concurrent course of action you are suggesting?" Cole asked with a cooler head.

"I would recommend two things, actually. You revisit the island to see what you can find out and also prove to us that Hollingsworth is not conducting secret tests. Then we can combine our resources to dig deeper into what is actually causing this." Morales paused. "Either Dr. Connors or I will accompany you and I promise you we will keep this strictly confidential if you agree."

"Let me think about this. I'm not trying to hide anything regarding these so-called secret tests you suggest. I can assure you that isn't happening," Cole said.

"I'm not taking his side, Mr. Hollingsworth. But he said our ocean is full of nonrecyclable plastics, and he thinks that somehow a portion is being funneled into the island. He has no idea how, but he suspects the interaction between the plastics and molten lava is basically vaporizing it into minute particles, which cannot be completely destroyed or burned off, hence, it has become airborne in the form of the mist. And now people are breathing it in as they are exposed, absorbing the microplastics into their lungs."

"Give me twenty-four hours, Doctor, and I'll get back to you. In the meantime, we'll take a trip back to the island to see what we can find out," Cole said. He was about to blast Almquist again when a lightbulb went on in his head. Somehow, it made sense. He couldn't believe what he was hearing, though. What if it were true that Lindsay and company were cleansing the ocean from the scourge of manmade plastic material and giving it back to humanity in an unfathomable manner, preparing the way for a new race to emerge into a more pristine world, if humanity failed to act.

"Of course, but please, Mr. Hollingsworth, do not delay too long. Many people's lives may depend on what you do next."

Cole called together his companions after Mario returned to the house. This was an unexpected revelation, and it was serious shit. At least with a more normal airborne virus, a cure—or at least a vaccine—could be formulated. This was Cole's initial reaction after learning more about the virus from Lindsay. But how did one formulate a vaccine for extracting thousands of microscopic, nonrecyclable plastic particles from a human body?

The men took seats on the back deck, awaiting Cole's next big surprise. Art had just left, and Cole called a serious meeting. It could only be big.

"Gentlemen, I just received a call from Dr. Morales, and he had some. . . um, rather disturbing news. They have discovered what they think made our pilots sick and where it's coming from. Morales brought in Dr. Conners, a highly respected virologist, and he discovered microplastic particles have infiltrated their lungs and are spreading to other vital organs."

Cole noticed the blank expressions on his companion's faces. Did they not understand, or did they not believe?

"And they think these tiny particles are coming from Hollingsworth Island and are being carried by the wind across the ocean in the form of toxic mist," Cole added.

"That doesn't seem possible, Cole. Is Morales sure this new specialist isn't mistaken?" Mario said, as though he was already in denial.

"Actually, it kind of does," Gamer interjected. "Everyone knows how much plastic is trapped in our oceans. Some of it breaks down over time into what is referred to as microplastics, and some enters the ocean from waste streams of certain products that are formulated from small beads of plastic resins. The last article I read about it said nearly nine million tons of nonrecyclable plastics enter the world's oceans each year—"

"Yeah, so what does that have to do with these so-called microplastics being in the air?" Rico interrupted. "How do they get from the bottom of the ocean into this green mist we've been seeing? I don't buy it."

"Toxic mist aside, microplastics enter the food chain in the ocean through tiny crustaceans called zooplankton, who mistake them for food. Zooplankton form the base of the ocean food chain and are eaten by larger fish. So, the microplastics eventually make their way to humans, who eat these fish. It is a vicious cycle, really," Gamer said.

"And who made you a professor of oceanography?" Rico said sarcastically.

"Rico, please listen to the man. He knows what he's talking about," Cole said, glancing at the boatman for help.

"Rico, in another life I *was* an oceanographer. My real name is Dr. Nikolai Kavrikov. I was born in Russia and grew up in the Ukraine until I defected to Sweden. I was betrayed by your friend, Andres Almquist, after he found out I was going to expose him for taking credit for other scientists' discoveries. The KGB came for me in the night, and I spent the next nine years in isolation in a shithole of a prison in Russia. I later escaped and ended up in the Caribbean. So, yes, I do know something about the ocean," Gamer said. He'd decided it was now or never and he was tired of lying to his friends. He needed to gain credibility so he could use his knowledge to help in Cole's journey, especially now that Art was gone.

Rico looked at the boatman sideways as if to say, *you're fucking kidding me, I don't believe it.*

Even Mario was stunned, although he had suspected for some time that there were deeper secrets the boatman was holding onto. Now it made sense.

"It was Gamer's assistance in the ocean that helped me find the original opening to the mountain. I couldn't have done it without him," Cole said, lending the boatman additional credibility.

"Okay, okay, I believe you. What took you so long to tell us?" Rico said, spitting tobacco on the deck.

"I apologize, gentlemen, but I needed to keep it a secret. Russia frowns on political prisoners who escape their clutches, and they have eyes everywhere. There is little they wouldn't do to get me back. I had to change my name. Please keep this knowledge to yourselves."

"Your secret is safe with us," Mario said. The driver turned toward Cole. "So, what do we do next?"

"We're taking a trip back to the island. We leave at daybreak. In the meantime, let's fire up the grill. There should be some steaks in the refrigerator. Also, I don't know about you guys, but I'm thirsty," Cole said.

No one needed further convincing, and soon everyone had a drink in their hand and were deep in discussion about how the hell tiny particles of plastic were the source of the problem.

CHAPTER EIGHTY-SIX

T HE SUN'S FIRST RAYS appeared above the eastern horizon as the four men climbed into the Eliminator. The water appeared on fire, myriad hues of gold and crimson. It was quiet, so very quiet, as though the planet was at peace with itself. The roar of the powerful engines as Gamer fired up the boat shattered the silence, bringing with it the harsh reality that things were not what they appeared to be in these tranquil, early morning hours.

Gamer guided the boat away from the dock, then quickly accelerated out to sea. There was no reason to delay, and they were soon doing eighty, skimming atop the sparkling waters, on a mission to find the truth. Little was said on their way to the island. The idea of an artificially created mist carrying billions of microscopic particles of plastics to infect the human race was still difficult to believe. What was even more daunting was the fact that Lindsay and her fellow angels were doing this intentionally. If this was true, how could the damage be reversed? This singular thought weighed most heavily on Cole. Would those already infected die, regardless of the outcome of their next actions?

While the others were still trying to work out the details in their own minds, Cole had come to believe it was all true. It might have been the dream he had the previous night, where a host of dark angels soared out from the volcano in all directions, carrying swords lit with fire, as if they were about to torch the earth, wiping the planet clean of human interference. Was it a warning? Would this be their next line of attack if humanity didn't capitulate?

Cole wondered how Art was faring, if he was truly committed to managing Cole's staff of reporters and environmental resources. He had promised Cole this would be his mission upon returning home, but would he even remember? Hopefully, Art's experiences prior to his latest visit would be enough to carry him forward, along with the letter Cole had written him. If Art no longer believed he was Cole's best friend and partner in this endeavor, would he care enough? Or would he retreat back to his practice of law and his pursuit of the Swanson sisters? Money and women were a strong pull and were much easier than fighting against the powerful elite, whose personal agendas were often in stark contrast to those of people committed to positive change. Cole could only hope.

Too soon, the specter of the guardian fire angel came into view—a glowing statue of scarlet energy, burning red-hot. Gamer slowed their craft, ever cognizant that this creature was not their friend, did not take orders from humans, and was at the beck and call of a higher power. If the being was so directed, their lives could be over in minutes, caught in the middle of a raging inferno as their boat turned instantly to fiery embers, spreading atop the waves like ash.

The creature gazed disdainfully down at the crew, as if they were pitiful, but allowed passage, following their every movement with focused, obsidian-colored eyes fraught with malice.

Gamer continued slowing his boat until they were barely moving, coasting slowly toward shore, awaiting first contact with Lindsay or whomever she sent to face them.

Cole stood at the bow of the boat, steeling himself for what was about to happen. He was prepared to challenge Lindsay but was unsure what her response would be—or if she would even show up. Perhaps she'd had enough and was just going to force them to figure it out on their own. If Dr.

Connors and Dr. Morales were correct in their diagnosis, they were already halfway there.

The companions waited nervously, in anticipation of something remarkable happening—a transformation, the opening of a hole in space and time, the emergence of celestial creatures beyond description. Who, or what, would appear next?

Without warning, the sky darkened above them, yet no clouds appeared. Something high above seemed to be moving, casting long shadows across the shoreline. As it grew closer, the rush of wings sounded. At first, Gamer thought a mammoth flock of seagulls was descending, drowning out the sunlight. Suddenly, a host of dark angels appeared, zooming and dive-bombing all around them, crisscrossing in their paths like grotesque bats. But bats didn't carry wicked swords alight with fire. Their ears were pointed, their white hair spiked, their wings tinged with shimmering silver. They soared closer, inspecting their uninvited visitors as if they were the infection.

Rico quickly unsheathed his machete to take a swing at the closest invader. Cole caught his arm in the nick of time.

"No, my friend, they are not here to attack us. They're here for another reason. Please don't evoke their anger," Cole said, recalling his dream—a dream sent by Lindsay as a warning.

Gradually, the flock moved away, forming a tight circle above the companions. And then, the transformation took place. The side of the mountain cracked open with a deafening roar, revealing a large crevasse and a scene so breathtaking, it did not register at first. A pristine landscape lay before the men, one Cole had previously witnessed. Only this time, it was filled with a swarm of unrecognizable creatures, including a host of both male and female angels, resplendent in blazing colors. It might have been a painting from the master impressionist painter Claude Monet, where light danced with colors as though alive, only in this case, the hues were even more brilliant.

Eagle-like birds with thirty-foot wingspans sailed above them. Large, reptilian-looking sloths moved gracefully on the valley floor, grazing on rich flora, while four-legged creatures resembling giant timber wolves sat on nearby perches as though they were keeping guard over their flock. A sense of peace and serenity hung in the air, like a fabric woven into the atmosphere that could actually be touched. All species present were at peace with one another, without conflict.

Out of nowhere, Lindsay emerged, floating toward Cole until she was only yards away. She opened her arms, spreading her wings, and light engulfed the companions until they were no longer conscious of the outside world around them. There was only light, and there was only beauty. Lindsay broke the silence.

This was life on Earth eons ago, before the infection set in, defiling the earth until all salient life forms were destroyed and the planet went dormant. Millions of years passed in silence and shadow, until a novel hope arrived, bringing with it a new species of animals and eventually humans, created in the image of our Savior. Humanity has a choice—one you men have been charged with initiating. Again, you might ask why you, but that's not the important question. It only matters that you have been chosen to fight for us. To save our blessed planet from total destruction.

The men stood paralyzed, unable to speak, unable to express their feelings. Who could have imagined such a thing? A miracle in the making—or was it a curse? One that would haunt them to their graves if they failed. And still they gazed open-mouthed at the pristine world inside the volcano, wondering what the future would bring and if they truly had a place in it.

Yes, Cole, the mist is carrying the particles of plastic that have been drawn into the mountain and repurposed to purge the ocean of its toxic waste—waste created by humans in their ignorance and indifference. It will continue until either the majority of plastics have been expunged from the water and no more are purposely dumped, and humanity makes a conscious choice to cease production of plastic products and turns to alternative materials—which exist, I assure you—and cleans up the oceans. This will be the first step in your new evolution as a species if you want to survive.

The next phase will be a vast reduction in the mining and burning of fossil fuels, though that must start concurrently. Not until these measures are in full force across the globe and governments agree will the virus stop and humans be cleansed at the same time as their planet. Everything will coincide, or continue to decline, until there is nothing left. There is no turning back now. Make no mistake, these irrevocable events have been set in motion. Not even I can stop it. We have all reached a point of no return. Fail to take action, and humanity will perish and the planet will become dormant once more. The next great cleansing is approaching. In fact, it has already begun.

Cole had finally regained the ability to speak. Taking a step forward, he addressed Lindsay. "What if we are unable to convince the most powerful governments to accept your terms? Terms, I might add, that will be nearly impossible to prove. Most governments will not rely on the words of a liberal press—especially the United States, with its current administration."

You have all the proof you need, Cole. Doctors have already discovered the virus is really an infection of microplastics. You need only to confirm that it is being spread by the mist created within this volcano. And then there is Hollingsworth Island. As you have already said, the military is planning an attack, and the time is growing near. The more the word spreads about the virus, the more it will drive your warships to destroy us. When the time is right, bring your film crews and let the world witness the power that resides here. Enlist the scientists and environmentalists around the world, who are just waiting for their time to arrive. You can make the world listen.

"It seems you offer us little choice. I promise you, we are facing staggering odds against success, but we are committed to this cause. I see no other alternative than to leave immediately and return to Hollingsworth headquarters to join with our publishing partners and begin spreading the word. I will direct our camera crews to organize and depart as fast as they can. There's just one thing, though. . . I don't know how much Art will be willing to contribute now that, um, you've changed him," Cole said.

True friendship never really dies, Cole, though it may be misplaced or temporarily forgotten. I'm confident you can make Art believe again. Do not despair over this. It is time to reengage your publishing empire to tell our story. Only you can accomplish this. Only you have been shown the truth. And finally, only you believe.

The pair gazed at each other for a long moment. There was really nothing left to say. It was time to leave. Cole had no other recourse.

"Please say goodbye to Cassie for me," Cole said, then added, "Thank her, too."

Tell her goodbye yourself, Lindsay said.

Another blinding flash of light lit up the surroundings, and the roar of wind nearly toppled Cole as the Light Warrior appeared before them, unfolding like a scene from a celestial battle of good versus evil, of gods and demons locked in mortal combat. Cassie, or what she'd become, appeared even more intimidating than before.

Cole's breath caught in his throat, and his companions stood frozen, like inconsequential statues.

"Cassie, I. . . I'm just so sorry we can't see this out together. I so hoped you'd be by my side. The sacrifice you made for me at the Bridge of Sighs can never be repaid. Thank you," Cole said, his voice cracking, drenched with regret.

Cole, remember what I told you on the Truett when you learned the truth about Lindsay, and later, Lindsay's explanation to you of an angel's power of reincarnation? One can choose to remain immortal or to return to the mortal life, just once. We may yet rejoin. Only time and the fates will tell. Until then, know that I love you.

Cole gazed up at the ethereal being, and his heart was suddenly consumed with overwhelming love. He had known for a while now that he and Lindsay could never truly be together again. Their paths were too dissimilar, their worlds too far apart. Lindsay, in her own enigmatic way, had given her blessing to Cole and Cassie to be together. Indeed, the angel had been responsible for them reconnecting. And now it was time to say goodbye again.

"I love you, too, Cassie. We'll find a way to get through this, and I will find you again."

Cassie's smile lit Cole up inside, and he believed. She had somehow lightened his burden and, in doing so, bestowed upon him a renewed sense of purpose.

Farewell for now, Cole Hollingsworth, until we meet again. . . if only in a dream. I will forever be by your side.

With that, she tossed Cole her other dagger. Cole watched in fascination as it floated unsupported toward him until it embedded itself in his left hand. They had been joined in a most mysterious way.

It never hurts to have two. It just may come in handy, the angel said cryptically.

With a second rush of wind, the sky around them quivering intensely, the entire scene suddenly vanished, leaving Cole and his companions adrift on an empty ocean, alone.

For a long moment, Cole gazed out at the surroundings, confused. There was no volcano, nothing but water in every direction for as far as the eye could see. Had they magically been transported out of the area, away from danger?

His thoughts turned inward. Cole had often wondered whether all he had experienced was real or imagined. None of it seemed possible. Was he just dreaming, or had he gone quite mad? The recent loss of his parents, followed closely by Lindsay's death—the only women he had ever loved before now—combined with the tremendous pressure of running the family empire his father had built. . .could all of this have brought him to the breaking point? Just how much could one person endure?

Cole supposed it was time to leave—time to go home. He needed to check in with Art and then with Bill Gaines. There was business to be taken care of. There was so much work to be done to convince the world to change its ways before it was too late. It could take him months to accomplish anything, to ignite meaningful dialogue among governments. But if this was to be his life's purpose, he had to try. Everything he had recently experienced had convinced him there was no other path to follow. He needed to return to what he knew best. He needed to make Hollingsworth Enterprises all that it could be and use it for good. He would leave first thing in the morning.

Cole floated along in a dreamlike state. One by one, his companions vanished into thin air, as if they had never been more than ghosts occupying space around him--images only he could see. He had become numb to it all.

Home was all that was left to him now. Home was where he belonged.

The story continues in book three, *Angel Wars: The Battle for Planet Earth*.

ACKNOWLEDGEMENTS

A SPECIAL THANKS TO MY wife, to family members, great friends, and to the readers of book one, *The Portal: Only an Ocean Apart,* who persuaded me to continue the story. Without their support and encouragement this book would not have been possible.

Thank you to the great team at Bublish, who answered all of my questions and skillfully guided me along the path to publishing my second book in this series. Their Marketing solutions are top notch.

Finally, a special thanks to Karen Phillips of Phillips Covers, who assisted in the book cover art in conjunction with the designers at Bublish.

www.ingramcontent.com/pod-product-compliance
Lightning Source LLC
Chambersburg PA
CBHW020008120726
47903CB00004B/1190